A PROMISING LOVE

"Good afternoon."

When Elizabeth looked to the foot of the church steps and found Tom smiling up at her, she was filled with excitement. How she longed to run to him! Instead, she descended slowly and returned his greeting.

Strolling together toward his carriage, Elizabeth told of how she'd passed the time since their last meeting. When she mentioned her niece's beau from the South, Tom looked distressed. "I am going mad wanting to hold you in my arms again, and you can talk of nothing but some Southern student Jane Anne fancies she loves!"

"Can't you see that if he loves her and wishes to marry her, I can go ahead with my own plans with a clear conscience?"

"But, Elizabeth, you're putting me second to your niece. We agreed up in the mountains that you will get your divorce and marry me. Was it just the mountain air? Does sea level suddenly make *her* future more important than your own?" Then he leaned closer, smiling wryly. "It's not entirely your fine character I'm in love with, Elizabeth. Can't you take pity on my yearning?"

With Tom's lips now only a whisper away from hers, Elizabeth began to feel a stirring within her that summoned a yearning of her own. . . .

ROMANCE AT ITS BEST . . .

LOVE ME WITH FURY (1248, $3.75)
by Janelle Taylor
When Alexandria discovered the dark-haired stranger who watched her swim, she was outraged by his intrusion. But when she felt his tingling caresses and tasted his intoxicating kisses, she could no longer resist drowning in the waves of sweet sensuality.

BELOVED SCOUNDREL (1259, $3.75)
by Penelope Neri
Denying what her body admitted, Christianne vowed to take revenge against the arrogant seaman who'd tormented her with his passionate caresses. Even if it meant never again savoring his exquisite kisses, she vowed to get even with her one and only BELOVED SCOUNDREL!

TIDES OF RAPTURE (1245, $3.75)
by Elizabeth Fritch
When honey-haired Mandy encounters a handsome Yankee major, she's enchanted by the fires of passion in his eyes, bewitched by the stolen moments in his arms, and determined not to betray her loyalties! But this Yankee rogue has other things in mind!

PASSION'S GLORY (1227, $3.50)
Each time Nicole looked into Kane's piercing dark eyes, she remembered his cold-hearted reputation and prayed that he wouldn't betray her love. She wanted faithfulness, love and forever—but all he could give her was a moment of PASSION'S GLORY.

FIREBRAND

BY
JANE
LEWIS
BRANDT

ZEBRA BOOKS
KENSINGTON PUBLISHING CORP.

For Wolfgang

ZEBRA BOOKS

are published by

KENSINGTON PUBLISHING CORP.
475 Park Avenue South
New York, N.Y. 10016

Printed in the United States of America

Part One

I

Elizabeth Aller Moss! I can see her now as she appeared to my four-year-old eyes on a certain memorable day in 1830: a slender yet full-breasted young woman who seemed even taller in a long, flowing skirt and high Empire waist, her abundant chestnut hair gathered up in a chignon above her strong, graceful neck. I can see those iris-blue eyes with their direct glance, and her smooth, fair skin which often had a flush of pink on either cheek due to her habit of walking briskly to all her errands, an unusual exertion for a young matron in her comfortable circumstances in the bustling, fast-growing city of New York.

I remember, too, the Moss house on West 10th Street, built before the Revolution by her husband Isaiah's maternal grandfather. It was one of a solid row of narrow brick houses, three stories high with windows only front and back. The lack of windows made the interior rather dim, a flaw not ameliorated in the front parlor by dull green walls against which the Hepplewhite chairs and settee sat below the mantel mirror reflecting a hint of daylight. No cheer was added by a portrait of the builder of the house, painted by one of those journeymen artists of Colonial times. I thought it a cruel face even before I learned that this revered ancestor had shot a man in a duel. The eyes were realistically moist, but no soul seemed to exist behind them.

It was in that room on my fourth birthday that I learned that Elizabeth Aller Moss was not my mother but only my aunt—my dead mother's sister. Later I found out that she had risked her own life to save mine, an act of courage that would link our destinies.

The truth came out because of a package that arrived for me by post from my Grandmother Aller who lived near Philadelphia. It was the first time I had received anything in the mail with my name on it, which added to my excitement. Beside me on the horsehair settee Elizabeth helped me remove the outer wrapping. Inside was a tissue-wrapped box, and inside that a small leather case. It held a large gold locket. It opened. I found within two painted miniatures: a blond girl and a brown-haired young man, both pink-cheeked and blue-eyed. I looked up from the puzzle. "Who are these people, Mother?"

She took the locket and looked down at the faces musingly. Then she held the locket open on her palm before me and pointed to the girl. "This is your mother, my sister Jennie. And this is your father, John Clark. They died within two weeks of one another when you were seven months old. So I brought you here to be my child." Her arm went around me, and she dropped a kiss onto the top of my head. "I love you just as dearly as they did."

Something inside me trembled. The locket faces seemed to belong to two dolls. "But if this lady is my real mother, what shall I call you? What shall I call Papa?"

"Your mother called me Liza. She was two years younger and as a little thing had trouble saying 'Elizabeth.' So you can call me Aunt Liza. And Papa will be

8

Uncle Isaiah."

I began to sob. She held me tighter, then gently dried my cheeks with a handkerchief drawn from the bosom of her dress of rosy silk and smelling of pomander. "It was wrong of me not to have told you this sooner, Jane Anne. But you started to call me 'Mama' as soon as you could speak and I let it slip past because I had wanted a little girl just like you. But the truth is that you owe your being to these two dear people who now are angels in heaven."

I had seen pictures of angels and imagined the two doll faces atop long white robes, large feathered wings at either side. I saw myself differently, one whose real parents were distant heavenly creatures. The room in which I sat seemed strange to me, the house no longer mine. I became anxious to please; my sweet disposition was noted by all.

Of Uncle Isaiah I was secretly a little afraid, and for a ridiculous reason: he had a crooked canine which was pointed, and when he smiled at me that tooth seemed menacing. Much older than my aunt, he had lines across his pallid forehead and at the corners of his small gray eyes, and he spoke in a thin voice. But at a distance he was a substantial, well-dressed figure in his velvet-lapeled coat, brocade waistcoat, and tight buff trousers that showed his slight paunch. In his high beaver hat he walked like a man of importance, chest out. He was a tobacconist, and sometimes smelled like the product he sold. But, as he boasted, he had other irons in the fire.

Along with richer men he had had the vision to see that Washington Square and lower Fifth Avenue and Broadway did not represent the last word in valuable New York land. A dozen years earlier he had managed to buy two lots on what he said would become a continuation of

9

Fifth Avenue, far to the north of the hideous brownstone castle at 37th Street built by a man named Waddell. Beyond that lone monstrosity, Uncle Isaiah told us, lay a wild landscape of rocky hillocks and dismal swamps with a few old Dutch farms where the land was tillable, together with the scattered makeshift shanties of immigrant squatters. But one day, he said, the inevitable continuation of Fifth Avenue would make his land worth as much or more than a richer man paid for one lot at the corner of 18th Street. "Who knows, if all goes well, I might decide to sell one lot and build on the other," he said, expansively. "Would you like to live in a mansion someday, Jane Anne?" Holding me on his lap, he smiled and stroked my hair.

"Yes, Uncle Isaiah."

"And would you now like to amuse me with a little song?"

"Yes, Uncle Isaiah."

I had a pretty voice, and one day he had heard me piping a ballad learned from the cook and had applauded, beaming at me. After that I was at pains to learn other songs I hoped would please him. He would lean back like a sultan in his chair by the fireplace, nodding while I entertained him. After he bought a Chickering piano my aunt quickly learned to play it and would accompany me. "A very pretty picture of domestic felicity," he would say. "I consider the four hundred dollars I paid for the Chickering money well spent."

That piano was not the only amenity to enrich the Moss home and others like it during the 1830s and early Forties. A machine was invented for cutting lake and river ice into blocks and soon a canvas-topped ice wagon was making its rounds to supply the new oak refrigerators like ours. The early morning milk cart with its big metal canisters became just as commonplace, the clopping of horse's hooves at dawn signaling a new day. Throughout the city narrow ditches were being dug by Irish immigrants for the new gas mains, although it was a long while before candles and oil lamps gave way to gaslight in homes. But the streets became brighter, as did hotel lobbies and public buildings. By the mid-thirties the dark Moss parlor had been transformed by my aunt: pale yellow striped wallpaper; ruby plush instead of horse-hair on the Hepplewaite chairs and settee; two narrow pier glasses flanking the door to the hall; and a new Brussels rug with a border of rose garlands. The Colonial past was erased with cheerful opulence.

But one object in the parlor remained unchanged. In the center of the mantel stood a large, lidded goblet called a "pokal" of a clear sea-green glass in which was blown a red rose surrounded by its engraved stem and leaves. The final marvel was a crystal drop of dew on one petal.

I knew that it was one of my aunt's most prized possessions. She had admired it as a child, she said, when it had stood on its own shelf built in the window of her grandfather Peter Aller's room, along with a flint-glass pitcher with a blue rim and handle. Both had been made by the famed Pennsylvanian ironmaster "Baron" Heinrich Wilhelm Stiegel, to whom Peter Aller was apprenticed as a boy in 1755. *"Der Mann der kann"* was Stiegel's proud motto and he proved it by inventing his widely used eight-plate stove and by improving the Franklin stove as well. But then his beautiful young wife died, and although "The man who can" named a new forge after her, and, perhaps, his Charming Forge too, it was said that his heart was broken. However, he began to experi-

11

ment with glassmaking and ended by owning a large glass-works from which spilled out an endless array of the finest glass in the Colonies: window glass, tubes and retorts for physicians and chemists, containers of every shape and size. And at last he created true works of art like my aunt's pokal. But he overextended himself and with the Revolution looming closer he could not raise money on his land or property. Finally, he was imprisoned for debt in 1775. The beautiful church he had once given to the State of Pennsylvania did not render his sentence less harsh. Bankrupt, he refused the help his former apprentice offered and survived for ten years by teaching school and giving music lessons.

"His only fault was a love affair with glass in the Age of Iron," my aunt said when she told me what a hero Stiegel had seemed to her as a child. He had been a striking man, her grandfather said, with muscles like iron but melancholy eyes. She had yearned to possess the pokal with the red rose from the moment she saw it. My mother Jennie had admired it too, and one day when she was five had asked their grandfather for it. He shook his head, and Aunt Liza scolded her for begging a gift, even though she herself had wanted to do the same.

"And your grandfather gave you the rose glass because you didn't ask for it," I said, wise to the moral lesson implied.

My aunt shook her head. "No, that was not how it happened." Her eyes left mine, as if there were some secret she did not wish to share, and then she went to the mantel to perform her evening ritual of lighting the candles at either side of the pokal so that the flames reflected in the mirror behind it made the red rose glow like a jewel.

But there was a momentous secret I did share: her

12

authorship of a novel. It was called *The Ironmaster's Bride;* she had completed it when I was too little to have been aware of stolen hours locked in her bedroom, but she had put it aside, dissatisfied. When I was six she began to write it all over again. One day when I was ill in bed with a catarrh I had wandered into her room and discovered her at work seated at a rosewood table by the window. She had sworn me to secrecy. I was to tell no one. "Not even Uncle Isaiah?" She said, "Particularly not Uncle Isaiah. I don't relish being scoffed at." My faith in her ability to do whatever she set her mind to made me inquire how she would be able to keep her authorship secret when her book was published. She smiled. "Oh, I'll just use a *nom de plume,* like George Sand." Her real name, my aunt said, was Amandine Lucile Aurore Dupin Dudevant. Why she chose a man's name, and such a plain one, she did not say.

On the nights when my uncle stayed late at his club, I loved to slip into their bedroom and brush my aunt's hair. While I did she would tell me about her day's events if she had been out of the house. I always asked about the "dandies," those young men in their swallowtail coats, long tight trousers, tall hats and frilled white cravats who aped English elegance with monocles they called "quizzing glasses" through which they ostentatiously observed any lady they thought pretty. "Any dandies today?" I would ask, passing the silver hairbrush down those long locks, coppery threads shining amid the brown. And she would laugh and say something like: "A dear little dandy much shorter than I who tried to look elegantly down at me while actually looking up!" At twenty-seven she looked no more than twenty, even in the fine clothes my uncle liked her to wear, for as men in New York grew richer, they wished their wives to dress so as to show it, to promenade with them on Broadway in elaborate bonnets with flowers framing the face, great bows under the chins, shining silk skirts and rustling taffetas gathered to puff-sleeved, tight bodices on which gold or jeweled breastpins often gleamed.

My aunt's "Bread Ladies," a name given them by a *Herald* journalist, were so attired when they went down to the Battery to meet a ship crammed with immigrants. My aunt felt a great concern for these poor people, many of whom, she said, could not speak one word of English, and she had organized a large group of her well-off acquaintances into a kind of club. The dues paid, along with any contribution extracted from husbands and rich friends, enabled the committee of several ladies to rush about buying out whole bakeries. The committee would then ride in a coach loaded with loaves of bread down to Castle Garden where ships were then landing passengers, and where they handed out bread and smiles to bemused foreigners. "A token of hope," my aunt said to me. "A gesture of welcome. Bread, my dear, speaks a universal language, like music."

The bitter December of 1835 forced the temporary suspension of these modest missions of mercy. The temperature fell to 17 degrees below zero by mid-month; snow packed all the streets and made most impassable, for there was no municipal department to keep them clear. Our kitchen range and several fireplaces were burning day and night, as in every home that could afford the fuel. On December 16th, coming home from the Pierponts—neighbors with several children, whose tutor I shared—I heard fire engines. I wondered how they could get to the blaze. At home, when I held my icy hands out to

14

the flames in the parlor fireplace I had the illusion that I was seeing in miniature the fire those engines were trying to reach. Very soon it sounded as if all forty-nine of the city's private fire companies were out in full force.

I was right in this guess, as I learned when Uncle Isaiah got home that night, having made his way with difficulty by various routes, the coachman sometimes stopping to shovel snow away ahead of the sleigh, an old-fashioned one with curly runners in which I loved to ride under a warm laprobe. In his high, excited voice he told my aunt and me that his cigar factory was threatened by a fire which had started in a five-story building on Merchant Street. It was blazing at every window before the first fire engine arrived and quickly burned to the ground. By then, however, the flames had spread to adjoining buildings. The cold was so severe that if the firemen stopped pumping water from the wagon's tank it froze solid. As for the hydrants, so little came out that attached hoses threw feeble jets less than twenty feet. Finally the firemen chopped holes in the ice of the East River and pumped water from it into long lengths of joined hoses. But it was too late for any remedy. By the next day the fire had raced from building to building and threatened Wall Street.

"The hub of the nation's trade!" Uncle Isaiah fumed. "The stock exchange, the banks, the import-export houses, all in danger because the Croton reservoir stands unfinished. A city surrounded by rivers, yet without an adequate water supply!"

"Then you must act to remedy this situation," I remember my aunt saying.

He was astounded. "I? Remedy it? I'm about to lose my factory building, unless a miracle intervenes. Why

15

should I remedy anything to benefit others after such a loss?"

The penny papers were full of it, with alarming pen-and-ink sketches of the burning buildings—but not as alarming as the sight from the third-floor window of the upstairs maid, Melonia, from which we could see the hellish flames to the south. Now men were working like demons, we had read, to clear the streets for fire engines as they chased the spreading flames. By the end of the second day Mayor Lawrence issued a plea to able-bodied citizens to man the pumps, for the firemen were exhausted. My uncle responded, hoping to save the old brick factory he had only recently bought. By then, fire engines were arriving from other parts of the state, from New Jersey, even one from Philadelphia.

But nothing did any good. Wall Street burned to the ground. Nearly seven hundred buildings were lost. So was the Moss Cigar factory.

Uncle Isaiah came home a devastated man and a weary one, and he sat slumped over his bent arms at the dining table beside a cooling cup of tea. He made me think of a child about to cry. It frightened me to see him so crushed. "Gone," he moaned. "The whole building is rubble and ashes."

"Better buildings than that one are being razed every day on purpose to make room for new ones," my aunt said, briskly. "How you can mourn the place I cannot see."

He raised his head. On his sooty face a smile began. "I can take out a loan with my uptown property as collateral. And there's the insurance, too." He stood, followed his slight paunch to the sideboard where a decanter always stood, and poured a glass of wine which

16

he raised in a toast to himself. "I'm not downed, not a bit. It'll take more than a disaster like this one to ruin Isaiah Moss." He tossed down the wine, then shook his head with a look of false pity. "But there are hard times ahead for some in this city, I can assure you of that."

The charred smell the fire left behind lasted a long while, and the devastation of block after block of once-fine buildings was sickening even to a child like me. But the bitter December and icy January left us at last; March winds blew chill February into the past, and ushered in a certain brisk, bright Saturday when I was allowed at last a privilege I had yearned for, to go with my aunt and her Bread Ladies down to the Battery in a coach full of fresh-baked loaves.

While she and I waited near the gangplank of the sailing ship from Europe, baskets of bread on our arms, my eye was caught by a strange-looking creature who in turn was staring at several well-dressed passengers who had just disembarked. He was a very old man, bent and white-haired, his jaw large and square. In knee-breeches, white stockings and silver-buckled shoes, he looked like a ghost from another day. "Is there among you a young woman named Theodosia?" I heard him ask in a harsh quaver. As the ladies looked at one another, shook their heads and drew back from him, my aunt took my arm and pulled me back. "That's Aaron Burr, the wretch who shot Alexander Hamilton in a duel by the questionable method of firing too soon."

I knew about Burr, and was excited to see him in the flesh. "And then he fled to Florida," I said proudly, "and later to Europe where he tried to persuade Napoleon to attack the United States. But who is Theodosia?"

"His daughter. The only creature he ever loved. She

17

disappeared many years ago on an ocean voyage; her vessel simply vanished. Ever since, Burr has haunted the Battery, waiting for the lost ship to come in. Don't stare at him!"

I tried not to. But I did not get to see a historical figure every day, particularly such a wicked one. By now the immigrants from below decks were disembarking, engaging the Bread Ladies' full attention, if not mine. I followed Burr, mesmerized. With my wide eyes on his white head as he queried another passenger about his daughter, I became suddenly aware that someone was watching me, and turned. A tall young man in a dark-blue coat, buff breeches and a beaver hat stood smiling down. "Is that bread for me?" he asked. I looked up into a pair of hazel-green eyes that glittered with light and mischief in the shadow of the hat brim. His hair was dark, to judge by the sideburns, and in the smooth bright skin of his cheeks two long dimples carved pleasant shadows.

"But you speak English," I pointed out, which evidently confused him.

"Do you imagine this prevents hunger?" he asked, his head cocked to one side. I now caught a certain lilt to his speech, a faint trace, perhaps, of an Irish brogue. But he did not look hungry.

"Our bread is meant to welcome poor immigrants who speak no English. Bread is a universal language, like music."

His face got a hard, clever look as he nodded. "Now there's a pretty and high-minded thought!" But his eyes had strayed from me to someone standing just behind me. I turned and saw my aunt. He removed his hat. For an instant of silence they stared at one another, then my aunt gave a light laugh. "It's Tom, isn't it? Tom

18

O'Casey." I instantly caught something false in her tone which puzzled me.

The hat he held was swept to his broad chest as he made a slightly exaggerated bow. "Your servant, Madame. Mrs. Moss, isn't it?"

"And what are you doing here in New York?" Her tone of light amusement seemed as exaggerated.

"Residing here, Madame, with a bachelor uncle engaged in the building trade which he has been teaching me."

"And your wife and child, I trust they are well?"

His smile faded. "My wife is dead of the cholera. My little boy died soon after."

"I'm sorry to learn that you've suffered such grievous losses. I did not know that things had gone so ill with you."

Aaron Burr now forgotten, I stood staring up from face to face, aware as a child can be that something unsaid hung in the air about them like a mist. "Ill?" Tom O'Casey smiled again. "Yes, one could say that. But being half Scot and half Irish gives me an advantage, for the Scot won't waste tears on spilt milk, and that Irish fellow in me suffers from optimism against all evidence to the contrary. And to tell the truth, I found I preferred carrying a hod to farming or tanning a hide any merry day of the week."

A hod carrier? He seemed too well-dressed and clean and well-spoken for that low, ill-paid occupation. My aunt, echoing my thoughts, said, "You don't look like any hod carrier I ever saw."

"Ah, well now, that's in the past. Now I'm in charge of the hod carriers, and have shown myself clever at scrounging up building jobs as well. You have a very

19

polite and pretty little girl here, may I say."

The sudden new tack took my aunt off guard, but she managed another social laugh. "This is my niece, Jane Anne. This is Mr. O'Casey, my dear."

"Ah, to be sure, she looks a good bit like Jennie. Any others?"

"Nieces? Not a one."

"Children."

"Not a one!" Suddenly she plucked a loaf from her basket and held it out to Tom O'Casey. "Here. A belated welcome to New York, and may all go well with you here."

"It's already going very well." Holding the bread, he eyed her from bonnet to skirt hem and back again. "Very well indeed!" Her cheeks were almost as pink as the small roses framing her face inside the bonnet brim as with a hasty farewell she took my hand in hers and hurried me away. But I kept staring back over my shoulder, saw Tom O'Casey greeting a little family of immigrants, Irish to judge from the man's red hair and heavy brogue, to whom he gave the loaf of bread. Around them circled several men each calling to the newcomers to follow him. "Runners," my aunt said, and I saw that she had also turned her head toward Tom. "Vultures who prey on new immigrants, take advantage of their innocence to lure them into hotels where they're grossly overcharged, even robbed." Her indignation had made her slow to a stop.

"Get along with you!" Tom told the runners. "These are friends of mine, so keep your paws off them." The burliest of the runners raised his knob-handled cane in a threatening gesture, but Tom seized it, tore it from his grasp, and hurled it away. The other two gave up as the

20

first ran to pick up his cane, then he too lumbered off in search of other prey.

"Isn't he brave!" I enthused. "Your friend, I mean."

She turned her head quickly and started toward the carriage where she saw the other ladies gathered, all watching. "How strange to encounter him by chance after so many years," she said.

The last loaf of bread had been given out, and we returned home, the women all eager to know about the handsome stranger my aunt and I had been talking to. "Oh, we knew each other as children," she told them lightly.

In the parlor at home she removed her bonnet before the mantel mirror, stood staring thoughtfully at her reflection. Absently, she put the bonnet down on the settee and went back to the fireplace to pick up a box of the new self-igniting matches, the "Locofocos" which had been in use for a year or so. She struck one and lighted the candles at either side of the Stiegel rose-glass.

"I'm quite certain Mr. O'Casey saw us together, Aunt Liza, and chose to break the ice by speaking to me first."

"Ah, well, that's neither here nor there, my dear. Neither here nor there." Her voice had a dreamy tone and she continued to study her face in the mirror with a cool scrutiny quite unlike the usual quick glances she bestowed on it. Beside her mirrored image the rose glowed, and her face illuminated by the candleflames had a mysterious and timeless beauty.

II

Elizabeth stared into the mantel mirror after she lit the candles beside her rose-glass. She did not see herself nor the dim reflected room behind her, but Tom at the Battery. How well he looked! What a handsome man he had turned out to be! Her hand went to her breast. She looked down at it, aware then that her heart was beating faster, it seemed, than usual. He was in this city, out there in the early night. He had been here five years. How many times had their paths nearly crossed? Where? When? Was he, at this very moment, thinking of her?

"Aunt Liza?"

"Yes?" She whirled to face the forgotten child. Jane Anne stood primly in her puff-sleeved pale blue merino dress, the correct two inches of lace pantalette showing below the hem. "I've been thinking about that gentleman at the Battery."

"Whatever is there to think about?"

"I'm quite certain Mr. O'Casey saw us together, Aunt Liza, and chose to break the ice by speaking to me first."

"Ah, well, that's neither here nor there, my dear. Neither here nor there." Elizabeth turned to the mirror and smoothed her hair. "I'd like a cup of tea. Ring for Mary, will you, dear?" She watched the obedient child hurry to pull the silk bell cord that hung between the upright piano and the door to the dining room, setting off a jangle in the basement kitchen, unheard up here. "And now you must change out of your street clothes and settle down to your lessons. You can get a good bit done before Uncle Isaiah comes home if you apply yourself."

"I decided that he might be a shy man. With ladies, I mean."

"Shy? Your uncle?" She felt herself smiling. She knew who the child meant.

"No, Mr. O'Casey. But then he didn't seem in the least shy with you. Quite the contrary, I'd say."

"Shyness with ladies was not a fault of his. Now skip!"

"Shall I take your shawl and bonnet upstairs to your room?"

"Thank you, dear." Divesting herself of them, Elizabeth lost the sense of being a stranger in her own home. The maid brought tea and lighted the oil lamp. In the Hepplewhite chair flanking the settee below the lace-curtained front window Elizabeth sipped the hot brew, eyes on her glass rose, passport to another place and time.

Old Peter Aller died at eighty-six when Elizabeth was twelve. In his will he left Jennie the rose pokal. That he had recalled her long-ago plea seemed to Elizabeth just one more proof of Jennie's power to charm. In a family where "pretty" was a word seldom used, golden-haired little Jennie had a way of getting her way. Elizabeth had yearned—oh, how she had yearned!—to possess the rose-glass, but had remembered parental injunctions against ever asking for a gift: Grandfather Aller had left to her the flint-glass pitcher with the blue rim. She knew Jenny's beauty had tipped the balance of justice.

From then on Elizabeth accepted her fate as the older sister of a charmer. She dressed primly in plain brown linsey-woolsey, her shining chestnut hair severely braided and hidden by a white close-fitting bonnet. No Quaker maiden avoided any touch of frill or finery more strictly. At thirteen she took to writing verses about the evanescence of beauty, the virtue of plain things like a pewter mug ("No flaunting silver sheen diverts the eye from this small vessel's humble majesty.") The simple life was lauded, transitory beauty deplored. The local hermit, a dirty dazed old fellow, was glorified for turning away from "life's gaudy Grails their seekers never find." Nuns fascinated her. In another place, of another faith, she might have become a nun, she believed, but alas happened to be a Presbyterian in Pennsylvania.

Her father, like her grandfather, was no churchgoer, his only religious remark being "In thy closet kneeling pray," but he did not object to his wife, of Scotch descent, attending her church with their daughters. Allerton had two houses of worship, Lutheran and Presbyterian. It had a Common School as well, for the foremost citizens of Allerton were sensible folk of Scotch or Dutch descent and saw no harm in erasing illiteracy by hiring a needy young man who could read, write and figure, live in an attic, and dine here and there. The first schoolhouse was a converted barn on the outskirts of town. Originally it had only two rooms intended to separate older from younger students, but soon it separated boys from girls due to an unfortunate coupling that was attributed to classroom propinquity. The little girls still walked chastely to and from school in pairs or trios; to stop to gabble with a boy was considered unchaste, giddy. Betsy Baker, the innkeeper's daughter, did that.

And so during childhood Tom O'Casey was a distant figure to Elizabeth and might have remained so, even though they attended the same church, for Tom's mother was a Dunbar and a Presbyterian. But the Dunbars and the Allers were not friendly. Long before the Revolution, when Allerton was only a handful of dwellings huddled together against Indian attacks, the men going out with flintlocks to farm their lands, a dispute had developed between the Allers and the Dunbars over a property line, settled at last to the Allers' satisfaction and giving them title to a certain hill where a sizeable vein of iron was then discovered. So bitter was the Dunbars' resentment that eighty years later the two families indulged in no more than a nodding acquaintance.

In a smaller town such distance would have been harder to maintain, but Allerton, by 1823, Elizabeth's fifteenth year, had grown larger than Lower Darby or Chadd's Fort—boasting, in addition to the schoolhouse and two churches, a circulating library, the old gristmill, a general store, a butcher shop, two inns, a blacksmith shop, a tannery and the Aller Ironworks. The main residential street was lined with pleasant Colonial houses like the Allers'; the two side streets with their smaller ones were clean and tree-shaded. But the Dunbars had chosen to remain in the old farmhouse more than a mile from the Dunbar tannery on Main Street. The house had been built by a Dunbar who had learned from friendly Indians their way of getting hides soft and supple enough to make jackets and breeches: cow brains did the trick.

To get to the circulating library Elizabeth had to pass the Baker Tavern and the tannery, and occasionally as she walked by with books in the crook of her arm she would see from the corner of her eye Tom O'Casey in the tannery doorway taking a breath of air, for after school he often worked there beside his father. In the manner of their mothers, they nodded formally if their eyes met. She had begun the task of reading all Shakespeare's plays, starting with *Romeo and Juliet* and the ancient disagreement between the Allers and Dunbars might have set her imagination at work. But Jennie, only thirteen, conceived a crush on Tom O'Casey, confided to Elizabeth one night with many a giggle. Even Tom's odd manner of dressing enchanted Jennie: he wore breeches and jacket of soft brown leather, like a man in the past century. When Jennie asked if Elizabeth didn't agree that Tom was quite the best-favored boy in town, Elizabeth replied aloofly that she was not in the habit of noticing boys at all and certainly not Tom O'Casey.

On a bright May Sunday three months after her fifteenth birthday this changed abruptly. Standing with open hymn book in church she heard a clear young baritone voice, glanced to her left and just across the center aisle saw Tom O'Casey with head turned above his hymnal to stare at her as he sang. He winked.

It startled her. She stared in disbelief. He winked again, his smile as daring as a kiss. She quickly looked down at the blurred words on the page, aware that her voice had stopped. Her prim serenity was gone. Wings fluttered inside her, like something trying to escape. She did not look in Tom's direction again.

But overnight she began to primp. She crocheted herself a wide lacy fichu, unbraided her hidden hair and washed it in rain-barrel water, brushed it with long dreamy strokes. She asked for a prettier bonnet, and next Sunday in church sat with eyes demurely lowered, but

27

with her whole being tense with hope that Tom had come to church and would notice how well she looked. Covert glances showed that he was not in his seat across the aisle.

Outside the church, while her mother congratulated the minister on his sermon, Tom materialized as if out of the sunny air. He was some ten feet away and just caught her gaze, then glanced toward the oak grove beyond the graveyard. She went to his side and silently walked with him past tombstones and into the shade of the trees. Strolling there, they were sometimes in the soft shade of lofty leafage, sometimes in sunlight, and the alternation seemed to add to her dazzlement. "You're not like other girls," he said. He praised her eyes, told her they were flag blue, "the flower, not the banner." He spoke with mockery of the old grudge their families clung to. "For a few acres of land near a hundred years ago are we supposed not to become friends?" To which she answered, "What's in a name? A rose by any other name would smell as sweet."

With a shade of bitterness Tom said, "But if my name were Dunbar instead of O'Casey, no one would ever call me 'the Irish tanner's son.'" Elizabeth nodded solemnly: his father had come to town as an indentured servant and was known to tipple too often at the tavern.

Before they left the woods Tom found a jack-in-the-pulpit, picked it, and gave it to her. Holding the delicate green lily with its upthrust central pistil she walked homeward in a daze of pleasure. She barely heard her mother's scolding for wandering off as she had, and with the tanner's boy at that.

Neither Romeo nor Juliet had prepared Elizabeth for the overwhelming emotion of first love. Stolen hours with Tom dwindled every other waking activity; the librarian commented on the rarity and brevity of her visits. When Tom took her hand as they walked in the early summer woods she felt his desire and hers tingle from palm to palm. Their first kiss left her so dizzy she had to cling to him or fall. He kissed her again for a long, long time and she knew with wicked exhilaration that she had felt the ultimate in carnal desire, or nearly so. When she thought of him, the verses that danced into her head had nothing to do with nuns or hermits.

Because they knew that neither her family nor his would look with approval on their attachment, they devised a secret means of communication; they left notes for one another in a hollow branch of an oak tree near the church. And sometimes in the evening after work at the tannery he would pass her house whistling an old Scottish tune which meant that he would wait for her by their oak tree. She would slip away and meet him there whenever she could. They earnestly discussed the necessity of telling her parents the truth so that he could openly call on her, yet she deferred it, wanting nothing to spoil the sweetness of what they had. Their secret love satisfied her romantic streak, and his kisses, though arousing inchoate longings, were still enough outlet for her passion.

But one Saturday afternoon when they went berrying together in the woods he drew her down to lie beside him in a grassy place amid a scramble of wild blackberry vines. They kissed and kissed, and at last he undid her bodice to bare part of one breast, kissing again and again, almost with reverence, the pale half-moon revealed. She let tender ecstasy devour her modest shock. At last only a shred of self-control remained to her, but she twisted herself away from his embrace, and stood up buttoning her dress. In a shaken voice she pointed out that she had to return with blackberries for supper and the sun had almost set. He lay back looking up at her with hungry eyes. "What harm if we stay a bit longer? What harm, Liza? I want to marry you. I need you. Now." He held his arms wide. "Come back here to me. Take pity on my pain." He was half-smiling, yet dilated pupils made his eyes look black. "Come to me. I'll never fail you, Liza. I'm yours, you're mine, and that's the truth of it."

Her whole being yearned toward him, and she took a step forward, then shook her head. "No. Get up."

"I'm up," he grinned. "Well up."

"That's base talk to a woman you say you love. I'll pick my berries alone, then." She swooped up a pail and left him there on the grass, her heart throbbing like a drum. But in an instant he joined her, and as they began to fill their two pails with berries a wild, cheery mood seized them and he suddenly put a plump, juicy berry into her mouth, and she did the same, and they laughed as their lips grew stained with purple juice. The sun had just set when they hurried homeward bathed in golden light.

The next day when she came home from school her mother confronted her, blue eyes flashing. A small woman, fair and quick-moving, Jane Aller had a deep-pitched Scottish voice. "And what did you gather along with those berries, Miss Sly? A bairn to disgrace us with, and yourself?" And she revealed that a spinster grimly gathering berries had seen them emerge from their hiding place, had heard their wild laughter as they fed berries to each other, and had hastened to tell Elizabeth's mother of the rowdy sight they had offered heaven and her own chaste eyes. "You used to play the Quakeress to a fare-thee-well. Was all that chaste modesty but a sham? How long have you been meeting Tom O'Casey on the sly?"

"I love him. He loves me. He wants me for his wife."

"Did you bed with him in the bushes?"

"No!"

"Then pray for a husband of substance, not the Irish tanner's lad."

"I love Tom. I want him for my husband!"

"Your wild, lusty feelings mean nothing. I had 'em when young, but wed your father as my parents wished. Cows have 'em, pigs do, and worms, for all I know. For shame, Elizabeth, behaving no better than a tavern tart!"

At supper that night her father pushed aside his pewter plate, lit his long-stemmed clay pipe, and said, "You'll see no more of Tom O'Casey, my girl." The puff of smoke he emitted reminded her of the preacher's sermon the past Sunday: hellfire awaited disobedient sons and daughters. But she heard such dread pulpit threats with ears that had once heard her beloved grandfather say, "Never act out of fear of hell or hope for heaven either; they don't exist."

"You're not being fair or just, Father! Tom's a fine and upright man who loves me dearly."

"He's seventeen without a penny in his leather pocket, with a father who drinks and a mother who's a Dunbar, and *they're* a mean, contentious lot."

"I love *him*, not his family!"

"But his family is what you'll get, along with him. As for love, you don't know what love is as yet. Many a lustful girl has wasted herself on a trifler and lived to regret it long. My duty is to spare you this grief, and I will. No more need be said. You'll not see Tom O'Casey again, my lass. I went to the tannery today and asked him to keep

31

his distance or displease me much."

She waited anxiously for Tom to defy her father. A week passed with no sign that he would. Her mother's surveillance relaxed as a crushed and silent Elizabeth seemed cured of her infatuation. And then one evening at sundown she heard Tom's whistle. Her mother was in the kitchen instructing the new scullery maid, her father still at the foundry, and Jennie nowhere about. Elizabeth slipped out and made a beeline for the oak tree where they ran into each other's arms, kissed, murmured words of love. Tom had a plan. He had no money. But he had an uncle in New York, his mother's older brother Barney Dunbar who owned a construction firm. Tom could write him, ask to become an apprentice. "I'll save my money and come back here and marry you. Would you wait for me, though?"

"If it takes years, I'll wait!" They kissed on it, she moved by his courage, he by her fidelity. It seemed most natural to lock her hand to Tom's warm, urgent one, follow him deeper into the woods than they had ventured before. The spring evening was uniquely balmy, or was it that their pounding blood warmed all the air around them?

The spot he said he had found by earlier exploration was a good way from their postbox oak, how far she never knew because she floated there on her own cloud of joyous excitement. On the soft new grass beneath an ancient tree he spread her cloak, and as he pulled it gently from her shoulders one of his hands brushed against her neck. The shiver that spread from there went right down her spine, and in moments they were lying side by side, each propped on an elbow, to feast on the beloved other face and the love in the other eyes. In only a moment

32

more their bodies had somehow melted together. Through the soft brown leather of his trousers she felt his hardness against her eager cleft that throbbed to welcome it in. With abandon she flung herself against him. His warm hands cupped her breasts that thrust against them as his lips and hers seemed to become one, merged forever. Mindless, she soared upward on wings of bliss. . . .

BLAM! The horrid sound of a musket fired quite nearby made them jerk and start like one hunted creature. Tom whispered, "I'll see who it is." He strode off in the direction of the sound. Shaken, quickly donning her cloak, she listened to Tom's voice and another but did not make out the words. Her whole being felt outraged by that hideous noise that had killed their ecstasy. In a few minutes Tom returned. "It was only old Phelps, out after a rabbit for a stew." Aware now of how late it was, she regretted that she had ever penned a poem about the hermit. They hurried out of the woods toward home, silent at first, then more cheerful as they realized that they had not seen the last of such bliss as the hermit's gun had ended.

The uncle's answer to Tom's letter asking employment was a grave disappointment. He had at present no need for a so young an apprentice. He knew Tom was needed on the farm and in the tannery. "Write me again in a year or two if you're bent on learning my trade," he wrote in a cramped hand.

"A year!" she wailed.

"Or two." Tom was leaning back against their oak; his arms went around her and drew her against him. He whispered, "If you were with child your father would be quick enough to post the banns." She felt his desire for her begin to throb and a thrill went through her. But her mother's "no better than a tavern tart" rang through her head. If she let herself be seduced like a low woman, would Tom still think well of her? And what would she think of herself?

"A year isn't so long. We'll wait it out like decent folk and try your uncle again when you're eighteen."

"But I wish, oh, how I wish you were mine right now."

"I am, in all ways but one."

In heartfelt letters left in the hollow of the oak they shared their secrets and their yearnings. She learned why he dressed by choice in leather: it was pride, his way of flaunting his father's trade out of resentment at being known as "the Irish tanner's son." Their secret meetings were few and brief, for often when he came by whistling at day's end she could not slip out, could only stand at the window and watch him pass, taller now than when he winked at her in church. My love, she thought, watching him go by. My true and faithful love!

Three days after her sixteenth birthday Elizabeth came home from the oak tree, Tom's note hidden in the bosom of her dress. A somewhat stout, well-dressed stranger with receding hair was warming his coattails by the fire. He bowed, staring at her from pale gray eyes that seemed to doubt the sincerity of his smile, marred by one crooked canine tooth. He stood very erect then, as if to display his waistcoat of rich brocade, or perhaps, she thought, to convey firmness of character. "This is Mr. Isaiah Moss, from New York," her father said. "My daughter Elizabeth, sir."

Isaiah Moss bowed again. "Miss Aller. As I was saying

to your esteemed pater, I am not one to dally. On a visit to Philadelphia I heard of the Aller Ironworks and its reputation for casting unusual equipment. So I hired a carriage and headed here forthwith as I am in need of a tobacco-shredding machine, built to certain specifications. Your father has kindly invited me to dinner, our business at the foundry being concluded."

Elizabeth could think of no response to this flow of information beyond a nod. The note from Tom was burning a hole in her bosom, so anxious was she to read it again. Isaiah Moss glanced at her father. "How pleasing to meet so modest a young lady. Those in New York are prone to chatter."

At dinner he talked little, ate steadily, but once fed leaned back with thumbs in his vest pockets, fingers thrumming his abdomen, and revealed in his high-pitched voice that he had made a real success of the tobacconist shop his father had left him and had opened two more, as well as selling certain inherited property so as to buy land on upper Fifth Avenue that would one day be worth a fortune. "And now I intend to have my own cigar factory; I have just purchased an old building for that purpose. Cigars, my friends, are all the rage in Europe now, where they are fast outmoding snuff. And they're sure to become even more popular here. I already have in my employ a couple of Cuban fellows, an *escojedor* who is expert at cutting up without waste the costly high-grade leaves used for the wrapper, and another adept at rolling the cut pieces around the cheaper filler, and who is at present teaching several Irish fellows the trick. But I need the shredding machine for the pipe tobacco I sell in my three shops." As Elizabeth stifled a yawn and saw Jennie grow rosy stifling one

35

of her giggles, Isaiah Moss paused portentously. "My ultimate aim is to manufacture a good ten-cent cigar." As this caused no amazement he added, "A *good* ten-cent cigar. At present there are none. A void exists between the vile five-centers peddled on street corners and costly imported Havanas which can sell for as much as a dollar apiece."

As Elizabeth's father got out his pipe, Isaiah Moss offered, "But I myself do not smoke. There are those who believe as King James did that tobacco is injurious to the health. I would prefer to forego a pleasure praised by Alexander Pope, Sir Walter Scott, the Byron fellow, and the late, great William Shakespeare than to risk doing my excellent constitution a damage."

Elizabeth's mother waved away a cloud of her husband's pipe smoke. "Mrs. Moss is most fortunate."

Isaiah Moss heaved a deep sigh. "Alas, I am still a bachelor. But at last I have reached that stage of prosperity which enables me to consider the responsibility of taking a wife. My mother, God bless her, has gone to her reward, and I rattle about a large house crying for a woman's touch. The house, I mean, of course."

Jennie lost her struggle with the giggles, muffled them in a napkin, and was excused from the table by her mother. Elizabeth envied her.

"I would like to show my appreciation for kind hospitality by inviting you all to the Arch Street Theater in Philadelphia tonight," Isaiah Moss was saying. "I noted that *Hamlet* is being played. Do you have by chance a penchent for the Bard of Avon, Mr. Aller?"

"My daughter Elizabeth does," her father said. "Mrs. Aller and I do not."

"In that case, would you permit me to escort Miss

ller, or is that presumptuous of a relative stranger?"

Without waiting for her father's reply, Elizabeth said,
Thank you, but I must decline."

"My daughter has need of diversion," her father said.
He turned to Elizabeth, his rather majestic, large-
featured face now iron-eyed. "It will be to your benefit to
spend an evening in the company of a mature gentleman." The letter from Tom seemed suddenly to be visible
through her bodice.

"I should think you'd enjoy seeing a play you have
only read," her mother added, nodding.

"I would enjoy *that*," she confessed.

It was quite exciting to dress in her best and to depart
grandly with Mr. Moss in his hired carriage, but she felt
disloyal to Tom as she walked down the theater aisle
beside a middle-aged gentleman from New York. Still, to
see *Hamlet* on stage was almost worth that uneasiness.
During the long ride home Isaiah Moss did a good bit of
boasting about the city of New York, which had outdis-
tanced Philadelphia in their long rivalry, with a population of over a hundred thousand. "You are not one for
badinage, I see," he said at last.

"I don't know what that means."

"Light and playful banter. It's a word often used in
New York, among the upper classes."

Did he regard his own remarks as badinage? She
turned her head to hide a smile. Now he was talking about
the population of his city once more, as though it somehow reflected well on him. "I believe that in another ten
years the number of residents will triple, although immigrants will account to a large degree for that increase.
They swarm in from Europe by the thousands each year,
particularly the Irish, though at least they provide us

37

with cheap labor."

It seemed to take forever to reach home. She thanked him for *Hamlet,* was relieved to learn he would leave for New York early next morning. "Duty calls," he sighed. "There are times when I wish I had been born an easy going soul like my father, content as he was with a modest income. Ambitionless, my dear mother was wont to call him. Yes, duty calls me and I must say a reluctant farewell."

Next morning she hurried to the hollow oak with a note telling Tom of seeing *Hamlet* with a tedious old New York gentleman, at her father's insistence. A note from Tom waited there. The penstrokes had dug deep into the paper, leaving inky dots.

Who was that man I saw you leaving with in a carriage? It was midnight when you returned. Is this an example of how I can trust you if I go far away to New York?

She left her note for him, went home feeling both guilty and angry. What right had he to assume she was shallow and uncaring? She waited two days but then went to collect his reply.

I do not think your father could have forced you to see *Hamlet.* Your protest must have been a very weak one. I cannot hire a carriage and take you to the theater. Nothing like that must ever happen again. It tore me apart.

She was still full of self-reproach at having failed Tom when Jennie danced into the room where she sat writing him a tender message. "You'll never guess! I just saw

38

Tom O'Casey walking along Main Street with that Betsy Baker. Oh, but she's a plump, saucy thing!"

The jolt was sudden and hurtful. "I don't believe you."

"It's true!"

Desperately, she raced to the oak tree, with a penned command: "Meet me here tomorrow at four without fail."

He did not deny having walked beside Betsy Baker. She had come out of the inn as he passed it, had fallen into step beside him.

"Jennie saw you. Everyone saw you."

"Well, to walk beside Betsy by daylight is nothing at all compared to spending a whole evening in Philadelphia with an old fop you never saw before."

"But I had no choice, short of making an unpleasant scene."

"Did I? Could I run away from her like a rabbit? Tell her to walk somewhere else? It meant nothing at all. You're blowing it up to put me in the wrong, too, because you pranced off to Philadelphia that night."

"No. I'm jealous, I think."

"So am I." They smiled then, and tentatively kissed, then less tentatively. "Oh, it's hard to have a man's feelings and not be regarded as a man yet." There was a nick on his cheek where he had shaved. Broad-shouldered in brown leather, he looked enough of a man for anyone. "But soon enough I'll be writing my uncle again." His face lit up. "And if he says yes, why can't we marry then, in Philadelphia? A secret marriage? You'll stay here while I'm up there getting started in my new trade."

"Maybe. Yes! Maybe!"

Their trust in each other fully restored, they carelessly

39

left the oak grove together, hands locked. Elizabeth's mother was kneeling by Grandfather Harth's tombstone, on which she had just placed flowers. It was, Elizabeth realized, the anniversary of his death. Jane Aller stood up slowly, her eyes riveted on them. Their hands parted.

Tom walked to her, staunchly. "Don't worry, Mrs. Aller. Nothing wrong has happened. I love Elizabeth. I want to marry her."

"Do you indeed? You've made a poor beginning as far as my blessing's concerned. Elizabeth, come home." Her silence as they walked was worse than any scolding. As they entered the house she said, "I'm deeply disappointed in you. You'll not go running after the tanner's boy any longer, my girl."

"He's not just the tanner's boy! Why do you keep calling him that? He's himself, and I will marry him or no one else, ever!"

"That might prove the better choice. As it happens, you may have another. Mr. Moss has just written to your father and me that you made a considerable impression on him."

"But I don't even like him! You know it's Tom I love!"

"I thought the same once, of a certain young man, when I was your age. I married your father instead. My parents saw that young man more truly than I. He turned out badly, a mere ne'er-do-well."

"How he turned out has nothing to do with Tom!"

"But it has much to do with callow youths who have not proven their worth."

The solution her parents found was swift. Elizabeth was informed that she was going on an extended visit to her mother's spinster cousin Amy in Philadelphia. "She's a dear, deserving lady, so good to Grandfather

Aller in his last years, and would welcome young company."

"I don't want to go to Philadelphia to Cousin Amy's."

Her father said, grimly, "The choice is not yours, but mine. So pack your clothes. We leave right after dinner."

She had books to return to the library and could stop at the tannery to tell Tom what had happened. She returned the books first. From the library steps, she saw exactly what Jenny had described: Tom strolling along beside the Baker girl. They were laughing. The pain of the sight made Elizabeth feel faint, ill. She stepped back into the library doorway, blind with tears, yet filled with the molten lava of her anger. She had loved a trifler! But never again would he have a chance to delude her. Never, never again!

In Philadelphia she struggled to uproot him from her heart, but wept into her pillow. Vindictively, she imagined him leaving note after note in the hollow oak until someone told him she was not in Allerton. But as the weeks passed it began to seem to her that she had been wrong not to let him know where she was, no matter who he had walked with down Main Street.

Her best effort was stilted. "My father has sent me to visit a relative in order to separate me from you. I saw you walking yet again with Betsy, so I am not sure you care where I am. It would not offend me to hear from you, however."

His reply was as terse. "Betsy Baker may have certain lacks compared to you, but disloyalty is not one of them."

Disloyalty! *He* dared to use the word?

Summoned by her father, she returned to Allerton a month later. After the city, the town seemed peaceful and

41

pleasant, and it was good to be in her own home again, in her own bed.

She was awakened from first sleep that night by the sound of Tom's whistle. Or had she dreamed it? She threw back the covers and ran to the window, but no one was looking up in the moonlight.

Next morning, a Saturday, her father told her that Isaiah Moss was coming to Allerton. "You have recovered, I hope, from your lust for the O'Casey boy. I informed him after you left for Philadelphia that you have a serious suitor, a well-off New York gentleman who asked my permission to marry you and received it."

Elizabeth was out of the house before anyone could stop her. Halfway to the tannery she found herself praying that Tom would be there. She had to tell him that she had not accepted any other suitor, had not even known she had one. And that she had not known until today what her father said to him. As she neared the tannery, Betsy Baker came out of the tavern and fell into step beside her. "If you're here looking for Tom, just let me tell you something, Elizabeth Aller. I'm expecting his baby. So don't think you can win him back, because he had to marry me."

Numbly, Elizabeth stared at three freckles on Betsy's pug nose, then at the girl's stomach, then ran. . . .

"While I realize that there is an appreciable difference in our ages," Isaiah Moss was saying, having moved to seat himself beside her in the significantly empty parlor, "this is all to the good as far as you're concerned, my dear, if I may call you that. I can offer you comforts and luxuries a younger man could not." As if to prove it, he dipped two

42

fingers into his waistcoat pocket and withdrew a glittering ring which he held up to admire, turning it so the facets of the diamond threw off bright flashes of cold fire. "An heirloom, worn by my dear mother. Nothing would make me happier than to place it on your finger in token of our engagement." She stared numbly at the bauble he offered to a broken heart. "You will find a bustling city like New York infinitely preferable to this somewhat buccolic town."

The distance of perhaps a hundred miles between New York and Tom's bride-to-be was more attractive than the idea of city bustle or sparkling diamonds. "I want an early wedding, as soon as possible."

He froze, his small gray eyes bleak. "Is there any *particular* reason for this haste?"

"Yes. I can't wait to get out of Allerton!"

The wedding took place immediately after services in the church where she had first thrilled at Tom O'Casey's wink. Many townfolk were there to see the ironmaster's daughter wed, and as she started down the aisle beside her father, she wondered if Tom were watching. She proudly raised her head, adorned with the usual wreath of flowers. Then she suffered a moment of panic; her feet would not move, but seemed to have taken root. If her father had urged her forward, she might well have turned and run back up the aisle and out of the church. But with stolid patience he waited there beside her. The arm to which she clung was like the iron it had hammered. She took a deep breath and looked up at him. He was looking straight ahead, his brow, nose and chin noble enough to be cast in bronze. In that moment she knew that though she might never love Isaiah, her love for Tom had ended in pain and disillusionment. She took a deep breath. Her feet moved her forward toward her only destiny.

The simplest of trousseaux was hers, for Isaiah explained to her parents that clothing in New York differed greatly from what was worn in Philadelphia where due to longstanding Quaker influence any color much brighter than brown was thought frivolous. It would be his pleasure, he said, to outfit his bride in a manner suitable to the city where she would now live. But her parents provided a dowry of five hundred dollars, linen bedsheets embroidered with her initials, a dozen solid silver spoons, a quilt made in a pattern originated by Elizabeth's great-grandmother and, of course, the Stiegel flint-glass pitcher with the sapphire-blue rim. It was only as she shut the drawer of the chest in her bedroom, and knew it was for the last time, that the finality of the step she had taken struck her in all its force.

The hired carriage was waiting below to take her on the first lap of her journey to New York. Outwardly calm, inwardly tense at leaving behind all that was loved and familiar, she went down the stairs and out the door. Her mother, father, Jennie, and half a dozen neighbors were waiting to see her off. Her mother surprised her by rushing forward to hug her with unusual warmth, and then to touch her cheek with a gentle hand, eyes bright with tears. Jennie surprised her even more. She rushed forward, flung her arms around Elizabeth's neck and began to sob like a child. "Oh, Liza, Liza, I think my heart is breaking. I love you most of anyone!"

III

Going up the six gray marble steps to the dark green front door of the house on 10th Street, Elizabeth could think only of the night ahead, the marriage bed. But Isaiah proved most respectful of her reluctance, even approving. Her shyness, he said, bespoke delicacy, and delicacy he regarded as the finest of female attributes.

It soon seemed that all she had learned from her mother of household tasks had been so much time wasted, for Isaiah had what he called his "staff!"—an Irish cook named Bridget, a housemaid named Mary, and a houseman called Fiddle, who soon left for a better post. "I did not marry to gain a servitor, but rather a lady of the house," Isaiah told her. "Among the better-off class of gentlemen here in New York it is the wife who sets the tone of the family. You will soon be called on by ladies who knew my mother, and by their daughters and daughters-in-law. I will have calling cards engraved for you which you will take with you when you return their calls, always within two weeks. As a merchant, I do not say that I am in the very highest social bracket, but we are not too far from it, for an ancestor on my mother's side was one of the earliest Dutch settlers here. As to your manners, I do not need to instruct you, for your deportment is quite correct if you will only learn to modify your robust manner of laughing."

The ladies duly called, and Elizabeth took an instant liking to one named Dolly Pierpont, who lived just down the street. Only nineteen, with snapping black eyes and most elegant clothes, she had to leave to nurse her first child, but urged Elizabeth to call as soon as she could. Elizabeth obliged the next day. As they enjoyed tea together in the cozy sitting room, Dolly spoke cheerfully of marriage. "It's all a game in which the wife exerts a show of make-believe authority as to household and social matters, leaving her husband free to make more money. We consume; they provide. But the joke is that the power they've consigned to us is not entirely hollow. Example: when a very rich man's wife like Mrs. Penrose decides to take a stand on some such issue as starving orphans, other females jump to aid her and to extract donations from their husbands who don't care a farthing about the orphans but have to show respect for Mrs. Penrose's husband's fortune by pretending to. Do you follow?"

By then the marriage bed had been endured, so appalling and grotesque an experience that Elizabeth was forever grateful to Dolly for defining her new life as a game. She was determined to play it with verve until she had children to give meaning to the marriage. Within six months she found her simple hair style copied by several ladies who had floundered ever since wigs went decidedly out. She obediently visited ladies who visited her, and on New Year's Day received guests from noon on, food and drink being amply provided. She kept the servants on their toes. But in her daydreams she was a mother with a varying number of children: five was her limit. She could see them quite clearly, those dear little faces. Sometimes

46

she even imagined that Tom was their father, that she and Isaiah had never married at all. For she could not hide from the fact that he had never aroused in her even an echo of the wild passion she had felt with Tom.

Isaiah was a cold man, although at times quite fatuous in his overtures to lovemaking, always performed in his long nightshirt. Her absence of passion pleased him, proving the delicacy of her nature, he said. On the night after receiving a letter from her mother mentioning that Tom's child had been a little boy, Elizabeth wept as Isaiah stroked her cheek, his preface to connubial encounter. After nearly two years she was all but sure her lack of ardor kept her from conceiving, although Dolly, nursing her second child, believed that with an older husband it took longer.

The day after Elizabeth's eighteenth birthday Jennie wrote to tell of her engagement. The letter had been written so fast that it was hard to make out in places, but it made clear enough an unjust contrast. Jennie had fallen in love with a fine young man of good family and her parents heartily approved. John Clark's great-grandfather came from Paisley, Scotland and had founded the Colonies' first spool-cotton mill, now grown to a thriving factory. Handsome, virile, and with a merry sense of humor, John was at the start of a promising career with an old Philadelphia law firm. "I am so happy, Liza, that I feel like a rainbow inside, high, high above plain old earth. But you know what I mean!"

Elizabeth remembered that feeling well. She read on, to learn that Jennie had met John Clark because she had disobeyed her parents. She confessed to Elizabeth that she had stayed for supper with a friend without permission, and on that evening John had chanced to visit the

47

girl's older brother. Two pairs of blue eyes met. "And I knew in that moment John was the man I was going to marry!"

Elizabeth was standing in the dim parlor, but clear and bright in her mind were the goblet with the red rose and the plain pitcher with the blue rim. They seemed to exemplify the truth about two lives; Jennie was destined to have her heart's desire, Elizabeth was not. "When John smiles at me, his eyes shining with love, I feel such joy I think I will burst, just simply explode with joy. Oh, Liza, you're the only one I can tell this to!"

Elizabeth's ears caught the stony thud of footfalls on the front steps. She suddenly could not bear to tell Isaiah about Jennie's joy. She rushed to the small coal fire in the grate. As if acting of its own volition, her left hand dropped Jennie's letter into the flames; her diamond ring glinted a sharp flash of light as the page caught fire, swiftly curled, and blackened. She turned to face her husband, Jennie's joyous message branded on her mind.

Valise packed to attend the wedding a month later, Elizabeth twisted her ankle going down the front steps, spraining it so severely she could barely hobble, even with a cane, for more than a week. But her mother wrote a long letter telling of the happy occasion: never a lovelier bride, a bonnier groom, a wedding feast so merry! Jennie wrote later that the only shadow had been the absence of her dear Liza. "John and I thank you for the beautiful silver pitcher which I shall always cherish because it came from you."

Two months later she wrote, "Our home is little to boast about, a small brick row house on a narrow street in a subdivision of one of the grand squares Penn laid out. But all within is warm and cheery. We have a young

Negress to do the hard chores, but I bustle about many household tasks which seem quite different than when I had to make my bed and dust and shine pewter at home. And John has built below the parlor window a little shelf where my pretty goblet with the red rose catches the morning light."

She had been married just ten months when her first child was born. "I have named her Jane Anne, Jane after our mother, Anne after John's. But you may be sure that if our next child is a girl I will name her for you."

Elizabeth composed a letter of congratulation, stressing her own life of relative luxury and describing her new bonnet from Paris, France, worn the evening before when Isaac took her to hear *The Barber of Seville*.

She did not confide that no such pleasure could compensate for her childless state, which Isaiah had at last made clear he attributed to some flaw in her reproductive organs. Deciding she must know the worst, yet dreading it, she made an appointment with a doctor. He found her constitution to be robust in all regards, but suggested that she imbibe wine with her meals, though not at breakfast. When she asked if he would examine her husband, he seemed surprised at the suggestion. Isaiah was more than surprised that night when she made the same suggestion to him: he was angry. Pacing the floor in his nightshirt, his thin, high voice discreetly lowered in case the maid was still about upstairs, he assured Elizabeth that a peccadillo in his youth involving a servant girl had made it very clear that he was capable of fathering a child. "My mother dismissed her, but being softhearted I contrived to supply money for the lying in, which I did by pawning a pair of valuable dueling pistols that had belonged to my grandfather." He wagged his forefinger at her, his eyes glaring. "No, I am not the cause of your childless state. And let me point out it is my loss, for I had counted on a son to take over the business I have built up from one shop and a wooden Indian."

She was stunned, not because Isaiah had tumbled a wench but because that long-past sin of his now proved her own incapacity to conceive the child she so desperately yearned for. From that night on she felt flawed. Jennie wrote that Tom's son was "a right pretty little fellow, by name Thaddeus, Tad for short." On a visit to Allerton she had run into Tom on the street. "He seemed quite down in the mouth. But why shouldn't he be? Gossip says he's stuck in that old farmhouse with two women who don't get along and a father who topes. And working like two men to keep it all afloat."

Sometimes a wicked daydream seized Elizabeth—that Betsy died and Tom came with his motherless son to New York to work for his Uncle Barney. And she and Tom met by chance, and she saw his little boy who looked just like him. She offered to take Tad to Washington Square to play, and then to start him on alphabet and numbers. Tom was grateful and Tad adored her. . . . Isaiah, of course, did not fit into the daydream at all, and had to die. She imagined a swift end: he simply fell down of a conniption fit at his factory. She gave him an impressive funeral, and was free. . . .

But the immorality of a happy future based on the murder of Betsy and Isaiah even though in fantasy prevented her from enjoying the imagined reunion with Tom and the acquisition of a foster son. Flawed! Not merely in the secret depths of her body, but in her mind as well! Sternly she forbade herself indulgence in this peurile, cruel daydream.

It was fortunate that she had a fondness for reading, for only through books could she escape the feeling that she was trapped in a meaningless life. For some time her hero had been Byron; she escaped to Greece where she met the curly-haired, large-eyed poet who limped toward her in a black cape, smiling. His club foot made them kin. Two lines of his haunted her, chanting themselves in her head: "The mountains look on Marathon/ and Marathon looks on the sea/ And musing there an hour alone/I dreamed that Greece might still be free." To what cause could she give herself, as he had given his life to free Greece?

But hers was a small and causeless world where women acquaintances bemoaned the servant problem, for daughters of one-time indentured servants preferred work in some factory to plodding around someone else's house twelve hours a day dusting, emptying slops, carrying water upstairs, cooking. A cook of any skill could command three dollars a week, free and clear! And they refused to be called servants, had to be called "help."

"What you can't do, a servant won't," Elizabeth told women who admired the shine on her andirons, her dustless table. Her mother's training had stood her in good stead, enabling her to achieve a smooth-running home for the husband who took pride in providing dresses and bonnets and a birthday brooch of garnets. Having learned that his mother had been a meager woman who suffered from chronic dissatisfaction with life, she imagined his generosities to be in part amends to a dead woman nothing had pleased. To her mother she wrote letters revealing her dissatisfaction with New York, the numerous fires, the unpaid volunteer fire companies who raced

51

one another to the blaze and then might battle for the honor of putting it out, the narrow festering alleys like Thieves' Roost, the lack of a municipal police department so that only privately hired watchmen patrolled the streets, the herds of roving pigs that served as garbage collectors. . . .

And then, abruptly, she thought she had found her cause. She went to the Battery with Isaiah and stood watching the shabby immigrants emerging from the hold of a vessel, clutching bundles, most of the women with shawls tied under their chins, some of the men with mustaches, all speaking strange tongues. She was touched by the smile of a woman who held in her arms a child of about two, wearing black shoes many times too large.

"Look at her and feel fortunate," Isaiah said. "She and her husband got together twenty-five dollars for passage and another twenty-five each to prove they won't become public charges immediately. They probably speak no English. The only thing they know may be farming. Without friends, family or industrial skills, they will have a bitter time to make ends meet, if they do."

And Elizabeth saw her cause. Education in the English language for immigrants. A school! Saying nothing to Isaiah, who had a way of scoffing at what he thought was impractical, she called the next day on the ample, benign Mrs. Penrose.

"A school for foreigners? Encourage this tide of people from places like Russia, Italy? Catholics and even Orientals? That is, *Jews?* No indeed, my dear Mrs. Moss. Let the word go back to their lands that here there are no streets of gold, and certainly no schools to teach them to take the bread out of the mouths of the poor of our own race and faith." Coldly, Elizabeth rose and bade farewell to that hard heart. "Wait, Mrs. Moss! Since you are so moved by feelings of charity, I am attempting to establish a lying-in hospital for the poor and unwed mothers of this city and will welcome your aid. At present too many die in childbirth, and others after trying to disembarrass themselves with skewers!"

Shuddering, Elizabeth went home in a miserable frame of mind. Life was so unfair! All those poor women dying to keep from having a child, and she, yearning to have one! That night at supper she sat facing the blue-rimmed Stiegel pitcher on the sideboard and inevitably saw in her mind its counterpart, the beautiful rose-glass that was Jennie's. Lucky Jennie, with a husband she loved and a child by him!

Isaiah sopped his bread in gravy. The empty bulge of the Stiegel pitcher behind him seemed to be balanced on his hunched shoulder. She smiled to herself. What would he say if he knew she had begun to write a novel? Barren her body might be, but her mind was not, and had recently started as if of its own accord to imagine scenes from the early life of a man much like the legendary Stiegel whose bride Death had coveted.

Elizabeth had completed a whole chapter when Jennie's luck changed.

For a week the New York papers had reported that typhoid fever had broken out in Philadelphia. This did not prepare her for Jennie's letter.

John is dead. Our parents are ill, my friends and neighbors had fled the city. I stood alone this morning at my dear husband's grave, yearning to be reunited with him. I have not eaten nor slept for days, am too weak, too ill, to flee this plague while poor little Jane Anne is still in health. Perhaps it's destined that we must both join her father. As to that, God's will be done. . . .

Shock numbed Elizabeth's mind, then ebbed; a dozen flashing images of her little sister followed: Jennie laughing, Jennie sobbing her farewell. God's will? No heavenly angel was going to descend to rescue Jennie and Jane Anne. Elizabeth dropped the letter to the hall table and ran up the stairs to pack her valise. Because she had been writing her novel, Jennie's letter had been lying unread on the hall table since the morning post came. But even if there were no stagecoach leaving for Philadelphia this late in the day she would be packed and ready to take the first one in the morning. Isaiah would surely read, as she had, the desperate cry for aid that lay under those weak, shaky lines of writing.

An hour later when he returned and read Jennie's letter he lowered it, frowning. "Can you be serious in proposing to go there? She does not exaggerate this epidemic. The papers all say it's the worst to strike that city since the yellow fever in 1793!"

"Do you intend to let my sister and her baby die?" Her amazement at his heartlessness was genuine although she had half-expected to have to overcome his caution.

"As she says herself, that is in the hands of God." He looked down at the letter and up again. "She may already be infected with this disease."

"But the baby's still healthy. Oh, Isaiah, if that child dies when I might have rescued her, I could never forgive myself!" She found her hands clasped prayerfully, like a woman in a melodrama.

"Your request is not sane. I will not risk my life nor permit you to risk yours by rushing into the heart of a plague. This I refuse. Absolutely."

"You don't have to risk your life. I'll go alone."

"You will not. I will pay for no such journey. God, not you, will decide the fate of your sister and her infant."

"God works through human agents!"

"Then you will have to regard me as inhuman." He thrust Jennie's letter into her hand and marched from the room.

The tears she had not yet shed flooded to her eyes, but they were less tears of grief than of helpless anger. She had no money, only accounts of tradesmen, at At T. Stewart's emporium. In her reticule upstairs jingled at most a few dollars, and the stagecoach fare to Philadelphia was ten dollars, each way. Moreover, she would have to hire a coach to take her to Jennie's house and back to the station again, and pay for her food enroute. She found that she was wringing her hands in anguish. Against her palm she felt the hard, cold lump of her diamond ring. . . .

With feigned resignation to the will of God she sat opposite her husband at supper, watched him swiftly devour a large helping of roast beef, turnips, potatoes, and bread. It occurred to her that Isaiah's God was a great convenience to him, for to that heavenly being could be delegated the task of coping with an epidemic and two fellow humans trapped by it.

As soon as he left in the morning she set off with her valise for a shop on Broadway he had once pointed out to her as the place where the thriftless got loans of money on their possessions. Behind the battered counter sat a little man with a gray beard and eyeglasses. He spoke with a peculiar accent, and it occurred to her that he might be a Jew. For her ring and the garnet brooch he lent her forty-two dollars and gave her a ticket with which she could redeem them. An hour later she was on the stagecoach bound for Philadelphia. She was sure she was doing the right thing and regretted only the unkind note she had left on Isaiah's bureau: "We seem to have different Gods. Mine tells me that caution can be only cowardice."

In Philadelphia she was the only passenger to get off the stagecoach, though a huddle of frightened people were waiting to get on. Their flight gave credence to the reality of Isaac's fears. The risk was real. She forced down her uneasiness, rode to her sister's house in an open calash driven by an old Negro in a high, battered hat. The streets were empty of strollers and few vehicles were abroad; people had evidently closed themselves in their houses, hoping to close the typhus out. The Negro looked mournfully back at her over his shoulder. "Us darkies got no choice. Got to make a penny as we can an' hope ole Yellowjack gonna spare us."

"Yellowjack? I thought it was typhoid."

"Us got both now. Ole Yellowjack sneaked back again." Uneasiness became a knot in her stomach; she suddenly saw herself as a wayward wife risking death against her wise husband's command.

At her sister's house, she gave the Negro a whole dollar to wait, knowing no time must be lost in getting her sister and niece and herself out of the city on the next north-bound stage. He eyed the black funeral wreath on the door, but nodded.

The door was opened by a young, thin Negress, a white kerchief around her head, another one tied over her mouth like a highwayman's disguise. On learning who Elizabeth was she admitted her, pointing at the staircase. "No room in no hospital. Your sister's up there. Front bedroom."

Tense with foreboding, Elizabeth opened the door and entered a dim room which one narrow shaft of sunlight entered through nearly drawn curtains. On the bed lay Jennie, hands crossed on her breast, a penny on each eyelid. Above the white nightgown her face was yellowish, and her golden hair was down like a little girl's. Too late! Elizabeth wanted to weep, to embrace that husk of Jennie, to beg forgiveness for . . . for . . . But the baby, where was she? Wildly, she stared about the room.

The shaft of sunlight touched a low cradle. She walked toward it, trying to steel herself for the sight of Jennie's dead infant. Plump, pink-cheeked, it lay with closed eyes. Then they opened, blue as the sky. The tiny hand that rested on the blanket reached up, fingers wide. They closed, trying to grasp one of the bright motes of dust dancing in the sunlight. Alive! A burst of relief filled Elizabeth as she bent forward, picked up the baby, and rocked her in her arms. Tenderness melted grief and fear. On the moist little mouth a smile budded. Cuddling the warm burden, Elizabeth hurried from the room after one last backward look at Jennie.

The mournful waiting Negro knew the way to the undertaker's. She told him her father, now ill, would pay him; this was acceptable. "They're put underground at once now. It's thought to reduce the contagion. A common grave. Will you attend?"

She shook her head. "How soon can you come for her? I want to leave the city today."

"Don't blame you for that. I'll do what I can."

Only an hour later, Jennie was carried out the door in a pine coffin. In the parlor Elizabeth held the sleeping baby, tears running down her face as she realized she could not see her sister interred, could not visit her ailing parents. All she could do had been done. The wry thought occurred to her that Isaiah would approve her caution as to leaving so rapidly.

"Mrs. Moss?" In the doorway the thin young Negress stood. She had removed the white napkin that had covered her mouth, as though the danger of contagion had left with the corpse of her mistress.

"Yes?"

"What's I to do?" the girl asked. "Where's I to go now?"

"Haven't you any family?"

"I's a slave, ma'am. Bought and paid for by Mr. Clark."

Owning a slave was now illegal in New York. But, still, this one had stayed with Jennie in her last illness when another might have fled. And there was money to pay her stagecoach fare. "What's your name, girl?"

"They calls me Melonia."

Elizabeth stood up. "Get the baby's clothes together, and your own. Please hurry."

"An' I'll bring a jug of ricewater and bread to sop in it," Melonia said, relief in her voice.

"What for?"

"The baby, ma'am. That's what I been feedin' her since her mama got too sick to nurse her no more." As she ran out it occurred to Elizabeth that Melonia might know more about infants than she did.

She went to the window to make sure that the Negro whom she had given another dollar was still waiting. He was. On the shelf below the window the rose-glass glowed. She remembered the first time she saw it, and the day Jennie had asked their grandfather for it. Lucky Jennie. Poor Jennie. The baby began to whimper, and she walked up and down the parlor, patting and rocking and crooning, and had a faint memory of seeing her mother do the same when Jennie was an infant. Whenever she faced the window the rose-glass caught her eye.

"I got the key so as you can lock up good," Melonia said from the doorway. "Low folks break into the houses left empty, robbin' and stealin' what they can. I better give that child some bread and ricewater afore we goes."

She took the whimpering infant. Elizabeth turned to the window, picked up the rose-glass, went to her valise and wrapped the Stiegel pokal in her nightgown. As she did so a shiver went through her. Disaster and death had come to that lucky child who had inherited that glass vase. Might misfortune as terrible wait ahead for her, its new possessor? She shook her head at the gloomy thought, quickly closed the valise.

Later, jammed haunch to jowl, the passengers began to relax from their tense postures after the stagecoach had jolted north some miles on the turnpike. A stout gentleman opposite took off his hat, mopped his brow, and looked at the baby sleeping in Elizabeth's arms. "You have a fine and healthy child there, ma'am," he said.

"Thank you."

On Melonia's brown face Elizabeth caught the hint of a sly smile, as if she had somehow guessed that it had pleased Elizabeth to be taken for the mother.

The nearer they came to New York, the more nagging were her thoughts of Isaiah. Would he be as charmed by Jane Anne as the stranger? Would he be charmed at all? Would the sight of his willful wife arriving home safe and sound overcome his anger at her disobedience? Oh, why had she written that unkind note? How could she cozen him into a pleasant mood? But in the woods they were passing there were dozens of dogwood trees in full white flower, and she gave herself over to pure enjoyment of those brides of the forest.

With the usual stopover at a tavern it was after sundown the next day when Elizabeth wearily unlocked the door of the house on 10th Street, rehearsing the speech she had been preparing to turn aside some of her husband's wrath. She whispered to Melonia to wait in the front hall, and carrying Jane Anne, on whom she had put a pretty little white lace bonnet, she entered the lighted parlor. A black-haired man in mustard breeches, wine-red jacket, and polished kneeboots stood up a moment before Isaiah did, his eyes glued on the baby in her arms.

"I see you went to Philadelphia." Her husband's lips were as thin as his voice.

The pleading speech had vanished from her mind. "My sister is dead. As you can see, her baby is well."

Isaiah remembered his good manners. "This is Mr. Lucas De Lange of Charleston, South Carolina. My wife, sir. My very disobedient wife, who has caused me deep concern for several days."

Mr. De Lange stared at Elizabeth out of eyes that were

dark blue, not brown as she had first thought. "Had you no thought as to your health, Mrs. Moss? Your very life? Did you not know of the epidemic there?"

"Yes, I knew. But there was no one else to aid my poor sister and my niece."

"Now that puts me to shame," Lucas De Lange drawled. "I started out for Philadelphia myself, but learning on shipboard that the typhus had worsened, I paid the extra passage to continue on to New York instead."

"No human life was in hazard in your case, sir."

"Quite true, only a business matter—to find a Northern merchant willing to contract with me for my tobacco crop." He flashed a glance and smile at Isaiah. "Which I do believe I have had the great good fortune to find."

Isaiah nodded. "You have shown me the advantage to both of us." To Elizabeth he said coldly, "I believe we can excuse you now, as we have further business to discuss."

Dismissed, Elizabeth wished Lucas De Lange a good night and returned to the hall where Melonia stood with the valises, the basket of soiled diapers, and her own bundle of possessions. Finger to her lips, Elizabeth moved so as to shield the slave's body with her own as they hurried past the door to the parlor and up the stairs. One unwelcome surprise at a time, she thought grimly, for she had seen no touch of tenderness on Isaiah's face when he looked at the bonnetted baby.

She improvised a crib out of her emptied bottom bureau drawer set on two facing chairs and lined with a quilt. "Mother of God!" Mary the maid stood in the doorway, mouth open.

Elizabeth explained her niece's orphaned state, and the Irish girl's eyes softened appropriately, hardened as she looked at Melonia. "Who's she, ma'am?"

"The nursemaid, and I want you to take her to the basement and show her where the laundry is done, and then make up the cot for her in the small rear bedroom on the third floor. And say nothing to Mr. Moss as yet, please."

Mary nodded. "Is the baby going to stay here, ma'am?"

"Of course." Doubt stirred; she suppressed it. "Is there any milk still fresh?"

"I think so."

"Then you may bring me some heated in a bowl with a spoon and a piece of bread."

When the servants left, Elizabeth changed Jane Anne's diaper, put on her tiny nightdress, and tucked her into the bureau-drawer crib, pulling the blanket up to the pink chin. A protective tenderness had replaced earlier fatigue. She marveled at the dewy sheen of the closed lids, the golden lashes. . . .

"Where did you get the money?" Isaiah stood inside the threshold at the other side of the improvised crib.

She put one finger to her lips, held up the other hand to show only the gold wedding band.

"You sold the diamond?" At his shrill indignation, the baby stirred.

"Pawned it," she whispered. "Please don't shout."

"Pawned the ring I gave you in order to flout me?" He stared at her bosom. "And the garnet brooch too?"

"They were mine to do with as I wished."

"By law all that you own belongs to me!"

"Even your gifts?"

"All!"

The baby whimpered, its head turning restlessly.

"Please, Isaiah, don't wake Jane Anne. It's been a very long journey."

"What do you intend to do with her?"

"Keep her. Raise her." Didn't he understand?

"It is in my home that you intend to indulge in maternity. I will have the final word in the matter." His nose pinched and he looked down at the child as if she were covered with dirt, pockmarked with disease.

Rage boiled up and overflowed. "Very well. If you are too cold and mean a man to find room in your heart for this poor little orphan, my own flesh and blood, then I will take her to my parents' home and I will raise her there. I swear to that! You cannot take this baby away from me, Isaiah. I'll leave you first!"

Her voice had gradually risen. Now a wail arose from the bureau drawer, a loud, ululating cry. She bent over, picked up Jane Anne, cradled her in her arms and glared as Isaiah. "There! Look what you did! Look how you frightened my poor little baby! How could you?"

Hands over both ears, he took a backward step, then turned and fled. In a moment she heard his footsteps thudding up to the third floor, heard the slam of the door of his study. As soon as he left the baby quieted down, then Mary came in with the milk, and minutes after eating some Jane Anne was asleep again. Elizabeth found herself too weary for any supper or even to unpack. She undressed, sponged the dust and sweat of travel from her face and body, snatched a nightgown from the heap of clothes she had taken from the bottom bureau drawer, and crawled into bed.

The baby's cry woke her at dawn and she went down to heat milk but found the kitchen stove not yet lighted. She brought bread and cool milk upstairs, and found Melonia rocking the baby in her arms. Still half-asleep, she put down the tray with the baby's food, crawled gratefully into bed again, and did not wake for another two hours.

Breakfasting alone in the dining room, she knew that her threat the night before had been a hollow one. Her parents might be willing to raise Jane Anne themselves, but would not condone her leaving her husband to do so.

"Good morning, Elizabeth."

As Isaiah took his seat at the other end of the table and rang the bell to summon Mary with food she tried to read his face. "Good morning."

The newspaper was folded at his place as usual; he opened it. She clasped her hands in her lap, closed her eyes. The paper rustled as he set it aside. "I presume you have a receipt for the ring and brooch?"

The ring! The brooch! What about the baby? "Yes, I do."

"Then I will redeem them for you today."

"Thank you."

Mary brought oatmeal, toast, a boiled egg in a china eggcup and poured his coffee. He attacked the oatmeal. She found her nails digging into the palms of the hands she held clenched in her lap. "Have you decided?" she asked.

"Decided what?"

"About the baby."

"I slept poorly last night. The couch in my study is adequate for a nap, but hardly for a good night's sleep.

64

Your irrational mood, and the peculiar odor young babies seem to have, left me no alternative but a night of some discomfort." He finished the oatmeal, pushed the dish aside.

Was he deliberately torturing her? He could not possibly believe that the quality of his night's sleep was now her deep concern. "The empty rear bedroom on the second floor would make a fine nursery. The south window gives sun in the afternoon," she said.

"Since sleep eluded me," he said, "I had ample time to think about the problem your sister's child poses. You have, I should tell you, a sincere admirer in Mr. De Lange. He considered your behavior most courageous. Rash, unthinking, but courageous. But I digress. Taking into account an apparent peculiarity of your physiology, I have decided that you may keep the child."

A burden of doubt vanished. She felt light as air. "Oh, Isaiah, for that I do thank you, with all my heart!"

Mary had entered to remove the dishes. She dropped a sketchy curtsey and smiled widely as she did when about to say what she feared was the wrong thing. "Have you told Mr. Moss yet, ma'am?"

"Told me what?" Isaiah demanded.

Elizabeth hid her sudden tension as she ordered Mary, "Stay with the baby and send Melonia here."

"Who?" he asked grimly.

"You'll see in a moment, and I think you'll be pleased." She thought the opposite, but smiled and nodded.

Melonia, in a clean white apron with a white kerchief tied around her head, approached the head of the table and curtseyed shyly to her new master. She was really,

Elizabeth thought, a quite neat and pretty girl, if too thin. Isaiah eyed her indulgently. "So you think you'd like me to hire you, I take it?"

"No need for any hire, sir. I's a slave girl, an' I guess you an' Mrs. Moss is my master and mistress now the Clarks is dead."

He shot Elizabeth a glance of approval. "Well done, my dear. Just when I begin to think your brain is addled from too much reading of fiction and poetry, you show me you're the sensible daughter of sensible parents. She's like money in the bank!"

"I was afraid you'd be annoyed, now that slave-owning is abolished in this state."

He frowned, shrugged. "I'll give her a token wage, just to observe the letter of the law." He turned toward Melonia. "You understand that? Your board and keep and a dollar a month for frills and furbelows, eh?"

Melonia curtseyed again.

When Elizabeth unpacked she found the Stiegel rose-glass, forgotten in the crush of more important matters. She decided to display it on the parlor mantel. In the dim room it did not glow as it had in her grandfather's window, and Jennie's. But its beauty could be seen by night after she raised it on an ebony pedestal taken from below a china vase, with a candle alight at either side. The rose came to life, its dew-drop sparkled.

Two intertwined lives, hers and her sister's, had finally produced the flower of compensation. To her had come the coveted rose after all, and to her had come a yearned-for child.

The bright dew-drop mesmerized her, a symbol of purity. Looking at it, the smug notion of compensation withered away. She saw herself as a despicable creature, tainted by envy of her sister. How long she had envied her! Tears came to her eyes, ran down her cheeks. She felt that ugly emotion leave her spirit. Staring at the rose, she promised herself and Jennie that she would be faithful to the task she had assumed, would raise Jane Anne to happy womanhood. "I swear it, Jennie," she whispered. "I swear it, my dear."

IV

On the night of the chance meeting with Tom O'Casey
Elizabeth sat down to supper facing her husband in his
place at the head of the table. He was eating as he always
did of late, like a starving man, now and then mopping
fiercely at his mouth with his napkin as if he might bite
that too. She found herself without any desire for food.
She had just supped on the past.

Isaiah leaned back, thumbs in his vest pockets, fingers
thrumming his paunch. He bestowed a benign smile on
Jane Anne. "Well, child, what have you done with yourself today worth mention?"

"I went to the Battery with Aunt Liza and the Bread
Ladies."

Suddenly Elizabeth found that she did not want Isaiah
to know of the meeting with Tom O'Casey. She could
make no sense of this, because even if Isaiah had some
inkling of a young sweetheart, he had probably never
known his name. She sat staring at Jane Anne, willing the
child not to mention Tom. Jane Anne glanced up at Elizabeth, wide blue eyes meeting her own. "Indeed?" Isaiah
prompted, and the golden head turned toward him.

"And you'll never guess who we saw!"

But why does it matter to me? Elizabeth asked herself.

"Aaron Burr! He was looking for his daughter Theodosia!"

A savage satisfaction lighted Isaiah's face. "So Bur still seeks his dead daughter, eh? That vile wretc murdered Alexander Hamilton, the one man who migh have saved this country from Jefferson's mistake notions of democracy. Hamilton knew that an aristocrac of the intellect is needed to govern a republic. But now what do we have, thanks to that bullet of Burr's? Jeffer sonian Democrats! And those dirty-shirt workies hidin under the skirts of that party now that their own miser able Workingman's Party has foundered and died away And we have the Tammany Machine Burr founded, s the great unwashed can connive against their betters With general male suffrage, which I deplore, Tamman can sway elections! Why, I ask, should shiftless fellow who own not an inch of land or property have a vot equal to that of a man like myself?" His voice was nov almost a scream. "I, who must now rebuild my factory a devastating cost!"

"Isaiah, you are not on a lecture platform," Elizabet reminded him. Ever since the awesome New York fire o last December his temper had been vile. He took it as great personal injustice that his cigar factory had burned she thought, and that he has to float a loan to rebuild, lik six or seven hundred other victims of the worst disaste in the city's history.

"And, worst of all, we have these idiotic abolitionist weeping crocodile tears over Negro slaves." Isaiah cas Elizabeth a bitter, provocative glance. "Your hero William Lloyd Garrison should have been locked up fo life in that Boston jail where they put him in 1831!"

"To save his life from a mob of anti-abolitionists who would have stoned him to death!"

"And a good thing if they had. His outcry for immediate emancipation of slaves was directly responsible for the Nat Turner rebellion in Virginia which caused the slaughter of some fifty men!"

"Fifty whites, you mean to say. You chose not to speak of the one hundred Negroes killed, too." She quoted Garrison: " 'In my stand against slavery I will not budge an inch!' "

"The only sane attitude as to freeing slaves is moderation."

" 'One might as well urge moderation on a man whose house is burning down, or whose wife is being violated!' " Elizabeth quoted again.

"Such strong language, Madame, in front of the child? Your abolitionists refuse to face facts. Northern industries benefit from slavery just as much as Southern plantations. More, I'd hazard, what with recent high tariffs on cotton and tobacco. And what's the South's answer to tariffs? Nullification! Senator John Calhoun of South Carolina wants each state legislature to have the right to veto any Federal law it deems unfair, and this with Senate approval by only four states! What happens to this nation? What happens to my tobacco business?"

"That you manufacture cigars does not justify the cruel oppression of Negroes," Elizabeth said.

"Negroes are an inferior species. You have only to look at them to know that: black skin, flat nose, thick gross lips, kinky hair!"

"You speak in caricature, which is dishonest. All Negroes do not have these features, and you know it."

He had the grace to look a bit chagrined, then frowned. "Be that as it may, I am now commanding you, Elizabeth to abandon those abolitionists you have been fraternizing with. The name of Moss is respected in this city. I will

71

not have it listed in the *Herald* as it recently was, along with those of the crackpots and fanatics at abolitionist rallies."

"Then I'll use a *nome de plume,* sir."

"Do not be pert!"

Jane Anne's small voice broke in. "I do so hate it when you are angry, Uncle Isaiah!" Mournful blue eyes looked at him; pink lips drooped.

Elizabeth watched her husband turn into a benign *pater familias,* reach down the table to pat Jane Anne's hand. "Your auntie is sometimes a very willful lady and I must scold her when she is." His cold eyes found Elizabeth's. "But I know she will obey me. Won't you, my dear?"

"Do you know what we're having for dessert?" Jane Anne quickly asked him. "Ice cream! Isn't that splendiferous?" With a dimpled smile she watched her uncle chuckle over the long word. The need to answer Isaiah's question had been deftly bypassed, and fortunately so, because the answer ready to explode from Elizabeth had been "No!"

She had contained it, and a smoldering resentment. She knew that the near-frenzy into which her husband worked himself over her attendance at an abolitionist meeting had less to do with their opposite political beliefs than with his need to feel potent and in control. The December fire that made cinders of his factory had been uncontrollable, the first devastating setback he had ever suffered, and it had changed him for the worse. Pompous self-satisfaction had ben replaced overnight by self-pity, and by fury at the injustice of fate, a rage which burst out in verbal attacks on more available targets. She could only hope that the change in him was not permanent, yet had the uneasy feeling that she was seeing a side of his nature that had always been there, perhaps unknown to him as well.

It was fortunate that the famous feminist's lecture fell on the night Isaiah played whist at the Union Club, taking his supper at City Hotel, and often playing on afterward. Elizabeth had decided that her niece was going to hear Fanny Wright speak, for Jane Anne was learning that charming manipulation of the male common to wives and bright Negro slaves. Jane Anne, of course, was delighted to be included, and as they rode toward Masonic Hall in a hired hackney coach Elizabeth told her how, when she was eleven, the Aller family went to Philadelphia to see that hero of the Revolution, the Marquis de Lafayette, on his triumphal 1819 tour of American cities. He was accompanied everywhere by Fannie Wright, a young heiress from Dundee. "Blond, beautiful and nearly six feet tall, she wore a slender Empire gown of yellow silk. Standing on the steps of Independence Hall she very nearly dwarfed the Marquis, then in his sixties. She was like a great ship in full sail. And as intelligent as she was beautiful."

Jane Anne seemed more taken by this sight of the city at night, but nodded.

"After Lafayette returned to France, Fanny Wright stayed here. She was an ardent abolitionist. She bought and then freed a number of slaves and established them, together with some white people, on farmland she bought. It was to be a utopia. She called it Nashoba."

"Why?"

"She wanted to show that both races could live in harmony on equal terms. No slaves, no masters."

"I meant, why was it called Nashoba?"

"It may be an Indian name. But her utopia was a disaster. The Negroes were confused without anyone to give them orders, and the whites fell to bickering about tasks and privileges." Elizabeth decided to delete the former member of Nashoba who spread the rumor that "free love" was practiced there. The rumor had made Fanny Wright the object of shocked whispers and lascivious jests. "Undefeated, she joined forces with a Mr. Owen, whose own utopia had failed, and they established 'The Free Enquirers.' Their periodical is widely circulated, and is dedicated to ending slavery, obtaining the right to vote for women and getting liberal divorce laws passed."

"Is that the periodical Uncle Isaiah won't have in the house?"

"That's the one. Now Fanny Wright has taken to the lecture platform, even though some stupid people consider it shameless of a woman to stand up and speak in public. But she is indomitable."

Staring out at the facade of Astor House, Jane Anne said, "Maybe I'd better not tell Uncle Isaiah where we went tonight."

Duplicity was like a third presence in the carriage. She had evaded telling her husband their destination, but would not counsel Jane Anne to equal evasion. "I admit I'm glad he is spending tonight at his club. But I would never suggest that you lie to your uncle or conceal from him anything he has a right to know."

Jane Anne looked at her then. "You didn't want him to know you met Mr. O'Casey, did you?" Guileless eyes stared up, lighted by the gaslamp the coach was passing.

"Not particularly." Her pulse had begun to race, pounded in her ears.

"I knew it, Aunt Liza! I can feel your thoughts some-times. But why didn't you want him to know?"

Why not indeed? "Mr. O'Casey belongs to another time in my life, before I knew your uncle. And I doubt that they would take to one another." She forced a laugh.

She felt a warm little hand touch hers. "My, but your hands are cold!"

"That's because I'm excited about hearing Fanny Wright."

They were early and got good seats in the third row. Soon Fanny Wright sailed to the center of the platform. The splendid young woman of 1819 had lost none of her beauty to the years, her shapely body clad in deep blue, her face intense in the wide flare of her bonnet brim. Her voice was resonant. "Ladies and gentlemen, I shall mince no words tonight. To begin bluntly, let me assure the women here that the clergy is our enemy." She ignored shocked gasps. "It is clergymen who down centuries have declared sacred the ancient chains that keep us in bondage. In bondage to the false idea that we are inferior creatures, fit only to be brood mares, houseservants, teachers or prostitutes." This brought a surge of mur-murs. "Yet at the same time the clergy utilizes women's slavish support to stay in power, and we gladly give it, denied by them the right to vote, to own property if married, or to divorce if miserably wed to mates who can beat us, rob us, or work us to death."

Elizabeth became aware that more was going on in the hall than boos, gasps and hisses. She turned and saw a number of dark figures flitting along the side aisles turning out the gas lamps placed at intervals along the walls. The hall was already quite dark and getting darker. "This is an old trick my enemies have used before,"

Fanny Wright announced, contemptuously. "The enemies of women love darkness, it seems. But they cannot obscure the light of truth. And truths I will speak tonight, if only one woman remains to hear me!"

Elizabeth had read in the *Free Enquirer* of the darkness trick, and opened her reticule to take out the small box of locofocos she had brought. She struck one of the self-igniting matches and held it high. Turning, she saw perhaps a dozen such flames behind her.

"Go on, Fanny," a male voice cried. "Let 'em have it!"

"Thank you, sir. I shall." In that thrilling voice she spoke of the disenfrachisement of women, linked it to the enslavement of Negroes, and to the use of child labor in mines, fields, and factories. Lighting matches and holding them high, Elizabeth was enthralled, but very soon her eyes began to sting, and she had to cough.

"Smudgepots!" Fanny Wright declared. "That is a new trick! The bigots will try to smoke us out since darkness proved unavailing!"

Jane Anne was coughing too. The noxious fumes filling the hall were already driving a few people toward the door. "Oh, please, Aunt Liza, can't we go outside?"

Elizabeth stood up, taking her hand. "Mrs. Wright," she called toward the stage, "I am Mrs. Moss and I would like you to have tea with me tomorrow!"

"How kind," the resonant voice answered through the smoky darkness. "Shall we meet at six at Astor House where I am staying?"

Elizabeth agreed, then took young Jane Anne home.

Her suite was an elegant one, all mahogany, mirrors, and velvet. In a tea gown trimmed in ecru lace Fanny Wright said she preferred her room to the Ladies Ordinary lounge, and had sent the chambermaid to fetch their tea. She laughed on learning that Elizabeth had seen her long ago with Lafayette. "I loved him dearly but would not have married him even if his outraged family had not opposed it. A play I wrote at nineteen called *A Few Days in Athens* first turned his attention to me, and then my looks. Good looks I was born with, but my brain has been cultivated by an excellent tutor when I was young, and by a wealth of reading. I fell in love with democracy and the ideas of Tom Paine long before I met the Marquis." Her eyes, as heroic in size as the rest of her, had taken in Elizabeth's stylish clothing as she spoke. "Forgive a personal remark, but I am surprised that you find my beliefs acceptable, Mrs. Moss. Beautiful women with prosperous husbands do not tend to believe that the vote can get them much more than they already have."

Elizabeth was startled.

"I have never thought of myself as beautiful."

"No? Then you have no mirrors or are deliberately blind to your virtues, a deplorable state. I suppose you had Puritanical American parents who taught you it is better to be good than clever, and that looks are of little importance? What a lie that is! Without my looks, do you imagine Lafayette would have taken me to America with him? Do you imagine that Franklin, Jefferson, even old Adams would have shared their views with me?"

"Somehow this is not the kind of conversation I imagined we would have," Elizabeth confessed.

"Did you expect a lecture on women's rights? I do that all the time. Occasionally I relish trivia and teacakes." The maid came in then with the tea tray and swiftly set a small table with a linen cloth, napkins, and silver. Fanny

Wright poured tea and passed the cakes. "I will hazard a guess, Mrs. Moss. You have found no appealing outlet for your energies, but may join the Free Enquirers group here in New York, if indeed you have not already done so."

"Or I may decide to write a novel about a woman like yourself," Elizabeth said, with a cool smile.

"You are a writer?" She seemed amazed. "But as for writing about a woman like myself, don't ever think of it. No one would believe you! The life I've led!" She threw back her head and laughed. "Just my brief marriage would make a novel. Can you believe that my former husband thought I should give up all male companionship except his own? I do not, of course, refer to bedding, merely to mental stimulation. He waited until our child was born to become a thorough tyrant. He considered that motherhood should separate me from any act except giving breast to an infant and the rest of me to his not remarkable mountings. To obtain a divorce from this possessive oaf was damned difficult, let me assure you. If he had only philandered, but, no, he was without spirit in that regard. Why does your own marriage dissatisfy you, if I may ask?"

Startled Elizabeth heard herself say, "What makes you think it does?"

"Happy wives rather rarely attend my lectures."

"My husband's temper is short of late, but that's all I can complain of."

The large eyes blinked. "Children?"

"We have a foster daughter. And now, if I may be equally personal, what of your own child?"

"Perfectly content with my relatives in Scotland at the moment, studying Latin with my old tutor. I miss her at times, but feel that I do her more eventual good than if I played at motherhood." She stared at something across the room. "Oh, dear Lord, look at that clock!" She rose, Junoesque and somewhat distracted. "I must squeeze myself into my corset and otherwise gird my loins to attend a soiree tonight." She held out a large warm hand which pressed Elizabeth's with what seemed affection. A moment later there was a tap at the door; Fanny admitted an older lady dressed impeccably for the evening, and Elizabeth was presented to the famous Mrs. Trollope, that severe and witty commentator on American manners and morals. In parting, Fanny Wright urged, "Write a book about a woman like yourself. Show the contrast between the appearance she offers the world and the realities of her inner life. I feel you have something to say."

Though I had little chance to say much today, Elizabeth thought, riding homeward in a hired coach. But she found herself savoring the larger-than-life gusto and candor of her hostess, and decided to join the Free Enquirers at once. . . .

An icy-eyed Isaiah was waiting in the parlor. "Where have you been?"

"Having tea."

"And with whom did you have this tea?" The false calm of his voice told her that he already knew.

"With a quite remarkable lady."

"Lady? I deny that term applies. I know who you had tea with. Fanny Wright! Do you deny it?"

"No."

"And you refer to her as a lady? That bawd? That lunatic? Who divorced her husband while carrying their infant in her arms? For no reason whatsoever!"

"He denied her the right to choose her companions."

"You call that a reason? I forbid you to ever set eyes on that strumpet again!"

"You may forbid, but I deny my obligation to obey." She felt calm and sure of herself, and turned from him to the door.

"I am your husband!"

"But not my master."

She went upstairs knowing that only Jane Anne could have told Isaiah of her destination. The child was caught between two fortifications.

At the head of the stairs Jane Anne stood humbly. "Oh, Aunt Liza, I'm so sorry! When he asked me where you were I just blurted it out. He was horrid to you!"

Looking down into the woebegone little face Elizabeth saw something Jane Anne did not know. The child had balanced her ledger. Having kept silent about Tom O'Casey, she had been impelled to lay an atoning sacrifice of truth on the altar of male authority. She bent to kiss the child's cheek. "No harm done."

She heard the front door slam below and knew Isaiah had betaken himself to his beloved Union Club. Men's clubs now flourished to such an extent that the *Tribune* had devoted an earnest editorial to the deleterious effect on home and holy matrimony. Husbands chose to smoke and drink and play cards with cronies in clubs, the writer deplored, instead of resting at day's end in the bosom of a loving family. Reading this, Elizabeth had known that the Union Club was a blessing to her marriage, for were Isaiah a man who rested every night in the bosom of his family, the weight would have been unbearable.

How testy he had become! He mourned the burned cigar factory as if it had been a palace and not an ancient structure in such poor repair that a workman had broken his leg when a rotten staircase collapsed under him. Her suggestion that he be reimbursed with enough money to pay for a doctor had met with Isaiah's astonishment. "These Irish get along. When he can walk again I may give him his job back, if I need him." But then the factory had burned and what had happened to the poor man she could not guess.

A week later Elizabeth left for an abolitionist meeting at six in the evening while Jane Anne was upstairs at her lessons. She had decided not to tell the child where she was going so as to spare her the burden of a guilty secret. It was Isaiah's night to play cards and sup at City Hotel, and she would be home long before he returned. She brought her parasol against the threat of rain, a most ironic precaution in view of the menace the night would offer.

The old building had been first a church, then a theater, was now a lecture hall. She was lucky to find a place at the end of one of the pewlike benches. Even the gallery was beginning to fill. It pleased her to see how many abolitionists were there even though she did not see the couple who were to have driven her home in their carriage.

The speaker had a fine command of language and well-timed gestures—hand raised toward heaven on noble phrases, pressed to his heart when sorrow was expressed, or clenched into a fist as he opposed tyranny. Boldly, he defined slavery as the gravest issue the nation faced or ever would, when from the gallery a voice with an Irish brogue shouted: "And what about jobs for the workingman? What about my wife and children what don't eat if I don't work?" Turning, Elizabeth saw a hatless, roughly clad man standing at the gallery railing, fist waving.

"That is not the issue we are here to address, sir," the speaker told him.

"What about the price of bread, then?" Another man had joined the first. "Up again! But do wages rise with it? No! How do I feed and house a family digging ditches at seventy-five cents a day?"

With effortful calm the speaker deplored the fact that too many employers exploited their workers mercilessly: there was a shoe factory in Connecticut that paid its female employees only seventy-five cents a *week* over and above the poorest of food and shelter. The rumblings in the gallery faded away. But then the speaker grew philosophical: "Condoning slavery has corrupted the moral fiber of the whole country, so that exploitation of others than Negroes has naturally followed. Pretensions to democracy are merest hypocrisy as long as Negroes are in chains. Hundreds of thousands of them were born here after 1808 when the slave trade was abolished. They are natives of this land!"

A voice roared from the gallery. "Sure, and you'd like to let loose all these niggers to take jobs away from us Irish and the bread from our mouths!" Elizabeth saw that he was leaning out over the railing like a gargoyle, his face contorted. "I'm a white man and a Christian and crossed an ocean to this damned city in hopes of an honest day's work! Speak up for us Irish right here in New York! Forget them niggers down South!"

Below, angry voices hushed him. In the gallery, friends slapped his back, yelled their agreement. The tension in the hall was as evident to Elizabeth as the darkness and fumes at Fanny Wright's lecture on women's rights. Desperately, the speaker proclaimed that he had nothing against the Irish and deplored their plight, but denied that freeing Negroes would rob the Irish of work.

Rough voices from the gallery jeered him. A bench was hurled over the railing to crash into the center aisle. A woman screamed. Cries of fear and protest inflamed the men in the gallery who responded by raising and hurling down another bench. This one, being frailer, broke into pieces. By now those seated directly below the gallery were on their feet, pushing their way toward the side aisles; Elizabeth heard someone sobbing. She could feel panic all around and in herself too, and knew a riot had begun and that nothing would stop it from reaching some dreadful conclusion. All around her people had risen, and she stood up too.

"Fire!" screamed a voice behind her. She turned and saw a wad of newspaper blazing atop the benches. Another was hurled flaming from the gallery as she watched. She found herself pushed into the aisle only half a dozen feet from the flames. The man pushing her mumbled an apology, offered her his arm, then broke into a run for the doorway, leaving her behind. Before Elizabeth reached it she had lost her bonnet in the crush of people jamming the exit and maddened by the smoke filling the hall. She was still clutching the parasol when she burst out into the street, only to find that she was not out of danger.

A gaslamp showed a melee of other escapees whom anti-abolitionists, lined along the curb, were pelting with mud from the gutter, angry epithets, jeers. She held her bonnetless head high as she started past that row of furious men. If she could reach the corner a block away she could hire a public coach or climb onto an omnibus, she told herself. Suddenly a young man with a limp hobbled from the curb to stand directly in her path. His face was pinched and wild. "I know you, lady. You're Mrs. Moss. I seen you with him once down to his factory."

"Kindly let me pass." She hid alarm with dignity.

He turned his head to shout to his companions, "Her husband kicked me out after I broke my leg on the job. Shall I let her pass, boys?"

There was laughter with hatred in it and a voice said, "Hold her 'til I give her a taste of mud." She felt something strike the back of her gown, then the side of her skirt, and looked down at a splotch of gutter filth, and knew she was afraid of the man she had once pitied. "I deplore your injury and the cause," she began, her voice low and quavering. Then she stamped her foot, angry at her own fear. "But I am not my husband! I did not throw you out!" She met the eyes of her accuser squarely. It was a stange moment, as if two people from distant nations had met without a common language. "Let me pass!"

The lame man was joined by two other rioters, grins showing in unshaven faces. "You'll have to beg prettier than that!" a squat man said. Beyond his head a tall beaver hat appeared. A cheery voice called, "Come on, lads! Let the lady through. She's a friend of mine."

The men turned, one said, "It's my boss. He's Tammany and he's for *us*." Immediately the others moved aside to open a path for her.

Tom O'Casey politely raised his hat, stepped to her side, offered his arm. "May I escort you home?"

"Thank you." Holding onto his arm was less a conventional act than necessity, for as they started toward the corner her knees seemed soft as thistledown and the blood was pounding in her ears like galloping hooves. In a moment the fast clopping of actual hooves on the paving neared and a fire wagon wheeled from the cross street, the helmet of the man at the reins silhouetted against a gaslamp; someone had evidently reported the blaze in the hall.

"Here we are," Tom said. "My noble steed and splendid coach." Below the street lamp stood a small black gig, its two wheels painted red, the patient horse standing with drooping head. Tom tossed a coin to the urchin guarding the vehicle, then handed Elizabeth in. As she tried to tidy her hair, disarranged when her bonnet was knocked off, she found that one long lock had come loose from the chignon and hung down onto her shoulder. She moored it as best she could with one of the hairpins remaining, then let her hands drop to her lap and gave in to a feeling of relief that she was safe and with no great harm done. Now it seemed remarkable that Tom should have chanced to be her rescuer. Only a few inches separated them below the gig's closed top, and she thought she could feel through her shawl the warmth of his body. As he urged the horse forward, slapping the reins on its rump, his arm brushed against hers. It did not seem possible to her that they were riding together through the light rain that had begun to fall.

"With your hair down on your shoulder that way I'm 'minded of a young girl I knew quite long ago." His deep voice was soft; the gentle patter of rain added to the sense of intimacy.

She struggled again with the escaping lock, and tried

for humor. "To seek her in me would be as hopeless as when old Burr goes haunting the Battery for a daughter drowned at sea."

He shook his head. "But that young Liza I knew didn't drown. Our past selves don't die, you know. They just get wrapped up in layers of time and circumstance, like cocoons. Do you remember the day in the woods when we watched a cocoon opening and saw a poor crumpled thing that crawled out and then flew off as a butterfly?"

She felt compelled to deny the memory. "A cocoon? A butterfly?" Again she tried to pin up the rebellious lock, and knew with the act that she wanted to keep her feelings under control as well. "Can one be both Tammany and abolitionist? That does seem a rare beast indeed."

"I don't pretend high motives for my political affiliations. I am in Tammany to become a precinct captain. After that my aim will be Assembly District leader, boss of a whole ward. After that comes the Executive Committee, and one of those men is elected boss of the entire county."

"So you have ambitions toward power if only over workingmen?"

He grinned at her. "My ambition is almost limitless. Studying architecture took up perhaps two hundred nights I could have spent at the tavern with my uncle."

"I respect ambition, if it doesn't make a man blind to all other values but the goal he's set his mind on."

"Oh, I'm far from blind to other values." He sounded amused at her prim comment. "Now and then I enjoy life right up to the hilt."

The metaphor plunged a sword into a scabbard, and for some reason she stirred uneasily, looked away from him and saw that the gig had turned into 10th Street. "How did you know where I live?"

For a moment he seemed at a loss, then smiled. "Dunbar Construction, my uncle's company, got the contract to put up your husband's new factory a month ago. His home address was the one he gave us, his office being ashes and charred brick."

So he had known where she lived when they met at the Battery two weeks ago, yet had not called. "You must be very busy now that the long winter's over and the rebuilding has started at last."

"True, I'm glad to say."

When the gig drew to a stop she could not remember if she had thanked him. "I am deeply obliged to you for arriving almost magically at the right moment."

"I guess fate offered us a second reunion, our first having been so brief." He turned his head to offer a bright smile which started a warmth in her that went sliding through her veins like fine wine.

"I won't ask you in," she said, as if this denial of hospitality also denied the reality of those feelings. "It's late," she added, at once aware that it was not.

"Do you mean you prefer this reunion to stay a private matter, just between the two of us?" He was only pretending confusion, she was certain.

"No! That's not what I meant at all. And now I must say good night." He started at once to get out. She laid a restraining hand on his arm, drew it back fast as if the sleeve had burnt her.

"Don't think of seeing me to my door in the rain. I beg of you."

Ignoring her, he jumped from the gig, circled it and handed her down. At the foot of the steps he removed his hat, bowed. "Good night, Liza. Sweet dreams. I know

87

mine will be sweet indeed."

As she unlocked the door with the key from her reticule her hand was unsteady. She hurried to the stairs, eager to get out of her muddied dress.

"Aunt Liza!" Jane Anne stood in the parlor doorway, her voice a plaintive wail. "What's happened to you? Where were you?"

"A riot, but I escaped."

Isaiah loomed behind the girl. "Your abolitionists again? Don't deny it!"

"I don't. Your anti-abolitionists set fire to the hall."

He beckoned imperiously. "Come here! I insist!"

"I thought you were playing whist tonight, as usual."

"I'm sure you did, and seized the opportunity to disobey me!" As she neared him he grabbed her arm, drew her into the room and whirled her around so she faced one of the narrow pier glasses flanking the doorway. "Look!"

The mirror showed a disheveled woman, hair tumbled down on one shoulder, skirt filthy with mud, mud on her shawl, and a streak of it on one cheek. To this creature Tom had talked of cocoons, the lost Liza, a sweet dream! She turned from the mirror.

Isaiah had moved to place Jane Anne between them, his hands resting on her shoulders. His expression seemed more smug than angry. "Look at this child. Observe her distress. She needs your guidance, your example. Yet tonight you have shown her disobedience and folly. You cannot behave so. You are a wife and a mother. And you must act like one." He lowered his voice to a solemn whisper. "Otherwise I will have to send Jane Anne away to a boarding school to remove her from your baneful influence."

Tears welled into the child's eyes. "I don't want to go away to boarding school! Oh, please, Aunt Liza!"

"Of course, you shan't!" She put her arm around the little girl, faced Isaiah. "I forswear abolitionist meetings in the future. That is a promise, Isaiah." She smiled down at Jane Anne, then with a grimace spread out her skirts. "Just look at this gown! And I was so fond of it!"

Isaiah drew a moral: "It's well worth the cost of a new one if you've learned that you can't touch pitch without being defiled. Those nigger-lovers being the pitch I refer to."

She winced, but continued to smile reassurance at Jane Anne, the hostage she had given to fortune—and to Isaiah Moss.

Part Two

V

On the day I first heard the word "Alamo" I had just been told at breakfast that in the fall I would attend Miss Boorman's Academy for Young Ladies as my friend Hope Pierpont had boasted she would do. She was six months older than I, and my elation was considerable for I had feared being left behind with Mr. Molesworth, the tutor, until spring. My joy met and overcame the news of a dreadful, distant massacre in Texas.

It was in March of 1836 that the Spanish word for poplar tree entered my nation's history and overnight became a synonym for unprovoked and cruel slaughter. Like every newspaper in the land, the *Herald*, the *Sun*, the *Tribune*, and the *Morning News* trumpeted and deplored the outrage. All of them pointed out that American settlers had been welcomed by the Mexican government years ago to a vast, long-neglected territory. Finally, inevitably, the American colonists had proclaimed their independence from Mexico, claiming that portion of the territory which their hard efforts had peopled, cultivated, brought to flower. This seemed reasonable to newspaper editors, my uncle, and Mr. Molesworth. But in March an invading force of 3,000 Mexicans under a General Santa Ana had come north of the Rio Grande and attacked those brave Americans, slaughtering 183 barricaded in an old Spanish mission, the Alamo. Then the bodies had been stripped, heaped in piles and burned. James Bowie and Davy Crockett, the famed frontiersmen and the former Congressman, had been among those dishonored dead. Public indignation knew no bounds: Was the massacre of those brave Americans to go unavenged? "We can't let those Mexicans get by with this!" my uncle warned. "There won't be any stopping them if we do!"

A hero emerged down in Texas who evidently agreed. Sam Houston and the men who had rallied around him, although gravely outnumbered, intended to hold Texas and meet the Mexican army of Santa Ana. Volunteers were said to be joining Houston's small, brave band daily, particularly from the South.

That this situation in Texas could have any effect on my aunt's life or mine was far from my thoughts on the day I first heard of Sam Houston and saw for the second time the handsome man my aunt had encountered at the Battery.

Bread was the pretext for Mr. O'Casey's visit. He arrived in the late afternoon to invite my aunt and me for a ride in his gig. "I think I have a task for you Bread Ladies that will do more good than handing out those loaves to arriving immigrants." I was instantly flattered to be included, though aware, as he must have been, that my aunt might not care to go jaunting with him alone. "And I think I can show you a part of the city you may not have seen."

"I believe I know New York quite well," my aunt said, "but it's a pleasant afternoon and I'm still grateful for your timely rescue from the rioters."

I was silent as we crowded into his red-wheeled gig to

ride southward. She had said nothing to me about who her rescuer had been, not a word. Her secrecy about having seen Mr. O'Casey again both wounded and intrigued me, for by then I was the proud sharer of a most important secret, knew that her novel *The Ironmaster's Bride* had been published under the *nom de plume* "Elissa Allaire" by the Boston firm Ticknor and Fields. "Your uncle shares Mr. Nathaniel Hawthorne's contempt for what he calls 'scribbling woman' so I must be tactful and choose the right time and place to tell him of this vice." She smiled. And she had added, "He and I are at odds about quite enough already." Pleased to be her confidante, I had nodded wisely. Sometimes it had seemed to me that she was attracted to causes sure to annoy him.

After a few minutes I came out of my sulk and remarked that she had not told me it was Mr. O'Casey who had brought her safely home that night. She bestowed on me her sweetest smile. "Didn't I? Really? I thought I had."

Very soon I was sorry I had come for this ride, as we entered that noisome slum area surrounding the once-lovely Bowery, a maze of narrow streets and alleys where poor immigrants, many of them Irish, managed somehow to exist. Mr. O'Casey said, "I have seen with my own eyes a small damp cellar room in which fifteen people of both sexes, including children, slept in turns on straw pallets. The musty smell of the place pervaded their clothes, their very skin and flesh. But I will not shock you with a sight like that. I'm taking you to visit a family somewhat luckier than most."

The gig drew up beside a decaying brick tenement building, the wheels nearly touching the walls on either side of the alley where a few gaunt men and boys silently gathered from nowhere to stare. Mr. O'Casey gave the nearest boy some pennies to watch the carriage, then took us into a door from which all paint had peeled and down a narrow hall that stank. He rapped on a door which was opened by the red-haired man he had greeted down at the Battery and saved from the runners. In his pale blue eyes I saw a combined look of despair and aggressiveness, but he mustered up a sketch of a smile and invited us in.

The tiny dark room contained a young woman in a worn shawl, a thin child of about six, another of perhaps three, a low bed with a clean quilt covering it, and a dropleaf table on which was a candlestick and four cups. An empty market basket yawned beside the door. The woman stood to offer my aunt the hard chair on which she had been seated; I was offered the other. Mr. O'Casey presented the Ryans to us. Mrs. Ryan bobbed a curtsey, Mr. Ryan made a stiff bow. "Brian Ryan is one of five sons," Mr. O'Casey said. "The portion of the much-divided family farmland he inherited comprised ten acres of poor soil. Potatoes are all he could grow to get a crop large enough to feed his family. Potatoes produce well, but are subject to blight. Such a blight spurred him to come here. He has had only three days work digging a ditch for a gas main. Seventy-five cents for a twelve-hour day. He's using up his savings to survive and can't outfit himself to go west in a Conestoga wagon as I first suggested. Here, Mrs. Moss, this fine little family is at present stuck." He turned to Brian Ryan. "Forgive me for describing your plight to a stranger, but she is a lady of kind intentions."

"All I ask," Mr. Ryan said, "is to get on my own two feet and do a good day's work at a steady job."

"And never doubt but he's a good worker," Mrs. Ryan told us.

The two little girls had been staring in wonder at my pretty dress and lace-trimmed pantalettes and straw bonnet. I made up my mind to part with two dolls and have the cook bake them some gingerbread men.

Tom O'Casey smiled. "I came to tell you that as of Monday, Brian, you have a job with O'Casey Construction for a month at least. Carrying hod for the bricklayers. I'll teach you how, having learned that along with just about everything else that goes with the building trade."

The change this news of a job made was astonishing. The wan children smiled, Mrs. Ryan clapped her hands, and Brian Ryan grew inches taller in a minute.

It was twilight when we drove out of the alley and turned northward. The wan faces of two little Irish girls had provoked in me a more poignant sadness than the deaths in Texas of two national heroes. When a lamplighter caused a corner lamppost to bloom with its flower of radiance I felt I was coming back to civilization again, to the part of it, at least, where I and people like me lived.

"Do you think the Bread Ladies might be willing to fill some empty market baskets for people like the Ryans?" Tom O'Casey said at last, and clucked to his horse, urging it masterfully around the corner.

My aunt's tone was cool. "I think you see me as an idle, fortunate lady who indulges in occasional kindness to immigrants. Or so your patronizing tone suggests. But the Bread Ladies remind this heartless city of the need for greater help. I am not one to sit back and wait for God or the rich to take care of the poor and the helpless. I believe I can assure you that my Bread Ladies will see to it that the Ryans and their neighbors do not starve. I cannot promise to feed all the immigrants in the city, but you did not expect that, I am sure."

His voice sounded properly chided. "A drop in the bucket is better than no drop at all."

"And I shall bring the Ryan girls gingerbread men," I offered. My aunt pressed my hand and he turned to smile. "And two dolls."

That trip to Ryan's alley produced more than food baskets, gingerbread men and two dolls. I am certain that *Kathleen of Killarney* began to take shape in my aunt's imagination that very night. It concerned the misadventures of a lovely young woman from Ireland who arrives at the Battery expecting to be met by an uncle. But he has died, so she finds herself alone in New York. Innocent and vulnerable, she is first employed as a maidservant, escapes seduction by her rich master, then works in a shirt factory where her virtue is assailed by a cruel foreman. Fleeing him she falls in with a richly attired woman of ill repute, but at last is taken into her home by a kind old lady somewhat like Mrs. Penrose who, finding she can read and write, turns her into a companion for her bedridden daughter, who proves to be a cruel liar, so that Kathleen is blamed for the theft of a valuable jewel. In the end, though, a fine young man of the upper crust proposes marriage and all ends well. My aunt assured me that the formula it followed was sure to become ever more popular—an innocent girl amid life's calamities, tearful at times (many times) but brave.

All but the heroine's name, nationality and hopeful arrival were in the future the following Sunday. My aunt and I went to the Presbyterian church together that day; my uncle dropped us off and continued to the Episcopalian. I was startled to see Mr. O'Casey take a seat in the pew directly across the aisle. His Sunday appearance was truly elegant; his frockcoat looked new, his cravat was a marvel of snowy perfection. In a moment my aunt saw him too. We had all risen to sing the opening hymn. She heard his robust baritone and turned. I stole a glance and saw that as he sang his eyes were on her. I could not believe it when he winked. A bold and roguish wink that made me smile in spite of a degree of shock. I felt my aunt stiffen like a ramrod.

He was waiting for us on the church steps when we came out. He approached, doffing his hat, and invited us to a dish of ice cream in the new ice cream parlor that had just opened on Broadway.

The smile my aunt wore was her social one. "To be seen in an ice cream parlor with a handsome bachelor is not comportment that meets my standards of wifely behavior."

His smile faded and left a bewildered look that made me almost sorry for him. He looked at me then with an expression that was hard to define. It was shrewd and held a hint of satisfaction. "We both know how much damage wagging tongues can cause," he said. With a fare-well nod he put on his gray beaver hat, tapped it to a jaunty angle, and left us, to be at once surrounded by several young ladies of the congregation who wished him to know of a church social to take place the following Friday evening.

For the rest of the day my aunt's manner was abstracted. She listened with vague eyes as my uncle boasted of the excellent job Dunbar construction was doing. "O'Casey persuaded me to put up a somewhat larger and costlier building than I had intended, but I find myself proud that my cigar company is to be housed in a structure worthy of my enterprise. All the men I know who lost buildings in the fire are doing the same, floating large loans and erecting better structures, thus turning a disaster into something like a triumph." He was smiling fiercely as he added, "It takes more than a conflagration to keep Americans down!" And with his Whiggish scowl, as my aunt called it, he pounded his fist on the table and added, "As those Mexican fiends down in Texas are going to learn to their horror and ruination!"

I had known that Dunbar Construction was the firm my uncle had hired to build his factory, but no one had told me that Mr. O'Casey worked for Mr. Barney Dunbar. I started to say as much, but something stopped me.

During the next week I saw little of my aunt. She had started on her new novel in earnest, had made herself a hideaway in one corner of the spare room between the front bedroom and mine. "I will not be at home to anyone for the next two hours or so," she told Mary, the downstairs maid after dinner. On my way home from the circulating library an hour later I saw from a short distance down the street that she was carrying out these instructions. It was Tom O'Casey who turned away as the front door closed and thudded down our front steps, face dark and thoughtful. He did not see me and in a moment the red wheels of his gig whirled him away.

VI

After dinner on a bright April afternoon, Elizabeth heard a bird sing outside the window. She went upstairs to the desk in the corner of the spare room and lit the green-shaded oil lamp, for the inner room had only a transom but no windows. She picked up her pen, dipped it in the inkwell, and began to copy the morning's penciled pages. But a restlessness had seized her. It was too nice out to stay inside. She had to have a walk. She had put on her bonnet and shawl when Mary toiled up to say that Mrs. Pierpont was in the parlor. "She insisted on waiting for you, ma'am."

In pale mauve trimmed with black silk braid that matched her hair and eyes Dolly looked like a picture from Godey's Ladies' Book. "What a lovely shawl! Is it new? Are you coming in or going out?"

"Out."

"Splendid!" Dolly stood up and settled her own shawl around her shoulders. "I'm a trifle put out with Robert. For a man with a seat on the New York Stock Exchange he can be most tight-fisted about spending money on a bit of travel. I'm going to have my fortune told. There's nothing like a little peek at the future to change one's mood."

"The Fisher sisters?"

"Of course. Who else? Do come along."

Although Robert Pierpont had provided Dolly with three children and a life verging on luxury, she had taken to seeking hints of the future in a velvet-curtained boardinghouse suite where the aroma of Chinese incense filled the air and tea leaves or Tarot cards whispered of dark strangers. The two Fisher sisters had arrived the year before from parts unspecified; a modest newspaper advertisement had informed New York of their psychic powers.

"We'll walk there," Dolly wheedled. "You always love a stroll."

As they passed along 10th Street below the little trees in their first hint of delicate leafage, Dolly prattled on about the mysterious ability of the older of the psychic sisters who had not impressed Elizabeth on her one earlier visit. "Only three months ago a dead husband spoke through Adela's lips, she being, of course, in a trance, and the widow all but fainted dead away, I assure you!"

Elizabeth remembered Adela Fisher well: sallow, with sad bulging brown eyes and an extraordinarily large bosom which the rest of her seemed to follow, drawn forward willy-nilly. Her younger sister Imogene was a dainty porcelain beauty of about sixteen, so much like a Dresden shepherdess that Elizabeth had felt she should carry a crook tied with a bow.

"Why do you suppose Imogene is afraid of Adela?" Elizabeth asked Dolly.

"Is she? I hadn't noticed such a thing."

"Perhaps that's too strong a word. But she's clearly dominated by her."

"Adela is a great deal older, and their parents are dead,

102

so isn't it natural?" Without waiting for comment, Dolly revealed that Adela had forseen the recent explosion of a Hudson River steamboat to the very day. "And didn't she tell you a good many things about yourself that were quite true?"

"Quite true." On the previous visit to the boarding-house suite Adela's Tarot cards had revealed that Elizabeth's destiny was in the hands of an older man, and that she was in close association with a fair-complected young woman, also that the death or illness of a dear one seemed, alas, indicated. It was clear to Elizabeth that Adela could have learned of Isaiah and Jane Ann from chatty Dolly, or perhaps from Clara Mason who was also among the trickle of devotees. In short, Elizabeth considered Adela Fisher a fraud, or perhaps merely a self-deluded woman who sincerely believed in her own mystical powers.

The aroma of incense met the Fishers' clients upon entering the second-floor suite, as well as the gleam of a large brass bowl on a stand by the door. Adela evidently considered this method of payment more genteel than coins doled into her hand. A neatly lettered card on the wall above the bowl specified the going fee for each method of probing the future or the beyond. Horoscopes had gone up: they were now a dollar and a half, Elizabeth noted. Adela followed her bosom toward her and offered a welcome in a voice deep as a foghorn.

Leaving Dolly to Adela and the Tarot cards, Elizabeth went to the corner where Imogene presided at a small round table draped with a lace cloth: her only forte was reading tea leaves. A dark blue velvet curtain hung from a brass rod and could be drawn to assure privacy for tealeaf secrets. Imogene wore pale blue with a ruffle at neck and wrists, and in the dim triangular niche formed when she drew the curtain the flame of the candle on the table wavered and made her shadow on the wall behind her move stealthily, as if with a life of its own.

"Drink off the tea, please, and give me the cup." Her small voice gained conviction as she spoke. After swirling the emptied cup three times, she frowned down at the contents, looked up. "I see a visitor. An unexpected visitor."

"Yes?" Who does not have unexpected visitors?

"It seems to be a man," Imogene said, peering down into the cup again. "He is wearing a hat." She was silent for a moment. "I see you surrounded by people, all sorts of people. I also see a journey, but that is some time off." She studied the leaves again. Elizabeth had the feeling that Imogene had forgotten all her coaching from Adela; she was like an actress who can't remember a line.

"Thank you. That was a very nice fortune, Miss Fisher."

"I haven't finished." Both Imogene's little white hands were pressing her temples now; a ruffle fell back to reveal a pale blue vein on one wrist. "This pattern here is confusing. But I seem to see trouble here. I don't know what, but it looks like you'll find a way out of the mess. There's also some kind of good news. Very good news." She looked up. "Sometimes what I see is almost like a story. But your tea leaves today . . ." She shrugged, looking plaintive. "They're just all disjointed like."

Elizabeth suddenly felt sorry for her. What sort of life was it for a pretty young girl, mouthing lies over the dregs in teacups? She opened her reticule and laid a silver half-dollar on the lace cloth.

Imogene's hand went out toward it, then drew back.

104

"You should put it in that bowl by the door. That's how my sister wants it done."

There was a sullen undertone, and Elizabeth realized that this method of payment gave Adela control over Imogene's modest earnings, and so control over her. "This is for you," she said. "I'll put something in the bowl as well."

Imogene smiled for the first time, showing small perfect teeth and picked up the coin. "I *do* thank you, ma'am. But in that case, won't you let me read your palm as well? I've been studying up on palmistry for near two months."

Elizabeth extended her hand, palm up, and learned that she would have a long life, at least two children, and a passionate affair of the heart. "See here?" Imogene said, pointing to a place in the center of her palm where the life line broke off then started again. "That means a great change ahead, though I can't say what." She looked up, hopeful of having given satisfaction.

Dolly was pleased with her fortune. As they walked home she said, "Travel in the near future! I do hope it'll be to Saratoga. Robert's been promising and promising that we can go again. Don't you simply adore Saratoga? It's simply the resort of resorts, isn't it?"

"Where the rich hob-nob with people pretending to be. Where parvenues from every state flock to promenade and boast later of having met a duke. Where pork dealers rub shoulders with financiers. Where—"

"You *are* hard to please! Did you get a nice fortune?"

"An unexpected visitor in a hat."

"Perhaps that handsome man you met down at the Battery? Did he ever call, by the way?"

"Yes. He and Jane Anne and I went for a drive to meet

105

the Ryans."

"Of course. I remember. But still, I would be careful."

"What does that mean?"

Dolly started walking again. "Jane Anne will be starting at Miss Boorman's Academy in the fall, won't she? Gone all day. Isaiah spends quite a few evenings at his club now, didn't you say? I do think simple opportunity causes more illicit affairs than passion, I really do."

"If I had imagined you'd manufacture a chance encounter and one call into an affair I wouldn't have told you about them." She was glad she had said nothing about the rescue on the night of the riot.

"Pray do not take that squiffy tone. You sound like Mrs. Penrose. But just don't forget what happened to poor Mrs. Draper. Isaiah Moss may not be the most exciting of husbands, but he *is* a husband, without which a woman's life isn't worth a brass farthing."

Elizabeth teased her. "Some women lead fascinating lives without husbands. Look at Fanny Wright."

"Surely you can't be serious! Fanny Wright? I know you seem to admire her, but she's really a sort of freak. And doesn't she have a large fortune? Without Isaiah, what would you do, dear?"

"Teach children, write novels, or walk the streets."

"Good heavens, whatever are we talking like this for? As though you'd ever be swept off your feet by this . . . this . . . What did you say his name was?"

"I didn't. It's Thomas Dunbar O'Casey."

"O'Casey? Oh, do forgive me! I had no idea he was Irish!"

"It isn't a crime." The woman's bigotry angered her. They had reached the Pierpont's house. Elizabeth

106

declined rather coldly Dolly's invitation to come in and continued west along 10th Street to her own house. Outside she saw a black gig with red wheels, very much like Tom's. She felt her heart take note of it, and ran up her front steps, unlocked the door. Mary was in the hall, ostensibly dusting the narrow table with its silver tray for calling cards. "There's a gentleman caller in the parlor, ma'am. Miss Jane Anne must have let him in, knowing you'd be back soon."

Tom! As she turned to the mirror to remove her bonnet and smooth her hair she found herself elated, smiling at her reflection. The gentleman in the hat had indeed arrived!

Tom stood up as she entered, dwarfing the room. His face was grave. She sent Jane Anne off to ask Mary to bring tea and then to study her lessons. Tom remained standing until she had seated herself in the ruby velvet chair flanking the settee. Clearly the manners of a gentleman had been learned along with the building trade, and good for him! She saw then that he was not his usual self, but quite pale and tense. "I've come to say good-bye, Liza."

"Good-bye? Where are you going? Why?" Her elation of a moment before had vanished, a burst bubble.

He was watching her steadily and leaned a little closer. "You're disturbed. I'm flattered."

"Disturbed? No, but I *am* surprised. You seemed quite satisfied with your life here when we first talked at the Battery."

"Since then I've had a falling out with my uncle."

"But where will you go? Back to Allerton?"

"Never. I suppose you know about Sam Houston?

That he will fight Santa Ana to the finish?" He watched her nod. "I decided today that I just might take myself to Texas and join his troops. God knows he needs men. And I have a hankering for the frontier."

"I don't understand. You're neither a soldier nor a Texan, and we're not at war with Mexico."

"Not yet, at any rate. I can't believe that you weren't outraged by the Alamo. Two hundred butchered Americans?"

"A hundred and eighty-three, according to the papers I read."

"Well, isn't that enough for you?"

"I simply can't believe you're throwing away everything out of admiration for Houston or outrage over the Alamo."

"All right, Liza," Tom smiled. "I'm leaving my uncle Barney high and dry to manage as best he can without me. I got him three fat jobs after the fire, and now he's red in the face and shouting about a hod-carrier I hired and a few bricks he thinks I paid too much for. But he needs me and I know it. So it occurred to me that a show of my fighting Irish blood—he believes that Irish blood is fighting blood, as some fools do—might wake him up to what I'm worth to him."

"So you told him you're going to Texas?"

"No, but I let the word get out at a tavern where he'll learn of it."

"Then it's all a bluff about going away!" She was delighted to have probed him—and relieved.

He shook his head. "You can't threaten what you're not ready to perform. I'm leaving this city, and that's for certain. Whether I ever work for Barney Dunbar again is a moot question. I won't if he continues to pay me less than I'm worth, and refuses out of caution or pure stupidity to understand what I want and why."

"What do you want?" Now the conversation was imbued with the frankness that had once existed between them, and she could not draw back into a polite distance.

"I want to get in with the big muck-a-mucks, the men with vision, civic pride! They're talking about turning a part of that wasteland to the north into a big public park with a lake, roads, pavilions, maybe a museum. What plums in the way of contracts that would provide! But Barney Dunbar is a simple fellow. He feels uneasy about people who've used silver forks all their lives. He won't invest in a decent office, a decent carriage, or spend what it costs to drink where the rich men do. He laughs at my ideas about the future of this city."

"What are they, aside from a public park and fat jobs for Dunbar Construction?" Now hostility toward his uncle had put a glow on his cheeks; she could almost feel the heat of his anger.

His fist was balled on one knee as he leaned toward her. "I want a municipal police department. A fire department, not forty-odd volunteers who race to a blaze and then may fight each other for the honor of putting it out while the building's burning to the ground! I want the Croton Reservoir completed and functioning at last. All those projects would provide jobs! I want a mayor elected with the brains to see that a horde of unemployed men is a danger in any society. A month or so ago a mob of workies broke into a warehouse and smashed so many barrels of flour that the street outside was knee-deep in it. And our mayor went out to confront them with sweet reason about the cost of bread. He and the State Militia men with him ended up pelted with flour so they looked like snowmen." Tom stood up, paced restlessly. "But with a strong mayor who could get some cooperation among the aldermen and the rich muck-a-mucks and Tammany, all working together instead of at odds. Wonders could be accomplished!"

"You're right, but what's in it for Tom O'Casey?"

He stopped dead, eyed her. "What a woman! Pretty as a picture, and shrewd as a lawyer!" He started to pace again. "Since long before the Revolution, this city's grown almost without plan. Tear down an old house, whack up another, no better built. Shoddy tenements for the poor going up by the dozens but almost no common schools. Gas mains by the miles; no adequate water supply. This is the biggest, richest city in this nation, and it's still an idiot child, slobbering on itself! You asked what's in it for me? I intend, by hook or crook, to be one of the men who have some say in the future destiny of New York. The tanner's boy who used to stink of manure and hides and get spattered with cow brains is going to sit at the mayor's table any day of the week including Sundays! Tom O'Casey, big in Tammany but close with the silver-fork folk. As Irish as Paddy's goat with the Irish, and *'bon giorno'* to the Italians, and *'Guten Morgen'* to the Germans. And in the rich men's houses I'll take a silver fork to their *pate de fois gras* and waltz with their wives and daughters as well as any European duke!" Tom's face was animated, his voice intense.

Elizabeth found herself applauding. "Bravo! Bravissimo!"

"And you'd best believe that I can do what I boast about!"

She leaned back, aware of having been carried away. "That remains to be seen, doesn't it?"

"You'll see it! And you'll see something else, Liza." He came to where she sat, dropped suddenly to one knee, seized both her hands. "You'll see the day when you walk out of this house for the last time. Right into my arms. That's what you'll see, Liza. That's what you'll do!" Sweat gleamed on his upper lip. His pupils were large with excitement. "The past is done. It doesn't matter now."

Numbed, she looked down and realized that their hands were locked, hers gripped in his, and she tried to pull them free. She heard her cold voice say with false amusement, "Are you trying to make me believe that you were my true and faithful love?"

He stood up abruptly, face and voice stony. "I was, Liza. That's the pity of it. I was."

"Is that how Betsy Baker got with child?"

He scowled, reddened. "You threw me away! Scorned me! I'd have taken Betsy or the devil's daughter after that!"

"Your memory is playing tricks on you. Your Betsy was with child before I agreed to marry Isaiah Moss."

"It's your own memory that's playing tricks, Liza!"

She was on her feet, but facing him. "Don't call me Liza! How do you dare to call me that?"

There was a faint clatter from the doorway. The maid entered bearing a large tray with the silver tea set, a plate of cakes. "Take it back, Mary. We're not having tea after all."

She stared. "No tea?"

"Too late. My guest is leaving."

"Yes, ma'am." With a look of confusion, Mary turned and departed.

Tom took a step toward Elizabeth, who stepped back.

111

"You said, 'Too late.' But it's not too late. Not too late for us to get back what we lost."

"I don't want what I lost. I have a life that suits me very well!"

"Then you're too easily satisfied! No children except Jennie's orphan! Old Moss is good at making cigars. You dress well and you have a good piano and your worthy charities. But is that any life for a real woman?"

She felt battered by his scorn. "I think you must be drunk. How do you dare to attack my husband?"

"One day, Liza, you are going to leave your old hobby horse for a stallion and be damned glad you did!"

His arrogance inflamed her. "You see yourself as a stallion, sir? You imagine I want one? You are in error. I want what I am lucky enough to have, a pleasant and civilized life most women would envy. I am no longer fifteen, ignorant of the world, the victim of mere feelings, no longer a child who believed in the promises of a boy who found a girl with fewer scruples. So gallop on your way, sir, and find another Betsy."

His face had flushed but his voice was cold. "The fine lady has spoken, is that it? You might convince me if I didn't know you so well. A passionate girl who kissed me as you did could never change into what you pretend to be. I'm not fooled by your masquerade, Liza."

He strode out. She stood with closed eyes and clenched fists, heard the front door slam and the rapid thudding of his boots going down the front steps. A hard knot of emotion was clogged inside her chest. She pressed a fist against it. She wanted to weep. Anger erupted. How had he dared? Oh, how had he dared to say such things?

*   *   *

It was a few days later that Isaiah complained of an unfair blow from fate. Checking progress on his new factory building that afternoon, he had learned that Barney Dunbar's nephew had left him flat. "The fellow kept all running smoothly. He had a way with the workmen being himself half-Irish. Everything's slowed down with only Dunbar in charge. It seems that O'Casey is off for Texas to join Sam Houston's soldiers. What he expects of that, short of a Mexican bullet in his brain, I don't pretend to guess. Don't tell me the Irish are not a strange breed!"

So it had not been a bluff after all! What had Tom said? "You can't threaten what you're not ready to perform." She told herself she was relieved that he was gone. But the phrase "a Mexican bullet in his brain" haunted her. She combed the papers for news of the fray in Texas.

It was a relief to learn that Sam Houston's valiant soldiers had won the battle at San Jacinto in mid-April. Santa Ana was captured and his demoralized Mexican troops had fled back across the Rio Grande, leaving the Americans in control of the territory they had fought for, and where the Lone Star flag of the Republic of Texas now proudly flew.

The *Herald,* the *Sun* and the *Tribune* outdid themselves in heaping praise on Houston and his brave men for the shattering victory—and only six weeks after the Alamo. They did not include any casualty list, for the obvious reason that dead Texans would be of little interest to New Yorkers. Elizabeth assured herself that there was no way Tom could have reached Texas in time for the battle, although nothing said he had not gone there.

But rationality did not control her dreams. Cruelly, she was one night a young girl in love with a young Tom and the next a distraught woman trying to find him in a

113

strange land supposed to be Texas.

On the night of the first of May she and Isaiah attended a charity ball. She and Mrs. Penrose had together persuaded the eccentric August Belmont to permit his ballroom to be so utilized. Many a ticket would be sold to those willing to pay a stiff price in order to later say they had waltzed in the famous home. Isaiah was among these. He seemed to take pride in the fact that Elizabeth had helped organize the affair, and complimented her appearance. She knew that she looked particularly well, in a new gown of amber silk, in advance of the mode with its wide skirt held out by a petticoat of bombazine, its low decolletage baring her shoulders and bosom. She had just waltzed with Isaiah, and was waiting with Mrs. Penrose and several others for him to bring her a glass of champagne punch.

"Mrs. Moss?"

The deep, resonant voice made a shiver go down her back. She turned. It was Tom O'Casey. Having imagined him in Texas it was as though he had defied space and time to appear before her, correct in his dark hammertail coat, a ghost.

He bowed to Mrs. Penrose, and Elizabeth had the notion he was going to ask that ample matron to dance, but he turned and bowed to her. "May I have the great pleasure of this dance with Mrs. Moss?" Words of refusal spun through her mind and vanished. Numbly she moved beside him to the floor where a dozen couples already swirled. She became aware of his hand on the small of her back. It moved slightly. She saw her long slender hand on his dark shoulder. The palm of the other rested in his palm. "You did not go to Texas, then."

"No, to Saratoga. To mix with nabobs and muck-a-mucks. In two weeks I landed a fine, fat contract. I came back and slapped it down on Uncle Barney's desk." He laughed. "He was grateful to see me, I can tell you. Things are starting to go my way now."

His arrogant, jovial tone was an offense; he had fooled her along with his uncle. His hand on her back moved again, very subtly, sending a quiver through her body. His other hand closed tighter on hers. Why was she here in his arms? "If you intend to mix with the elite, you should really take a few dancing lessons."

He misstepped, losing the rhythm, but recovered it. "I did."

"Then you must have learned not to grip a lady's hand quite so fiercely."

His hand at once relaxed. But the one on her back still pressed it, the largest, warmest hand in the universe. He smiled down at her. "As you can see, I've forgiven you!"

"You've forgiven *me?*"

"For throwing me out of your house in your panic."

"In anger! You offended me deeply." Over his shoulder she caught a glimpse of Isaiah standing with a glass of punch in his hand.

"Why are you dancing with me if you still hold a grudge?" Tom asked.

"A grudge? You *do* flatter yourself!"

"No grudge?"

"I am dancing with you because a lady will never humiliate anyone if that can be avoided." She was aware that she sounded like a book of etiquette.

"Why do you lie to yourself?" He was smiling. On her back his hand moved again, a caress.

"Lie? I? A strange accusation from someone who deceives people with tales of joining Sam Houston!" Her

115

anger was hard to contain. "Not that it mattered to me one iota!"

"There you go again! Another lie!" Head tilted to one side he was smiling as sweetly down as if he had just paid a compliment.

"I find you offensive, and I see my husband waiting with the champagne punch I asked him for. I'm quite thirsty." She tried to slip from his arms. He pulled her strongly to him.

"The dance has not ended." With set jaw he waltzed her past Isaiah. "It should not be seen as an offense if an old friend tells you the truth about yourself. I watched your face tonight when you turned and saw me here, alive. You're not dancing with me because you're a lady, but because you're a woman with feelings for me you pretend aren't there. It's a terrible wrong you do to yourself and to me." As if his suppressed anger lent him agility, he circled the floor with vigorous steps she had to follow and even managed some skillful twirls that whirled her skirt wide. When the music stopped he quickly offered his arm and walked her back to Isaiah. He bowed, thanked her, greeted her husband, and left.

Isaiah frowned at his retreating back. "What's O'Casey doing at the Belmont's ball?"

She took the punch, sipped, managed a cool voice while her heart drummed. "Since it's a charity ball I presume he bought a ticket."

Tall, angular Cornelius Ferris, one of the richest bachelors in New York approached and requested a dance. Isaiah beamed, for the Ferris fortune had long impressed him—along with the man's seat on the New York Stock Exchange. Nearby, Elizabeth saw Tom waltzing with a young lady who looked up at him with

116

dazzled eyes.

". . . polka?" Mr. Ferris was saying.

"Pardon?"

"The European polka is all the rage in London, and sure to be so here, I do believe."

"I do believe you are right, Mr. Ferris. Such a cheerful, invigorating dance, isn't it?" Tom was no longer in sight; Isaiah, looking pleased with himself, was now waltzing with Mrs. August Belmont. For a heavy man he was extremely light on his feet.

Suddenly, the evening stretched ahead, seeming interminable. Like the rest of her life.

Elizabeth dated her insomnia from the night of the Belmont ball. Long after Isaiah was asleep she lay tormented by one thing Tom had said to her: "Why do you lie to yourself?" She could still feel the warmth of his hand on her back. She hated him—yet she did not. She admired his ambition—yet she despised his trickery with his uncle. She remembered vividly how Tom had looked at seventeen, and in the next instant could recall nothing but his old-fashioned leather breeches. At four in the morning she got up, lighted the chamber candle by the bed, and went down the hall into Jane Anne's room.

The girl was sleeping on her back, one arm flung up on the pillow. Her closed lids, lashes fanned on her cheeks, had a faint sheen. Elizabeth remembered a baby in a bureau-drawer crib. The innocence of the child's face touched her as the infant's had, and gave her back a sense of her own true identity. She had long ago assumed responsibility for another life—and by doing so had become the self she now was, a woman justly offended at

117

being attacked by a man's unruly desire. Lashed into a frenzy by his own boastful ambitions, Tom had included in them possession of her. To keep face with himself, he now believed that her outrage had been a defense against unacknowledged desire for him. So he was the one who had lied to himself!

Satisfied, she returned to bed and soon fell asleep.

The next night she read until three; the lamplight waked Isaiah who demanded darkness. On the third night he was angry. It occurred to her then that it had been a year or more since he had demanded his conjugal rights; why did they share this bed? Perhaps, she said, they should have separate rooms just now. He agreed that for the present it might be a sensible idea. "I need eight hours of uninterrupted sleep in order to face the many problems that beset me!" He decided that the third-floor front bedroom would be his, at least for the time being. Next day she set herself the task of refurbishing the neglected room, which, he said, had been his as a boy.

By June she was spending several hours every day with *Kathleen of Killarney*. Mrs. Penrose's new charity proved most helpful. Elizabeth spent one afternoon a week as instructor and confidante of the young prostitutes Mrs. Penrose hoped to redeem by teaching them the duties of a housemaid. She had rented a loft where they slept. It was in her own kitchen that they learned to make simple foods such as toast, gruel, boiled eggs. In the vast Penrose dining room they learned to set the table. They dusted her parlor weekly for practice. The pretty red-haired Irish girl whose first two years in New York encompassed more misadventures than a reader would have believed stole some table silver from her benefactress before vanishing, but left Elizabeth a treasure-trove

118

of abuses and disasters, many of which were undoubtedly true.

In stories of a young girl facing life's dangers, a wise and kindly older man or woman always interceded to offer a way out of difficulty, though good sense and courage on the girl's part were required. Would Mrs. Penrose recognize herself, perhaps be angry? But Elizabeth could not worry about that. It was amazing how swiftly the plot fleshed itself out. More amazing was the way *Kathleen of Killarney* served to make the reunion with Tom O'Casey assume its proper proportion. It had been an episode, no more. Absolutely nothing more!

VII

The night my aunt and uncle went to a ball at the Belmonts' I went to her wardrobe, took down a gown of rose silk and put it on. I did up my hair atop my head and posed on tiptoe before her cheval glass holding the dress tightly around my waist from behind. I stretched my free arm toward my reflection, a fan of carved ivory swinging from a silk cord around the wrist. "Good evening, Mr. Belmont. Dance with you? I'd be most delighted." I attempted a waltz with an imaginary partner, but stumbled on the dragging hem of the gown, much too long. Returning to the mirror, I flipped open the fan, half-hid my face as an etiquette book showed, and fanned with small swift motions of the wrist. But when I took off the dress I was just a girl in white batiste pantalettes and an underwaist as flat in front as an ironing board. It would be years before I would waltz at a real ball or even put my hair up. How I wished that time could be folded like a fan so that the next five years could be squeezed together into only a month!

That September I was enrolled in Miss Boorman's Academy for Young Ladies. She was the spinster daughter of the very rich family that built one of the first mansions in Washington Square. Thin, with frizzy bangs, she seemed to have frozen into the style of her girlhood: high-waisted Georgian gowns with slender skirts and short puff sleeves. She saw the distinction between a girl and a young lady as absolute. To turn girls into young ladies was her calling in life, she said. Comportment was the word she most often used. A young lady never laughed loudly, never spoke loudly, never took long steps. "Comportment and sincerity, these will always mark a lady," she told us at an assembly the first day. "Here you will learn how to behave in polite society without any taint of falsity. *Tres bien?* To that you will reply, *'Oui, Mademoiselle Boorman.'*"

"*Oui, Mademoiselle Boorman,*" we chanted sincerely.

Afterward she spoke to each girl privately in her office. To me she said, "I hear you have an ear. If so I may recommend that you take voice lessons with dear Mr. Gatti who in his youth sang at La Scala." It was gratifying that when he heard me sing a dozen notes he leaped up from the piano stool to shout, "Thanks to God, a real voice at last!"

"I knew *that* when you were five," Uncle Isaiah said at supper that night, with some contempt for an Italian's opinion.

After he had bought the Chickering piano which my aunt learned to play quite nicely, it was Melonia's idea that I offer my uncle a concert one evening. She was upstairs maid by then. It was from her that I learned of my uncle's absolute authority. "You gotta set yo'self to stay on his good side, Missie. Look nice, talk nice, act nice. He got power over you like over me." My shoe had come undone and she knelt to tie it, looking up at me with earnest round brown eyes. "Remember this, he ain't never 'dopted you." So I sang for my supper that night, which seemed to please him greatly. By the time I was at

Miss Boorman's my childhood fear of my guardian seemed foolish. Not only had I learned to charm him, but his absolute authority gave me a pleasant sense of security. I was proud of his new factory building with two marble pillars, completed a year after the fire which had devastated the old one. His anxiety about money which I first noted a year later troubled me profoundly.

On New Year's Day of 1837 my aunt and uncle did not entertain, but merely followed an old custom and hung a pretty red-ribboned basket on the front door below the brass knocker so that those who came could leave calling cards. "Panic" was a word one began to hear rather often as the year of 1837 toiled through a rainy spring, a muggy and humid summer. At that year's charity ball my aunt wore the same dress as to the last, though the amber silk had lost none of its style and elegance. This year, Uncle Isaiah said, the usual August holiday at Cape May or Asbury Park was out of the question. "Are we poor now, Aunt Liza?" I asked.

"Poorer than we were," she said, "but still luckier than most." I knew she had finished her book months before, and that once again her insomnia had its grip on her on many nights. That day her blue eyes each wore a bluish shadow beneath as she explained to me the cause of the panic. "It was caused by President Andrew Jackson's mean revenge on the United States Bank. Its president pumped bank funds into the campaign of Henry Clay. Clay lost. Jackson succeeded in withdrawing government funds from that bank, causing its collapse. The result of this was that each state bank began printing money at will. The more there was the less it was worth, you see." I did not but had no interest in further explanation.

My aunt's insomnia was not the only change I became aware of as the months passed. Although she continued with most of her charitable obligations, she did so without enthusiasm, giving only listless attention to my glowing reports of Miss Boorman's Academy.

The sudden death of her father was what jolted her from this apathy. From one day to the next she packed to leave for Philadelphia, to attend his funeral and comfort her mother. Uncle Isaiah decided that his urgent business matters prevented him from accompanying her, and that I should not leave school. During the three weeks she was gone I missed her dreadfully. The very house seemed to miss her, for Bridget and Mary became slack. Drinking endless cups of tea at the kitchen table or disappearing when they pleased on personal errands while grates grew choked with ashes, dust filmed surfaces or rugs went unswept. Melonia kept the upstairs as neatly as ever, but refused to do the work of the other two servants. My uncle seemed too abstracted to notice anything, spending most evenings at his club.

When my aunt returned, he inquired eagerly about any patrimony she might have received, was bitterly disappointed that no cash at all would be forthcoming. Her father had left the Allerton ironworks to her mother; managed by a former apprentice, it would provide an ample income for the widow. A one-third share in the family home would be Elizabeth's at such time that the property was sold; her mother intended to live there with the spinster cousin who had kept house for old Peter Aller in his last years. "He certainly might have done better by his only child," Uncle Isaiah remarked.

"A daughter married to a well-off husband? Why would he feel the need to provide for me?"

As I brushed her hair that night she confided what her mother had told her: her poor father had died of a broken heart after several lesser attacks, the first following immediately after the day the Liberty Bell was rung in 1835 and cracked—for the second time. It was to the Aller ironworks that the task of mending the bell had been entrusted, the bronze castings done there being of such good quality. My Grandfather Aller told Congress that the bell should be re-cast. If merely patched, it would crack again. But they wanted the same bell mended. So he complied. It was rung. And it cracked. "He went against his better knowledge, did not stand up for what he believed. So he died blaming himself for the crack in our Liberty Bell," my aunt told me.

But her mood brightened. It was wonderful, she said, to see how the little town where she grew up was expanding, almost a suburb of Philadelphia now. And she had seen again the remarkable Fanny Wright. After a lecture in Philadelphia they had supper one night at her hotel. "We discussed, among many other matters, the recent independence of Greece after so long a struggle for freedom. Eleven long years after Byron died there! She gave me a magazine containing an article that fascinated me. It told of the Grecian women who had been slaves under Turkish rule, sometimes in harems. The huge and often hideous black eunuchs in charge of the harems were slaves too, yet sometimes ruled their decadent masters. Oh, it was fascinating, fascinating! And now those Greek slave women have suddenly found themselves free. How does a woman who has known such tyranny cope with freedom?"

I saw that my aunt was herself again, full of life, cheeks glowing. I hugged her. "Oh, it's so good to have you

125

home again, Aunt Liza!"

She returned the hug, then held me at arm's length to ask, "Would you be very unhappy if I were to go away again soon, and for a longer time?"

"Yes! Why, you only just got back!" A thought comforted me. "And besides, I doubt that Uncle Isaiah could afford it."

"I'm going to tell you a secret. I have a bank account. Under the name Elissa Allaire. Most of the money I earned from *The Ironmaster's Bride* and *Kathleen of Killarney*. So I can afford this trip I want to take. And oh, Jane Anne, I do have such a yearning to travel! To see a part of the world I've only dreamed about!"

"What part of the world?" With a sinking heart, I thought I knew.

"Greece! The isles of Greece! Where burning Sappho loved and sung!"

If she had said the Antipodes I could not have been more dismayed. "Does Uncle Isaiah know?"

"No! And you're not to say one word."

I nodded, reassured. Although some of the wives of the city's wealthier men had visited England and even made the Grand Tour that included Paris and Rome, I was sure that Uncle Isaiah would put his foot down on Greece, and hard.

As if my thoughts had summoned him, I heard his heavy footfalls on the stairs. Gray-faced, shoulders slumped, he plodded into the room, looked vaguely toward the dressing table where I stood poised hairbrush above my aunt's cascade of shining hair, and spoke the words thousands of other men were to speak or had spoken. "I am facing ruin. Total and absolute ruin. I cannot meet the payment on my loan."

"Ruin?" My aunt spoke the word as if it were Greek.

"R-U-I-N! Ruin! Disaster! Damn that glib O'Casey! He convinced me to put up a larger building than I had intended. I should have trusted my own good judgment. With a smaller mortgage I wouldn't be facing foreclosure."

"But the old building was insured, wasn't it? Why did you need so large a loan?" My aunt rose to go toward him.

The question seemed to anger him. He sank into a chair, bent to undo one shoe, removed it and tossed it petulantly aside. "Don't you know the total cost of the damage done in New York by that fire? Over 22 million dollars! Nearly every insurance company went bankrupt. Mine was among the first. Not a penny from it! I had to take out a loan to rebuild. The country then was in a state of false prosperity. President Jackson had closed the National Bank down, distributed the money among his pet state banks. But then a rash of state banks sprang up. They began issuing their own banknotes. The inflation that resulted caused prices to soar. Business fell off. Stocks went down in value as they were unloaded. As men began to default on loans, banks took over mortgages. That's what's going to happen to me. I'll lose my factory; I may lose my property uptown that I used as collateral. But why am I talking like this to two females?"

"I thought your tobacco shops were doing well," my aunt said.

"I'm weary, weary," he groaned, and got up and walked to the bed, lay down. "Business is off thirty percent." He rolled his head on the pillow, eyes looking wildly about the room. "Before I know it, this house will have to be sold. We'll end up like those hand-to-mouth couples crowded together in some boardinghouse."

"And your railroad shares?"

"Worth less than I paid and going down daily. Oh, God!" He covered his face with both hands. I had the terrified feeling that he was going to cry like a child, but he merely lay there with his hands over his face as if blocking out all around him he could help himself forget the ruin he foresaw.

"I can offer you three thousand, seven hundred dollars," my aunt said. "Will that help?"

His hands dropped from his face. He sat up slowly, staring up at her. "You received an inheritance after all! You deceived me!"

"I did not."

"Then where did you get such a sum?"

"From my writings. It's been accumulating in the Merchant's Bank. Royalties."

"Writings? What writings? What do you mean?"

"Two novels and some trivial short pieces."

"You earned that much *writing?* Why didn't you ever tell me you were indulging in this hobby?"

"Because you would have discouraged and scorned me."

"I wouldn't say that."

"I would. And before you tell me that what is mine is yours by law, I offer you that money here and now if it will help to tide you over."

"It will!" Smiling, he got off the bed, seized her hand, kissed it like a gallant in days gone by. "It will stave off disaster for a while, and that's all I ask." He grinned. "Oh, I'm going to pull through this panic! Because men will smoke, once addicted. They may not buy clothes, they may not pay the butcher, or the rent, but they'll manage ten cents for one of my cigars and this you can bank on!" He patted her cheek. "Someday I'll find the time to read one of those lucrative products of your pen."

"And someday when you're on your feet again, I'll ask you to return to me the money it earned. I have a particular use for it."

"And what is that?"

"Oh, it doesn't matter now." She spoke lightly, but the animation that had lighted her face as she spoke of Greece was gone. For my part, I was relieved on two scores: I would not have to live in a boardinghouse, and my aunt would not go sailing off to that distant land.

The very next day she succumbed to an attack of quinsy so severe that she could not speak above a faint whisper for a month. For two weeks she did not swallow a bite of solid food, but survived on broths. She lost many pounds, but the end result was beneficial. The slim waist of a girl of eighteen was to prove a boon as far as the fashions of the Forties went, for they were full-skirted with very tight bodices, but unlike most women my aunt required no corset.

The Forties were to bring other changes far more significant. . . .

My aunt had struggled with her novel about the Greek slave girl, but at last gave up. Without realistic locales, she said, it lacked all verisimilitude. After my uncle's financial affairs had greatly improved, she asked for at least a part of the nearly four thousand dollars she had turned over to him, but there seemed always a good reason why to do so at that particular time would impose a great strain.

The time came, however, when my uncle could afford to entertain again. As the depression of 1837-40 receded, the social life of New York returned to normal, or even more so. As if echoing the growth of his city and his nation, Uncle Isaiah's pomposity swelled a bit along with his abdomen and jowls. His railroad shares soared in value as hundreds of miles of tracks began to crisscross the eastern part of the continent. At the Union Club he hob-nobbed with the great men of New York on somewhat better footing. I. Moss, tobacconist, had survived in good style a panic that had swept many men under, their names all but forgotten.

Tom O'Casey was also making something of a name for himself. His uncle's construction company bought out and swallowed up a rival, and was bidding on more and more important jobs. He had succeeded in gaining social acceptance, so that my aunt was surprised by running into him at functions where once she would have least expected to see him, she said. Among other dowagers he had charmed was Mrs. Penrose, at first by generous donations to her charities, then by his expression of views she shared. When she took tea with us one afternoon she told us how many young women of good family were absolutely smitten by him. "Not much good it will do them," she added, stirring sugar into her tea. "The poor man has apparently no wish or desire to marry. He's not a bachelor, you know. I mistrust bachelors in general, cold selfish fellows in my opinion. No, Mr. O'Casey is a widower. Yes, widowed very young. Lost wife and child within a year. The impression I have is that he loved his wife so dearly that he will never wed again."

"Indeed?" my aunt said.

"He has altered my preconceptions concerning the Irish. Of course, he's not entirely Irish, which I am sure has something to do with it. Tammany, yes, this I freely admit. He commands an entire precinct, I believe. But it was a revelation to learn what Tammany hopes to do for the working man. He proposes that there should be compensation for those injured on the job, which I must say is a novel and most humanitarian idea. Oh, I really cannot say too much about Mr. O'Casey, Elizabeth."

"So I see," my aunt said.

After Mrs. Penrose had a third cake and left, my aunt remarked, "Apparently the only woman in New York Mr. O'Casey cannot charm is me."

"Or me," I said. "His boldness is a trifle *déclassé*." I used the word proudly, a new and most stylish word at Miss Boorman's.

She took the wind out of my sails. "Are you planning to turn into a snob? Pray do not. It would sadden me much. Mr. O'Casey is many things, perhaps, but he is not and never could be rightly called *déclassé*."

The onset of womanhood was not too alarming in spite of Hope Pierpont's dark whispers about pints of blood. My aunt had already explained that it was a perfectly natural occurrence, and when I asked what the use of it was she said it meant that when I was married I would be ready to have a baby.

"How soon can I wear my hair up?"

"When you're a little older."

"How much older?"

"Let's say when you're sixteen."

The spring of 1840 was memorable for another reason. Uncle Isaiah came home one evening looking pleased. The tide, he said, had turned, at least for Moss Cigars. He hastened to add that he contemplated no rash expenditures. "We will have to remain content with the simple

131

pleasures for some time yet."

After an almost unbearably hot August and September, the simple pleasures winter offered were welcome. One was to go ice skating on the pond formed by a stream that fed Croton Reservoir, completed at last, its high buttressed walls most impressive. One cold, brilliant Sunday afternoon my aunt and I were dropped off there by my uncle. (He could again afford to pay a coachman.) There was a small business matter he was going to see to, but would return in an hour or so. I had to puff to keep up with my aunt, a splendid skater and very striking in her full skirt and jacket of scarlet wool, her hands warm in an ermine muff, relic of more affluent days. Side by side, we skimmed around the pond amid skaters of all ages. From the corner of my eye I saw how my aunt drew and held the glances of two handsome gentlemen in mufflers and red noses who stood like a number of others at the pond's rim to watch. I imagined one saying to the other, "Who can they be, that exquisite lady in red and the fair maiden in blue beside her?"

With a swish of blades on ice, someone joined us, skating along beside my aunt. "Good afternoon. May I take a turn of the pond with you?" It was Mr. O'Casey, rosy-cheeked and bright-eyed in a red stocking cap and long muffler. At the same moment that I recognized him I heard Hope Pierpont calling me. She stood at the edge of the pond just ahead, waving. I missed my aunt's reply as I skated off toward my friend.

Her dark eyes sparkled like her mother's as she confided that she had come with her brother in hope of running into a friend of his. "And if he's here and asks to skate with me, I'm going to." Within minutes a tall boy whose voice had not quite changed emerged from the throng to continue at her side. From that moment on my friend ignored me utterly. A lump of hurt lodged in my throat as I left them to skate to the pond's center where some people were practicing figure-eights. Mine were nothing to boast of so I left them showing off theirs and made for a narrow inlet, devoid of skaters and edged by bare dark trees.

The stark seclusion exactly fitted my mood. I practiced my figure skating but imagined myself singing to an audience of hundreds at Mrs. Penrose's next benefit concert at the Academy of Music. Then I would no longer be a person with no one to skate with. And Hope Pierpont would be glad to be known as my closest friend!

Later, I could not remember the ice cracking under my skates. In one instant I was envisioning a vocal triumph and the next minute found myself up to my chest in icy water, floundering and terrified. The shock was so sudden that I lost my voice and could only gasp a weak cry for help. My full, wet wool skirt seemed to be trying to pull me deeper as I clutched the edge of thin ice which broke off.

"Don't panic!" a shrill, familiar voice commanded. "I am here!" A frenzied glance showed Uncle Isaiah on the near bank. "Do not flounder about. The water is not very deep." As he spoke the tip of my skate touched bottom and some of my terror vanished. My guardian and rescuer was now making his way a few feet onto the thick ice near shore; he cautiously lowered his bulk to kneel while he untied the long white muffler from around his neck. "I can come no closer. I will toss you one end of this. Grasp it and cling tight with both hands. I will draw you out of the water onto thicker ice. Do you understand? Don't wiggle about. Just let me slide you along."

My teeth chattering now, I nodded. It took three tries before I caught the end of the muffler. Grim-faced, he carefully pulled me toward him, hand over hand. A strong heave pulled me right up against him. He made a choked sound. Suddenly both his arms were around me and he was hugging me to him, kissing my cheek, my forehead, my mouth. I forgot that I was soaking wet, freezing cold, for his passion dazed me and filled me with uneasiness.

Abruptly, he released me. Two boys were skating toward us, from the mouth of the inlet beyond which skaters whirled oblivious around the main pond. "Is she all right?" a young voice demanded.

"I must get my niece home at once," he told them. "Can you aid me to my feet?"

"But what about Aunt Liza?" I asked.

"I'll send the coachman back for her."

As I shivered under a lap robe in the carriage he sat looking out the window, spoke to me without turning. "Kindly make no mention of my emotion to your aunt. She is a wayward lady and must not guess I am so soft-hearted. I would lose all control, and we can't have that, can we?" He had turned his head to look down at me, his smile both ghastly and roguish.

"No, Uncle Isaiah." I had heard the false tone adults use when lying to a child but did not understand the cause, since my aunt *was* a "wayward lady." In fact, she was now skating with Mr. O'Casey.

At home I was the center of a flurry of activity. Kettles of water were heated by Bridget and Mary to fill the copper bath tub in the second-floor watercloset, while Melonia helped me out of my icy wet clothes in front of the roaring kitchen stove. Lying in hot water was blissful

134

and made me very drowsy. So did the hot toddy Melonia brought me as soon as she had tucked me into bed. I was barely aware of anything at all when Aunt Liza rushed in, white as snow, blue eyes huge blurs of anxiety. "I am the apple of Uncle Isaiah's eye," I told her—and myself.

That winter my voice improved greatly. From Mr. Gatti I learned quite a bit of Italian and all the pretty vocal trills then in mode. A petite figure with golden curls to my shoulders and dressed in the pastel shades my aunt said suited me, I was quite often asked by my uncle to stand by the piano, played by my aunt, and sing for apparently delighted guests. I always worried that he had me sing too long. All the etiquette books I had read warned against undue demonstration by any young lady of her musical ability.

Aunt Liza had grander ideas than mere parlor concerts. She envisioned my fascinating future as a diva or at least a famous concert singer. "You have a talent and you must continue to develop it. One day you might sing before the crowned heads of Europe. Think of it! A life of travel, of independence, of excitement!"

Of course, no such future as she imagined appealed to my uncle. This I learned when I was fifteen. A wealthy man of taste and sophistication heard me sing after supper, and delighted my aunt with his opinion. While my voice, he felt, was not large nor full enough for opera, it was certainly of concert quality. "I have certain connections," Mr. Ferris said, "and I will be delighted to arrange her first concert. At the Academy of Music, let us say."

As my aunt smiled, my uncle frowned. "You mean,

for pay?"

"She would receive a fee, surely."

"I am glad to say my ward does not have to demean herself by selling her talent to the public!"

My aunt stared, then leaned impulsively forward. "I would like to remind you . . ." She leaned back, choked down the words she had been about to utter, but I thought I knew what they were. Pay she had once received for her talent had seen him through a crisis. She smiled at the gentleman who liked my voice. "Then perhaps you can arrange a first concert without a fee."

"I do not wish Jane Anne to sing in public at all," my uncle said.

But he could scarcely refuse to let me sing at a charity benefit organized by Mrs. Penrose. And so one night shortly after my fifteenth birthday I found myself standing with shaky knees on the lighted stage at the Academy of Music at Fourteenth Street and Fifth Avenue beside a large piano played by Mr. Gatti. Moments before, my aunt had told me, "Do not think about the size of the audience. Think about the meaning of the song. You are singing to give pleasure, just as you do in the parlor at home." All those faces were most intimidating, and I think I would have been lost without those words. But after Mr. Gatti's reassuring nod, after the first notes rippled out, the meaning of the tender ballad he had decided I would open with took over my being. Other songs poured easily out, for the applause after the first had been most heartening—and surprising, too, because until then, despite my aunt's visions as to my future, I had believed my modest talent equal only to pleasing my family and uncritical friends.

I think my aunt was more excited than I at the favorable comments in several papers. The *Herald* was most kind. "Of those singers, pianists and violinists who generously gave of their talents at the Academy of Music, one stands out radiantly in this critic's mind. Miss Jane Anne Clark, a demure and childlike figure in pale blue, rendered with compelling charm and finesse several songs ranging from a simple ballad to a rousing Italian boat song which would have taxed the vocal ability of a far more mature singer, but to which she proved more than equal."

"You see, Isaiah?" she said that evening. "It would have been a crime to bury her light under a bushel."

He dashed the paper down. "She's too young! Far too young! I don't want her standing on a stage, leered at by men!"

The unexpected result of my first public appearance was a flurry of young gentlemen callers.

Most came armed with notes of introduction from irreproachable matrons. Unfortunately, the first three came on a Sunday afternoon when Uncle Isaiah was at home. He scorned them all as mere "quizzers" grown bold, and decided that my first public appearance would be my last.

VIII

When Tom O'Casey skated up to ask her if he might continue beside her, Elizabeth felt no great surprise; it was as if this precise moment had been inevitable. "I can't prevent it, can I?" She forced herself to avoid his gaze, to concentrate on the frozen plume of her breath, to contrast it with the warmth of her hands hidden in the plump pouch of her ermine muff.

He laughed, and her head turned sharply. "You said exactly what I expected you to say." In his red knit stocking cap and muffler he looked boyish. The chill had brought bright patches of color to his cheeks; his ears looked cold. "But I still dare to hope that after more than five years you have forgiven me."

She stared ahead. "Let me see. For your lie about going to Texas? Your mad boast that I would leave my husband for you? For calling me a liar at the Belmont Ball? Which?"

"All three."

She offered him a cold stare. "What I find hard to forgive is that you convinced my husband to overextend himself financially. He assumed a loan much larger than he intended."

"Who knew a panic was on the way? Or a depression? Or that most insurance companies would go bankrupt? I don't pretend I did."

"I don't know why I'm discussing this with you."

"I do. You want to blame me for your husband's sins."

"He happens to be a very upright man!"

"Two of the Seven Deadly Sins are Pride and Greed, aren't they? They more than I made him build a big brick factory with two Doric pillars in Vermont marble." He was smiling again.

"And you did nothing to persuade him?"

"All I could."

"And which sin lay behind your persuasion?"

"Covetousness?"

"I don't understand."

"'Thou shalt not covet another man's ox or horse or ass or wife.'" His head turned to meet her stare; he smiled. "Before you get angry, let me say that I treated Isaiah Moss no differently from any other man I deal with. A better building for him meant more profit for me, true, but it was also a benefit to the city. Out of the fire of '35 came better buildings than the ones that burned. And completion of the Croton Reservoir. And a municipal fire department. A police department is next. New York has woken up at last to its crucial lacks."

Two young boys, racing, cut sharply in front of her. She braked with her rear skate, then swerved. Tom's arm went around her waist to steady her, and then they skated forward; this was the one place where such an embrace could cause no comment. She felt her body stiffen. He asked, "Do you want to know why I said such outrageous things on the day you didn't give me any tea?" His arm stayed around her.

"I prefer to skate alone."

"I was in a strange state that day, full of anger at my

140

uncle and afraid my outburst of temper at him had wrecked years of work."

"Take your arm away, please."

He continued to ignore her, as if too engrossed in what he was saying to her. "I swear to you I had no intention of saying what I did. Things came out of me I hadn't known I felt. It was like being possessed by a demon." His warm, urgent voice was counterpoint to the cold slither of the blades of their skates moving in perfect unison, as if they had practiced skating together to be ready for this moment of confidences.

She felt breathless from the triple exertion of skating, speaking and containing sudden emotions. When she opened her mouth no words came out, only her frozen breath. Like the others circling the outer rim of the pond, she and Tom seemed to be on a carousel, only it had whirled them back in time. His head was turned toward her and the frozen vapor of his breath mingled with hers. "I'll forgive your demon if you assure me he will never appear again." She felt blood rush to her face, and her words seemed to hang on the air like her breath, a visible blunder. They presupposed other meetings in the future.

"No demon of mine will ever trouble you again." There was a smile in his voice.

Her eyes slid to his face. What did that mean? That his feelings had changed? She quickly stared ahead again. An almost languorous mood had come over her; she suddenly yearned for warmth, flames cheerily crackling.

"Would you like some hot chocolate?" he asked. "I know a small Viennese refectory that has the best in the city."

Had the man read her thoughts? Or the demon? "I'm here with my niece, as you know."

"My invitation includes her, of course."

With anxiety overcoming any other emotion, Elizabeth found that Jane Anne was not circling the pond. Hope Pierpont remembered seeing Jane Anne practicing figure-eights, and pointed to the inlet. They all skated there and at its far end saw the patch of dark water rimmed by snags of ice. As Elizabeth stared with a sinking heart two boys came over to tell them about a blond girl who had fallen in, rescued by a stout gentleman who had just minutes ago taken her home.

Later, Elizabeth could not remember what she and Tom said to one another during the tense drive to the house on 10th Street, where she found Jane Anne already in bed, hugging her doll. Her voice was drowsy. "I'm the apple of Uncle Isaiah's eye," she murmured as her eyelids closed.

Guilt for neglect of the child began to gnaw at Elizabeth, for it might have been a tragedy but for Isaiah. She hurried up to the third floor, found him swaddled in blankets in his easy chair, his feet in a basin of hot water. He sneezed as she entered, sipped his hot toddy. Expecting criticism she got none. His mood was glum, his manner distant; he had been reading his Bible.

Abruptly she recalled that Tom was waiting downstairs. On learning that Jane Anne was fine he nodded. "Then we can have our hot chocolate?"

"I think not."

"Why not?"

"I don't think it suitable."

"Not all married ladies are so strait-laced."

"Then take one of them for hot chocolate."

"But I prefer to take you."

"I'm afraid your preferences don't alter a thing."

"I find your primness ridiculous, Liza. It sits ill with your modern attitude toward women's rights. Why do you put yourself behind a purdah like this? There has to be a reason I don't know. And I wish to God you'd explain it."

Every word seemed to wound. "I owe you no explanation at all."

They parted coldly at the door. "I'll call to find how Jane Anne is," he said.

"Don't."

She was instantly sorry as soon as the door closed behind him. Why had she forbidden him to call? Every married woman she knew offered hospitality to bachelors. Dolly Pierpont said they offered in return a flattering remark or two that made her feel less stodgy. But Tom was not just any single gentleman. He was a man she had once loved, a man whom her husband detested. And Jane Anne knew both particulars. She was at the delicate age, no longer a child, but not yet a woman. She would not benefit from a foster mother who entertained a former lover.

Next day Jane Anne was quite well enough to attend class at Miss Boorman's. Isaiah was at work, the cook at the butcher's, and Mary the downstairs maid was visiting her sister. The house felt empty, although Melonia was up in her room working on the quilt she was crocheting. Elizabeth walked to the window of the parlor to look out at 10th Street, and saw at the foot of the bare tree near the front steps a small bird hopping feebly and dragging one wing, a robin that had not flown south. She ran out, picked it up, felt its heart pulse against her palm. The clatter of an approaching carriage frightened it. She held it closer, stroked its tiny head with one forefinger to soothe it.

"Liza!"

Tom's gig stood at the curb. He leaned out to say, "Take a look at the Personals in the *Herald* tomorrow." Then he drove away.

Nothing could have kept her from reading that newly inaugurated column of cryptic messages, usually signed with a first name or initials. Boldly, Tom's stared up at her: "I will love you until the day I die. T." She felt her heart leap and thud, and saw him as he had been when he first said those words to her, on the day they gathered blackberries, the day he kissed her breast. If no spinster had heard their laughter, might everything have come out differently? Her good sense reasserted itself: it was not the spinster who had parted them, but Betsy Baker, pregnant by Tom.

A week after the first message, a second appeared which proved him no marvel as a poet: "Our hollow oak may now be dead and gone, but he who hid there words of love lives on." A week later she was annoyed to read: "I am no reader compared to you but I have come across the words: 'The truth shall set you free.'" She made up her mind not to read the column again. Next week the message was: "Striving, I strive toward you. T."

She began to feel a menace in his singleminded pursuit, which seemed a kind of mania. She started to write him a note to tell him his messages in the *Herald* were absurd and must stop. Her own pen stopped as she saw the trap she was falling into. He must not know she had ever read them!

But as weeks became months she found herself looking forward to her weekly salutation from Tom. Some made her smile, some made her frown, but all made her feel desirable, someone quite other than Mrs. Isaiah Moss.

During that winter she took pleasure in the robin's slow return to health. The rumpled feathers grew sleek, the wing healed so well that one day when she let the bird out of its cage it flapped its wings and flew a few feet, from the floor to the bed. When the first days of spring had warmed the air she knew it was time to let it go, took it to the spot where she had found it and held it high on her cupped palms. It gave a little jump, spread its wings and took to the air. She watched it soar away, and felt both sorry and glad.

That evening at the Free Enquirers' meeting, held in the loft studio of a well-known sculptor, Tom O'Casey walked in. He smiled, took a seat, and listened with apparently eager attention to the news that Elizabeth Cady Stanton, mother of seven, was dedicating herself to getting a law passed in New York State that would allow married women to retain control over their own property. He chuckled with the rest as reference was made to the article in the *Tribune* by Margaret Fuller, the brilliant editor of the *Dial* and much admired by Horace Greeley who had let her announce in his paper that women should be permitted to do any kind of work they were fitted for: "Let them be sea captains if they can!"

"So then you are really with us, Mr. O'Casey?" a frail spinster asked him.

"Heart and soul."

To Elizabeth, he seemed woefully out of place among the twelve women and five men devoted to women's rights. She accepted his offer of a ride home to tell him so. "I consider it immoral of you to utilize that noble little group for base motives."

He turned to stare. "What motives do you mean? I

believe in women's rights. When you have a name like O'Casey that enables people to look down on you as an inferior, you don't have to read many issues of the *Free Enquirer* to know that women are even worse off."

She still doubted the purity of his motives. "I happened to read a number of your personals in the *Herald* and found some quite amusing."

He nodded. "I knew you would."

And then, abruptly, the messages stopped. A week passed, two, three. A number of women with names like Sadie or Emma begged husbands to come home. Gus wanted Dan to know that the money was now in the bank. Adelaide was begged to return to her loving father, that all would be forgiven. But "T." no longer had a word to say.

Two weeks later he appeared at the lyceum she frequently attended, although she had to admit that a lecture on Greek architecture might well have been of more interest to him than to her. Between the Free Enquirers and the lyceum they saw each other at least twice a month. He was always friendly, never presumptuous. She could not help but compare him to the other men in attendance; he stood out head and shoulders from the rest. It did not escape her that other women were quite as aware of this as she.

Not until she emerged on a rainy afternoon from Mrs. Penrose's loft and her weekly session with her child prostitutes to find Tom waiting at the curb in his gig did she realize that he had some way of knowing where she was on a given day. "You are far too omniscient. How did you know I'd be here today?"

Smiling, he refused to say.

"It's not pleasant to feel that I'm being spied on!"

"If that were true, it would indicate more than a passing interest on my part, offensive to your sense of propriety. So I shall continue to insist that I happened to pass just as you came out of the building without an umbrella."

"But that is too much to ask me to believe." She was irrationally pleased, knew she was smiling, but could not help it.

"Believe what you wish, my dear," he said.

It was not in the Personals column that she read the words that abruptly altered their relationship—but a headline on the third page: COLLAPSING WALL INJURES BUILDER.

A dilapidated tenement on Broad Street was being razed to allow for a new and modern structure when a brick wall collapsed, severely injuring Mr. Thomas O'Casey of the Dunbar Construction Co. On the premises in his professional capacity. Mr. O'Casey had just entered the half-demolished edifice when he was knocked down by a cascade of tumbling bricks and buried under them. Still unconscious, he was removed from the debris for medical attention. . . .

Removed for medical attention to where? The hospital? His home? Where did he live? She threw down the paper, struggled against mindless anxiety. One thing was sure; she could get to the Dunbar Construction Company in a hired coach; those coachmen knew the city well.

But when she reached the doors of a weathered and unprepossessing old warehouse in front of which lounged several rough-looking men, she regretted impulse. What could she say? To whom? She knew she was about to make a spectacle of herself, reveal her feelings like a foolish girl. Good sense returned in time. She tapped on the coach ceiling, told the driver to return to 10th Street, and entered her house as if it were a haven hoped for during a long and dangerous voyage.

Neither the *Herald*, the *Sun* or the *Tribune* had a word in the next three days about the condition of the injured builder. Nothing. But wasn't no news good news? If he were dead or maimed for life, that would surely get mention. All she could do was wait patiently to hear from him. She waited without patience, her nerves playing tricks on her. Was he deliberately trying to torture her with suspense?

Invited to the Pierponts for supper, she sent Jane Anne on alone with the maid and ate alone, for Isaiah was, of course, at the Union Club. After Mary had cleared the table, she stayed there, inert. Aware that she had chosen this gloomy seclusion, she faced the Stiegel pitcher on the sideboard, symbol of her marriage and her life. She felt tears coming to her eyes, wanted to put her head down on her arms and cry. The door knocker sounded. Mary and Bridget were down in the basement kitchen, so she went herself to the door and opened it.

Tom stood there. He removed his hat. His head was wrapped in a bandage. She took a step back. He crossed the threshold, opened his arms. She walked into his embrace. His arms closed around her. His lips came down onto hers. His mouth was warm, firm. Her eyes closed. For three heartbeats the kiss held. He released her. She stepped back. The shock of their contact made her voice tremble. "I read about your accident."

He bent his head, pointed to the top. "I had a lump big enough to bowl with. And a hard head, which was lucky."

She felt strange, as if some other woman had suddenly inhabited her skin. She gestured toward the parlor. "Won't you come in and sit down?"

He seized her hand, bent, and kissed the back, drew her toward him. Holding both her hands he said, "That is not the question and you know it. What are we going to do, Liza? What are we going to do about ourselves?"

"Do?"

He pulled her to him. "Oh, Liza, Liza! I've waited so long. We love, we need. For sheer dogged patience I deserve a trophy. You don't belong in this house, and I don't belong in my lonely room. What are we going to do?"

Behind him the knocker was rapped three times; a light, girlish laugh followed. Elizabeth went past him to open the door on Jane Anne and the Pierpont boy, who had escorted her home. "We have a visitor," she said lightly. "Do you remember Mr. O'Casey?"

IX

As my sixteenth birthday neared my aunt and I changed
roles before her mirror, for she had not forgotten her
long-ago promise that I might put up my hair at that age.
She achieved a soft chignon which allowed a few curly
tendrils to escape at each side of my face. I was delighted.

My uncle was not. "Why rush her out of innocent
childhood? She still plays with her dolls at times. And in
my opinion she looks very much prettier with her hair
down."

"I do not!" Economically, I denied both his state-
ments. "I'm too old for dolls and too old for curls down
my back. Please, do be reasonable, Uncle. No one my age
at Miss Boorman's wears her hair down anymore."

"You will wear it at home in the manner that pleases
me," he decided, and opened his paper with a great
rattling sound.

So I did, but only for a few months. Because his ban on
my ever again singing in public collapsed when Mrs.
Penrose (I believe in collusion with my aunt) brought to
tea one Sunday the wife of an enormously rich financier
who asked my uncle if I might sing for her guests at a
soiree she was planning to hold. Among the guests would
be a Rhinelander, a Schuyler and old John Jacob Astor, to
say nothing of Fanny Kemble, the English actress who

was currently the toast of New York. He could not resist. The result of my second public appearance was another influx of beaux, these from the very best, or at least wealthiest families.

I wore my hair defiantly up, began to enjoy their visits, poured tea with grace, and listened to various young men expatiate on the least important topics of the day. A young lady proved her good breeding by listening to a young man prove his respect by saying nothing worth hearing. "You're really having a great success," my aunt observed. "The young men of New York are the despair of mothers with daughters. Perhaps because of the recent depression, they seem bent on staying bachelors forever. One gentleman caller a week is regarded as popularity, and you've had four." She gave me her most roguish smile. "I guess I'm going to lose you to a husband sooner than I thought."

"Not to anyone who's called so far," I said.

My disinterest in my admirers was wild enthusiasm compared with my uncle's opinions of those he chanced to encounter. "His eyes are too close together, a sure sign of slyness. . . . He is light-waisted, a driveller. . . . Don't be fooled by his fine clothes. . . ."

And then Benjamin Mason called. He was the scion of a wealthy family whose most recent social gesture had been described in the *Herald* as "a sumptuous soiree where the *haute monde* cavorted until a late hour performing both the waltz and the new European Polka." But Benjamin was modest and intelligent and a student of medicine, soon to open his own practice. Slender, with warm brown eyes, he did not chat of nothings. My aunt was charmed; I was enchanted. "Nonsense," my uncle said, when I told him of Benjamin's virtues, not forgetting to mention his family's wealth in case my uncle did not know of it, although that was unlikely. "You're too young to have any judgment at all about young men." When my aunt pointed out that she had been little older than I when she married him, Uncle Isaiah said, "But you were far more mature. Jane Anne is still a child."

But a child was not what I felt like with the doctor-to-be. I kept his bouquets until the last flower withered. And one day after he had conversed of more than trivia, his eyes clearly telling me of his devotion, his controlled ardor, I asked him to stay to supper, convinced that my uncle could not fail to be favorably impressed.

I could hardly have chosen a less fortunate night. My uncle arrived home fuming because his Irish employees, taking heart from a recent "workies" parade were asking for a slight increase in wages. Having seen the factory, with its loud and furious chopping machine that sliced up the big leaves sending a fine dust of tobacco sifting down over everything including the long rows of cigar rollers working away like so many machines themselves, I felt the few extra pennies a day they asked was not unjust. I said so, knowing that Benjamin deplored what he called "exploitation of labor."

"You know nothing of business," my uncle said, rudely. He turned to Benjamin, who had nodded in agreement with me. "Nor do you, sir. These men who work for me are illiterate, dirty, and ungrateful that I provide them with the means to earn their daily bread."

"They also provide you with the means to earn yours, sir," said Benjamin.

"You sound like a Jeffersonian Democrat."

"I am, sir."

153

"I thought as much." Darkly, my uncle served himself with gravy and said no more.

Made nervous by my uncle's dour mood, and trying, I believed, to steer the conversation into other channels, Benjamin chose the field of medicine. He happened to refer to the amputation of a limb, which he called a leg, and at which he had assisted that morning. My uncle stared at him with apparent fascination.

After supper, I duly sang three songs. Benjamin watched me with adoring eyes. Then, rather abruptly, he stood up and asked my uncle if he might speak with him privately. My heart gave a leap and seemed to turn over. I knew, I was sure, that he was about to ask for my hand in marriage.

"Come upstairs to my study, young man," my uncle said.

While we waited my aunt came to sit beside me and held my icy hand. In a very short time the two men returned. Benjamin gave me a sad, bemused look, and very shortly left. As soon as he had gone, I confronted my uncle. "Why did he look at me like that? What did you say to him? Did he ask to marry me?"

"He did. I gave him short shrift. I said, 'The worst fate that can befall a young lady is to marry a man who is no gentleman. You, sir, are no gentleman. My answer, therefore, is no.'"

The wail of anguish that filled the room was mine. His smug face melted and dissolved in my tears.

"Talking of severed limbs at the supper table!" His growl produced from me another wail.

I felt my aunt's arms around me. "You made him nervous, and so he just mentioned the first thing that came to mind," she said.

"Showing bad judgment as well as bad taste. I suppose you noticed that he said *leg?* Not limb, but *leg?*" My uncle's voice oozed distaste.

I could not deny that, and, weeping anew, fled to my room.

Two days later a messenger delivered a note from Benjamin. He wrote that in view of my uncle's dislike of him he could only accept the dismissal of his hopes. He added that it was perhaps unfair of him to seek to tie me down before I had had the opportunity to meet a larger number of young men.

"I don't want to meet a number of young men!" I told my aunt, weeping. "I want to be engaged to Benjamin Mason!"

My aunt read the letter again, then looked up at me thoughtfully. "You could let Benjamin know your feelings. Do you love him enough to elope?"

I stared. Defy the guardian I had tried all my life to please? "Elope?"

"You have to ask yourself if you love Benjamin enough to defy your uncle."

I looked at the letter in her hand. In bowing so easily to my uncle's dismissal had Benjamin shown a certain lack of courage? "No, I don't believe I love him enough to elope," I said. This proved a true evaluation, as I learned three months later when I met a gentleman from Charleston, South Carolina: Jonas Lucas De Lange.

My uncle had brought Jonas home to supper after they finished their business talk at the cigar factory. In his soft South Carolina drawl our guest, despite his narrow delicate face and slender though tall body, conveyed to

155

me, at least, great strength of character. He was also extremely handsome, and I could not help but contrast his restrained way of chewing with that of my uncle. His business visit had been delayed, he said, by the necessity of stopping off in Philadelphia where his younger brother was attending the university and had fallen ill of a mysterious and debilitating ailment. "He's now on his feet again, and I continued here."

"Your wife did not accompany you?" Aunt Liza asked.

"I have no wife, Mrs. Moss."

A surge of elation made me feel faint. I saw my uncle's look of alarm. "I always thought you Southerners married younger than we in the North. A matter of climate."

"Our climate does not cause youthful marriage but dread diseases you up here are spared, such as malaria and yellowjack." His pale skin was lightly tanned from outdoor duties. I knew that since the death a dozen years ago of his father he had been running the De Lange plantation. I knew, too, that he had been very generous about several deferred payments on tobacco shipments during the recent depression. His hands fascinated me, long and tan and slender below spotless white cuffs. I ventured a question.

"Why does your brother study in Pennsylvania?"

He looked beyond my shoulder, his tone remote. "The college of sciences there is quite famous."

After he had left for his hotel my aunt assured me there was no reason why my question could have offended him. I then asked, "Did you have the impression that he was at all taken with me?"

"I certainly saw that you were taken with him."

"I'm so glad Uncle Isaiah likes him."

"It gives me hope he won't chill this one off," she said. We had never put into words what by then we were both uneasily aware of: whether my guardian knew it or not, he had slated me for spinsterhood. His love for both my aunt and me was tempered by pride in us. I saw this most clearly when she played and I sang for guests; he all but gloated as he watched their charmed faces. We were his precious jewels, safe in the cottonwool of his proprietary affection. He would not easily open his hand and let me go as I had seen my aunt do with a crippled bird she had found and nursed until its broken wing mended.

Yet I was twittering with eagerness to fly, and ripe with the awareness that however well I sang, love was a woman's best fate, marriage her true destiny. What lay beyond the altar was dim to me, for the secrets of the marriage bed were not discussed by persons of good breeding. That word referred to manners, to knowledge of etiquette, not to the begetting of children. At Miss Boorman's school, members of the opposite sex were regarded primarily as dancing partners and as social entities to be dealt with according to set maxims: "Do not giggle. Do not chatter. Do not draw attention to yourself in any manner when in public." The somewhat outmoded "language of the fan" was taught us, the fan's main use being to conceal real emotion yet titillate while doing so. My aunt's books enlightened me a little more than many novels I had read. These books, from current romances to the wonderful works of Jane Austen, tended to end at the altar. To be in love prior to an engagement was, however, quite acceptable though somewhat daintily dealt with, which caused me to regard the inward flutterings aroused by Jonas De Lange as occasioned by love at first sight, a phenomenon my reading had extolled.

He called the next afternoon. I had read that many Southerners are descendents of Cavaliers and rather hoped for a noble ancestor for Jonas. He smiled as he said, "Louis De Lange, who came to Charleston in 1697, was the boisterous son of a French baron, a Hugenot and, for a short time, a privateer. My mother is a Harth. English, that is. By now, Charleston is something of a melting pot. Many Scotch-Irish, Spanish, and German families, and a large number of Jews." I thought it charming that he had brought two bouquets, one for my aunt and one for me. But next day he brought one for me alone, pink roses in a frill of paper lace.

It was clear to my aunt that he was delaying his return to Charleston on my account, for he had earlier mentioned that his swift return there was mandatory. "And certainly that hotel offers no inducement as to comfort, used as he is to two homes, the town house in Charleston and the plantation house upriver."

Having made a trip to the library to learn all I could about Charleston, I displayed my knowledge by saying that the name of the plantation must indicate that it stood on the Berkeley River, named after the early English governor of the vast Virginia territory, then comprising South Carolina too. Jonas smiled. "It is indeed on that river. But spelled differently: B-A-R-C-L-A-Y. My ancestor Louis De Lange spelled it phonetically, you see, according to the pronunciation he heard. He learned his error, but, it is said, refused to change a letter."

I continued to display my knowledge by remarking that tobacco seemed an unusual crop for that area, Virginia being where it was mainly grown. "And North Carolina," he agreed. "The De Lange tobacco fields are indeed unusual. So is the fact that most of our crop is sold directly to Mr. Moss rather than being deposited in a Virginia warehouse. That is most unusual. But so are the De Langes, I must warn you."

"Warn me?" I asked.

He looked confused. "Did I say that?" Our eyes met. He was seated on the settee, I in a chair flanking it, and my aunt was not present. Jonas leaned far forward to take my hand gently in his. I sat staring down at our two hands, mine resting on his palm, which was warm and seemed faintly to throb. "In all my twenty-nine years, Miss Clark, I have never until now met the young lady I wished to marry."

Stunned by the suddenness of his declaration, I could do nothing but stare at him, my other hand going to my thudding heart.

And that was the moment Uncle Isaiah chose to arrive home. By the time he came into the parlor Jonas was again seated decorously on the settee. He rose to say, "Good evening, sir. I came to ask if I might take Miss Clark to a concert tonight."

"Alone?" My uncle could not have looked more astounded if Jonas had suggested a voyage to La Scala in Italy.

"Yes." Standing tall in his dark frockcoat his whole being denied that my uncle could consider him anything except a proper escort for me. Had Uncle Isaiah met his match?

"I believe my wife and I will also attend," he said.

"Not possible, I fear. I bought the last two tickets."

I was delighted. Going alone with Jonas smacked of high romance to me, and of incipient freedom from the restraints imposed on a young unmarried woman. Seated beside him at the Academy of Music where I had sung only six months earlier I felt years older than the child who had warbled those songs. Heady, heady evening while the violins soared, while my heart melted in ecstasy whenever I glanced at Jonas and found his eyes on me!

At my suggestion we walked the short distance home: I wanted to prolong by that much the first such evening of my life. I found myself telling him of the short shrift my gentlemen callers had got from Uncle Isaiah intending to warn him of what he might face in the way of objections to any engagement.

Jonas, too, was candid. "My younger brother Leo is something of a renegade and so a deep disappointment to my mother. All her maternal affection long ago transferred itself to me, it seems." He smiled. "As she sees it, there is not a single girl in all Charleston worthy of her remarkable elder son." The smile faded. "But, joking aside, her health has been poor since my father's death. The shock of learning she is to have a Northern daughter-in-law will be considerable. So for the present, my future hopes must remain a secret between the two of us."

I nodded, smiled, and concealed a deep disappointment. My own future hopes had been for an engagement everyone knew about, particularly the girls at Miss Boorman's to whom I would display a pretty ring. "And I imagine you could not tell my uncle your intentions until you've told your mother."

"How sensitive you are to another's feelings!" We had reached the door of the house on 10th Street, and I reached up toward the brass knocker, but he stayed my hand, turned me toward him. Our first kiss was more exciting than I had imagined any kiss could be. His mouth was soft, and like two delicate animals with a life

160

and feelings of their own, our lips coupled. When at last we parted, I dizzily held myself upright by the cloth of his coatsleeve, he whispered in a shaken voice, "Oh, Jane Anne, my dear! I would like to marry you tomorrow! But wisdom tells me our future happiness depends on my carefully preparing my mother for the inevitable. I want her to welcome you eagerly to Barclay Shore, to love you as the daughter she never had."

Again I managed a nod of false agreement. He released my hand and, smiling down at me, rapped the knocker against the door.

After he left for Charleston, I felt forlorn. It was hard not to tell my aunt of the secret understanding. I lived for the days when his letters arrived: long, long letters, telling of his day-to-day life, his remarkable ancestors. Each time I read one the lurking fear that he might forget me, or that I had been only a passing fancy, was dispelled. Some lines were to me like poetry: "The cicadas have tuned their tiny fiddles to fill the warm night with a shrill pulsing music that as a child soothed me to sleep. Then I imagined sometimes that the wonderful sound was emerging from the open pale lips of the magnolia blossoms on the tree outside my window." Such lines made me hope my letters to him would not seem trivial or disappointing. I chose to use a quill pen of my aunt's and as I wrote the ivory-white ostrich plume would occasionally stroke my cheek, exciting memories of the touch of his hand, his lips.

X

Those unwary moments of physical closeness which Jane
Anne's return had shattered did not alter the nature of
Elizabeth's relationship with Tom. He continued to turn
up where she was from time to time, and always smilingly
refused to reveal how he had known where she would be.
One day she found out.

Dolly Pierpont was expecting her fifth child and faced
months of relative isolation. No lady worthy of the name
would be seen in public after her interesting condition
became apparent. Aware of having neglected her friend,
Elizabeth stopped by one afternoon, was admitted by the
maid and went straight back to the sitting room.

Tom O'Casey rose from an armchair, stood smiling at
her.

She turned, befuddled, to Dolly, who stood up, rotund
and smiling. "I believe you know Mr. O'Casey? Do
excuse me a moment while I look for my white yarn."
She held up a baby's bootie, attached to a knitting needle,
moved sedately to the door and out.

"How long have you known the Pierponts?" Elizabeth
asked.

"Mrs. Pierpont and I met two years ago. She was
gracious enough to invite me to tea. I've called on her a
number of times."

The secret of his omniscence was now clear. "And you pumped her about me."

"Of course."

"One scarcely knows whom to trust these days." She sat down; the familiar room seemed suddenly as strange as a setting on a stage onto which she had wandered, unfamiliar with the play.

"Some of us trust our own feelings," he said.

"Reason is a more stable faculty, I think."

"Does reason tell you there would be anything wrong in joining me Saturday morning for a steamboat ride up the Hudson? Just to Tarrytown? To dine at a pleasant old inn and return well before dark?"

Dolly's voice said, "The meals they serve are so good, it's scandalous. Six full courses. Robert and I have been there several times." She flourished a hank of yarn as if that had really been the cause for absenting herself.

"The boat sails at nine," Tom said.

"It will sail without me."

"Are you sure you won't change your mind?" His casual tone made it a polite persuasion.

"As sure as I am of my own name," she smiled.

He left soon after and she turned to Dolly. "You never told me Mr. O'Casey was on your list of callers."

The knitting needles were clicking, the baby's bootie resting against the swell of Dolly's abdomen. "Oh, didn't I?"

"It seems to me a curious oversight." The swollen belly of her friend seemed a barrier between them, which had never been true before.

Placid, unashamed of duplicity, not even recognizing it as such, Dolly held up the bootie, gazed at it with a gentle smile. "I do think there's nothing that touches me

164

more than a little baby's foot."

The bootie suddenly enraged Elizabeth. "We weren't talking about babies' feet. We were talking about Tom O'Casey's visits here. Why did you let him pump you about my affairs?"

"Goodness, did I? We did mention you a great many times. It's quite clear that he thinks the world of you, Elizabeth. Did I offer you tea? I seem to have a mind like a sieve, these days." She gave a complacent sigh and put the bootie aside. "Or perhaps a glass of wine? We have some admirable Tokay just now."

"Thank you, no." Elizabeth stood up.

"You're not leaving so soon?"

"We seem to have nothing to say, Dolly. I asked a question and you offered me tea and Tokay instead of an answer." Looking down at her friend she felt in perfect control of her own emotions.

"Did I? Well, I *did* let Tom O'Casey pump me about you. I told him about the Free Enquirers, your passion for those boring lyceums. I knew I was making it possible for him to see you from time to time."

Elizabeth sank back into her chair, staring. "But why?"

Dolly shook her head. "My heart has often ached for you, my dear. Isaiah is a very tiresome man. A good provider, a churchgoer, most successful in business, but dull. Dull as ditchwater. Jane Anne is nearly grown and gone. You've made a life of it out of bits and pieces, this and that, never complaining. Why shouldn't you have an admirer? This isn't the Middle Ages!"

Such words from Dolly seemed like brutal blows. "So you connived with Tom O'Casey out of pity for me, is that it?"

165

"Facts are facts. You're almost thirty-five, even if you don't look it. Thirty-five, Elizabeth! Your life is half over. Out of the blue comes a former sweetheart, unmarried, charming, handsome. Doesn't that seem to you like a gift from the gods? And if you were quite discreet, what harm would be done?"

They stared at one another over an unspoken word: barren. "Then you consider that my flaw gives me license other women don't have?"

"Doesn't it?"

"You've become a very worldly woman, haven't you?"

"Lord, how can I help it, living in a city like this? Robert tells me all sorts of things at night in bed. Do you know there's a bordello a few steps from staid old Washington Square? Yes! A Frenchwoman runs it, very modishly dressed." She leaned forward. "Do you know that in the most respectable hotels women live who are mistresses of apparently respectable men? And you must know about those discreet houses of assignation where ladies in heavy veils slip in to meet their lovers." She heaved herself to her feet. "I'm ringing the maid to bring us tea. No! Tokay. I feel in that mood." She came to where Elizabeth sat, bent to kiss her cheek. "Oh, my dear, I guess I feel that you deserve a steamboat ride to Tarrytown. Tell me, what's the harm in that?"

Elizabeth sipped the wine. It was excellent. Thirty-five years old. Half a lifetime. Opposite, Dolly prattled of nothings, her old self again. From the hallway came the sound of children's voices.

On the gleaming new white triple-decker steamboat other New Yorkers strolled in holiday mood. At the Tarrytown

166

inn the old waiter in knee breeches and peruke took them for man and wife. The food was as scandalous as Dolly had promised. On the way back to New York they stood near the prow looking out at the Hudson ahead. Her hand was on the rail; Tom's hand covered hers. "You know, don't you, that you're going to have to choose me or send me on my way for good?" His voice was low.

"Choose you? Do you mean become your mistress?" Her own words startled her. She turned to face him, pulling her hand free. Lightly, she said, "I'm not the sort of woman who puts on a veil and slips into a house of assignation."

His eyes, narrowed against the low sun, looked hard and cunning. "I keep wondering, what sort of woman are you? Your life with a sterile husband seems to me a strange form of self-immolation."

If he had struck her she could not have been more jolted. "Why do you assume he's the sterile one?"

"You don't seem . . ." His voice trailed off.

Coldly she enjoyed his confusion. "Apparently you failed to charm Dolly Pierpont into telling you *all* my secrets." The steamboat whistle blew. The sound seemed derisive.

The earlier easiness between them limped like a cripple until the steamboat reached the wild wooded north end of Manhattan. Staring out over water dappled by sunset light, Tom said slowly, "If all you'll ever grant me is a platonic friendship, then I'm not the man for you, Liza."

They parted with polite farewells. She thanked him for a pleasant day; he thanked her for her company. She knew the bitter truth. In revealing her flaw she had become undesirable to Tom, a kind of freak, a woman who was not a woman at all.

A week went by before a messenger boy appeared at the door with a note; she recognized Tom's writing on the envelope and tore it open while the boy waited for a reply.

My dearest:

I write this in the hope that you return my love. Be brave, curse Plato, and meet me at Darby House tomorrow at five. It is two doors from the mouth of McDougal and our room will be in my name. Will you be there?

Tom

Every reservation crashed down like the wall that had buried him. "Wait," she told the messenger, and ran upstairs to the box room. At the table where she had written so many words she dipped her pen in the inkwell and wrote one word: "Yes." She folded the page, sealed it in an envelope, and wrote Tom's name across it. She ran downstairs, gave it to the messenger, closed the door. Within less than five minutes she had changed her life forever.

The next morning she went to A.T. Stewart's and bought a bonnet with a dark veil. . . . A mysterious, face-less woman looked out at her from the cheval glass; she might well be taken for a lady in mourning instead of one on her way to an assignation. Or would everyone who saw the veil guess the truth?

The clock hands pointed to a quarter after four. She could not wear the veil as she left the house; of what had she been thinking? She undid the two pins that held the veil in place and tucked it into her handbag; as she walked toward Broadway she felt light as air, free of all doubts at last.

In the coach she re-attached the veil, her hands a bit

shaky. She had told the coachman to let her off at the corner of McDougal, not in front of the Darby, but as she paid him his shrewd glance and a certain tone to his thanks seemed to mark her as a woman about to meet her lover. She walked into a small, dim lobby, tastefully furnished with mirrors, mahogany, brocade drapes. An old man who looked regal came forward to meet her. "Yes, Madame?" His bow was courtly.

"I am looking for Mr. O'Casey." How small her voice sounded!

"Yes, Madame. May I show you to your room?" A courtly gesture indicated a corridor to the rear of the lobby. She preceded him along it. Smoothly he unlocked a door, and with another gesture presented to her an impeccable bed-sitting room, dark red draperies at the window, a high carved mahogany headboard, a refectory table set with wine, glasses, a bowl of fruit. Bowing himself out, the old man softly closed the door.

The room was soundless; it might have existed in the middle of a wide desert. She walked nervously to the fruit, touched a ripe pear, a purple grape, then turned to the mirror and saw a mysterious veiled stranger. If he cared so deeply, why was he late? With the thought, the room turned sinister. How many assignations had it seen? How many couples had been locked in illicit embraces on that wide bed?

What was she doing here?

She opened the door, hurried down the corridor, across the dim lobby, and out. Her only fear was to encounter Tom arriving. She walked several blocks and then paused to throw back the dark veil. She knew she was right. She had too much self-respect for that room at Darby House.

Tom would have to understand.

But she had no chance to explain. The next lyceum lecture apparently did not merit his attendance. The Free Enquirers inquired where he was. Nor had Dolly Pierpont seen him since the day he proposed the trip up to Tarrytown.

Elizabeth had no alternative but a short note sent to him at Dunbar Construction Co. in which she confessed her distaste as she had waited alone in a house of assignation. "Please try to understand. I know it must have been a disappointment to you, and I am sorry for that."

His answer was terse. "You said yes, but meant no. You are as you are, and I am as I am. So be it."

Reading those words an actual pain shot through her, as sharp as a knife-thrust. Tom had left her forever! A gray mist seemed to close in around her. It would take some time to get used to not seeing him; it was as if he had gone to a distant place where she could never go.

At first Elizabeth was surprised that Isaiah had invited to supper so handsome a young gentleman as Jonas De Lange. Then she found her husband had assumed him to be married. She saw Jane Anne watch the stranger with parted lips as she had once watched Benjamin Mason.

His narrow, sensitive face suggested to Elizabeth a man who might forever remain a bachelor, to the regret of quite a few Southern belles; he spoke of his mother a number of times and mentioned a younger brother in an almost paternal way.

She was amazed to learn from Jane Anne that an understanding existed between them. After he returned to Barclay Shore numbers of letters were exchanged, and

Elizabeth was amused and touched when Jane Anne asked to use her pen with a white ostrich plume to write to Jonas. The letters she read aloud to her revealed a man capable of obduracy, and one whose emotions had been deeply stirred. With a curious, hollow feeling, Elizabeth knew that before long Jane Anne might be gone forever.

"Thirty-five. Your life is half over."

The only news of Tom was reported to her—and all the city—on the second page of the *Herald*. Cornelius Ferris was to erect a new home at Fifth Avenue and 28th Street.

The Ferris mansion will be neo-Grecian in style, and will display art works Mr. Ferris is planning to purchase in Europe next spring. Indoor bathrooms with both hot and cold running water are contemplated, and the cost of the residence will exceed fifty thousand dollars. The task of erecting what will surely be this city's newest "show-place" has been awarded the Dunbar Construction Company.

A month later she read in the same paper of the sad death of Mr. Barney Dunbar. After celebrating in his favorite tavern, he unwisely chose to walk the short distance home, was coshed, robbed and left to die in the gutter. His sole heir was his nephew, Mr. Thomas Dunbar O'Casey.

Later it seemed strange that the death of a man she had never seen should have led to a series of events which crucially affected her. Tom became an employer instead of an employee, and as owner of a profitable business his status soared. He could choose between the Knicker-bocker Club or the Union Club. His preference was made clear to Elizabeth one night at supper by a wrathful

171

Isaiah: Tom had become a member of the Union Club.

"Sponsorship by only two members in good standing is far too lax a method," he fumed. "I have always preferred the black-ball. That way, one secret, adverse vote can keep out an undesirable applicant." He gobbled the last bite of pudding, then pushed the dish petulantly aside. "Irish hod-carriers today, Jews tomorrow!" He scowled at Elizabeth. "I well recall the night he had the crust to ask you to dance at the Belmont's. Of course, it was a charity affair and a few of the *hoi polloi* got in if they coughed up the price and had the gall to attend."

Elizabeth did not delude herself that he was suffering from jealousy of a younger man engendered on that night and smoldering ever since. She knew his envy was of another sort: Tom's elevation in life had jarred Isaiah's belief that to have been born poor or Irish or both was part of God's wise plan. He believed in a universe in which the well-off male of Dutch or English ancestry was justly superior and divinely favored. He was a snob, no doubt, a bigot, no doubt. But such shortcomings must conceal some hidden sense of inadequacy. Watching him chew, she wondered what it might be.

A few nights later he triumphantly announced that he had put O'Casey in his place. "He joined several other gentlemen and myself at the City Hotel bar, invited by none other than Mr. Cornelius Ferris, something of a crackpot despite his money. A few jests were exchanged. I recalled one concerning Tammany, and told it." Isaiah grinned. "It's about an Irish hod-carrier who had worked his way up in Tammany so that he found himself attending a large banquet. The first course was consommé. Paddy spooned it up like the others. The entree was macaroni au gratin, which he forked in. Then a broiled

172

lobster was served to each guest. Paddy stared at it in horror, threw down his napkin and announced, "I have drank your dishwater and I have ate your worms, but I'm damned if I eat your bug!" Isaiah chuckled, eyes bright with malice. "But I'm *damned* if I eat your bug! He'd never before seen a broiled lobster, do you see?"

Elizabeth heard a clatter as her fork struck the plate.

"Poor Mr. O'Casey," Jane Anne said.

Isaiah looked uncomfortable; a forefinger loosened his collar below flushed jowls. "Well, of course, as a gentleman I turned to him and said, 'No offense meant, sir.' To which he had the ill-grace to reply, 'But much offense taken, sir.' And then he left."

Staring at her husband, Elizabeth compared him to the man he had insulted. "I didn't know you were so eager to make enemies."

"Since I never want O'Casey as a friend, what harm's done?"

She found herself standing at her place. Feelings she had crushed down for years made her voice tremble. "Your bigotry disgusts me! I am sickened by what you call a joke! Sickened, do you understand?" She left the table and ran up the stairs to her room, slamming the door. The long cheval glass showed her a woman of thirty-five with a bitter face.

But what good did it do to be angry about such cruel bigotry? None. Without thought of consequences or implications, she went to her desk got out a sheet of stationery, dipped her pen in the crystal inkwell. She hesitated only a moment about the salutation then wrote:

Dear Tom:
I have just learned of Mr. Moss's insult disguised as a

173

jest. I will not be able to condone my silence if I do not tell you that I am ashamed of what he did and offended by it. I offer my congratulations at your election to the Union Club and trust that no further bigotry will mar enjoyment of your membership.

Sincerely yours,
Elizabeth

XI

I loved Jonas De Lange. He loved me. There was no doubt
at all of that for many months. He wrote delightful letters
except, perhaps, when the topic was tobacco. And he was
candid with me and did not spurn my girlish curiosity.
His renegade brother Leo, he assured me, was studying
medicine in Pennsylvania not just because the school
was good but because he was against the enslavement of
Negroes and disliked living where it was practiced. This
might have been caused, he wrote, by the fact that at the
very young age of three Leo had chanced to see a slave
tied to a whipping post and lashed nearly to death. "Not, I
hasten to add, on the De Lange plantation. We have
always treated our slaves well, both the field hands and
house servants. My father cut dead in the street the man
who had that slave so severely mistreated." Of his
mother's frail health he had less to say. She had never
really recovered from the shock of his father's sudden
death, resulting from a fall from his horse. It was during
the year after that tragedy that ten-year-old Leo had
taken to running away and finally disappeared from the
Ashley Military Academy for many months. I could read
between the lines to see that poor Jonas at eighteen had to
step into his father's boots and run a large plantation,
comfort an ailing bereaved mother, and search for a run-

175

away brother.

But as the long months passed letters began to seem a poor substitute for Jonas himself. My letter to him expressing this brought two full pages concerning the fact that he had to be on hand to see the new tobacco field properly readied for planting and the new crop then safely past its infancy. My eyes plucked key words and phrases: "Logs burned to ash—ash plowed into soil—seeds planted—transplanted four feet apart—green tobacco worms—picked off by hand—pulled in half. Cutworms next gnaw the roots right through—must be troweled out. Then the plants are topped—and sand leaves removed—they must be 'suckered'—every leaf that grows after topping has to be plucked off—harvest—cut leaves dried on scaffolds in open air—hung in the tobacco barn—smoked over oak or hickory logs—finally graded, packed into hogsheads.

"So you see, my dear Jane Anne, that there is truly no rest on a tobacco plantation. There is also Mother's health to consider. Lately she has had alarming spells of faintness and lassitude for which there seems no medical remedy. . . ."

My aunt had guessed that there was an understanding between Jonas and me; it was a great relief to acknowledge it and to share some of my feelings concerning the delay in any formal engagement. That Jonas was sincere she did not doubt: it was the ailing mother that troubled her. But she was cheered by the fact that there was a Charleston town house where the De Langes lived during the worst of summer heat and during a social season of balls, banquets, concerts, and plays. "With two roofs, there's no need for you to be always under the same one with an aging Southern belle who faints."

This brought to mind the only flaw in my daydream of marriage to Jonas. "But, oh," I told my aunt, "I'll miss you so dreadfully when I go South to live!"

"Don't worry. I intend to visit you!" She spoke with such emphasis that I realized that my marriage would widen her horizon, and provide a legitimate escape from Uncle Isaiah.

His railroad shares had again soared in value; his cigars were being exported to tobacconists in several other states; he now had three shops in Manhattan, one in Hackensack; at his club he now hob-nobbed with wealthy men he had only bowed to before. He spoke in a propriatory way of his country's splendid destiny after Lieutenant J.C. Fremont rode west over the Oregon Trail and returned to report to his President and his nation that a vast rich wilderness reached to the Pacific. "And we will settle it!" Uncle Isaiah boasted. He was equally staunch after Marcus Whitman, a minister who had founded a settlement in Oregon rode on horseback across an entire continent to urge President Tyler that he must act at once to prevent the territory's annexation by the Hudson Bay Company. My uncle's fist thumped the supper table. "Tyler must not vacillate on this!"

"Henry Clay would not have vacillated," my aunt said. She had been disgusted when in 1840 the Whigs had discredited President Martin Van Buren as a sybarite wallowing in a White House bedizened with satin settees, French bronze lamps, gilt eagles, ice cream vases, and gold goblets "while the people starved!" The Whigs had then ignored the great Henry Clay to nominate a malleable nonentity from Ohio, endowing him with a log cabin like the popular Andrew Jackson. But old "Tippecanoe" Harrison had caught a cold at his inauguration and died after only thirty days in office; he was succeeded by the other half of a campaign slogan, John Tyler. A Southerner and old-fashioned states' rights Jeffersonian, President Tyler now opposed the Whigs' hot desires for a new National Bank and for government roads; and Tyler might well ignore Uncle Isaiah's desire for the Oregon Territory, as my aunt pointed out.

"Who knew Harrison would die?" my uncle demanded.

"The joke was on the Whigs," my aunt said. "You hoped for a puppet, but God cut the strings."

"God has little to do with politics."

Nor did most New Yorkers in the mid-Forties. We were more interested in P.T. Barnum's museum of paintings and freaks, taking sophisticated pleasure in seeing through its amusing humbug. And in the new envelopes in which letters were enclosed instead of being merely folded and sealed with a gob of hot wax. And in the minstrel shows, the polka, and phrenology, that amazing science whereby character traits were revealed by the bumps on the human skull. Spiritualism was gaining new devotees daily, and Adela Fisher was now something of a local celebrity.

Hope Pierpont, like her mother, had been to the Fisher sisters' boardinghouse suite any number of times. I had not, because my aunt said that soothsayers offered mere generalities that would apply to most lives, people being more alike than they prefer to believe. By the time I went with Hope to have my tea leaves read by Imogene, the younger sister, I had begun to believe that some mystery lay behind the continuing absence of my beloved Jonas. I hoped for the comforting news that I was sincerely loved by a tall dark gentleman.

Although Hope had told me Imogene was very pretty,

178

nothing had prepared me for so exquisite a young woman with such elegant taste in dress. Lilac silk with tiny white pearl buttons down the bodice contrasted beautifully with cornsilk hair and alabaster skin. In her velvet-curtained corner the scent of her perfume all but overcame the aroma of incense. But her reading of the tea leaves seemed rather mechanical. "I see a change in the near future. Someone is going to pass into or maybe out of your life."

"Which?" I could think only of Jonas.

She peered more closely at the dregs in the cup before her. "Out, I think."

"Can you tell if it's a man or a woman?"

She suddenly seemed to really see me, her large pale blue eyes peering into mine. "Got a sweetie, don't you?" Her small mouth was quirked in a smile. But then she was all business, frowning down into the cup so that the two little lines between her brows made her look older. "I cannot say for sure, but it appears to be a man, someone very close to you."

Humbug, I thought. Just nothing but humbug! I yearned to say he was not close to me but in South Carolina, and scarcely heard her further prophecies of an unexpected guest, a letter of importance, and a possible journey in the near future. Suddenly she yawned, quickly covered her mouth with a slender pale hand on which gleamed a pearl ring surrounded by tiny brilliants. I complimented her on it quite sincerely and perhaps a bit sadly: I would have loved to have had such a ring to flaunt.

She held her hand out to look at it. "It was a gift from the wealthy old lady I read to and things like that." She yawned again. "Do pardon me. She had a bad night and I

179

was reading until all hours." She peered dully into the teacup. "I guess that's all, Miss Clark."

As I opened my reticule she shook her head. "No, no, you must put the money into that brass bowl by the door. That's how my sister wants it." A strange look came into her eyes; they looked almost smoky, so dull did they become, but she was smiling at me very prettily revealing her beautiful white teeth.

Although I went home telling myself that Aunt Liza was right, that fortune telling was a mere foolish game, the remark that someone was going to pass out of my life seemed to have one possible implication. Jonas was in the process of passing out of it. He had proposed on impulse. He now regretted doing so. Unable to hurt me by confessing this, he hoped I would grow weary of waiting and be the one to break off our secret understanding.

The very next day Mary, our downstairs maid, gave notice. After a bitter row with Bridget, the cook, on whom she had been on bad terms for some time, she had been offered a job as parlor maid in a Fifth Avenue mansion and had accepted. "But I won't leave you in the lurch, ma'am," I heard her tell my aunt. "I had my young cousin Annie come here to have a talk with you and she's waiting down in the kitchen now."

It was ridiculous, but my mood lifted. Someone was indeed going out of my life, but it was not Jonas! On the contrary, a few days later he sent me a sapphire ring (my birthstone) and a letter that made my heart leap.

In a month more I shall be in New York. At that time I will ask your guardian's permission to marry you. If he proves as difficult as you fear then we shall elope. My mother is at last prepared to welcome you as warmly to

Barclay Shore as I have for so long wished.

But after my first elation passed, I began to find the thought of going to faraway Charleston a bit dismaying. I suddenly realized how much I would miss Aunt Liza, my uncle, Hope and Aggie Pierpont, all my friends at Miss Boorman's, and even Miss Boorman herself.

"Charleston is not the moon, dear," my aunt said.

"If Uncle Isaiah refuses to give his permission, then I'll have to elope. No lovely wedding party with a flower bower!"

"If you love Jonas, no such thing matters. If you do not love him, then you must tell him so at once."

"Oh, I do. And if I can't marry Jonas, I'll never marry anyone at all!"

She smiled although her eyes looked unamused. "At your age I said almost those very same words about someone else."

"About Tom O'Casey?"

She looked shocked for a moment, as if I had revealed knowledge I should not possess, but then nodded, brightly. "I imagine all young ladies say those words at least once."

"Except for the very plain ones," I pointed out sagely.

"If we leave at once there will be time to shop at both A.T. Stewart's and Wanamaker's before they close. We must make a start with your trousseau."

That very afternoon we found a charming fabric, pearl-gray French silk, satin-backed and so woven that the shining inner side made long diamond shapes on the outer. And we found a pair of flat-soled gray slippers to match. We took the silk straight over to a French dressmaker who said she could have it ready in two weeks. I was delighted at the first fitting, for she had made the skirt very full and piped the tight bodice with shell pink satin. She would also make up another dress to the same pattern, a blue batiste for everyday wear and perhaps more suitable for the climate of Charleston. Moreover, although I wore my sapphire on a chain around my neck, the ring hidden in my bodice from Uncle Isaiah's eyes, I had shown it to the Pierpont girls and they were most impressed. The only flaw in those serene days of early September was that I heard nothing more from Jonas.

On the day I brought the gray dress home my aunt was out so I put it on to show Melonia, "I do hope it's quite suitable for the South."

"It's suitable for you, Missie, and that's for sure. Makes your waist even smaller than it is. I recalls a Virginia gentleman sayin' about his lady, 'She's got a waist you can span with yore two hands and a behind that wouldn't fit in a washtub!'"

I told her that remark was very vulgar, but went to my mirror to admire my small waist and wonder if my behind were too small for Southern taste.

The following night I had an excuse to try on my new dress again, an invitation to a soiree where I would be asked to sing. I had to be certain that the bodice was not too tight to draw a deep breath in. As I slipped the dress over my head and felt the rich silk glide into place over the stiff bombazine of my petticoat, there was a knock at my door and then the new maid Annie peered around its edge to offer me the most wonderful words I had heard in ages. She was smiling, and her red hair and every freckle seemed to glow in the lamplight: "Mr. De Lange is waiting downstairs, Miss."

He was early! And by some miracle he had arrived at the very moment I put on my new, beautiful dress. I rushed over to the mirror to arrange my mussed hair. I remember that it seemed to take forever to button my gown's twenty small pink satin buttons before I could see, touch, and kiss my dear, dear love.

XII

Elizabeth found herself regretting the impulsive note to Tom O'Casey, particularly after five days had passed without any answer. The one that arrived via messenger one morning was brief.

Your kind letter, Elizabeth, meant more to me than I can say. May I call at five today?

The fellow waited while she penned an answer: "I shall be delighted to receive you at five." She was ready at four-thirty. She buffed her nails, and went to her dressing table to smooth on a little "pearl powder," and became sure the bedroom clock had stopped. At three minutes before the hour the new downstairs maid knocked. "A gentleman just called, ma'am, and I remembered to put him in the parlor like you said."

"Good." Annie sometimes left guests standing in the hall. At the parlor doorway Elizabeth stopped to compose herself. Her heart felt strangely light and a pulse in her throat was fluttering.

He stood at the mantel, hat in one hand, turned. He looked older, with shadows under the cheekbones. "That color becomes you." He sounded tense, but that was natural. Months of absence needed to be bridged.

"Thank you. I see that Annie forgot to take your hat."

"No matter. I'll be leaving very soon."

Some of the lightness left her, but she said, "Do sit down just the same."

"You may not want me to when you know why I've come."

"Because of the note I wrote you, I assume." Some of the lightness had left her spirits.

"I came to tell you about your husband's mistress."

"Isaiah?" As if the floor had opened at her feet she stepped back.

"Isaiah Moss. The pillar of society, the churchgoer, the upright fellow who plays so much whist at his club."

She shook her head. "Oh, no! Not Isaiah! You're mistaken."

"You don't believe me?"

"No!"

"Will you believe her?"

She took another step back from him. "Do you think I'd visit such a woman? Even if she existed?"

"I can have her here at once."

"Here? In my home?" She looked about at familiar walls. "Never."

"Then wherever you wish. She's outside waiting in my carriage."

"Do you imagine I'd believe her?"

"I think so, unless you prefer to cling to your false illusions forever, to tell yourself I'm a conniver, she a liar and your husband all he pretends to be."

A jumble of emotions jostled within her as she stared at him, then turned and went to the front door and out. At the curb, instead of the old red-wheeled gig stood a new black cabriolet, shining in the late afternoon light. Aloft, a young ruddy-faced coachman sprang down to open the door of the carriage for her. At the far end of the seat a woman looked out of the other window, her face hidden by the sweep of a lilac satin bonnet brim. Tom handed Elizabeth in. As the carriage began to move forward the woman turned her head. Elizabeth stared at the porcelain face and pale blue eyes of Imogene Fisher.

"Good day, Mrs. Moss," she said, rather shyly.

"What are *you* doing here?"

Imogene spoke rapidly, as if to get it over with. "I came to say you have a husband that's not a bit what you think he is. And that's God's truth, Mrs. Moss. Your bad old husband went and got him a girl and it was me." From her reticule she drew a lacy handkerchief and wiped away what might have been a tear from under one eye, watching Elizabeth as she did. "I never set out to have a man buy me pretties and all. I truly did love the first one. He said he'd marry me but he was already wed."

Imogene! Elizabeth looked out the window as the cabriolet passed a gray stone church in a strange city. Confession seemed to have Imogene in its grip. "In Boston, see, I was seduced when I was only fifteen by the scion of a rich old family I met in William Lee's ice cream parlor. That's why Adela and I came down here, our parents being dead and all."

"And your sister doesn't know about your present— situation?"

"You mean my room at City Hotel? Oh, no! She wants to think I get my pretty things from a wealthy invalid lady I stay with sometimes." She returned her handkerchief to her reticule. "But I've broken off with Mr. Moss. Your husband's not a nice man. Maybe with you he is, but not with me. When I told him to stay away, the mean old thing tried to take back this brooch he gave me." She tipped her head to look down at a large pearl and several diamonds in a gold setting which adorned her bosom. "It goes with my ring, see?" Elizabeth looked at the pearl ring. "But I'll tell you the truth, it was a bad day for me when I let him buy me that shawl. I'm a person with some feelings, not just a tart he could of found under a corner street lamp."

"You don't have to keep on with this kind of life, Imogene." Amid all Elizabeth's roiled emotions, the concern for young girls of the streets surged up.

Imogene shrugged. A bored look dulled her face. "Adela's always been mean to me, always and always. And I don't too much care for reading tea leaves, Mrs. Moss. It's taxing, thinking up all those things to say."

The carriage stopped and Elizabeth looked out at the boardinghouse where the Fisher sisters practiced their psychic arts. Imogene said, "I read tea leaves for Adela three times a week. And please don't tell her about what I told you, because it would kill her if she knew for sure." The smiling coachman opened the door on her side and she bent forward, gathering up her skirt to descend.

"Wait, Imogene," Elizabeth commanded. "Why did you tell me about my husband?"

Imogene cast back a wise look over one shoulder. "I don't mind pleasing a gentleman like Mr. O'Casey. And I always remembered how nice you was to me one day long ago. Don't let it upset you too very much. Men are very strange creatures, I've found."

She left behind a scent of stale roses. Elizabeth leaned back, her eyes closed. The other door opened, and Tom got in beside her. "I rode with the coachman. Are you all right?"

"I think I'm angry."

"Quite natural, I'd say."

"At you."

"Of course. The bearer of bad news never gets thanked."

"Don't think this will change anything between us."

"It already has."

"You did this for revenge, didn't you? Revenge on Isaiah for humiliating you."

"His attempt to humiliate me only angered me. I had been told by a fellow club member that he had replaced Imogene's former protector. It was not difficult to verify this."

"But your revenge was incomplete until I knew."

"The letter you wrote about that bad joke of his told me you had stayed undefiled by his bigotry, his arrogance. And it told me you still care for me."

"I did when I wrote the letter. Now I see you as a ruthless and vengeful man."

"For God's sake, Liza. You know revenge wasn't the whole reason I came here today, or even the most important one."

Her battered emotions could not tolerate his nearness, nor the sudden gentleness of his voice. "Just be aware of this. My husband's morals have nothing to do with mine."

"God knows that I'm aware of your high standards as to morals, my dear. I assure you that to cuckold Isaiah was not my aim when I decided to discredit him with you."

"I don't care for your language."

"I could not think of a clearer way to put it. I'm sorry to displease you."

"I wish to be taken home at once." Talking had held at bay harsh emotions crowding within her. Now, suddenly, she wanted to weep, to rage, to scream. She pressed her lips tightly together and clenched her hands into fists.

When they reached 10th Street the sun had set and dusk was thickening. The new maid had forgotten to draw the drapes at the parlor window when she lit the lamp. The coachman opened the door for Elizabeth. She hastily descended, ran up the steps to the front door, hammered with the knocker, then wondered what she would do if Isaiah had come home early. Annie opened the door. Elizabeth heard her ask if she would be wanting her tea now. She nodded, hurried up the stairs to her bedroom, shut the door, and stood looking dazedly at the four-poster bed. It loomed large. With closed eyes she remembered nights she had endured what women had to. Her mind used to rove through a pleasant woodland where she always came to a clear stream leading to a pool where a fat bullfrog sat on a lily pad blinking bulging eyes. He dived into the water as Isaiah heaved his body away from hers, a mere flat lily pad where a bullfrog had been. Had those perfunctory nighttime encounters represented to him a husbandly duty? She heard her own harsh laughter. Outrageous!

Someone tapped at her closed door. Annie said, "Tea's ready in the dining room, ma'am."

Not wanting tea, she still went downstairs, sat in her usual place while Annie filled her cup. "Thank you, Annie."

"You still have on your shawl and bonnet, ma'am."

"I'm rather cold."

"Should I light the parlor fire, then?"

"All right."

She sipped tea, her mind a riot. Directly ahead on the sideboard stood the flint glass pitcher with the blue rim. She stood up, walked toward it, lifted it high above her head in both hands and dashed it to the floor. It smashed in an explosion of bright scattered shards. She looked down at them, raised her skirt and stepped over them and left them behind.

She reached the front hall as the door knocker sounded. Annie came running out of the parlor, round freckled face alarmed. "What was that terrible noise, ma'am?"

"I broke the Stiegel pitcher. Sweep up the pieces. I'll answer the door."

Tom's coachman stood there. His grin faded as he saw her face. Touching his hat with its perky cockade he said, "Mr. O'Casey asks, would you care to join him for a bite to eat at Grenell's?"

For generations, Grenell's had been the finest of New York's public dining places. He ordered the famous terrapin soup and the canvasback duck. They ate to the musical tinkling of the ice in all the water glasses. Mrs. Trollope had commented on the American love affair with icewater. She had also said that while at table the food being consumed should not be discussed, whether good, bad, or indifferent. Defying her, Elizabeth praised the duck. As she did she saw Clara Mason staring at her from a nearby table and offered a gracious nod. It occurred to her that she was behaving with admirable poise. She could taste the duck only intermittently; one bite was delicious, the next void of flavor. The wine had the same peculiarity. She agreed to Baked Alaska for dessert and heard Tom order champagne. As they ate they spoke of trivia. The Masons were staring again. It might not be long before Isaiah learned that she had broken bread in public with Tom O'Casey.

He leaned toward her, voice low. "Do you have any idea how much I yearn to hold you in my arms? This very instant?"

"Sauce for the goose is sauce for the gander? Only I am not a goose." Even as she spoke so tartly she felt a slow unfolding of desire for him. "Your campaign seems rather heavy-handed. The revelation of my husband's affair is followed by this sumptuous meal which I presume is to be followed by your attempt to arrange an assignation, though I can't believe you would be so brash as to hope I'll succumb this very night. Or do you? Is it to be Darby House once more? Or have you selected a place you think I'll have less objection to?"

As she spoke Tom's face underwent a series of changes, from puzzlement through amazement to alertness. "I see I haven't made myself clear. I want to marry you."

"Marry me?" Shocked numb she stared at him.

"You sound surprised."

"But that would mean divorce!"

"Better than bigamy." He was smiling.

"Divorce." She whispered the word. It had a strange sound. Yet she knew she could not continue with a marriage to a hypocrite. Isaiah, the whited sepulcher. Her mind flinched away from him.

"See an attorney tomorrow." Tom leaned toward her, his face ardent, intent. "Isaiah won't fight you. He can't. He knows he's an adulterer. He knows Imogene Fisher is quite capable of acting as your witness. He'll let it go by default."

"But there's still the scandal to consider. And there will be one."

He shrugged. "My shoulders are broad."

"But Jane Anne's aren't. The child I raised and dearly love."

"She's not a child anymore."

"But why should she suffer for what I do? She loves a Southern gentleman. He will be in New York in another week. If Isaiah does not give his permission to the marriage, they will elope. She will be in Charleston, free and clear of what happens here."

A waiter cleared his throat. She looked up. The champagne was poured. Tom raised his glass to her; Elizabeth raised hers. The rims touched with a tiny musical clink amid the surrounding tinklings of ice in water glasses. "I will love you, Liza, until the day I die."

Her eyes filled with tears and she saw their glasses part through a mist. The champagne tasted not of sorrow but the hope of joy.

Outside, the night was brisk but beautiful. A rising moon hung low above the city. She did not hear his instruction to the coachman. She found she did not care where they went. The day's strong emotions, the fine meal, the love Tom had expressed in the words of long ago all made her amazingly carefree. There was even a certain excitement in the notion that she, Elizabeth Aller Moss, would soon be that anomaly, a divorced woman. She shivered slightly. Tom's arm slipped around her shoulders; she leaned back her head and looked up into his face.

But his eyes were directed at something outside the carriage. "Look," he commanded. He was smiling.

She saw a pillared portico, pale in the moonlight, like an ancient Greek relic transported to the new world. A lone night watchman by his small fire might have been some shepherd camping amid ancient glory. "The Ferris mansion," Tom said. "By spring it'll be finished, a feast for all eyes inside and out. It'll make my name in this city. I'll be able to do well by you, Liza."

He had turned his head to look down at her, leaned closer. Her lips reached up toward his. An intense thrill ran the length of her body as his arms circled her, held her closer. To her astonishment, she felt her eyes flood with tears. A hard sob wrenched itself free. Gently he pressed her head down against his shoulder. "Let all the tears out, dearest one. And then we can laugh together."

But there were not so very many tears and soon he was kissing her again. He did not suggest Darby House or any other place for a rendezvous. For this she was both glad and sorry.

He saw her to the front steps of the house on 10th Street. He bowed, then wished her sweet dreams. She went up the steps feeling altogether another woman from the frenzied creature who had smashed the pitcher three hours earlier. She knew it was not the champagne that made her so light-headed but the day's sudden reversal of her whole existence after the revelation of her husband's character.

Her key was in her reticule, and she unlocked the front door and walked into the hall, but stopped. The tableau that confronted her was like a curtain scene from a play. At the foot of the staircase a young man she had never set eyes on stood holding Jane Anne in his arms like a drowned child. Her head was back, her face white, eyes shut. He turned with her toward Elizabeth. His face was stern and pale, his hair jet black. Against the dark gray of his coat sleeve she saw a wide black funeral band.

"She fainted on the stairs but I caught her." His voice was deep, his eyes dark blue. "My name is Leo De Lange. I came to tell Miss Clark that my brother Jonas is dead."

Part Three

XIII

By the end of his second year of medical school it had become plain to Leo De Lange that in the two hundred years since Harvey's discovery of the circulation of the blood, medicine had not advanced at all. He so wrote his brother Jonas. "The lancet and the leech kill more people than gunpowder!"

"To hell with the lancet and the leech," he announced to a group of his classmates who had met in his boarding-house room to study together below the grisly smile of a shellac-tan skeleton on a stand. "To lance a vein and remove blood from a patient will merely weaken him, not help the ailment. Leeches are just a slower way of procuring the same bad result. Look at George Washington! He came home on a winter day with a fever and sore throat. Both got worse. On the day he died, four different bleedings were done by three different doctors. The last said he got very little blood, and it was thick and dark. By then poor George had no blood left! So he died at sixty-eight. Unlanced, he could have lived."

"So you say, but who can prove it now?" one man demanded.

"What we know is that he died with no blood in him. It stands to reason that blood circulates for other purposes than its own activity. The first President of this republic

199

was robbed of his blood and his life by three doctors, and that's shameful."

"You're too much of a rebel, Quassia," another said, and everyone smiled or laughed outright. The nickname had been pinned to Leo because of his defense of Quassia cups, often peddled by quacks. Tooled of a wood with a bitter taste, a Quassia cup was to be filled eight or ten times a day with water that was let stand half an hour, and drunk. The wood gave the water a medicinal taste, of no use at all. But the water itself was beneficial, Leo insisted, especially in the case of a kidney complaint. "If George Washington had been treated with Quassia cups instead of the lance and leech he might have lived another dozen years!"

Leo also denied that tomatoes were poison and ate three "love apples" a day for several months to prove it. He slept with his window open, denied that night air was a malign force. "Ill-ventilated, stuffy rooms *are*," he insisted.

It was at the start of his third year at medical school that Leo learned something about himself which for a time knocked all his former arrogance to the ground, left him shaken and insecure.

Anatomy class. The cadaver he was to dissect was of a woman, a derelict creature fished from the Delaware River. Scalpel in hand, Leo made the first abdominal incision, cutting through the skin of the abdomen. His gorge rose at the faint stench of formaldehyde and rot that was exhuded. He continued, jaws clenched, through the next red layer of muscle. Sweat ran into his eyes and he stopped to wipe his forehead with his forearm, saw in a quick flash the feet toed out at the ends of skinny legs growing misty. He shook his head to clear it, saw the sharp nose with black nostrils pointing at the ceiling, the deeply sunken eyelids. Someone made a joke. He fainted.

He came to as he was being helped up from the floor; he endured a few comments about lily livers and Nancy-boys and went home from class feverish. He awoke in the morning with a sore throat and burning forehead and blamed his weakness of yesterday on illness. It was several days before the fever abated, and then he found himself again standing at the dissection table, looking down at a male cadaver, this time. The same inner shaki-ness gripped him, but he gritted his teeth and accepted the scalpel to slice through muscle to the viscera, gray-blue, coiled like a knot of fat snakes. He had to stop, his hand shaking now with a fine tremor. The doctor teach-ing them touched his arm and took the scalpel from his hand, which continued to tremble.

That night, for the first time in his life, he got drunk in the tavern the medical students frequented and had to be carried home by several classmates. In the morning he was too ill to leave his bed; he had a fever again, and an ague. The widow who ran the boardinghouse came her-self to bring him broth; she said if he were no better soon she would call in a doctor. He knew no doctor could cure what really ailed him. Not the effects of too much alcohol, not the grippe, as she suspected, not malaria. No: to study medicine had fascinated him, but to practice it was beyond him. Sights worse than a dead man or woman lay ahead, and deeds would be demanded of him more terrible than cutting into dead flesh. What would he do faced with a living person whose leg had to be amputated? Could he do what was required of him, hearing screams and howls of agony?

A deep melancholy pervaded him. All his years of

study wasted! As soon as he was well enough to sit at his writing desk he composed a letter to his brother admitting his despair. "I seem to have a deep streak of cowardice. I am afraid of cadavers. Without completing Anatomy, I am done for here."

But the anatomy instructor, who had studied medicine in Edinburgh, proved kinder to Leo than Leo to himself. The teacher said he had seen such a reaction several times before. "By the time you open your practice you may be able to avail yourself of Dr. Crawford Long's great discovery."

"What is that?"

"The use of ether in surgical procedures. Crawford Long was a student of mine. He graduated in '39 and after a year at a large New York hospital he returned to Jefferson, Georgia, to open a practice. Recently he wrote me a very enthusiastic letter. He had removed a large tumor from a patient's neck after having had the man inhale ether, and the patient had felt no pain at all. Dr. Long got the idea from one of those ether frolics while he was a student: everyone giggling after inhaling this gas. He happened to burn his hand severely on a lighted cigar but felt nothing. More experiments are needed to learn to gauge and control the stuff, but I think he has stumbled on something of major importance. So have courage, De Lange! Don't let your recent experience in the dissecting room overwhelm you."

Leo had obtained Dr. Long's address in Georgia and had begun a correspondence with him about ether by the time Jonas's letter concerning love arrived a few weeks after their brief reunion in Philadelphia.

I confide in you the fact that in New York I had the

good fortune to meet Miss Jane Anne Clark, the foster child of Moss and his wife. Jane Anne's exquisite singing voice would alone have captured my heart, but in addition she is both pretty and intelligent. To my great good fortune, she took to me as strongly as I to her, and we have a private understanding. I am now trying to accustom Mama to the idea that I wish to marry this young lady. Hard going, because Mama laughs as if at some boyish joke, or else pretends to believe that I have fallen into the clutches of a Northern siren who collects hearts on a string. It also seems that Moss is unwilling for Jane Anne to marry me, or, indeed, anyone. But come Hades or high water, Leo, I am going to make her my wife before the year is out!

But it was neither hell nor flood that kept Jonas from his heart's desire, Leo discovered nearly five months later. The letter from his mother was brief: Jonas had caught yellow fever. "I now fear for his life. Oh, come home, Leo, to your poor mother!"

She had not exaggerated. Leo returned to Barclay Shore to find his brother yellow, wasted, delirious. But as Leo sat by the bed achingly aware of how little he had appreciated the kindness and decency of Jonas, there came a brief, lucid moment when the half-closed eyes found his. The parched lips opened. A hollow whisper said, "Go to New York, to Jane Anne Clark. Meet her. Marry her. You will never know a finer young woman."

Leo swallowed the lump that closed his throat. "You're the one who will marry her, Jonas."

"No." The eyelids closed. . . .

At the funeral in the Charleston cemetery where five generations of De Langes formed a small town of tombstones, the Negro who had been Jonas's personal slave since their boyhood hurled himself sobbing into the open grave. Leo, holding his weeping mother upright, envied the slave Jerome, able to let out his grief. Leo's was bottled up inside, painful and unexpressed.

The following day Leo's own boyhood slave, Henry, came to him in the same bedroom where he had learned from Leo how to read, write and figure sums. For the past two years he had been invaluable as overseer, Leo knew. "Did your brother tell you why he went up there to New York?" Henry asked.

Flat on his back on his boyhood bed Leo shook his head. He felt spent, listless and every memory of his brother's kindness ached. "A business matter I think he said."

"He and I figured out one day that old Moss was gettin' too much of a bargain on our bright leaf. With U.S. tariffs what they is, unless he ups what he pays us, we're better off usin' a Virginia warehouse and lettin' them sell it in Europe."

"And did Moss agree to pay more?"

"No, sir. Told your brother he'd have to think on it, and then comes a letter sayin' there's nothin' finer than a long-time business connection and he couldn't pay a cent more."

Leo sat up. "I have another reason to go to New York. I'll see Moss. How much more do we need?"

"At least one-fifth more per hogshead."

"That much?"

"Yes, sir."

"Don't call me 'sir' because it makes me feel I ought to stay and run this plantation. But I intend to be an absentee landlord."

When Emily Harth De Lange learned that he was

leaving she stared in horror. "What kind of a son are you?"

"Not the son Jonas was."

"I'll never forgive you. Running off before your brother's cold in his grave!"

"I'm doing what Jonas asked just before he died."

"To leave your mother here alone?"

"To see Miss Jane Anne Clark."

The words of her dead son were sacred, irrefutable. Yet with bitter eyes she said, "I knew from the day I bore you that you would never be a comfort to me. You're not like your father, not like your brother, not like my Daddy. You're a renegade. That's all you are, a renegade turning your back on everything you ought to cherish!"

Her angry eyes were faintly bloodshot and she smelled sweetly of wine, first prescribed when his father had died. It was the wine, he believed, that had caused her to send Henry out to the fields to pick tobacco and himself to Ashley Military Academy when he protested this waste of a house servant who could read and write. He remembered his escape from Ashley and smiled. "Yes, I'm a renegade, Mother." Still a pretty woman at forty-eight, she had never remarried. Instead she had turned Jonas into her make-believe husband. Poor Jonas!

"I'll say good-bye tonight, Mother, so as not to wake you in the early morning when I leave."

In spite of the hard front he had put on, a certain remorse dogged him during the journey to New York. He kept telling himself that he was carrying out his brother's last wish. At least Miss Jane Anne Clark would learn of her loss from his lips rather than the cold page of a letter.

A freckled maid admitted him to the Moss home and went upstairs to find the girl. He waited in the hall. The wait was brief. He heard above the light patter of footsteps, then saw a lovely little figure in pale gray descend the stairs more than halfway, then pause. Her blue eyes went from his face to the black band on his sleeve. As he told her his name he had started toward her, and when she crumpled and fell forward he was close enough to catch her, lift her in his arms. He stood there a moment looking down at her brown lashes against a white cheek, at a golden-brown tendril of hair that was somehow touching because of its artfulness. At the same time he was very aware of holding in his arms the girlish body his brother had loved and longed for. A great gush of sorrow choked him; the terrible fact that Jonas was gone forever from this earth was more agonizing now than at the funeral.

He felt a gust of air as the front door opened. A woman came toward him, her eyes wide, her lips parted. Her full skirt seemed to fill the hall. When he told her who he was and why he had come she went so white he thought she might faint too. "Oh, my poor child!" She went to a door to the left, opened it. "Carry her to the settee in the parlor, Leo." When he had obliged, Mrs. Moss knelt and took the girl's limp hand in hers. With the other she stroked the pale forehead. She stood abruptly. "I must get the smelling salts, I think. I'll only be a moment."

He stood looking down at Jane Anne's face, a ghostly triangle in the dim room, the face his brother had dreamed of. He could not take his eyes from her. She moaned faintly. He knelt beside the settee, took her cold limp hand.

A high, thin voice spoke from the doorway. "In God's

name, what is going on here? Who are you? What are you doing to her?"

He stood up to face a paunchy man with icy eyes and a chest like a pouter pigeon's. "I am Leo De Lange. My brother Jonas is dead. The news was too much for his fiancee. She fainted."

"Fiancee? No, no! You're mistaken! They were not engaged—no, no."

Mrs. Moss had returned with the smelling salts. She swept into the room and confronted her husband, her blue eyes blazing. "They were! With my blessing! And would have married with or without your approval. Do you lack all decent feeling? This bereaved brother came all this way to tell us Jonas is dead, and all you can do is deny the engagement?" She whirled to Leo. "Please overlook his rudeness, if you can."

Mr. Moss looked ready to choke on his high collar. "I, rude?"

"And heartless!" She turned to kneel again by the settee, to wave the smelling salts under Jane Anne's nose.

The girl's head turned to one side then the other and her eyes opened. She held out her arms. Her aunt embraced her with soothing sounds.

"Of what did the poor fellow die?" Moss asked.

"Yellowjack." Leo went to Mrs. Moss to say, "I believe the syncope Miss Clark just suffered means she should be in bed. Would you like me to carry her upstairs?"

"You?" Moss cried. "If she is to be carried, I shall carry her."

Jane Anne's voice was faint but resolute. "I can walk."

When the two women had left the room arm in arm, Isaiah Moss asked, "And did your poor brother suffer greatly?"

"Yellow fever is not a pleasant disease to die of." Leo found his dislike of Moss so intense that he decided then and there to spend the night at a hotel. "I have a business matter to settle with you, but it can wait until morning."

"At my factory, then. You have the address."

"I do. Please tell your wife I'll stop in tomorrow before I leave for Philadelphia to see how the patient is faring."

"Good-bye," said Moss.

Leo had never before been in New York City and sauntered south on Broadway, marveling at the great number of vehicles of all sorts even at this late hour, from an ancient ox-cart to jaunty little one-horse gigs, sleek cabriolets with liveried coachmen aloft, even a few grand coaches that might have belonged to royalty. The omnibusses with their big rear wheels carried as many as fourteen passengers apiece.

A single room at Astor House cost two dollars. That all the rooms boasted gaslight did not seem to warrant such extravagance. He took an omnibus down to City Hotel, at 115 Broadway. It was an immense hostlery, five floors high with over seventy rooms, he learned. The cost of a room was little less than at Astor House but included meals: breakfast at eight, a six-course dinner at three, tea at six and supper at nine. In the large lobby there was a counter where guests registered. As Leo approached the clerk there was talking to a grizzled man in a nautical cap, a packet-ship captain, Leo quickly gathered, just returned from Europe.

It was after ten, too late for supper, but off the lobby was a bar with a cage-shaped buffet where a busy attendant dispensed drinks to gentlemen who then stood there to toss them down or went to a table to read their papers or talk politics. There was a vacant chair beside the sea captain, and Leo took it. He learned that City Hotel was the favorite New York hostlery of packet-ship captains, Toby Rudge being no exception. Back in 1794 it was a hotbed of revolutionary conspiracy, then it catered to the rich, the stylish, and the leaders of New York's literary and scientific circles, he said. Since 1836 it had enjoyed the patronage of the first private club with permanent rooms of its own, the exclusive Union Club. "But in that same year, a scandal struck the place. Murder. Yes, the gory, cruel murder of a pretty young doxy in one of the hotel rooms. Jewett was her surname. The first name I forget. In the past few years I've noted a few changes for the worse. The old place seems to be deteriorating a bit. But the food stays ample. And just recently they've started giving you room service at a small extra charge. Only hotel I know where you can get it." The captain winked. "At times this is handy, if you take my meaning." He got up and went to the bar for a refill and brought a hot toddy for Leo, too. That made him philosophize a bit. He advised marriage, though himself a bachelor still.

Warmed by the toddy and the friendly captain, Leo read awhile in bed. He had packed a book by an English writer named Dickens. Despite his sorrow he found himself chuckling over the adventures of Mr. Pickwick and his friends.

The Moss cigar factory, of dun-colored brick with white marble columns flanking the doorway was to Leo substantial proof that Moss could afford to pay what Henry had suggested. In an office on the first floor Moss sat at a roll-top desk reading a newspaper which he thrust aside with a great rattling as Leo came in. He rose with an amiable smile, the disaffinity of yesterday having vanished overnight. "Mrs. Moss is most put out with me and says I have been inhospitable to let you go to a hotel. Accept my sincere apology. Sit down. Have a cigar." Broadly beaming he offered a humidor choked with the famous ten-centers.

"I never smoke in the morning. Shall we get down to business?"

"By all means. First, let me remind you that Barclay Shore tobacco and Moss Cigars have enjoyed a mutually prosperous association for over seventeen years, through thick and thin, through panic and depression, and—"

"I'm not a sentimental man where money is concerned, so let me get to the point. Unless you are able and willing to meet the price I can get in Europe and elsewhere, that long association must end."

Affability faded away. "But your brother and I agreed to let things stand as they are for the present."

"But I do not." A sudden thumping from a machine on the floor above gave Leo the impression that the very building was furious. "You have been getting top-grade bright-leaf Burley for your outer wrappers at damned little more than you pay for low-grade filler. You know it, I know it, so there's no more to say except that the new price for bright-leaf is 20 percent above last year's."

As Leo stood up briskly Moss rose slowly, sour-faced. "This ultimatum I shall have to consider with care. My solution may well be a cheaper outer wrapper."

"Which may in the long run cost you in sales, but you know better the risk of lowering the quality of your cigar."

Apparently that hit a nerve, for Moss said, "Your brother was in all regards a gentleman. I see you and he have little in common."

The image of a girl in pale gray descending the stairs leaped into Leo's mind. "He's dead, sir, leaving me to contend with."

By day the Moss parlor was most pleasant, an elegant yet cheerful room where ruby velvet and pale golds kept out the cold north light from the front window. Only a minute after the maid left him there, Mrs. Moss flowed gracefully toward him. She held out a long slender hand, very white in contrast to her violet sleeve. "Sit down and have some coffee with me, do." As she spoke the freckled maid came in with a silver tray. As Mrs. Moss poured he sniffed freshly brewed coffee, cinnamon rolls. "Sugar? Cream?"

"Black, thank you."

A girl's voice spoke from the doorway—Jane Anne Clark, in blue today, her bonnet rimmed with corn-flowers. "You were quite right about taking a walk, Aunt Liza. It did make me feel better." She came toward them, nodding at Leo as he rose. "I'm so glad you came back. Thank you for catching me yesterday. I've never fainted before in my whole life. It took me unawares." She sank down on the settee.

"That's a very pretty bonnet," Leo heard himself say, and sat down beside her.

Her hands flew up to it. "Heavens, I am in a state. Sitting in my own parlor with my bonnet on!" She took it off, set it down in the space between them. Her upward glance was appealing. "You may think it odd that I'm in blue today, but I own no black clothing. I notice you're not in mourning either, though."

"A parade of grief in ebon garments? No."

"Aunt Liza says yellow is the mourning color in some country—I forget at the moment which, and white in another. This does seem to make more sense than black, if one considers the immorality of the human spirit."

"Immorality?"

"Immor*tal*ity, I meant to say."

Tears filled her eyes and he yearned for words that would comfort her.

"Blue becomes you," he said.

"Thank you. It's said to be a blonde's color, along with pink. But I don't care for pink. I think it's too artful."

"Artful?"

"Like candy roses."

He laughed. "I was prepared for all the noble sentiments death seems to inspire."

"If I feel them they are not for display." She took the cup of coffee her aunt held out and raised it to her lips. Her hand was not steady and she had to lower the cup to its saucer, wait a moment and then try again.

Mrs. Moss had risen. "I must leave you now, Mr. De Lange, but please stay for dinner with us. We dine at two-thirty. I fear we Northerners must seem most inhospitable to a Southerner like yourself."

"I am only Southern by birth, not inclination."

"Now that you must explain." She sank onto her chair again.

"I'm an abolitionist."

She beamed at him. "I, too. My husband, alas, is a Doughface."

From the corner of his eye he saw Jane Anne's small hand delicately fingering a cornflower on the bonnet between them. "A Doughface?" he repeated.

"You surprise me, Mr. De Lange, for the term was coined by John Randolph of Virginia and refers to a Northerner who approves of slavery."

"Of course. I know the term." He turned to Jane Anne. "Which are you? Doughface or Abolitionist?"

"I agree with my aunt. Slavery is wrong. But life is hard for freed Negroes. We have a great many here in New York. I feel particularly sorry for the poor little Negress corn girls. They sit on the curb with buckets of hot corncobs they sell. Sometimes I feel that they might be better off on a Southern plantation like Barclay Shore."

"Then you don't think I should emancipate my slaves as a matter of principle?"

"Where would they go? How would they live? I don't think freedom to starve is worth much."

"As I learned at ten when I ran away."

"From the military academy after your father died?"

"Jonas told you about it?"

"Just that you ran away."

"Ashley Hall was a terrible place. We younger boys had a teacher named Blaster. Yellow teeth, thick eyeglasses, and a heavy hand with his cane. There was a little fellow named Morgan who was terrified of him, so he was caned often. Blaster's method was to grab a boy by the hair, haul him out of his seat, and whack him hard across the rear. Many times. After little Morgan hanged himself—"

"Hanged himself!"

"With his stockings from his bedpost. After that, I

213

decided to ruin Blaster. One night I got a razor from an older cadet and shaved off my hair. With a black sock, glue and patience, I contrived a wig. It might not have fooled many but Blaster. As I said he was near-sighted. The other cadets knew something was up but not what. When Blaster asked where the Magna Charta was signed, I looked out the window like a student who doesn't know the answer and hopes to be overlooked. So of course Blaster called on me. I looked him in the eye and said, 'Morgan.' He repeated the question and I repeated the answer. He turned red, then white, and foamed at his mouth and descended on me. He seized my hair to yank me to my feet. And it came off in his hand. Moreover he went reeling off backward and fell down. I sat there with my bald head gleaming in the morning light, smiling. The other boys went mad with joy. Laughter rocked the walls. Someone gave an Indian whoop. Blaster fled to the headmaster's office. I found myself on the carpet, tried to convey to him that Blaster's guilt over driving little Morgan to suicide had made him hear that name instead of 'Runnymede.' But I learned I was to be expelled. Nothing happened to Blaster at all. So that night I tied my clothes to my head and swam the Ashley river and headed north.''

''Don't stop there! What did you do? How did you manage to live?''

''It was early summer so there was fruit. I begged at farms, stole from orchards and gardens, earned a few cents here and there. Ended on the docks of Baltimore hoping to stow away on a ship, but fainted from hunger. A kind man who owned a warehouse took me in, fed me, and gave me a job at four dollars a month to keep his books. He also bought me dinner at a nearby tavern and I slept in the warehouse, in a large packing case with wire mesh over the opening to keep out the rats. There my brother found me after several months. I told him I would not return to Barclay Shore, but at last we struck a bargain. I would return to the South if I could go to college in the North. I also wanted my slave Henry taken out of the tobacco fields where he had been most unfairly sent, being a house slave. Jonas agreed, and kept his word, too."

He saw her eyes mist up and added: "Later, much later, I learned that on the night in '31 when I swam the Ashley and started north, Union troops marched into Charleston to put down an uprising. The South Carolina Convention had already met to consider outright secession." He laughed. "While I was seceding from the South, my state was close to seceding from the Union."

"Could it really come to that?" she asked.

"Yes. I think Charleston is where it will begin. We were the first to secede from Great Britain, you know."

"I notice you said 'we.'"

"There you have my plight, Miss Clark. Born a Southerner, yet doomed to think like Garrison."

"Secession would mean the end of this great nation." Her look was earnest, and her small hands were clasped anxiously. He wanted to take one in his, kiss it, comfort her.

"How great must be seen," he said. "We've lived nearly seventy years on pride in our great past and its great men. We have to manage to forge a future in an industrial age which did not exist when our Constitution was written . . ."

"Mr. De Lange?" He turned to see Jane Anne's aunt in the hall doorway. When she had left them he had no idea,

215

so intense had been his focus on her niece. "Do you like roast lamb?"

He stood up. "I must confess to you that Mr. Moss and I had a disagreement at his factory this morning. I don't feel much like dining at his table."

"*My* table, if you please! The factory is his realm. This home is mine. I decide who shall be entertained here. If you refuse my invitation I will be very unhappy."

"Then I accept with thanks."

A small fire blazed cheerfully in the dining room grate. As Leo spread his napkin, he felt his boot strike something hard and slippery, bent down to retrieve a long shard of glass. He then did not know what to do with it, and placed it by his knife.

But Mrs. Moss had seen it. "That's the unswept remainder of a small domestic accident yesterday afternoon. I broke a pitcher."

Jane Anne's eyes went to the sideboard. "The Stiegel pitcher? Do you think it might be mended?"

"No, it can never be mended." Her aunt spoke calmly and served soup from the tureen into bowls which the freckled maid brought to each place.

He heard the front door open and close, Jane Anne suddenly leaned toward him. "That's my uncle. Don't say a word about medicine at the dinner table. He considers that indelicate." Suddenly her face was bright pink, but he had no notion why.

After Isaiah Moss had eaten ravenously and in almost total silence, he leaned back in his chair, thumbs in his vest pockets, fingers thrumming his paunch. A thin smile appeared. "Your brother mentioned that you're a student of medicine. A most interesting career. You must have many a tale to tell."

"But none that I can tell before two ladies at the dinner table."

"I am sure my husband appreciates your delicacy," Mrs. Moss said blandly. Leo glanced at Jane Anne, who stared down at her ice cream, a small dimple showing in one cheek, and he felt that she, her aunt, and he were in secret collusion.

After Moss had left, the three of them returned to the parlor where Mrs. Moss sat at the piano and rippled out a few bars. "Jane Anne, do sing for us, or Mr. De Lange will think we're a pair of bluestockings."

"I don't believe I'm in voice, Aunt Liza."

"Perhaps not, but do your best. Our little Southern medley, I think."

Obediently, Jane Anne took her place by the piano bench, hands clasped below her breast. In a voice that was silvery touching she sang two songs undoubtedly written by a Northern composer: a pickaninny was lulled to sleep underneath a silver Southern moon; a dead Quadroon was mourned by the man who had loved her. Then she turned and whispered to her aunt, the tempo changed, and suddenly he was hearing Italian words, trills and high notes—opera! At the end Leo stood up, applauding.

"Fanny Kemble praised Jane Anne's voice most highly," Mrs. Moss said with pride. "'New York's sweetest little songbird,' she called her."

"Aunt Liza! You're embarrassing me!" Jane Anne pleaded, her face pink.

"Forgive me, dear, but I'm very proud of you for singing so well in spite of your grief."

He decided that the musicale had been intended more for Jane Anne than for him. Wisely, her aunt had impelled her to pick up one thread of her life again.

In Philadelphia he wrote to Mrs. Moss, thanking her for her hospitality. The letter to Jane Anne sounded so stilted that he tore it up. It was a few days before he tried again, but that one seemed no better. Strange, because he had told her so many intimate things. Soon his normal existence was swallowing up hours and days, then weeks. In addition to his regular studies he was engrossed with private experiments with ether, using himself as guinea pig. The trick was to measure what amount of the gas could blot out the pain of pin jabs in his forearm without producing maniacal laughter.

The letter from Grandfather Harth was terse. "It is urgent that you return home at once. I despair for your mother and fear she may be near death. Your brother is gone. She has only you, now. Do not fail her, or me."

XIV

All the way on the packet ship to Charleston Leo kept telling himself that his mother was not really dying. He went first to his grandfather's house on the Charleston Battery. The old man gruffly confessed that he had exaggerated her condition. "But it was the only way I knew to get a son of your ilk to perform his duty. Your poor mother never recovered from your father's death, and the death of Jonas was too much for her. Her heart broke. Her mind went. She was once the prettiest girl in Charleston. I can't bear to look at her now." Bitterly, he drank the last of his port, his mouth turned down at the corners, gray hair unruly above ruddy cheeks.

"After my father died she took heavily to the wine bottle," Leo said. "Is that the case now?"

His grandfather did not seem to hear. "And aside from a duty to your poor mother, you have another, an inherited responsibility, Barclay Shore. By your brother's will it's yours and your mother's in equal share, damn it. Oh, Henry's a good manager, I don't deny that—but a Nigra, nonetheless. It's just not fitting, in no way fitting."

"Has my mother been drinking heavily since I left?"

"You're an unnatural son and an unnatural Charlestonian! I should never have underwritten this Northern education of yours. You belong on that plantation. What do you want to do, burn it down? Solve your problems that way?"

"Don't tempt me."

"If you leave now you can reach Barclay Shore not long after nightfall. I'll let you ride old Bruno."

On the river road as he neared the plantation the tall trees on either side closed above his head and he felt smothered. He was filled with a dim panic, as if the land itself were reaching up leafy arms to enfold him, pull him into itself. There was a full moon and when he saw Barclay Shore the house glimmered a sickly white; the piazza rail seemed stretched in a grin of triumph. Its prodigal had come back to it.

The smells claimed him too: smell of the slow river, of the old rice paddies, of the tobacco fields and smoke from the slave cabins, different from any other. And when the front door was opened he was aware of the mingled scents of old wood, old rugs, the vinegar-and-oil polish used on the furniture for generations.

"Welcome home, sir."

"Don't 'sir' me, Henry. How is my mother?"

"Bad off. Mostly in her bed this past week."

"Wine? Bourbon? Rum?"

"Doesn't matter none to her. Any does her, or all, though of late she seems to favor just plain corn whisky. This last time's the worst ever. Her brain's turned. Sees things not there. Hears things, too."

"Doesn't my grandfather know? And the relatives?"

"Mostly she struggles herself together to put on a kind of front when they call. But they know. Only they don't want her to know they know."

"Do you think she's awake still?"

"Most surely. Wakes nights, walks the house some-times."

"Then I guess I might as well go up to her."

Henry's big hand touched his shoulder, dropped. "Try not to feel too bad about what you're going to see."

Upstairs, Leo paused outside his mother's closed bed-room door, his hand cold on the doorknob, his throat dry. He knocked, waited, took a deep breath, walked in. "Mother?"

On the big four-poster a huddled form curled up with its back to him stirred, half-turned, one white arm flung out across the covers. On the table at the far side of the bed an oil lamp with a green shade was turned low. Leo came closer, smelled whisky and violets and another odor, sweet and deathly. Aware of his presence, his mother pushed herself into a sitting position against the huddle of pillows. Around her white, puffy face her dark hair was straggly and damp. Coming closer he could see a red network of veins on the cheek nearest the lamp. Her large brown eyes had shrunk into pouches of flesh; her eyebrows seemed sparse. She stared dully, then gave a sudden smile and opened her arms. "Jonas! My Jonas!"

"No, Mother. It's Leo."

"Leo?" The sound of the two vowels was plaintive. Her arms fell to her sides like things of wood. She gazed at him a moment, then nodded. "Yes, it's Leo," she announced. "Jonas is dead." Her right hand reached out, closed on a stemmed wine glass, half-full of what looked like whisky. She raised it to her lips, eyes closed, sipped like a lady at a dinner party, then tossed all of it down, head tipped back. She wiped her mouth with the back of the other hand. Her voice was clear, her articulation perfect. "A little wine for the stomach's sake, as it says in the Bible. Is it the Bible? Or is that from Sir Walter Scott?" She blinked at him. "What in the world are you doing back here?"

"Grandfather wrote me you were ill."

"Ah, Daddy. Yes, I did mention to him that I would like to see my only living son before I depart this miserable life. I do believe I did say that." Tears filled her eyes. "I am dying, Leo. Do you know that?"

"I know you're drinking yourself to death, yes."

"You always were a cold and heartless boy. Not one kind feeling under your skin except for Nigras."

"But you picked a miserable way to die, Mother. Your looks are gone, your mind is going, and that's only the start." As he spoke, anger mounted. He strode to the bed, flung back the covers while she stared in horror. Her distended abdomen could have belonged to a woman six months pregnant. "You're liver's just about gone. That means the kidneys are failing too. Soon you'll be jaundiced, yellower than any Chinaman."

"Indecent!" She was curled up small, arms crossed on her breast. "You're indecent, uncovering your mother like that! What's in your mind, you indecent boy?"

He flung the covers back over her. "There's only one chance for you, Mother. Total abstinence. Teetotal sobriety."

She laughed. "Go back north to your teetotalers."

"No, I'm staying. I give you a choice. You will drink every drop of whisky I give you. Or else you will not swallow anything with even one drop of alcohol in it. Which will it be?"

She smiled mockingly. "I do believe the first seems more temptin'. Every drop of whisky you bring me."

"All right. We start now. Where's the bottle?"

Watching him cautiously, she edged herself to the far

side of the bed, reached down, and with some effort pulled up a stoneware whisky jug. "Just pure old corn whisky. My Livvy goes and gets it for me from the still."

He took it, filled her wine glass. "Drink it all."

With a gleeful look, she sank back, raised the glass to her lips. He went to his old room, unpacked the few articles he had brought, returned. Outside he heard an owl hoot, and the sound of the crickets. "Time for another."

"Too soon."

"Hold out your glass, Mother. A bargain's a bargain."

"You'll just make me too sleepy to hear about any of your wonderful doings up North."

He filled the glass, held it out to her. "Drink. Drink and die, Mother. That's what you want. We'll speed up the process." As he spoke, a dreadful thought struck him: did he want his mother to die? All he had to go on was his own single experience with drunkenness, wine and then whisky. After that the very smell of either had brought on nausea. This seemed to him to support the story he had heard in medical school of a doctor who had cured drunkenness by giving massive amounts to drink until the patient vomited while reluctantly raising a last glass, and from then on abstained.

His mother's eyelids were drooping now. When he filled her glass yet again, she shook her head, lips clamped shut. But he stood patiently holding out the glass until she took it, angrily drank, fell back to her pillows with a moan, head turned away from him. Soon she began to snore.

He left her door open, went to bed down the hall leaving his wide too. He was awakened in the morning by the sound of his mother vomiting into her chamberpot.

After a time her feeble voice called for Livvy, but before the old servant could have heard her, he appeared instead, picked up the whisky jug, filled her glass. "You look even worse than you did last night, Mother." He held out the glass. She seized it in a shaky hand and he noted that her fingernails were grimy; two were broken off. She swallowed the liquor like a woman taking a bitter medicine, thrust the empty glass at him, then fell back onto her pillows. He refilled the glass.

"I don't want any more corn whisky at this hour!"

"We agreed you will drink what I pour for you. I poured; you drink. It's all or none."

She sipped very slowly, sighed. "You don't understand. No one understands. It all went away. Everything I cared about. Lucas, Jonas, my looks, my figure, any joy to life there ever was. It's not fair, not fair what happened to me, Leo."

"When your brain is pickled in alcohol that won't matter any more. You'll lie here like a vegetable with poor Livvy changing your wet sheets only you won't know about that or anything else."

"Stop! What an ugly thing to say to your own mother!"

He filled her nearly empty glass. "Drink up."

She took the glass, laughed, and suddenly threw the whisky in his face. He turned his head away and shut his eyes, one of which burned like fire. As he ran to the washstand to grope for the ewer and fill the basin her laughter was merry as a girl's. He sluiced the affected eye with cold water, again and again, then turned, toweling his face dry.

She was sitting up in bed, smiling. "Did that hurt?"

"Like hell!"

She tilted her head in a parody of her old flirtatious manner. "I think I am going to try your other method, Leo. No whisky at all. I really do think I will try that now. I was tired of drinking and drinking before you ever came back."

A sudden elation filled him. He tossed aside the towel. "Good for you!"

Eyes downcast, she plucked at a corner of the sheet. The sight of her lashes against her veined cheek reminded him of how she had once flirted with his father, with Jonas. Her voice was like a little girl's. "Do you think I'll ever be pretty again?"

"The most beautiful woman in Charleston!"

On the second day of her abstinence she went into a seizure; her body convulsed then straightened out. Her face was blue-gray. He knew enough to leap for the bureau, seize her tortoise-shell comb, and hold her tongue clamped down so that she could not swallow it and choke to death. When the convulsion passed she was unconscious; he held her in his arms, rocked her gently. She opened blurred eyes, spoke his name, then slept. When she woke he fed her milk with a spoon; she swallowed obediently, her eyes on his. He added corn syrup to the milk next time, fed it to her every hour for the next two days. Always in dread of another convulsion, he had a cot brought to her room and slept there lightly. On the morning of the third day he had Livvy bathe her and bring her a soft-boiled egg. That night he himself brought her a supper tray—soup and a little chicken and rice. He ate his own supper with her at a table by the window. "Perhaps just a little wine?" she asked. "I've always had wine with supper, Leo. Ever since I was fifteen."

"No wine. Nothing at all with alcohol in it. That's your enemy. That's your poison."

"But why? Why should it turn against me?"

"God knows. I don't. But it happens. To all sorts of people. You're one."

She was petulant for a while, but then they talked about other matters. On the next day she was up and about, in an apparently good mood. She had washed her hair. He went to talk with Henry, came back, and found her in the parlor, a glass of wine in her hand. He strode to her, snatched it, hurled it against the wall where it shattered, dribbling wine down. "Oh, such a mess you've made! That stain is never coming out of that wallpaper!"

"Good. Look at it often."

"Jonas was always such a loving little boy. You never loved me, Leo. Why is that?"

"Did you love me?" The words were unintended.

She regarded him thoughtfully. "You always seemed like someone else's child. A foundling. You exasperated me to no end, again and again." She smiled. "But, yes, of course I loved you. Mothers love their children, no matter what." The angry capillaries in her cheeks were less noticeable, or had she hidden them with rice powder? That would be a good sign, that she was beginning to care how she looked. Suddenly he had to know, and walked toward her, hand out to touch her cheek, find if it were powdered. Her hand reached up and caught his, surprising him. She looked up at him over their locked hands. Tears were brimming in her brown eyes. "This is very hard, Leo. All the memories are too sharp." A tear slid down her cheek, left a shining path where the rice powder

226

had been. "Don't leave me yet," she whispered. "Promise!"

"I promise."

In a month the change in her was heartening. She had softened her black dress with a frill of lace at the throat; above it her face looked fragile but lovely. One afternoon he took her out rowing on the river and though she used a parasol the sun still gave her a faint flush that seemed to him the glow of returning health. She confided her knowledge that something was wrong with her long before Jonas died. "I would wake in the dark and lie there hearing some night bird in the tree outside, knowing that some terrible disease had taken away all my willpower. So many, many times I drank too much. Long ago I began to hide a jug in my wardrobe. But I swear to you I didn't know it was the drink that was making me another person altogether. I thought the drinking was just a symptom of this mysterious illness of mine." She leaned forward to touch his hand as he thrust the oars forward. "You're a good son, Leo."

He pulled back on the oars and her hand dropped. "But not as good as Jonas, I guess."

She smiled shyly and anxiously at him from the shade of the ruffled parasol. "Just don't go running off to the North all at once." Her left hand went up and pressed against the white frill over her heart; her gold wedding band gleamed. "I just couldn't stand that. Not yet."

"Not yet," he promised.

Another month passed, and life at Barclay Shore had resumed its longtime pattern. Learning of Leo's return, relatives and friends began appearing, "Just droppin' by." Leo discovered that seeing these people who had known him from infancy was pleasant; their soft voices soothed him, and he was touched by their recollections of some minor childhood episodes he had forgotten. A number of them made it clear that they regarded his peculiar preference for a college in Philadelphia as just boyish foolishness, forgivable now that he had resumed his proper place in their world. Rufus Pinckeney, grand-nephew of a former governor and owner of a cotton plantation further up the Ashley was a frequent guest. He was startled when Emily refused wine. "I just seem to have lost all taste for it," she said with a conspiritorial glance at Leo. But without him, would she have refused?

Alone one night on the piazza after his mother had retired he sat looking out over the river, remembering the night long ago when he swam the Ashley, clothes tied to his shaven head. And it seemed to him that his student years which began with that flight from cruel injustice had now come to an end. Wasn't his grandfather right? With Jonas gone, didn't his moral duty exist here at Barclay Shore?

Suddenly restless, he got up and walked to the tobacco field, stood close to the nearest row of plants, nearly as tall as he. He reached out between the big, heavy leaves and touched one sticky-stalk. As he withdrew his hand and felt the viscous, pungent sap between thumb and forefinger, he remembered his father doing the same thing, recalled his satisfaction when the stuff was thick, strong-smelling. The first De Lange in Charleston, Louis the privateer, had tried to grow tobacco without much success. His son had failed too. Henri De Lange had gone to Virginia where it had by then been grown for a hundred and fifty years to learn all he could and produced the first bumper crop as a result. His son Jerome had carried on, then Lucas, then Jonas. Now it was Leo's turn. Any other destiny had been chopped off like a sand leaf by the death of Jonas.

The round moon's bland face seemed to be aware of his conclusion and to approve. Does a moon nod benevolently? he wondered. This one seemed to.

That night he dreamed he was riding again along the river road. At first he was terrified when the leafy branches overhead began to lower slowly, the ones ahead barring his way, but then two branches closed around him like arms, drawing him against the tree trunk and to his amazement it was not mere bark but warm human flesh, soft, a woman's. . . .

The next day found his mother in a pensive mood. "Can you believe it's nearly time for the Governor's New Year's ball in Charleston? This will be the first year I've ever missed it. The first since I was fifteen! Even after your daddy died Jonas and I put in a brief appearance. I remember when I was eighteen I went with a ragin' fever, lied to your daddy about how I felt. I was expecting Jonas, too. The fever gave me a fine color and I had a merry time of it, dancin' with all the young men."

He knew then what she wanted of him. Her face was no longer puffy, her eyes were clear. Not a thread of gray showed in her hair. "You want to go to the New Year's ball, don't you?"

"How would it look, with Jonas gone less than four months?"

"As if you were bearing your grief bravely."

"Will you escort me?" Her eyelashes lowered, then rose.

"I have no clothes."

She sat thoughtful for a long moment. "There's Jonas's."

229

"He was half a head taller."

"But your shoulders are just as broad. It's in the shoulders where the fit of a coat starts, Leo. As for the trousers, old Martha can shorten them." On 'shorten' her voice broke; she shook her head and went on brightly. "But you must dance with me. I just can't bear to join the old ladies by the wall just yet."

"I don't dance."

She stood up, held out her arms. "I'll teach you!"

He shook his head. "I'm not graceful."

"Of course you are! One thing you always had, Leo, is fine coordination. Your daddy often remarked on it. Come on, if you really want me to go to the ball! I'll show you the waltz step, so simple."

It seemed to him that he could see the two of them in the parlor, his mother humming and then counting, "One, two, three; one, two, three," as he moved stiffly, a hand at the back of her waist, his sweating palm feeling the boning of her corset, the other hand holding hers aloft as they whirled. "Da da da, *tum* da-da, *tum* da-da . . . that's fine, Leo. Why, you're a born dancer and never knew it!"

In her black lace, hair beautifully coiffed, she smelled of violets. Her eyes were bright, and she wore an amethyst pendant, encircled with pearl. In his brother's altered black suit and white cravat he entered the ballroom at her side, proud of her. Old friends offered welcoming words and smiles. The inevitable moment came: the first waltz. The floor filled with dancers. He feigned great interest in watching them whirl by. "Leo?" she commanded, sweetly.

It was quite different from the parlor lesson; the large orchestra playing an unknown Viennese melody, sweet and dizzying with the whirling of other dancers on the polished parquet floor. But in only a few minutes his feet seemed to remember how to move adeptly and his body responded to the sway of his mother's, and the pair moved so smoothly and swiftly it was like flying. He smiled down into his mother's upturned face and knew that memories of happy dances with his father were flooding her mind. Above glittered thousands of crystal tears in the chandeliers, and he felt the power of a magical past extending back in time for more than a century and a half. Or was it the champagne he had drunk that made these dancers tonight seem like the living counterparts of South Carolinians dead and gone, their vanished lives given significance by tradition observed at the Governor's Ball?

Rufus Pinckeney, now a widower, had been watching them. "Your mother is a most seductive lady," he observed as she was waltzed away by a beaming bachelor.

His mother was silent for a while as they rode back to Barclay Shore, Henry at the reins of the ancient carriage. He soon found this was not from weariness or any bittersweet nostalgia. "How glad I am you persuaded me to attend the ball! How very glad I am! I swear, those dear people just simply fed my soul! And the music, and the lovely gowns, all of it! My heart doesn't feel withered anymore." She looked up at him with the shining eyes of a young girl. "I'm so glad I have you, Leo, even if getting you born all but killed me!"

As he went to sleep that night he half-hoped he would dream again of those seductive trees—such a comforting dream, so clearly telling him that his roots were deep and inescapable. But instead he dreamed for the first time since his return of Jane Anne Clark; she was singing to him again but could not make a sound.

It surprised him, because of the dream, to get a letter from her, mailed on the last day of the old year.

My Dear Mr. De Lange:

I do not know why I am writing to you after the several months that have passed since any communication between us, but find myself recalling your concern about your mother's condition which has caused this lengthy interruption of your studies in Philadelphia. Has her health improved?

Life here continues much as always. My aunt has found a new cause which somewhat angers my uncle: they are on opposite sides, as usual. As you probably know, an anti-Catholic group calling themselves the "Native Americans" is trying to get a law passed barring all naturalized citizens from ever holding any public office, and extending their residency here before they can become citizens to 21 years. Brutal riots have been staged by these bigots. In Philadelphia they have killed 24 innocent people and burned down two beautiful old Catholic churches.

My aunt, as you may have guessed, is *anti*-Native American, to a very strong degree. To urge the mayor to put down any further riots in this city, she has organized a group of men and women of her own persuasion. Last evening they met here, my uncle being, as usual, at his beloved Union Club. Unfortunately, he returned early, in time to hear a spirited discussion which linked "Native Americans," Negro slavery, child labor, broken treaties with the Indians, and the denial to women of the right to vote. My uncle attempted to reason our guests out of their convictions as to human rights, but came off very badly and ended stamping upstairs in a huff.

I could not help but agree that he is truly short-sighted in his wish to discourage people not born here by denying them citizenship within a reasonable time. If, as he believes, this Union should in time be extended to the Pacific Ocean, then who shall cultivate that vast terrain? Mere immigrants, lacking any stake in the country's future because they lack any voice in its government? How solid a Union would this condition eventually result in? It seems clear to me that the franchise must be extended to all without regard to birthplace, color or gender. Yes! Even to women and Negroes. But as one who abhors slavery, I am sure you agree with that.

And it does appear that with the election of President Polk the westward extension of our country is certain. It is said he was provoked when Tyler, in his last weeks in office, robbed him of the glorious gesture of annexing Texas, that republic opting at last to join the Union. His eye, all say, is on California, ever since Frémont brought back to Washington his glowing reports.

On the dark side, of course, is the threat of a war with Mexico, although it is believed that Polk hopes to acquire much of her northern territory by purchase, and indeed has an envoy at her capital making such an offer.

Good heavens! I am astounded at the length of this letter, which began as a simple inquiry as to your mother's present state of health. However, I shall send it on to you, well aware that you may think me a garrulous and even forward young lady who boldly ignores the suggestion as to proper etiquette: to wit, that the female of the species is better seen than heard. I wonder, shall I ever see you again?

Yours most sincerely,
Jane Anne Clark

Leo looked up from the letter, saw the river flowing to the sea. He was lodged in a backwater in the river of time! Great events were taking place of which he knew almost nothing. Of the "Know Nothings"—the Native Americans—he had heard. Of more importance to Carolinians than them or than President Polk was the graying John Calhoun, still struggling to justify States' Rights with a strong Union.

Leo read Jane Anne's letter again. He was reminded of his outrage as a boy of sixteen when he read how President Jackson convinced the Indians of Georgia to leave their ancestral lands, coveted by whites, to cross the Mississippi to its far shore and beyond. Four hundred had died horribly when a steamboat's boiler exploded. Then thousands perished during their long march westward. The promised government funds were never paid them.

As a child he had rebelled against the blind, malignant oppression of the helpless. But now, out of a sentimental notion as to where his "duty" lay, he had forgotten what every fiber of his being had once known: his country could never be a great one so long as injustice to human beings was condoned by those able to see it for what it was.

He wrote at once to Jane Anne Clark:

Your most welcome and informative letter I regard as providential, and it had a profound effect on me. Of this we will speak further when I see you again. My plan is to settle certain matters of great importance here, and then return to my studies. As soon as I have been able to make up for much time lost, you may be sure that it will be my great pleasure to again visit New York for the sole and single purpose of enjoying the company of a young lady

234

who so splendidly flouted etiquette.

Yours gratefully,
Leo De Lange

The next morning he rode to the Pinckeney plantation to ask if he still had any interest in owning Barclay Shore.

Tall, graying, with a nose like George Washington's, Pinckeney said, "I tell you, Leo, these tariffs on cotton are cruel. Why, what it's come to is I'm no more than a vassal working for the benefit of the Northern mill owners! Tobacco, though, that's another story. One's a bit better off. I can't manage a lot of cash down on your tobacco land and Nigras but I can pay the balance off gradually, a nice steady little income. Think we can make a transaction?"

"I'll let you know soon."

Leo found his mother reading Sir Walter Scott in the parlor. He was tired; it had been a long day. He sat facing her. "Did you know that Rufus Pinckeney wanted Barclay Shore?"

She closed the book. "What are you getting at?"

"He still does. I don't have to worry about how he would treat the slaves, because he shares my father's opinion as to treating them with decency. And you've always seemed to like it better in town."

"Are you standing there talking about selling Barclay Shore to Rufus? Do you want your daddy and Jonas to turn over in their graves?"

"I don't think the dead stir an inch about anything on earth, Mother."

She stared in outrage as *Ivanhoe* slid from her lap to the floor. "If we sold Barclay Shore, what would we be then?"

"I don't understand."

"What would we *be*? What would *I* be? Now I know who I am. Everyone in Charleston knows who I am. A plantation owner. So are you. It's what we *are*. Living in town I'd just be your father's widow. My father's widowed daughter. Poor Emily." She made a vicious simper. "Poor Emily. She was once mistress of the De Lange plantation, you know."

"But I am no longer prepared to stay here so as to preserve your status."

She stared with hurt, cold eyes. "You intend to go back North again?"

"I must."

She lowered her lashes. "I knew you were bound to leave me, all along."

"So the question is: what's to be done about this plantation? I won't stay here to run it, and you can't."

The lashes snapped up. "Who says?"

"You did."

"Well, that's just not true! With Henry, I can manage quite well." She stood up, gazed about her, smiling. High on the walls the portraits of Henri, Jerome and Lucas De Lange stared out. "I wonder what they'd say if they knew that a woman and a Nigra are the only ones left here who care a fiddler's damn?"

On the packet ship Leo stood at the stern watching the islands off Charleston recede, fade, disappear. Once more he was escaping, this time not the South alone, not merely Barclay Shore, but a seductress who had turned Jonas into a substitute husband. Did his last words mean

236

to urge escape from their mother as well as marriage to Miss Jane Anne Clark?

Such thoughts disturbed him; he turned and walked toward the ship's prow so as to look ahead, toward his future. One thing was sure. He was in no position to marry anyone, and would be lucky to catch up with the rest of his class after missing so many months of lectures and laboratory assignments. With the cold breeze in his face Leo felt resolute. He would succeed, he vowed.

Part Four

XV

Feelings Elizabeth could barely control boiled up in her the morning after Leo De Lange left for Philadelphia. She had waited until nine to go down to breakfast in order to avoid her husband, but he was still at the table. He had discovered that the Stiegel pitcher was missing. "I questioned Annie. She said she found it in pieces on the floor night before last, and swept them up. She says she did not break it."

"No, I did." Elizabeth fought the impulse to tell him it had been no accident. Her teeth were gritted, her hands clenched with the effort at self-control.

"A pity." Isaiah shook his head. "Stiegel glassware has greatly increased in value."

"Since you bring up the matter of money, I ask you again to return to me the funds I lent you six years ago."

"You choose a most inappropriate time to ask me to indulge you this whim."

Vividly, she saw the pearl brooch on Imogene Fisher's bosom. "The time will always be inappropriate unless you curtail your own whims." Her anger threatened again to explode as she realized that the money earned at her desk had bought a jewel for a prostitute. "Be a man about town if you will, but not with money I earned."

"Man about town? What gave you that notion?" Now

he looked uneasy, but hid it with a belated smirk.

"People will talk."

"But you are too intelligent to listen to vile gossip."

"I am also too intelligent to be deflected from the topic we were discussing. Money. My money. Either you are a man of your word or you are not. I know that your financial crisis is long since over. You can afford many luxuries now. Is integrity beyond your means?"

He reddened; his chest puffed out. "Why can't you accept the legal fact that as a married woman what is yours is mine?"

"Still, you did promise me to return the money when you could. I believe that verbal agreements are legally binding. And I do have a witness to our transaction."

"Witness?"

"Jane Anne." By now her hidden rage had turned, by control of it, to icy calm. Money can free the spirit, she told herself.

"What do you need this money *for?*" Isaiah demanded. "Don't I provide amply for your needs?"

"That is not the issue. The issue is that you can afford to keep your word to me. I am demanding that you do." Her heart thumped dully; she feared that if she lost this struggle she would hurl Imogene in his face; she might turn into the virago who had smashed the Stiegel pitcher.

"I may be able to scrape up a third of the sum. Say a thousand dollars."

Good! He was beginning to negotiate. "I want it all. Deposited to an account in my name alone. I will forgo the interest it might have earned me."

He stood, threw down his napkin. "Well, I should hope so! I should certainly hope so!"

"Today," she added. "I want this settled today."

"Impossible!"

"Why?"

"Because I may not have time to get to my bank today, only to indulge you in this whim."

"Don't, pray, speak of indulging me. You are merely keeping your word."

"And any man I know would call me a fool for doing so!"

In the doorway he turned to glare back at her. "I see now my great mistake. As I crushed your abolitionist activities, I should have crushed your feminist affiliations as firmly." He took a step toward her. "One other matter. I must take you to task for offering hospitality to that Southerner as you did night before last, without regard for my wishes in the matter. Leo De Lange is a renegade, so described by his own brother. A black sheep. And he has designs on Jane Anne. When I entered the parlor I caught him staring down at her in a most lustful manner as she lay there on the settee."

"How you slide away from the issue! Money, not lust is the subject."

He turned abruptly and left with no farewell, and she went upstairs to see if Jane Anne had begun to stir. Her tormented sobs had awakened Elizabeth in the night, and she had spent a long chill hour beside the poor girl's bed, assuring her that time would prove her friend, that her grief would pass. She was still asleep, her favorite doll Eliza beside her.

It was three days later that Isaiah produced a bank draft for two thousand dollars. "That is absolutely the last cent I am prepared to turn over to you at this time, so take it or leave it. I do not know another husband who would be so generous about a wife's foible."

She picked up the money: better half a loaf than none! "Yes, husbands tend to be more generous to women who are not their wives, don't they?" She met his shocked stare with what she hoped was an ironic smile. Feeling shrewd and worldly she banked the money that afternoon; along with royalties earned by *Kathleen of Killarney* since Isaiah had recovered financially she had nearly three thousand dollars. Enough to go to Greece as she had once yearned to do, if it were not for Jane Anne, and Tom.

Tom had as yet to be told that Jane Anne's marriage would now never take place. He must surely understand that they could not add to her first great grief a divorce that would mean the dissolution of the only family she had ever known. Elizabeth sighed. The heady, freed feeling slowly deflated. Marriage was not the only trap that held her; she had a child to consider.

"But she is scarcely a child any more," Tom said after her message to him had brought the coach and smiling coachman to her door late that afternoon. Side by side as she and Imogene had been five days earlier, she and Tom now rode north. The day had turned nasty; a fine snow had begun to fall, blown here and there by gusts of wind. "I believe she was eighteen this September?"

"Her precise age is not the point. I will not behave so as to hurt her."

"If your divorce is going to hurt her, then she will have to be hurt sometime, and there's no way around it."

"But not now, not when she's so torn in her feelings, so vulnerable!"

His hand covered hers. "I understand. Of course I understand. We've waited so long, a little longer won't matter." He turned his head to look out the carriage window at the snow. "This cursed storm is going to delay progress on the Ferris mansion; I can't have roofers up there in such weather. And yet it must be finished by the first of May; that's the agreement. My whole future—our whole future—depends on my ability to fulfill what I promised." He faced her. "I don't have the slightest hesitation about marrying a divorced woman. President Jackson did, and it didn't harm his great popularity. But I'd just as lief have a happy, house-proud Cornelius Ferris singing my praises when we challenge public opinion."

Now the snow was mixed with hard sleet that stuttered against the frosted windows of the cabriolet; Elizabeth shivered, wiped a clear patch with her glove, looked out at the improbable brownstone Gothic towers of the Waddell castle. Lights glowing at the windows and the whirling white snow gave it a look of authenticity, as if royalty really lived there, or perhaps a princess from a childhood fairy tale, still awaiting the prince who would rescue her from the spell that held her imprisoned.

One bleak December morning Elizabeth woke early with fragments of a troubling dream flitting about her mind like bats, flitting into shadows and vanishing. All she could remember was a man in tattered clothes shouting, "Too late! Too late!"—and then turning his pale face away to cover his eyes with bent arm in an actor's gesture of despair. At that moment she recognized him as Henry Clay.

The Whigs had finally nominated him. But the campaign issue was whether Texas should be annexed to the United States. All the Northern Whigs were against it, leaving Clay trying to straddle the issue. A hard task, she thought, for a man who had said, "I'd rather be right than be President." And impossible against an opponent like the Democratic candidate, James K. Polk, solidly for Texas annexation along with all the South. To say nothing of Oregon: "Fifty-four-Forty or Fight." The final blow to Clay's hopes, though, came from the abolitionists whose Liberty party ran a reformed Alabama slave owner against him and cost him the New York vote, which cost him the Presidency. Poor Clay.

She got out of bed, found herself shivering, put on a robe, and opened the curtains to look out at the uninspiring facades of the narrow brick houses across 10th Street, the bare branches of its few trees. "Bare ruined choirs where late the sweet birds sang." Unbidden and unexpected came a memory of the lofty oaks under which she had once walked with her girlhood sweetheart. Too late for Clay and too late as well for she and Tom?

She found another reason for despondency. Jane Anne was not herself yet and had been stunned to learn that Leo De Lange had returned to Barclay Shore for an indefinite stay and apparently had no wish to continue their acquaintanceship. To Elizabeth this was an equal disappointment. How closely intertwined their lives had become! Jane Anne's joys and sorrows were felt almost as keenly as her own, proving that as a mother she had not failed.

Jane Anne was to sing for Mrs. Penrose soon and Elizabeth decided that a new gown was needed to replace the gray one which had so sad a memory attached to it. Later that day they went to a draper's shop to see the new French yardage he had advertized. One small white hand touched an exquisite silk unrolled on the counter but

Jane Anne turned abruptly and looked into Elizabeth's eyes, her own tear-glazed. "When will I stop being unhappy?" She looked again at the fabric. "It's such a lovely shade of blue!"

The connection was lost on the puzzled draper, but Elizabeth was sure that she understood. Leo De Lange would never see that blue gown. She thanked the merchant, led Jane Anne to the door. In the street Jane Anne ignored the gust of wind that made them hold onto their bonnets, that iced their cheeks and made tears come to their eyes. "Oh, Aunt Liza, I thought I loved Benjamin Mason. I was sure I loved Jonas. Yet here I am halfway in love with Leo De Lange. Am I a very shallow woman?"

"You're not a woman yet, dear, just a young lady."

"Do I dare write Leo after so long?"

"Why not? A Christmas note, perhaps."

"But what if he doesn't answer this one, either?"

"Then you'll know more than you do now." And so will I, she thought. And Tom.

It was a sadness for both of them that they would have to pass Christmas day apart. "But next year will be different," she said.

"I wonder." Tom looked sullen.

"Of course it will!"

As usual, Christmas dinner with the Pierponts was a cheery, bountiful feast. New Year's Day was, as usual, celebrated at the Moss house, the guests appearing all afternoon in various stages of inebriation. But at least Jane Anne was happy again. After much vacillation she had decided that Christmas was too transparent an excuse for writing to Leo De Lange (although she had really, she confessed, been hoping for a Christmas greeting from him to which she could respond). She composed a long letter which she mailed on the last day of the old year. The young gentlemen who called the first day of the new one were greeted with a demure sparkle. Elizabeth guessed that it was caused less by their presence than by renewed hope of a letter from Leo.

Though supposedly a Grecian beach it looked like a stretch of the Jersey shore: Cape May or Asbury Park. Walking alone there Elizabeth was filled with sadness, not for Byron but for his friend Shelley, the drowned poet. Ahead was a heap of charred timber, the remains of the funeral pyre Shelley's friends had made to burn his poor, fish-gnawed body. Then, striding toward it from the other direction came a man in a long dark cape. Byron? No, Tom O'Casey, hair tousled by the breeze. "Why this Godforsaken beach?" he asked as he neared. She gestured gracefully toward the ashes of Shelley's pyre, and told Tom how the flames had consumed all the body but the heart, which did not burn. "His heart did not burn," she repeated, nodding significantly. Tom leaped over the ashes between them then, embraced her, folding the cape around their two bodies like closing wings. She knew they would spend the rest of their lives together and a great joy filled her. . . .

She woke later than usual and lay there luxuriating in the pleasure the dream had brought. A tapping at the bedroom door was unwelcome. Without asking permission, Melonia rushed in, a dim figure in the curtained room. "Oh, ma'am, I do think Miss Jane Anne's terrible sick! I passed her door just now and heard her moaning, and she was talking to herself, words that made no sense to me at all! I felt her forehead and it was hot like fire!"

Elizabeth rushed to her niece's room to find a physician already there.

"I would say typhoid fever," the doctor said, "Even though there are not the usual rose spots on the chest or abdomen. But typhoid's all over the city, you know. I suspect the Croton Reservoir water. It's full of all sorts of animalcules, also pollywogs and even small fish. But at any rate, whatever this delirium and fever is caused by, this young lady belongs in the hospital."

From Jane Anne's bed across the room came a childlike voice. "My mother and father died of typhoid. But I won't, will I, Aunt Liza?"

Elizabeth went to the bed, bent to stroke the girl's burning forehead. Panic thrummed in her. "Of course you won't!" How brisk she sounded! How assured! Could life offer such an irony: the promise to Jennie kept and Jane Anne dead at eighteen of the same disease?

Later, at the hospital, Elizabeth stayed by Jane Anne's bed stroking the hot forehead, then bathing it with cool water a nurse brought; and she listened to a long babbling discourse concerning Jonas and Leo De Lange, a white kitten Hope Pierpont had promised her, a stain on her gray dress. At last she was given laudanum and fell into a deep sleep.

The first thing Elizabeth saw when she got home at dinnertime was Isaiah's new black hat, silky pile gleaming, on the hall table.

He rushed out of the parlor, wild-eyed. "The servants told me it may be typhoid. Is it? I beg you: what does the doctor say? It must be serious if he put her in the hospital. Oh, God! She must not die! That dear pure creature, so young so delicate!" Fear of his own powerlessness trembled in his voice. "I must go to her at once!"

"She was asleep when I left. Before that she was delirious."

"If we lose her, I'll never forgive myself!" Elizabeth was startled to see that tears filmed his eyes. "Are you coming with me?"

"I just left there."

He nodded, opened the door, hurled himself out. Willy-nilly, as if Jane Anne were their own flesh and blood, they were knit together by her peril. His self-recrimination struck Elizabeth anew. Did he imagine Jane Anne's illness to be God's punishment for trysts with Imogene? It then occurred to her that he had foregone his dinner, something she had never before seen him do.

"Ma'am?" Melonia stood at the foot of the stairs, having come silently down, her hands tightly clasped against the bib of her white maid's apron. Her voice was crushed, barely audible. "Tonight's prayer meetin' at my church, and all of us'll pray for her."

An irreverant remark of Grandfather Aller surfaced: "Religious folk will always pray for relief of your distress; it makes them feel good and costs little." As though from a great distance she heard herself thank Melonia. She went up the stairs fighting down the irrational urge to promise her Maker she would give up Tom if Jane Anne got well. In her room she knelt by the four-poster to pray. All she could manage was "Don't let her die, please, please let her live!" She got up from her knees heavy with guilt, as if she had failed to do what would have prevented Jane Anne's illness. What? Drain the Croton Reservoir?

In the endless, anxious weeks that followed she saw Tom only twice. He became almost as unreal to her as the dream-man in the Byronic cape. Daily she went to the hospital, sometimes twice a day. Once she saw early daffodils on the table by the bed; the card told her they were from Tom. But no flowers, no letter from Leo De Lange had arrived by mid-February. Even allowing for the slowest conceivable delivery, Leo must have received the letter mailed on December 31st. That same day a lucid Jane Anne asked her to write Leo De Lange that she was ill. "Perhaps something happened to my letter to him," she said. "Of course, he may just be dilatory about answering because he has no interest in me whatever." From the doorway Isaiah's voice rasped, "Nonsense. The fellow's not a fool, even though unworthy to touch the hem of your gown."

Elizabeth turned to look at him appraisingly. A thought as to the delayed letter was stirring as the doctor came in, hurried but smiling, to tell them that the fever had at last abated and Jane Anne was now out of danger. In a few days more he could release her to convalesce at home.

There was a stumbling sound; Isaiah was clutching the footboard of the bed, his face gray, hand on his chest. "It's the relief," he said to the doctor. "The blessed relief." Elizabeth found herself nodding. Blessed relief, indeed!

"You didn't tell me," Jane Anne said. "Will you write Leo, Aunt Liza? Or do you think it's better to wait a bit more?"

"Let's give him another week."

She rode home with Isaiah in his carriage, having gone to the hospital by omnibus. The inkling of doubt that struck her in the hospital returned. She turned her head to look at him. He now affected a cane and sat with both hands propped atop its gold handle. "Did you confiscate a letter from Leo De Lange to Jane Anne?"

His head turned very slowly, one massive jowl overhanging his stiff collar. "I am profoundly offended that you would ask me such a thing."

"But did you?"

"What would be the point?"

"To nip off any budding romance."

"I have larger concerns, madame, than a callow rapscallion's letters to my niece."

Huffy as he sounded, she noted that he did not directly deny her tacit accusation, but merely dodged it with pious generalities.

Jane Anne came home on February seventeenth, after seventeen days in the hospital. Many pounds thinner, she pecked at her food. She had interest only in the postman's knock. Anxiously she pounced on any letters, sadly put them down on the hall table and turned away, shoulders slumped, face wan.

Elizabeth began to be angry at Leo; how could he be so mannerless, so heartless? The note she wrote was terse. Had he received Jane Anne's letter of December 31st? If so, had he answered? "She has been very ill with typhoid fever, from which she is slowly convalescing. Your strange silence leaves us both concerned that all is not well with you."

A week passed, two, three . . . at last a letter from him arrived, postmarked Philadelphia.

Dear Mrs. Moss:

Certainly you must think ill of me if your niece has not received the letter I wrote in answer to her long and interesting one, which I cherish. My reply was sent from

Charleston on January 11, the day I received hers and should have reached her on or about the 22nd.

Thank you for letting me know of this contretemps. I have sent her a reply, long overdue, and close to the letter I wrote from a full heart at Barclay Shore.

The reason I am so late in answering your letter is that you sent it to the plantation after I had left for Philadelphia.

It seemed to Elizabeth that she could actually see the color returning to Jane Anne's cheeks as she read this message. "But what do you suppose could have happened to the letter he wrote me on January 11th?"

"We may never know, dear." Their eyes met; Elizabeth looked away as though her suspicion of Isaiah might show in hers.

Although Jane Anne's spirits were greatly improved by hearing from Leo at last, her body lagged behind. Her appetite did not return, as if the triple shock of death, supposed rejection, and severe illness had imposed a symbolic self-destruction. Finally the doctor suggested a popular remedy: sea air. A holiday on the New Jersey shore would work wonders, he believed.

Tom's sympathy for Jane Anne had been waning. When he learned that soon Elizabeth would be off with Jane Anne to Asbury Park, he exploded. "That girl! All your love and concern has gone to her for too long. I swear I'm never again going to try to deflect a trickle my way. Go to the Jersey shore with your beloved make-believe daughter. Spend the whole summer there if she so desires. I'm through begging you to get a divorce. I'm through waiting for the moment when you'll put me first!"

Shocked at his anger, she spoke soothingly, told herself he was tired, overworked. "You won't see a lawyer about your divorce," Tom scowled, "Nor will you become my mistress. And now you disappear with your niece for an indefinite time to Asbury Park. What man will put up with this forever?"

"It's not an indefinite time, only a few weeks."

"Why can't she go to your mother's?"

"Sea air, the doctor said."

They were in his cabriolet where they had kissed, embraced, shared confidences half a dozen times while that smiling coachman of Tom's drove about the city. But tonight rain spangled the windows and ran down like tears. She looked at his profile, in sudden silhouette as they passed a streetlamp. Why couldn't he understand that this was not the time to abandon her foster child?

"Tom?"

His head turned. "Yes?"

"Things will work out for us, you'll see."

"Things don't just 'work out' for anyone. People have to work them out, which can involve hard choices. I think I've waited long enough for you to act on that truth. Long enough!"

They parted without a farewell kiss, although he walked with her to the front steps as he had the night of the riot, so long ago. She was heavy-hearted as she packed to leave a week later, having heard nothing more from Tom.

On a balmy April afternoon she sat in the sand at Asbury Park beside her convalescing niece. They wore their new bathing costumes, pantaloons to the ankles, and over

254

that, full-skirted dresses to the knees. Jane Anne's was deep blue with a sailor collar, Elizabeth's maroon. Nobody had braved the chill ocean, although "promiscuous bathing" was a new and daring pastime among sophisticated New Yorkers and bare white female feet twinkling in the shallows where the waves broke was a deliciously naughty sight, as a popular journalist had rhapsodized. Elizabeth and Jane Anne covered theirs with sand that was still warm from the sun.

It was time for Jane Anne's afternoon nap, but Elizabeth could not bring herself to leave quite yet for the boardinghouse; she pointed to a sandpiper skittering angularly on the wet sand where a wave had retreated. "On a day like this it's good to be alive!" she said, and shaded her eyes to look at a small sailboat scudding along in the sparkling sea.

That was when she saw the wide-shouldered man with touseled dark hair striding toward her through the shallow foam of a receding wave. He wore a short-sleeved knit pullover and tight trousers to the calves. Her heart stopped beating, or seemed to, then thudded heavily. It seemed strange that Tom O'Casey's bathing clothes were the same maroon as her own.

He stood at her feet smiling down, backed by the wide sparkling ocean. A wave crashed; a surge of excitement filled her. A seagull screamed overhead, down the beach children were laughing.

He sat down at her feet, then stretched out on one side, his head propped on one muscular arm, looking up into her face. His skin had a rosy flush which made his eyes seem quite green. "I decided to take a short holiday. I left Brian Ryan in charge. He's become a very capable assistant, you know."

The nearness of his scantily clad body made her rather giddy, her eyes mesmerized by the wide yellow band across the chest of the pullover, which exaggerated the pectoral muscles beneath. "Don't you think Jane Anne is beginning to look like herself again?" she asked.

He cast her a careless look. "Thinner, but quite healthy now, yes."

"Thank you again for the daffodils, Mr. O'Casey," Jane Anne said.

"You're welcome." Now his eyes were on Elizabeth's bare left foot; she covered it with a heaping double handful of sand. He sat up, brushing sand from one elbow. "What about a walk down to the pier, ladies?"

"No, it's time for Jane Anne's afternoon nap. Doctor's orders."

He jumped up, held out a hand to each, pulled them to their feet. "Good. Jane Anne can have her nap and we'll have a walk."

The sunlight, the salt smell of the sea, the handful of strollers on the little boardwalk all combined to make a walk the most natural thing in the world. Elizabeth and Tom went with Jane Anne to the rambling boarding-house fronting the beach, then crossed the sand to nearly the water's edge where a little girl and boy were building a sand castle. Elizabeth could think of nothing to say; Tom's presence after their last parting said much. She looked down at the wet sand, firm underfoot. Their arms brushed, and a shiver went through her. They walked in step toward the weathered piles of the pier, black where the waves reached the old wood. It was farther off than it had first seemed. She looked back and saw the double trail of their paired, arched footprints. The sea breeze whipped loose a lock of her hair which lashed her face.

She stopped to anchor it; his hand reached out and brushed it back into place. "Do you want to go on to the pier, or back?" he asked.

The words derived a deep meaning. Back to Isaiah? Back to the house on 10th Street, to the pretense she had endured for Jane Anne's sake? "To the pier," she said, exhilaration rising in her with every step she took. They reached the pier and continued under it. In its heavy cool shadow the salt smell of the sea was captured, and the thud of a breaking wave echoed. They faced each other and his arms went around her and drew her into a close embrace. Their lips met, their mouths melted together, and they clung in a long kiss as wave after wave broke against the seaward pillars of their roof. Then she heard nothing, eyes shut, her body aware of his, yearning to be closer. Faint, dazed, surprised to be here in his arms, she opened her eyes. Then she ran out into the warm sunlight on the other side of the pier, dazzled by it, by the diamonds glittering on the ocean, and by her own joy. She knew that nothing could have been different, and that nothing was ever going to be the same.

As they walked farther and farther from the boardinghouse where Jane Anne lay napping, he confessed that he had been unreasonable. "I know you are not a woman to traipse off with no concern for her child's future. I am willing to be more patient about the divorce. I offer a compromise: a fellow at the Union Club has promised me the use of his cabin in the Catskills for a week or two in May. Perhaps you could get away at the same time. I mean, stay at the resort hotel nearby. Could you? Would you be willing to?"

His kiss still warm on her lips, she nodded, entranced by the delight she saw in his eyes.

XVI

There are moments in life we never forget. The most memorable I have yet known was when I ran joyously from my room and down the stairs expecting to see my beloved Jonas below. A stranger's face looked up. I saw the black band on his arm. He spoke his name. I knew Jonas was dead. I felt myself falling. I do not remember Leo catching me. My past and future were split apart that night; the past lay dead with Jonas and the future became dark.

All that I had read of love assured me that good women love but once. And so for some time I could not admit to myself the nature of my feelings for Leo; I told myself that I naturally admired him for having had the courage of his convictions since the age of ten. Although no doctor would agree, I am almost sure that the discouragement of his silence after the long letter I sent him on December 31 left me vulnerable to the fever that laid me low, left me a wraith.

The mystery of his silence proved mundane: his reply to that letter of mine had been lost in the mail. I read and re-read the one he sent to replace it until the folds were so flimsy they tore. He was struggling to make up for months lost from his medical studies due to his mother's mysterious illness. When I deplored to my aunt the absence of any hint as to when he might come to New York again, she advised me to be glad he could not. "To say you look like the last run of shad would malign the poor puny things!" I went to the mirror and took a long look. She was right. The doctor urged sea air to restore my appetite and color.

In Asbury Park the sudden appearance of Mr. O'Casey was a surprise to her, and to me. I had uneasy feelings concerning him. It was time for my tonic and nap when he appeared, so they walked with me to the boarding-house then crossed back over the beach to go for a walk together.

From the verandah I watched them walk side by side toward the ocean, sparkling in the afternoon sun. The distant, smothered crash of a breaking wave had a forlorn sound. I felt abandoned; Leo's last letter had lacked fervor. He had expressed his disbelief that malaria arises from noxious marsh gases. As my aunt and her friend grew smaller and smaller, my eye fell on the spyglass mounted on a tripod near the porch railing. I applied my eye and in a moment found my quarry. They were heading for the pier. After a minute they stopped walking, stood facing one another, talking. The breeze loosened a strand of her hair; his hand went out and brushed it into place.

That simple gesture made a shiver go up my spine. I realized that I had never seen her husband exhibit such tenderness.

A cough made me turn guiltily. I told the owner of the spyglass, an old gentleman who liked to watch birds, that I had been observing some terns and he told me to feel free to do so any time.

Up in my room I did not nap. I lay pondering the

mystery of love. At Miss Boorman's we all knew of the family so refined that the legs of their grand piano were called "limbs." Their daughter ran off with the coachman. No one could imagine what she had seen in the coarse fellow. I had no difficulty imagining what my aunt might see in Tom O'Casey. Was he the man she should have married? The answer came to mind so promptly that I felt disloyal to my guardian.

That night at supper I saw she had been so long in the sun her cheeks seemed to have a permanent blush. "Where did you and Mr. O'Casey go today?"

"Go? Oh, beyond the pier, quite far beyond."-

I was glad when he left for New York after two days. My aunt was abstracted for the rest of our holiday, like a person not wide awake, caught between dream and reality. It reminded me of the way she was when writing. One day when she sat beside me on the beach, her chin propped on her hugged knees, eyes on the wide Atlantic, I was reminded of the voyage to the Isles of Greece that she had once yearned to take. And now, at last, my uncle had returned a good part of the money she gave him then, for he had boasted at dinner of his generosity in doing so. "You could go to Greece at last, couldn't you?" I asked.

"Greece?" She gave me a wandering look as if I had mentioned Madagascar or the moon.

"Your book. *The Greek Slave Girl.*"

"I no longer want to write about a slave girl." Her smile seemed to me as mysterious as that of the Mona Lisa, extolled by the art teacher at Miss Boorman's as epitomizing both wisdom and purity.

And so I was surprised after we returned to New York when she remarked at the supper table that her holiday with me had whetted an appetite for further travel. "I've been a stick in the mud for too long, ever since I had to give up that trip to Greece."

"Greece?" He stared. "Don't you know that the matter of succession to the Austrian throne may lead to war any day now? The Italians are in a state of rebellion. And France may be on the edge of a second revolution. You cannot go to Greece. Where is that girl wi' the dessert?"

"Did I say I intended to go to Greece?"

He did not hear. Annie had appeared with three stemmed glasses of ice cream and a chocolate cake, which my aunt began to slice. Eyes greedily on it he said, "Brighton, perhaps. London."

"In late May the Catskills are charming, they say." She handed me a piece of cake to pass to him.

Fork ready, his eyes followed it. He nodded.

"The Pierponts have been there several times," I offered. "Hope just loves the old inn where they stayed near Peekskill."

She nodded, "Dolly Pierpont tells me the steamboat trip up the Hudson was pleasant. A stagecoach meets the boat and takes one the rest of the way most comfortably."

"They have horses and cows and wonderful cream, Hope said," I added.

His ice cream gone, Uncle Isaiah leaned back and patted his abdomen on which the stretched vest threatened to burst its buttons. "I, of course, can contemplate no trip to any mountains. I must keep my nose to the grindstone."

My aunt's look seemed very cold. "But you have diversions here I lack."

"Diversions?" He looked uneasy.

"Your club. Whist. City Hotel."

He coughed. "The Catskills, eh? Much more sensible than Greece or Brighton. I don't mind shouldering the modest expense."

"No, I will pay," she said.

"Out of *your* money?" He smiled bitterly.

"Yes."

For some reason I had understood from the start that she intended to go there alone. She left in a flurry of excitement. My uncle and I took her early one morning to the dock. As she waved her handkerchief to us from the white vessel's rail I wondered again why she had decided on the Catskills and why my uncle did not seem to object to her going off so soon again without him. As I watched the *Iron Witch* glide off below two dark clouds that billowed back from her tall smokestacks, I had to suppress as ridiculous the notion that my aunt was leaving me forever.

After taking me home, my uncle left for his factory. The house had never before seemed so confining, so dark, so much like a prison. I went to Miss Boorman's now only for music lessons. Almost all my friends had left, too, many of them engaged or even married. But my talent for singing seemed only a useless mockery. My uncle would not permit me to use it as I wished.

A Mr. Mandel heard me sing at a charitable event and approached my uncle with an enthusiastic plan: he would pay me to tour several cities with his revue. Of course, my uncle had been outraged and very rude. But the entrepreneur came the next afternoon to give me his card and remind me that at eighteen I was no longer a child, was free to sign an agreement with him. He believed as did his friend P.T. Barnum that the time was ripe for a pretty young singer to make a name for herself. One of the cities on his itinerary happened to be Philadelphia. The first day after my aunt left I was almost ready to take the leap.

Shocking news from Leo made me forget everything else. Two weeks earlier he had been temporarily suspended from the university due to an unauthorized experiment with ether. So he had come to New York to see me. But my uncle had refused to tell him where I was. Disappointed, Leo had returned to Philadelphia. "It was just as well, perhaps, because I was speedily forgiven by the powers that be. I must blame my own impulsiveness in coming without word to you beforehand."

My anger at my guardian knew no bounds. I could not wait to vent it, but went at once by omnibus to his factory. In his office there I waved Leo's letter in his face. "You didn't tell me he came here, not a word about it!"

"It slipped my mind."

"I don't believe you! It couldn't have! It would have meant so much to me to have seen him! You have no understanding of my feelings, none at all!"

As he tried to convince me he had only acted for my good, I looked at him and saw a stranger. All my life I had tried to please him, but now what he thought of me did not matter. "If you have damaged my friendship with Leo De Lange, I'll never forgive you!" With a flounce of my skirt I turned and hurried out half blinded by my angry tears.

I felt only a little better after writing to Leo and to my aunt. That night at supper my uncle and I were as cold and formal as enemies who have met at an inn or hotel by mischance. I passed him the butter; he passed me the turnips; he spoke of the sudden change in weather; I merely nodded, allowing the roll of thunder to confirm his observation. My first fury had passed, and I was a little awed by the anger I had shown that morning, yet I was far from ready to apologize for my disrespect.

It was he who apologized, or nearly so. After supper he asked me to join him in the parlor, and there, standing with his back to the hearth he tried to justify his treatment of Leo De Lange. "You are not a young woman of earthy nature, my dear. No, yours is a delicate nature, suited to certain demands marriage entails. I do not mean to suggest that you should never marry, only that the choice of a husband is far more critical than you suspect."

"I doubt that Leo De Lange came here to ask me to marry him," I observed.

He ignored this interruption. "There are very few men in this world of a refinement compatible with your purity. I could not bear to see you tarnished by crass hands, and I have more than one reason to believe that this De Lange fellow is the last man on earth I should consider as a potential husband for you."

"You don't know Leo De Lange, not at all. How can you judge him as unsuitable?"

He smiled sadly. "I believe I know him far better than you do. I think I know the nature of that mysterious illness about which Jonas was somewhat secretive. I am certain that Leo is a lustful young man."

"I fail to see how that illness has anything to do with his character."

"Of course you do not, and that is as it should be. Suffice to say that I have put two and two together to my own satisfaction. I urge you to forget him. Set your sights higher. He is not of the same moral fiber as his brother. He is not for you."

"I cannot promise to forget him. I will not even try." I am sure I looked calmer than I felt, hands clasped in my lap.

A frown made his face forbidding. A louder peal of thunder was followed by the sudden slash of rain against the window. The slight fear of him I had felt as a child tensed my body as he said, "I can already see the inroads en this slight contact with the fellow has made on your isposition."

"Because I will not deny my true feelings for him in order to please you?"

His eyebrows arched. "*Will* not? Do you forget that disobedient children are whipped?" He forced a smile, showing the crooked tooth, and took a sudden step toward me. "I would not like to be forced to such an extreme. Nor would you like to feel my cane across your little posterior, would you?" The threat seemed to be only in jest, but it alarmed me. He took another step toward me. "You would not be the first disobedient young lady to demand such punishment for her own good!"

As thunder crashed again I struggled between a deep humiliation and the knowledge that it was Wednesday night—that Melonia was probably at a prayer meeting, my aunt in the Catskills, and the other two servants by now down in their basement rooms. It was as if my uncle and I were alone in the house, and I at his mercy. I stood up, eyeing him warily.

The parlor door opened and Melonia stood there, attired for church in a cast-off bonnet and gown of my aunt's. She curtsied, then clasped her hands beseechingly. "Mr. Moss, sir, would I be askin' too much if the coachman took me over to my church?"

266

Fortuitously, she offered the absolute dependence and abasement I had denied him. He conceded her request, advising her to get no idea of making a precedent of tonight's dispensation. I slipped past her out of the parlor, went up to my room, and then, feeling silly as I did so, turned the key in the lock.

For the rest of my aunt's holiday frequent showers depressed me unduly. Leo's letter in answer to mine explained quite fully the reason for his interest in ether. After reading it I felt like crying. It could have been written to a male friend just as well as to me, I thought. It seemed clear that my uncle had succeeded in discouraging whatever ardor Leo might have felt. And how did I know he had ever felt any at all?

XVII

Jouncing toward the Catskill resort in a stagecoach that made up in speed what it lacked in comfort, Elizabeth read as best as she could an article in the *Harper's Magazine* she had brought. The writer was an English nobleman seeing Elizabeth's country for the first time. She felt herself an exemplar of his theory.

Most Americans are peripatetic people. Though some rural folk may never venture more than twenty miles from home, the more urban citizens think nothing of hurling themselves in splendid steamboats or by railway trains or in the ubiquitous stagecoach hundreds of miles on the smallest pretext. I am told that even twenty years ago, a race meet in Flushing, New Jersey drew a crowd of 120,000. The American stagecoach ventures everywhere on roads we in England would not dignify by that name. The travel-battered passengers descend like invalids but soon revive under the spell of some new scene. It is as though Americans are by nature aware of the vast size of the continent they occupy and thus view casually a journey that would span an entire country in Europe.

Descending in front of the hotel, "travel-battered," her eyes hopefully sought Tom, but he was not there, and somewhat dispirited by this, she carried her valise up the steps. Nor did he appear that evening. She passed the next day taking a walk with strangers amid rural scenery, eating the ample midday dinner with due admiration for the rich cream and famous peach cobbler. Seldom had she felt more alone. And then he suddenly appeared. Outsiders could pay to eat there, so that Tom's presence went unremarked except for her accelerated pulse and sudden animation. Like everyone, he was dressed much more casually than in town. His soft shirt was tied with a black silk neck scarf under an open jacket, and her own white linen waist and skirt made her pretense of ease less difficult. They sat opposite one another at a long table. She could not taste the food she put into her mouth. Once their eyes met and locked and she could not take her gaze elsewhere for a long minute. There was never much conversation among the guests as they ate, and only their full preoccupation with the viands could have prevented general notice of that thrilling, silent reunion.

After tea, sunset strolls were popular, if less so than rocking on the verandah. Without a word, Elizabeth and Tom strolled off together. "I have borrowed that cabin I spoke of," he said. "It's less than two miles along this road, then into the woods a way."

"I see." They continued to walk. The evening was balmy, the sunset splendid. A low burnt-orange moon rose very quickly, shrinking smaller and turning to silver. She knew that at any moment she wished she could turn back. Dusk thickened. The cabin, when they reached it, was of logs, so extremely rustic that its owner might well have decided to run for President. When she said so, Tom laughed. The sound of his laughter mingled with the chuckle of a nearby brook. "Do you want a look inside?" She nodded. He put the key into the lock, but then had trouble turning it. Tense as a tuned fiddle-string, she did not know whether she wanted the door to open or stay shut. Kisses in a closed carriage were one thing, but to step into this cabin was another matter. With a grating of metal on metal the key turned. Tom pushed the door open then stood aside for her to pass. She entered a darkness that smelled of wood ashes.

He struck a match, lit an oil lamp with a red glass shade. There was a big fieldstone fireplace, an oval rag rug on a hand-pegged floor, a table and two chairs by the window, a couch facing the hearth. In an ell was a wide bed with a patchwork quilt. Above the mantel hung deer's antlers, a five-foot span from tip to tip. Arms wide, Tom came toward her, and fear swamped a rising joy as he embraced her. Their kiss was nothing like the one below the pier. Aware of her lack of response, he released her. "I don't like those antlers," she said.

He turned to look up at them. "Why not?"

"I think of a poor dead deer, killed for sport."

"But I didn't kill it."

"It's dark out. I think we should be getting back to the inn."

"As you wish, my dear." She felt calm as soon as they had started back. She was not George Sand; sinful freedom alarmed her now that she faced its imminent reality. The hotel's lighted windows ahead were safety. "If you have more comfortable shoes," Tom was saying, "we'll explore the woods tomorrow morning."

In the open air, below leafy boughs or sunlit sky she felt merry and at ease with him, knew that he was remembering as she was happy times when they were young. They came upon plump mushrooms, praised simple wild-flowers, found a tarn deep in the woods and so well concealed by surrounding ferns and shrubs that it seemed like their own singular discovery, unseen by human eyes since Indians had wandered here.

It was Tom who found the wild berry vines. Only a few berries here and there had ripened enough to eat, but as she plucked one and pressed it to her lips a past day burst up from memory and she saw the young Tom lying with his hands clasped under his head, promising to love her forever. She tasted a remembered tart sweetness, felt sad, then joyful. "Oh, Tom," she said, "At this moment I feel that it is right to be here with you. I did not feel that last night, but today I do." She saw another ripe berry, bent to pick it and offered it to him.

He opened his lips to take the berry, kissed her fingers. "'Life, liberty and the pursuit of happiness.' Don't you see? We're claiming our birthright at last."

"That sounds very grand. Too grand."

"Why? It may be wrong to speak ill of the dead, but your father and Betsy played hob with our lives when we were too young and too vulnerable to cope with their willfulness and deceit. Your father willed you into marriage with Isaiah Moss. Betsy, for her reasons, deceived me into a marriage I never wanted. She lied to you if she said she was expecting my child before you became engaged to Isaiah. But they're dead and gone, and life has been kind to us at last. I see it as just and right for us to be exactly where we are at this moment!" His arms were around her then, he held her tenderly, kissed her gently. . . .

The next day the hotel packed a lunch basket and he brought wine; they picnicked by their secret tarn, lay back amid the ferns, hands locked, talking about their bright future together. At first it seemed only make-believe to her, but by the end of another day of woodland exploration she found that she felt like the Liza she had been—hopeful, vivacious, merry. The long years of her marriage were what seemed unreal now. Even the nagging need to provide for some sort of security for Jane Anne before leaving Isaiah could not dim her sprightly mood. "Look!" Tom pointed to the gray cocoon hanging to a twig. They watched it, hoping to see for the second time in their lives a butterfly struggle free. To her it became a mystic need, for it would mean that the self she now felt herself to be had reality, and that a human being can struggle free of its cocoon even after many quiescent years. And she knew that the cocoon meant much the same to Tom. So intent were they that the first spatter of rain caught them unawares; they had not seen the thunderheads piling in the summer sky. He picked up the picnic basket, took her hand, and they hurried, partly protected by branches above, toward the road that led to the inn if one turned right, or to his cabin to the left. As she preceded him down the path she did not know which way she would go, but then turned left. The dirt road was unprotected by trees for the most part, was already turning slippery. Thunder rolled; she thought of Haw-thorne, of Rip Van Winkle and the dwarfs with their ninepins; she did not think of the cabin to which she, not Tom, had chosen to go.

They reached it drenched. Dismayed, she put her hands up to her wet hair, unpinned it, and shook it down while he knelt to light a fire. As the flames began to crackle upward he turned. "You now have a choice. To sit in wet clothes and catch cold or to accept my robe and avoid one. Choose, Liza." Smiling, he pointed to the dark red robe hanging from a peg on the wall by the bed.

"And what will you wear?"

"Dry trousers and a dry shirt."

"Common sense tells me to accept your robe."

"I'll watch the fire intently while you change."

But as she unbuttoned her dress and let it drop to the floor and undid her damp camisole and petticoat, she felt as if his eyes were on her, glanced over her shoulder, saw him standing with his back to her, staring at the fire. The robe felt good against her skin; it was of a soft flannel, its warmth welcome in the chill the rain had brought with it. Turning, she saw that he had opened a bottle of wine and was filling a glass. The red wine glowed in the firelight as he held the glass out to her, and she was reminded of the glow of her glass rose. Seated on the couch she sipped the wine, basked in the fire's bright warmth, and resolutely kept her eyes from looking up at the antlers above. But she could not resist, and with a start she saw that the antlers were gone.

"I took them down," he said, joining her. In his white shirt, hair curly from moisture, he looked Byronic, a poet, not a builder. "I didn't like them either." He raised his glass. "To Liza and Tom and their pursuit of happiness."

"Why do you speak of us in the third person?"

"Did I? I don't know why." Something was disturbing him; he sipped his wine and then said, "I almost feel the gods are laughing at me."

Puzzled, she drank the rest of her wine in silence, waiting for his advance, tremulous and expectant. But he stayed slumped in his corner of the couch and stared at the fire. She became uneasy in the silence, broken only

274

by the heavy splatter of the rain, the intermittent thunder. At last a clap just above the cabin made her jump, startled him from his brooding thoughts. "Tom! What's wrong?"

He turned his head; his smile was slow and sweet. "Our luck has found us," he whispered. "Don't you know that, Liza?"

A sudden yearning for his arms, his kiss stirred and glowed in her just as lightning glared blue through the window and another peal of thunder shook the house. "Luck?" she whispered. "I chose to be here."

It seemed that her arms opened to him just as he flung himself toward her and clasped her in his. A delicious thrill shot through her as he kissed the side of her throat, her ear, her cheek, her mouth while gently he eased the robe from her shoulder to kiss her bare breast. There was no moment in which to dread the finality of this encounter, for his gently stroking hands sent wave after wave of tender passion through her. Easily, softly, smoothly, he pushed away the cloth that hid her body from his eyes. "I want you naked," he whispered. "Naked for me. I want to be naked for you."

"Yes. Yes!" Her eyes were on his dazzled ones as he stared at her body lying in the open robe while he undid his shirt. Almost solemnly, as if performing a rite, they stood facing one another in the firelight, then hurled themselves into each other's arms. As their warm skins touched, exquisitely, not a hint of shame was in her, fully naked before a man for the first time. The long kiss took her out of time, and then he moved suddenly to lift her in his arms, to carry her to the bed. "No! By the fire. Oh, please, by the fire!" she pleaded. He nodded. On the couch, his face above hers, her mind started a familiar journey, a journey to a pretty woods where she had walked in fancy on those nights when Isaiah had demanded his conjugal rights, but she came back to the present, to the firelight, to Tom, his face above her looking down half in shadow, half warm and bright, one emerald eye, one dark. She wanted him. "Oh, yes, yes, my dearest love!"

The strangest feeling she had ever known was his slow and gentle penetration; no force, no thrust, no crushing weight, nothing to escape, no hurt; he gave a little gasp once, eyes wide on hers, and then hers closed and little by little the rhythm quickened, and then she was gasping, and the prickle of ecstasy glimmered up her body from the soles of her feet, bursting out of her mouth in a sudden cry of joy as her loins seemed to melt like wax in flame then rush up to meet his thrusts again, again, again . . . "God," he gasped at last and lay spent as she was, spent and glowing, smiling at the discovery of such pleasure, astoundingly found yet again on the wide bed as birds outside trilled salutes to the storm's end.

The rest of their week was a succession of idyllic days. She returned to her bed at the hotel the night of their first, wearing the bedraggled white dress that had dried before the fire while they had tea and toast at the table by the window. But soon the rustic cabin seemed like a home to her. Tom brought in provisions from a grocery store in Peekskill so that they could be independent of the hotel. She quickly lost all fear of being an object of scandal; her comings and goings seemed of little interest to the other guests. The joy Tom gave her, each time unique, changed her universe. Stifled sensuality burst from her; she loved to stroke his skin, to smother him with kisses as they laughed amid tumbled bed covers.

They could not get enough of the outdoors either; after the storm, the weather seemed to bless their union of body and spirit with sunny days more like perfect June than mid-May. On their long rambles they shared a hundred secrets. Not once did any sense of sinfulness disturb her celebration of carnal love. Nor did she let bitter thoughts of wasted years arise; it was enough that they had found each other despite the living and the dead. Only as the last night of their holiday approached did a dark mood seize her. "I could not bear it, if this were meant to be all," she whispered as they lay back in the ferns beside their secret tarn.

He sat up, looked sternly down at her. "Meant to be? What does that mean? That some mysterious power guides our destiny? We do. You do. It is up to you to act so as to bring about our marriage, Liza. No more temporizing."

"I think you are what Henry Clay called 'a self-made man,'" she said, reaching up to stroke his cheek.

He seized her hand, kissed it. "What's wrong, then, with being a self-made woman?"

"Oh, I'm far from that. Conventional beliefs have shaped me up until now."

"Then damn them, confound them! You can make your life what you want. A divorce, what's that? A bit of scandal, a rustle of whispers, and then it's over!"

"I know. And I promise to see the lawyer as soon as I return to New York."

His kiss was swift and sweet and she forgot her dread of the moment when she must tell Jane Anne the truth that involved the shameful word "divorce."

XVIII

When my aunt returned I noted at once the great change in her appearance; her eyes glowed softly, her smile was radiant and a certain briskness had been replaced by an easy, flowing grace. It was her complexion that made her seem almost a stranger, for already lightly tanned by the sun at Asbury Park it was now darker, giving the blue of her eyes a jewellike intensity. She could not say enough for those lovely mountains, for the crystal-clear tarn she had found, surrounded by ancient trees, for the wild flowers and the mushrooms she had picked in those deep woods.

"I'm glad you had such a lovely time," I said. "Here it rained nearly every day."

Her hand, wearing the kisses of sunlight I had not shared, came out to stroke my cheek. "It seems such a long time since you've brushed my hair for me. Would that be too much trouble, dear?"

I knew she was offering me the chance for a confidential chat, and seized it. As the silver-backed brush stroked down her long hair I told her how Uncle Isaiah had discouraged Leo from seeing me. "Not that I suppose he would have come all the way to the Jersey shore to do so. I got a letter from him the other day that was all about ether."

279

"Ether? A gas, I believe?"

"And about a doctor named Crawford Long, who has used it to perform surgery without pain to the patient. Leo thinks ether will surely revolutionize medicine and dentistry. He's quite bitter about the cautious attitude toward its use on the part of the medical profession." Suddenly the brush stopped moving and I began to cry.

"Jane Anne! What's wrong?"

"I don't care about his old ether!"

"He obviously regards you as an intelligent young woman, and his friend."

"I don't want to be his friend! I love him! I love him passionately. Oh, it's so hard being a woman!" I tried to continue brushing her hair, but she took the brush from my hand and put it down.

"Did he say nothing about wishing to see you again?"

"Nothing!" And I told her then about the day I had almost decided to accept Mr. Mendel's offer of a tour with his revue.

Thoughtfully, my aunt braided her hair for the night. "The trouble is that you're between a life and a life and that's no life at all."

"Mr. Mendel mentioned that his troupe will soon play in Philadelphia. I think that's why I was tempted."

"And you could visit Grandmother Aller and Cousin Amy."

"But wouldn't that look very much like pursuing Leo?"

"You would be there in pursuit of a musical career. The visit to your grandmother would serve to hide the truth from your uncle. Do you know this Mr. Mendel's address?"

I nodded, filled with hope and excitement.

"Then I'll send him a note by messenger inviting him to tea tomorrow. We'll see if he'll agree to a trial concert for you in Philadelphia."

He duly arrived, not a very cultured man, but an enthusiastic one, with a slight German accent, a grease spot on his lapel, and a perfectly dazzling gold watch chain. He had arranged tours in England, France and Austria, he spoke four languages, and ever since he heard me sing at a benefit concert he envisioned me charming thousands. "I have a nose for what people want, and this country is ready for sentiment, sweet sentiment, a little song bird like Miss Jane Anne Clark." As for singing in Philadelphia, he had already booked his troupe of minstrels into a theater there for the first two weeks in July and could easily, he said, make a spot on the bill for me.

"The pay will not be magnificent," he twinkled. "This is the chance for her to try her wings."

Never in my life had time gone so slowly than until the day when my aunt and I left for Philadelphia. We took a packet boat, the weather being very warm for stage travel. I scarcely noted the ocean breezes, split between two excitements: seeing Leo once more and my first experience singing in a real theater where people had paid money to be entertained, and not for the sake of charity, either.

Knowing Leo was in the audience was a spur to do my best; that three members of my family were with him offered comfort. I followed a blackface singer in a checkered jacket, high hat and white cotton gloves. His voice was deep, his Southern accent heavier than that of any real Negro I had ever heard. His last song, my cue to be ready to walk onstage after my introduction seemed to me to concern a tragedy, but brought gales of laughter:

"Then Ah comes from mah work around a four o'clock/ Knock at de door but de door is locked/Open de window an' mah baby is dead/With a six-foot Nigger in mah foldin' bed!" He had to pause for the laughter to subside enough for the final refrain to be heard: "As I walks dat levee round, round, round/As I walks dat levee round, round, round/As I walks dat levee round, round, round/ I'se a-lookin' for dat Nigger, an' he must be found!"

As he exited past where I stood in the wings his big grin was wiped from his face as by a magic hand; his eyes were sad and he was sweating. On stage I was announced as "the sweet young song bird from New York." I tried to imagine I was only at the Academy of Music or at someone's soiree, but the whole feeling was quite different, and as my accompaniest began the introduction I felt that the tender ballads Mr. Mendel had insisted upon had little chance of entertaining the people out there who had found hilarious the dead Negress and the search on the levee for her killer.

But as I sang I felt a kind of warmth steal over me from that audience, a kind of affection. When I finished my last song I could see the first row of faces beaming up at me while hands clapped with enthusiasm. Giddy, I bowed to left, to right and to center as Mr. Mendel had told me, and sailed on air into the wings. There the blackface artist had lingered and he grinned down at me to say, "You sure has got it, little lady. The real moxie!" I had no idea what "moxie" was but thanked him anyhow.

That evening made a wonderful beginning for my stay in Philadelphia, though the repetition of the same songs during the ensuing nights became tedious. As for Leo, between his studies and my full evenings, we saw less of each other than I had hoped. Our best time together was the Sunday when he and a friend who had a small sailboat took my aunt and me down the Delaware. I had brought a picnic basket my grandmother packed. It was as Leo and I ate sandwiches on the stern deck, my aunt being at the tiller, that he revealed his disapproval of my lowering myself to sing with fellow artists like those who had preceded and followed me. "You're simply too fine to take part in a revue like that, Jane Anne."

"You sound like Uncle Isaiah. He thinks I'm too fine for almost anything but singing in his parlor."

"In that I can almost agree with him."

I felt saucy, exhilarated by sun, air, and his presence. "I'm not nearly as fine as either of you think, not as delicate, either."

He looked at me broodingly out of those curious, dark-blue eyes, but said no more. As we sailed back he showed me how to steer, which brought us very close. But he did not take advantage of this in any way.

Too soon I would be gone and all those miles and months would separate us again. But what could I do? Inspiration struck me as the intensity of my emotion mounted. He was shy with women. That must be it, for I could swear that the perspiration beading his forehead was not only from the sun. Yet I could not turn my back to the tiller and throw myself into his arms.

"My nature is such that I do not entirely trust females," he said. The stilted words came out in a voice roughened by his emotion. "But I trust you, Jane Anne."

"Enough to come for a picnic with me next Sunday in the woods near my grandmother's house?" It was pure inspiration, and came, I am certain, from the special feeling my aunt had for that bit of primeval forest. She and I had walked there on a visit years ago and I

283

remember how well she knew those woods, even down to a hollow near the branch of a certain oak.

"Picnic? Yes, I'd like that very much," Leo said.

Better than the oak grove my aunt favored, I liked a green dell near a stand of birches. Leo carried the basket with our dinner of chicken, sandwiches, fruit and cake. For drink there was both wine and lemonade. To my delight the dogwoods were in white bloom, and in the lush grass tiny bluettes grew, and he did not talk about medicine once.

Instead we spoke of my singing career. I faced a decision: to return to New York or continue to Baltimore with the revue. It did not surprise me that Leo favored the former, and vehemently.

"I seem to have a talent for singing. I may as well use it," I said. "In fact, it would be wrong of me not to. Quite a bit of time and money has been spent on its cultivation."

"Use it by all means," Leo said, "But not in Mr. Mandel's Ethiopian Revue. It's beneath you, and that's all there is to it."

"Unfortunately, no other opportunity just now offers itself." The words came out calmly yet seemed to me so flagrant a hint that my face felt on fire with blushes.

He looked at me steadily, so that I wanted to hide my face in my hands. Instead I found one hand held firmly in both his. "I'm sure that will not be true for long."

But did he refer to my career as a singer or my life as a woman? The spatter of a raindrop on my cheek startled me and abruptly ended our conversation since summer showers can turn to torrents in minutes. We scurried into my grandmother's house just before this one did. He stayed for tea but left before supper.

My decision had already been made. I would return to New York with Aunt Liza.

He saw me off. My aunt boarded the packet ship on some pretext, leaving us alone together. "Seeing you again has meant a great deal to me, Jane Anne," he said, and suddenly leaned forward and kissed my cheek.

"Do you think you can come to New York soon?" The packet ship's whistle blew. I felt bold and also desperate.

"Not before the end of August. Until then I'm working as a sort of apprentice to the surgeon who teaches us anatomy."

"You be sure to write to me, then!"

"I shall."

"And somewhat longer letters, please." The gaze of his steady eyes made me daringly honest. "And less about ether. I care about what happens to *you*."

"I don't write very well, but I'll do my best." Then he blurted, "I'll always do my best for you, Jane Anne."

I waved to him from the ship's railing, smiling merrily, but not at all sure if he had referred to mere future friendship or something nearer to my heart's desire. One thing was sure. August was going to be the longest month I had ever, ever lived!

XIX

Before Elizabeth and Tom had left the Catskills they made the plan to meet every Friday at one on the steps of the Presbyterian Church. It was only a short walk from Elizabeth's home and the meeting would seem to any passerby to be a chance encounter. They could then walk down the street and around the corner to where Tom's cabriolet waited. On the Friday following her return from Philadelphia she arrived early. The day was so warm that her parasol did little good and she went up the steps to stand in the meager shade of the recessed doorway. Anticipation of Tom's arrival reminded her of those first two days at the Catskill inn, except that now the longing to see him was unaccompanied by the anxiety that had dogged her then.

Foolish fears! She closed her eyes and felt a smile on her lips as she remembered delicious moments with Tom in those mountains. The hidden pool gleamed cool in memory and then the sight of his body glowing along one naked side in the firelight. . . .

"Good afternoon!" She opened her eyes and saw Tom at the foot of the church steps. He doffed his hat, bowed, and ascended to her, smiling. The excitement of her reverie filled her and she yearned to kiss those lips, but could only return his greeting. As they strolled to his cabriolet she told him of Jane Anne's success as a singer. "And Leo is not so disinterested as she feared. He assured her he looks forward to visiting New York at the end of August."

"I am going mad wanting to hold you in my arms again, and you can talk of nothing but some Southern student Jane Anne fancies she loves!"

"Can't you see, my dear, that if he loves her and wishes to marry her, I can go ahead with my own plans with a clear conscience?"

"Your conscience! Doesn't it tell you that you're treating me badly? Putting me second to your niece? We agreed up in the mountains that you will get your divorce and marry me. Was it just the mountain air? Does sea level suddenly make *her* future more important than your own?"

"Tom, be fair! What difference can a mere six weeks make to us?" They had reached the cabriolet. As Tom opened the door she heard footsteps approaching and moved her parasol so as to hide her face from the passersby. Inside the carriage she continued: "I don't think you could love a woman who would rush to divorce and bring down all that scandal on the innocent head of a young girl in a torment of love for a man who may not feel the same for her."

Tom smiled wryly. "It's not entirely your fine character I'm in love with, Liza." He leaned closer, his voice warm and cajoling. "Since you now confront me with a longer wait than I counted on before you leave your husband, can't you take pity on my yearning?"

"No!"

"But it does not make sense! We have committed adultery. The die is cast. If we are cautious . . ."

"No. I told you in the mountains that I will not indulge in secret meetings while I'm living under Isaiah's roof. I cannot live with him and share your bed and that's that."

"So I'm to suffer because of a young man from Charleston I never set eyes on! It's ridiculous! Suppose he doesn't care for her? What then?"

"Then I decide between her singing career or a higher education."

"Education? To what end?"

"I don't know, Tom. But I won't abandon her."

"No, only me! Aren't you afraid you'll lose me to a woman who can put me first instead of second?"

She felt a pang at the thought. "Should I fear that, Tom?"

He smiled. "Never."

Her feelings about a secret rendezvous proved less delicate than her mental reservations. By mid-August she had seen him twice more on the church steps and once inside, where it seemed to her that boyish eyes of long ago stared at her over his hymnal. A heat spell had set in, unremitting. She got out of bed one night, pulled off her nightgown, sponged her hot body with cold water, and lay down naked, cooling her face and body with an old ivory fan not used for years. She found herself yearning for Tom's arms.

The next day was Friday. Dressed in white linen she toiled sedately below her rose silk parasol toward the church while sweat trickled down between her breasts. She had paused in the poor shade of a small tree when a shining black cabriolet pulled up to the curb, the young liveried coachman aloft. Tom got out, took her arm, aided

289

her in. She leaned back, against the leather seat gratefully.

Beside her he reached for her hand, kissed it. "I'm going mad with this longing! I've never known anything like it! For God's sake, forget your finicky scruples!"

"But where can we meet? I won't go to one of those houses of assignation! I refused to be a nameless lady in a heavy dark veil."

He pressed something into her hand. She looked down at a key, with a card.

"My house. Today at five. If I'm delayed, let yourself in."

At the appointed time the hired coach let her off at the mouth of the narrow, dead-end street paved with gray flagstones; the brick wall of a public stables formed one side, on the other stood perhaps half a dozen small cheek-to-jowl Dutch houses, much older than the one on 10th Street. Tom's also had a dark green door. Using the key he had given her she entered with a hard-beating heart. Directly ahead a narrow staircase ascended; to the right was a small dim parlor. "Come up!" called Tom's voice. As she went up to him her desire mounted. She went through an open door into a bedroom decked with flowers—on the bureau, the table by the wide bed, the windowsill. Tom wore a wine-red dressing gown. Laughing, he opened it like two wings at either side and enfolded her against his naked body.

She closed her eyes as a dream and reality blended. She was aware of his fingers unbuttoning the bodice of her gown as her nostrils savored the deep scent of roses, the piquant whiff from a bowl of garden pinks. "Did you buy out a florist shop?"

He shook his head, easing the straps of her camisole off

her shoulders so that her breasts were freed, bared to his touch, filling his cupped hands. Solemnly he kissed each one and then her lips. Her own rising ardor made her aware of the heat of the room. "Oh, for that cold ocean at Asbury Park, or our tarn."

Kissing her throat he did not seem to hear.

"I hate being half-dressed like this."

"I prefer you bare." He lay back, smiling. "Strip, slave!"

"Don't call me that even in fun."

"Then I'll be your slave. Command me."

"Bring me our mountain pool."

"Will you accept a sponge bath? Perfumed water?"

"I will."

In moments she was naked and he was stroking her with the soft, cold sponge. In the basin floated a chunk of ice. He had planned this delicious relief. A second large basin of white enamel stood on the floor by the washstand. She stepped in, took the sponge and filled it and squeezed it so the water sluiced down her body. "Delicious!" She opened her eyes. He was pouring wine into the two glasses on the bureau: chilled white wine, quite dry. Sipping it, she watched him step into the basin, squeeze the sponge above his head so streamlets slid down his face and chest and flat belly to be lost in the dark triangle. The hard work he had done most of his life had carved his flesh into arresting planes of muscle, the pectorals classic as a statue's, the thighs hard and shapely. "Turn around," she commanded. He did, and she admired the small neat buttocks, the wide shoulders. "You are beautiful," she said.

He looked back at her over his right shoulder, heavy black eyebrows arced in surprise. "Beautiful? Me?"

"You, my dear. Please kiss me."

Their cool skin soon warmed. His hunger for her fed hers for him. They mounted together to an ecstatic height. The fountain gushed warm life, hot joy. Tension ended in a slow collapse to peace.

Now a whisper of breeze stole through the open window to offer a delicate caress, and she thought of a fat little Eros with stubby angel wings hovering above the smiling naked lady of a Renaissance painting. What a wonderful painting she and Tom would make, she in his arms like this. I am a shameless woman, she thought, although the phrase had lost any evil connotation. "Do you consider me a shameless woman, Tom?"

He opened a drowsy eye. "Not nearly shameless enough."

She settled her head on his shoulder again, smiled, and drifted off on the tide of satisfied desire. . . .

Twice more during that humid August she went out the green door of the house on 10th Street to enter the green door of Tom's home. It was while she was lying in his arms, Leo De Lange's visit only a few days away, that a plan occurred to her that would provide for Jane Anne's immediate future if Leo did not return her love. Mount Holyoke College for young women would provide a sanctuary and would offer studies at a high intellectual level, to say nothing of contact with new friends. Safe in South Hadley, Massachusetts, she would be spared much of the shock of the divorce and all the ensuing scandal. Since 1836 Mount Holyoke, first of its kind, had gained increasing cachet.

"What are you pondering about?" Propped on one elbow, Tom was smiling down at her by the light of the bedside candle.

"Leo De Lange arrives Saturday."

"If she were your own daughter you could not be more doting!"

"You sound jealous!"

"I am."

"Don't be, my dearest. You have no reason."

They talked of other matters then. He was pleased that Cornelius Ferris was at last returned from Europe with art works and furnishings for the mansion that had been finished since June.

"I'd love you just as dearly if he'd hired someone else to build his house."

He smiled and his hand came out to slide along the curve of her shoulder and down her arm, sending through her the same delicious tingle of pleasure she had felt as their arms touched on the afternoon they had walked along the beach toward the shadow of the pier.

XX

Shaken but exhilarated by his first ride on a railroad express train, Leo arrived in New York an hour earlier than he had expected, unconcerned about the several cinder burns on his coat.

The chugging, the noise, the shriek of the whistle, the clang of the locomotive bell had thrilled him, and the densely packed passengers, fifty to the car—all kinds of people sitting shoulder to shoulder—only brightened his enthusiasm for this newest mode of travel. He saw as rightly democratic the principle of one-class tickets in a country that professed to believe in human equality. Crushed between a portly man in a high silk hat and a rawboned farmer, Leo gazed out the small window at scenery that flew past at more than twenty miles an hour. More than six thousand miles of track had been laid in the Eastern states; already two lines pierced the Alleghenies, inching toward the Mississippi River. Elated, he knew that the railroad would unite his country, now only a loose-knit collection of separate states, each insular and suspicious of the rest.

The whistle blasted, the train slowed slightly, perhaps for a cow on the track ahead. Leo smiled to himself, comparing the huge locomotive with its urn-shaped smokestack pouring out a black cindery cloud, its ornate cowcatcher, boxcar, and five passenger cars with the absurd little two-decker canopied omnibuses of only fifteen years earlier. Then there had always been an open platform stacked with cotton bales between the passenger cars and the locomotive, padding in case of a crash. A band had always played cheery music to calm the anxiety of the riders.

Leo turned to the farmer. "In the Thirties when a locomotive collided with a cow, the locomotive had to be sent to the repair shop. Now the railroad company has to pay for the dead cow."

The farmer nodded, aimed a ringer at the brass cuspidor. "Never killed none of mine, though there was a close call once."

The man in the high silk hat joined the conversation, an authority. "Bridges. Railroad bridges. That's the big need now. Rivers wedded to railroad lines. New Orleans has hogged the nation's trade long enough. Steamboats did that. More goods shipped out of there last year than was handled by the entire British Merchant Marine. Cheap freight costs on the steamboats. But now a new day's dawning."

New York itself offered Leo a day of brilliant sunlight that glorified the best of the city and glided its worst. He was still a full half hour early when his hired hackney reached Tenth Street, but his impatience to see Jane Anne again prevailed over courtesy. It was not quite one o'clock when he knocked at the dark green door, valise in hand, spirits high.

The freckled Irish maid admitted him; Elizabeth Moss came to welcome him into the parlor. "Jane Anne's gone to the jewelers' to pick up a locket he mended." The tension she exuded made her smile seem perfunctory. "I know I should ask you if you wish to refresh yourself after your journey, but I won't. I must take advantage of this chance to talk to you alone." She closed the door leading to the hall. Anxiety began to stir. What was wrong? "Sit down, please." He obeyed. She remained standing. "I'll come right to the point. What are your intentions toward Jane Anne?"

The blunt question, and from a woman, rattled him. "I like her very much. I look forward to knowing her better."

She shook her head, sank into the chair flanking the settee, leaned toward him. "No time for all that. Before your visit ends you must decide whether you are going to marry her."

In spite of his astonishment he spoke sternly. "Why are you asking me to make this commitment at this time?"

"I wish there were time for a long, charming courtship. There isn't. This home is about to dissolve. I must make plans for her. It will be either a life with you or Mount Holyoke."

Stunned, he did not know what to ask first. "Mount what?"

"The woman's college."

"College? For a woman? What's the point?"

"The point is that she cannot remain here after I sue my husband for divorce."

Shock numbed his mind for an instant. "Divorce?"

The parlor door was flung open; a radiant Jane Anne stood there in pale blue. On her bosom a gold locket gleamed.

"Oh, you're early! What a lovely surprise." Unseen by her niece, Mrs. Moss raised her finger to her lips.

297

He stood, went toward Jane Anne, took her outstretched hand. Looking up at him, innocent of the knowledge he now possessed, she became more than just pretty to him; she became the innocent victim of her aunt's extraordinary decision, a victim he had the power to rescue. He smiled down at her. "I came by railroad. The new express train. And I saw the shape of the future of this land!"

Her marveling blue eyes looking up inspired him to span the mighty Mississippi with a suspension bridge, send railroad tracks reaching out across the vast prairies to the far Pacific Ocean. The railroad, he told her, would unite not only their nation, but the world!

After the midday dinner at two, a meal unattended by Mr. Moss, Jane Anne was bent on sightseeing. "We must see Jeremiah Gurney's new gallery of daguerreotypes. The walls are simply covered with likenesses of famous people. Authors, politicians, the President, and even Queen Victoria of England. And I do want to see Mr. Goelet's home at 19th and Broadway. Peacocks and golden pheasants stroll on the front lawn. Or did. I heard that during a recent 'workies' riot old Mr. Goelet became frantic with fear that they would storm his mansion. He thought the peacocks such clear evidence of his wealth that he had his servants pluck out their tailfeathers so they could masquerade as ordinary birds."

"A tall tale," Leo offered, rewarded by silvery laughter.

"I think Gurney's Gallery will be enough for this afternoon," her aunt suggested, "particularly since I plan that we visit Barnum's Museum tonight." It pleased Leo that Jane Anne did not argue the point as a forward girl might have done, but demurely agreed. It more than pleased him that Mrs. Moss decided not to accompany them to Gurney's. They spent a pleasant hour there, both deeply impressed by the likeness of the haunted eyes of Edgar Allan Poe. Several well-dressed ladies greeted Jane Anne and asked after her aunt.

Before tea there was time to stroll around Washington Square, a pleasant park surrounded by solid-looking three-story houses. She pointed out the one belonging to a rich eccentric bachelor whose shabby torn window curtains had offended his neighbors. Two doors away was the Boorman home, one of the oldest on the square, which was first an old Dutch cemetery, then a parade ground, she said. "I'd like you to meet Miss Boorman, but I hesitate to visit her today. She's somewhat old-fashioned and I fear that to stroll in with a young man to whom I am not even engaged might upset her." Then her small gloved hand went to her mouth, and she stared over it with shocked eyes, cheeks flushed with embarrassment. Hastily she spoke of a visit next day to Hoboken on the ferry. "There's a little railroad and a big carousel and it's such a pretty place!"

"Are you forgetting that I'm only here until Monday?"

She looked away so that he could see only the sweet curve of her cheek, the soft tendril of hair that had instantly touched and charmed him. "I wish I could," she said softly.

"Next time I'll plan to stay longer." It was a shock to remember that "next time" could not be earlier than Christmas holiday, that by then her aunt's divorce might already be a reality.

To Leo's pleasure they had a hearty tea at six without Mr. Moss, who had gone to his tobacco store in Hackensack. They rode in style to Barnum's Museum in the

Moss coach, which would then go to the ferry landing to await Mr. Moss's return from New Jersey. "But a friend is going to meet us and drive us home," Mrs. Moss said.

The stuffed white whale hanging on chains from the ceiling, the woman who weighed five hundred pounds, the great ape, the albino lady, the "What Is It?", and other wonders were viewed by gaping tourists and smiling New Yorkers delighted to show their sophistication by observing that the whale had probably been whitewashed, the fat woman padded, the albino bleached, although they could not explain away the "What Is It?"—a creature whose hands grew from its shoulders, whose short, thick legs supported it in a grotesque jig. It had brown eyes, and looking into them Leo felt the same disagreeable sensation of an unjust superiority he had often felt looking into a Negro's eyes. Jane Anne turned suddenly away. "I can't bear to look at him!" she whispered. Her face was sad. "He knows he's a freak. It's painful to see his suffering eyes."

Leo yearned to enfold her in his arms, comfort her. "I feel the same."

"You do?"

"Men and women share many of the same emotions."

"Yes, I suppose they do. Though I believe Uncle Isaiah would point out to us that the poor fellow probably makes a quite good living out of his deformity. Then he'd find out how much a freak earns in a week. Oh, dear, that sounds most disloyal, doesn't it?"

For the first time he remembered that her aunt was with them. He turned to where she had stood and stared about the huge gaslit hall with its many exhibits and its throng of people clustered at each or moving from one to another. Then he glimpsed Elizabeth standing below the

300

white whale beside a tall dark-haired man with a bold, handsome face. Jane Anne had seen them, too. "That's Mr. O'Casey. My aunt and he were acquainted long ago when they were young."

A cluster of people passed between, gaping up at the whale's belly; then Leo saw Mrs. Moss and Mr. O'Casey coming toward them. She presented Leo to the older man. Shaking that strong, hard hand Leo looked into a pair of clever green eyes and knew he was being evaluated, and that to do so might be the reason Mr. O'Casey had met him here tonight. "Do I pass muster?" Leo asked dryly.

Unruffled, O'Casey grinned down at him. "I'd say so."

Elizabeth Moss pretended not to have heard. "Well, Leo, have you had enough of freaks and humbug?"

His day had begun at five so as to catch the early morning train. "I have."

"Then allow me to drive you all home," O'Casey said. "My coachman is waiting outside."

In the cabriolet Jane Anne was subdued. It did not surprise Leo that she expressed a wish for an early bedtime as soon as they had finished their late supper. His room was between hers and her aunt's; in bed the two women alternately troubled him. Despite the divorce Elizabeth Moss was bent on getting, he did not consider her a light woman. He wished her well, yet resented her demand that he declare his intentions. What had he to offer a wife? Wife! The word alarmed yet excited him.

Leo slept late and arrived at the breakfast table, having hastily washed and dressed, moments before Isaiah Moss finished his coffee and rose to leave—for his church, he announced. His smile was almost genial as he said, "Perhaps, Mr. De Lange, a breath of air before you

301

partake of breakfast would not be amiss? Will you cross the rear garden to the coach house with me?"

Leo knew it was a command, bowed in acquiescence, and followed Moss to the rear of the hall and down to the small garden, walled on two sides; the main house and the coach house enclosed it on the other two. The grass at either side of the brick walk and the rododendrons against the walls seemed barely to hold their own in so sunless a spot. In its center, Moss paused, turned, and faced Leo. "I will speak briefly and to the point. If this visit of yours indicates that you have serious intentions toward my ward, forget them. I will never agree to an engagement with you, and on this nothing could possibly change my mind. I believe in being honest, as you see."

"Jane Anne is eighteen. She herself has a voice in the matter."

"If she should defy me, if she should despise the protection I mean to offer her, then, sir, I shall disinherit her. My estate, as you surely know, is considerable. Not a penny will be hers." His icy smile of triumph showed Leo that he believed the loss of Jane Anne's prospects would discourage his suit. "Have I made myself clear to you, De Lange?"

"To the point of insult," Leo said. The young man turned his back on Moss and went up the back steps in a boiling rage. But he was nonetheless aware that the effect of Moss's threat was the exact opposite of what the man had hoped. It had crystalized Leo's decision to propose to Jane Anne before he returned to Philadelphia.

After church, he and Jane Anne walked to the old Goelet farmhouse. Large and quaint, it evoked pre-Revolutionary times more emphatically than even the oldest houses on 10th Street or in Washington Square.

On the wide green lawn beyond a low stone wall gold and silver pheasants seemed prettily arranged to please the onlooker; and then, strutting slowly, appeared two male peacocks, their tails fanned splendidly, in contrast to a cluster of smaller pea-hens, drab and brown. Jane Anne had brought from home a bag of dried bread to feed them, and she leaned out over the wall to toss a small piece of bread to the lawn, near one of the peacocks which had made its stately way toward where she stood. As if amazed, the gorgeous bird peered with one eye at the bread, then pecked it up, waited for another. The girl laughed in delight. "Oh, see, Leo! Grand as he is, he's not above a bread crust." She tossed another, smiling, then aimed one toward the shyer peacock. "But the poor pea-hens, they have nothing!" She pulled a handful of bread bits from the bag, reached far out to scatter them as close to the pea-hens as she could.

Seeing her, so artless, so young, so unaware that her world was about to change forever, he was deeply touched. Leo took the bag of bread from her hand and put it down on the wall. He held one of her hands in both his and found again how small hers was, how delicately boned. "I . . ." His voice stopped, to his dismay. He stood staring down into her trusting eyes. The moment lengthened. He heard the dry rustle of a fallen leaf. "I love you. I want to marry you."

"I'm glad."

The words, so honest, so simple, electrified him. When he kissed her this time it was on the lips. They felt like warm rose petals. And then a peacock screamed, hideously. Startled, he released her and they both turned toward the sound. The bolder peacock stood only a few feet from the wall, its multi-eyed, splendid tail staring at them. They burst out laughing at the same instant, and Jane Anne reached for the bag of bread and shook out all the crumbs onto the grass. As the peacock fell to, Leo kissed her again.

As they walked back toward 10th Street, a belated excitement struck him as he realized the finality of those few words he had spoken. He looked down at her hand, resting against his dark gray sleeve, her arm linked through his. So white, like alabaster, her hand adorned the dull wool; such a pretty hand, such a protected hand. . . . "Do you love me enough to live very simply for another two years or so?"

"Of course!" Her face was earnest. "I know I am capable of much more than has so far been required of me, and I would rather live simply with you than grandly with anyone else on earth."

The yearning to embrace her was intense, but a matriarch approached on the arm of an austere gentleman in eyeglasses, so he only covered her hand with his. "It will be only a boardinghouse, my dear."

She smiled. "Decidedly preferable to Mount Holyoke College. Aunt Liza has been praising it to the skies lately. But I truly don't believe I'm cut out to be a bluestocking, do you?"

To the pretty uptilted face, to the tender young bosom on which a gold locket gleamed, he said heartily, "No!"

As they neared the Moss house it was hard to believe that he had mounted those eight steps only the day before, exhilarated by his first ride on a railway express train. At equally breakneck speed he had been propelled into the most important commitment of an entire lifetime.

Sobered, he realized that she did not know what marriage to him would cost her. "This morning your uncle said that if you marry me he will disinherit you."

She smiled. "Did he also happen to say that the worst fate that can befall a young woman is to marry a man who is no gentleman?"

They burst out laughing at the same instant. A moment later and with very few words they had decided to miss Sunday dinner and ride the ferry over to Hoboken where, she assured him, the carousel would simply take his breath away.

XXI

The day Leo proposed marriage was the happiest and most dreadful day of my life.

The joy came first. My aunt's delight was an added bounty. She hugged me and said, "How glad I am that you are to marry the man you love!"

Knowing that she had not I almost felt guilty in my happiness. "I understand," I told her. "Perhaps better than you know." As a woman who had just attained the status of an engagement, however ringless at the moment, I felt I now merited her confidential candor; for a blind woman would have seen that her marriage was a total fiasco now, and that Tom O'Casey loved her.

But she turned from me to Leo to tell him how pleased she was. On learning that we wanted to go to Hoboken she was perfectly wonderful, although I know she had chosen our Sunday dinner with care. Now she would have to eat it alone with her husband. "Wouldn't you like to come?" I asked.

"Fifth wheel to your coach?" She shook her head, smiling.

Leo and I had a joyous time together and when we returned at eight that night found we had been invited to supper at the Pierponts. Mrs. Pierpont's lively dark eyes rested often on Leo and it pleased me to see that so sophisticated a New York matron clearly approved of my fiancé. Hope was a bit green, but glad for me. After supper we played Seven Up at the round table in the sitting room, the three eldest children and Mr. and Mrs. Pierpont and Aunt Liza and Leo and I, and all was cheery and heartwarming, quite the best impromptu celebration I could have wanted.

It was near eleven when we returned home. A sleepy Annie admitted us, saying that my uncle had only just got back and had gone upstairs to his study. After the easygoing evening with the Pierponts it was sobering to be faced now with the task I had set myself. I hurried up to the third floor trying to convince *myself* that I could convince *him* of Leo's worthiness.

He was at his desk, poring over an open ledger by the light of a red-shaded oil lamp, his face as stoic as those of the two marble busts atop the bookcase to my left. I suddenly felt sorry for him, left out of the Pierpont's celebration and up here counting his pennies. "Yes? What is it, Jane Anne?"

Like most American young ladies, I had read in more than one etiquette book the proper manner in which a daughter should inform her father or guardian of a proposal of marriage. Hands gracefully clasped below the bosom, rather as though I was about to break into song, I cleared my throat. "I am here to tell you that Mr. De Lange has asked me to be his wife. I reciprocate the feelings of love he has expressed. But I would be an ungrateful young woman, considering the care and affection you have bestowed on me, dear Uncle, if I were to fail to ask your approval of my marriage to him."

He had shown no emotion during my speech, only nodded once or twice as if hearing familiar music. Then he closed the ledger with a slam. "Another would-be doctor of medicine! Do you imagine this to be a noble profession? One that ranks with law, architecture, religion? It does not. Most doctors are mere quacks, trading on ignorance, peddlers of dubious nostroms and leeches. I doubt that De Lange could support a wife except for income derived from his family plantation as an absentee landlord."

"It is not his profession, or lack of it, that I wish to marry, but *him*."

"Not long ago you were equally bent on marrying his brother."

"I was younger then and mistook affection for true love. I know now how much stronger are my feelings for Leo."

"Feelings! If the fate of the human race depended on the *feelings* of inexperienced young women, we would not have reached the state of civilization we have attained."

"I realize you are not very fond of Leo, but . . ."

"I despise him!"

"But you don't have any reason to!"

"Ah, but I do. He is a traitor to his heritage, a turncoat, a renegade. There is nothing I more despise than a Southern abolitionist. I despise them even more than I do those who befriend the foreign Catholics who swarm to these shores and hope to see this land ruled by the Pope of Rome!"

"Your political opinions have little to do with my future happiness." I struggled to stay calm. Anger at him was rising.

"I expressed my opinion of the despicable young man you desire to ruin your life with."

"He is not despicable! He is admirable! And if you

309

refuse to give me your permission to marry him, I'll marry him without it!" Beyond all caution, I was quivering with disappointment. Where was the affable man who once had stroked my hair and talked of the mansion he would one day build for me?

He stood behind his desk now, glaring down. "I see that a pale, romantic face and a pair of broad shoulders have blinded you to all else. Weigh them against what I now tell you, miss. Marry him and you will never inherit a penny from me. I so informed him this morning, but evidently he hopes I can be wheedled by you into a change of mind. No chance of that! If he wants a penniless orphan, then he will marry you. Tell him that. See how eager that makes him for wedding bells."

"It doesn't matter to him, and it doesn't matter to me!" I felt my chin trembling as it had when I was a child. "I hoped very much for your blessing, however grudging. But I see now that I'll have to marry without it. And I will!"

As I turned to leave his shrill voice commanded, "You will not! I will not be defied!"

A glance over my shoulder showed a face radiating such anger that I quickened my pace, almost running to the staircase. I was halfway down when I heard him just behind me. As I reached the second floor, his heavy hand fell on my shoulder. I opened my mouth to scream, but his other hand clamped itself over my lips. Roughly, he tugged and blundered me across the carpet to the door of my room and pushed me inside. I was so numb with shock that my knees buckled and I fell to the floor. As I did, I heard the key turn in the lock, the scrape as it was removed. Still I stood, ran to the door, tried to open it. Yes, locked in! Locked in like a bad child, the bad child I had never, never been. I felt tears running down my face as I beat with my fist on the door. "Let me out!" Silence answered. With my ear pressed to the crack of the door I could hear the shrill sound of his voice downstairs, and Leo's deep one, but I could not make out their words.

I groped my way to the lamp by the bed, found the box of matches and lit it. By its glow I looked longingly at the window that overlooked the rear garden. But even if I succeeded in letting myself down by the device of two bedsheets tied together, where would I go? I lay down on my bed, fully clothed, and pictured the scene below. I imagined my guardian ordering Leo from the house, then excoriating my aunt for having condoned my infatuation. An hour passed, and with it the wild hope that Leo would rescue me by means of a stepladder. There was a soft tapping at my door; I ran to it and heard my aunt's voice whisper that I was to go to sleep, that all would be well. Sadly, I undressed and crept into bed, wondering what the morning would bring, and how long I was to remain my uncle's prisoner.

It was nine in the morning when the door was opened. My aunt rushed in, behind her a short man in a leather cap—the locksmith Leo had hired, she told me. "We must pack in a hurry. Leo is waiting downstairs. A packet ship for Philadelphia leaves the pier in less than three hours."

I put on my clothes in such haste I scarcely had time to feel excited. By that time Bridget and Annie and Melonia had brought in from my aunt's room the Saratoga trunk she had bought when she hoped to go to Greece. Quickly yet calmly my aunt sorted my clothes, discarding several old dresses, while I decided which other possessions I could not part with.

There was a knock at the door; the driver of the coach Leo had hired stood there to take my trunk downstairs. A few more items were added and then the lid was slammed shut. The sound reminded me of unbelievable reality: I was leaving forever the room that had been mine for as long as I could remember.

The trunk departed between the coachman and Annie; my aunt had also vanished, so I stood and looked around at the flowered walls, the bed with its dark spool bedposts, the washstand with its marble top where long ago I had stood on a footstool to wash my face, the table where I had done my lessons, the window from which I had watched the smoke and flames of the great fire. Tears filled my eyes: how abruptly my life had changed! Then: "Hurry," my aunt's voice commanded. I turned and saw her in her bonnet in the doorway. She held a package wrapped in white tissue, tied with a white bow. "Hurry!" she said, again, and I followed her down the front stairs wondering how in the world she had managed a wedding gift.

In the lower hall Leo was looking up just as he had the night I first saw him, and my heart turned over, stricken by love and by memory. Annie, standing by the trunk while the coachman mopped his brow on a big red kerchief, began to sob and Leo spoke to her kindly and took one end of the trunk to help the coachman carry it down the front steps. Aunt Liza and Annie and I stood in the doorway.

Two young toughs, black trousers very tight, high black hats pushed to the backs of their heads to show off their long curly hair, abandoned their poses of casual waiting at the foot of the steps of the house next door. They closed in on Leo who was at the bottom end of the trunk. One doubled his fist to hold it under Leo's nose. "Put it down, mister."

Leo set down his end of the trunk and the coachman at the upper end followed suit. As Leo stepped to one side, the trunk slid down the steps to come to rest at an angle, the lower edge against the pavement. At this moment the thug menacing Leo swung his arm back as if to hit him. The blow never landed, for I saw Leo's head dodge and his knee rise, and in the next instant the man who had tried to hit him was curled up on the paving, moaning. As his friend closed in there was a shrill whistle. The watchman who patrolled 10th Street ran toward us, whistle in his mouth, nightstick raised. From the other direction came a police officer, the morning sun glinting on his large copper badge. Thus discouraged, the second thug turned and ran across 10th Street, pell-mell. "Was he tryin' to steal your trunk, now?" The watchman asked Leo.

"Apparently," Leo said calmly. "Though what he would do with this young lady's dresses, I don't know."

"Sell 'em, sir. Sell 'em!"

"No such thing!" the injured thug gasped, as he carefully arose. "A gent, he hired me to keep his girl from running off, he did. Mr. Moss, it was."

"An absurd story," my aunt said. "I am Mrs. Moss. My husband would never do such a thing."

"You don't know your husband, lady," the thug blustered, and bent to retrieve his high black hat, brushing it with an elbow.

The police officer grasped the thug's sleeve. "Come along and tell it to the sergeant down to the City Jail."

They departed, the coachman and Leo got my trunk onto the coach, and I embraced Melonia and Bridget and Annie, all standing there looking woebegone. Leo was looking at his watch. "With a bit of luck, we may just make that ship before she sails!"

Aunt Liza came with us. I had not realized the traffic would be so thick, nor that an excavation for a new gas main would cause a detour. We got our tickets and got aboard, trunk and all, just as the whistle blew. My aunt and I embraced, and she gave me the white-wrapped package and wished me joy. Leo and I found a place by the shoreward rail whence I could see my aunt among others there waving off voyagers. The ship pulled away from the dock; her figure grew smaller and smaller and soon was no bigger than my doll Eliza which I had tucked at the last moment into my trunk.

I looked down at the white box, held it near my ear and gently shook it. It was the size and shape of a shoe box. "It's quite heavy," I told Leo. "I wonder what in the world it is."

"One way to find out is to open it."

He held it while I undid the white ribbon and took off the paper. It was a shoe box. A nest of crushed tissue paper filled it. In that nest lay the Stiegel rose glass, the lid nested separately. Reverently I took it out and held it up in the morning sunlight which turned the rose into a glowing jewel. I was so deeply moved that tears came to my eyes. Then I told Leo about the man who had fallen in love with glass in the Age of Iron.

Part Five

XXII

In the outer office of Haggis and Harris a young clerk on a high stool at a slanted desk scowled as he copied a brief with a scratchy pen. He told Elizabeth she would have to wait, pointing with his quill to a hard wooden bench. But at last the inner door opened. A fat man smoking a cigar emerged, chuckling; he sobered on seeing her, politely raised his beaver hat, paused to expectorate into the brass cuspidor, and left. "You can go in now," the clerk said.

Harris was long-faced, neatly and somberly dressed, with a small tuft of hair in each ear. On seeing Elizabeth he rose behind his desk to bow her to a chair facing it. "Mrs. Moss, is it not? With what problem may I aid you?"

"I wish to divorce my husband." The words sounded remarkable, and would have even without his stare of astonishment.

"Divorce?" His hands began at once to tidy the documents spread out on his desk. Papers arranged to his satisfaction, he leaned back and placed the tips of his fingers together so that Elizabeth thought of the game: "This is the church, this is the steeple . . ." He tipped his long head to one side and offered a pale smile. "You are not the first lady to express such a desire."

"Is that intended to put me at my ease?" She bit her

lip; she had not meant to sound so pert.

He removed his smile. "Why do you wish to take this drastic step?"

"Any affection which once existed between my husband and me has long since vanished. We share the same roof but that is all."

He shook his head. "Incompatibility is adequate grounds for divorce in only one state I know of: Vermont. In New York it is insufficient as a complaint. This I am inclined to regard as fortunate. Incompatibility in some degree seems to be almost as common as marriage itself, and must be borne with patience, I fear." His smile had returned, a tolerant one.

"What about adultery?" She felt a blush burn on her neck and face. Would her face tell him she was guilty too?

He leaned forward in a confidential way. "You are a mature lady, Mrs. Moss, and you strike me as a quite intelligent one. No intelligent female divorces an otherwise satisfactory husband for adultery. I am aware that such a liaison must be most disturbing to a lady of quality such as yourself, but I assure you that the chagrin you now suffer can be counted on to pass."

"I am not suffering chagrin. I am offering you the grounds you need to get me a divorce."

He leaned far back, and again formed a church steeple with his fingers. "Have you made due allowance for the fact that men are so fashioned by nature as to be prone to passionate impulses the fair sex is spared?"

"Is adultery sufficient grounds for divorce in the state of New York?"

"It is. However, the way in which women of your class as well as those of far lower social standing deal with a husband's adultery is to ignore it. The illicit liaison often peters out and things settle down as before. But a woman who divorces for this cause faces contempt and ridicule."

"How soon can I obtain a divorce on those grounds?"

His hands parted; the church was razed. With a sour look he asked, "With whom did the alleged adultery occur? A prostitute?"

"I guess she might be called that."

He leaned forward over his desk, the tufts in his ears alert. "Did you happen to catch them *in flagrante delicto?* This is, in the act?"

"No."

"In that case, where is your proof?"

"She confessed the affair to me in person."

"But were there any witnesses to the actual liaison with your husband?"

She shook her head. He seemed fond of the word "liaison."

"No witnesses? Only the word of a doxy? Inadequate, in my opinion. Her mere allegation is not worth—if you will pardon the expression—a coon's hoot in Hades, even if she could be prevailed upon to testify against her client, which I doubt. That is, if your husband should deny said allegation—which we can assume he will."

"But why would any woman admit to such a thing if it weren't true?"

"Can anyone hope to understand the mentalities of these abandoned creatures? I assure you that among the lower order of humans false accusations are far from uncommon."

His cheerfulness more than his words enraged her. "Mr. Harris! Do you have any idea how difficult this is for me? How hard it is to speak against the man with

319

whom I have spent more than half my life? Do you think I would be making this allegation if I did not believe it?"

"I am sure you do. But mere belief on anyone's part, be he the President of this republic, is, under law, totally inadequate without the firm support of evidence." His eyes had become vague; one hand reached out toward a pile of documents at which he stole a quick glance. It was clear that more important matters now claimed his attention.

She stood up. "You seem very facile at raising objections to the divorce I am bound to get!"

He also rose—a short man who sat tall. He spoke with deep sincerity. "If so, that is because I do not want you to go through the agony and notoriety attendant on this most unusual legal procedure only to fail in the end. You have no witnesses, no proof, no case! But even if you did, divorce is so rare a solution for marital difficulties, and I include gross physical cruelty, arrant neglect to provide, drunkenness, and other matters I shrink from mentioning out of respect for the delicacy of your feelings."

She leaned toward him, her voice angry. "The long and short of it is that you do not wish to take my case. Isn't that it?"

His mouth soured, corners turned down. "Without your offering any proof *of*, or reliable witness *to* your unsavory allegation and therefore facing the strong chance of losing the case in the event that your husband contests your charges—yes, I fear that is my position. But believe me when I say that I am also considering your future welfare. Do not, in a fit of anger at your husband, turn yourself into a disgraced woman, a pariah doomed to live beyond the pale of decent society!"

"I consider it a greater disgrace to ignore the truth I

know and live a lie." How righteous she sounded!

"Yet thousands of women are doing just that, as we speak."

"Then the society which demands such sacrifice of principle is evil and corrupt!"

"But we cannot change the society in which we must live, can we?"

"Not by conforming to its unjust demands, sir!"

His eyes widened; he looked delighted. "Ah, I think I begin to see the light! These suffragists have infected you with their wild theories. What a pity! I assure you, Mrs. Moss that before females can divorce without paying a stern price in shame, we will see them voting and have a Catholic in the White House!"

When Elizabeth reached the street she was shaken with anger and disappointment. These emotions melted into uneasy doubt of Tom, who had spoken so airily of a swift divorce. Yet at the same time she yearned for the comfort of his reassurance that in Harris she had encountered an unusual lawyer, a man whose sympathy did not extend to ladies of quality who wished to sever marital ties. Feeling ghostly in the afternoon sunlight, she walked to the street corner to wait for an omnibus or coach. All the passersby seemed to be hurrying toward pleasant destinations; a messenger boy, letter in hand, ran past. She turned and hurried back to the building she had just left, and where she had noted the sign of one of the city's messenger services when she entered earlier. The note to Tom she penned at the counter was brief. "The lawyer refuses to take my case. What now? I shall await your answer at home. E."

The narrow facade of the house on 10th Street had a look of prim solidity, and would survive the rebellion of a wife who challenged the sanctity of marriage.

She remembered the first time she had come up these steps as a bride of sixteen. A slow anger began to uncoil. Into her mind leaped the image of the banner of the rebel colonists, the sinuous snake: "Don't tread on me!"

The door was flung open. Isaiah stood there, glaring at her from icy eyes. He was hatted for the street, gold-headed cane in hand. He raised it in one fist as if to strike her, but lowered it. "I know everything. You connived with that Southern scoundrel. You released Jane Anne. My wishes meant nothing to you, nothing! Where is she?"

"On her way to Philadelphia. She will stay with my mother and marry Leo there. All you can do is accept it with grace and wish them well." She entered the hall. The faint smell of roast mutton greeted her.

"Never! I knew him for what he was the first time I set eyes on him, staring at her as if she were some slut!"

"And of sluts you should know!" The coiled serpent had struck of its own volition.

His cheeks flamed from jowls to eyeballs. "I fail to take your meaning."

"I mean Imogene Fisher."

The flush ebbed. He shrugged. "I deny knowing any such woman." Now he was quite calm, chest puffed out. She remembered Harris saying that the word of a prostitute would not be taken against the denial of a man like Isaiah. "What vile lies have you listened to?"

"I have listened to Imogene herself."

His calm proved insubstantial: he stared. He bluffed: "Indeed? I have no notion why she would traduce me in this way unless I piqued her vanity by refusing her solicitation one night at City Hotel after I left my clubroom there. 'Hell hath no fury,' et cetera. It astounds me that you would give credence to such vile rubbish."

"I do not intend to be a complaisant wife."

"Nor am I a complaisant husband! I have just been told by George Mason that you were entertained in public by Tom O'Casey. At Grenell's, no less, where all the best people still go." Isaiah pointed his cane at her. "I have lived long enough, madame, to know that secret sin begets suspicion of sin in others. A chaste woman would not have believed a harlot's lies. And if I considered that Irishman worthy to duel with a gentleman I would post him in every newspaper in this city!"

"We're not living in the eighteenth century. Dueling's illegal, and you know it." But the killer grandfather stared from his pale eyes.

"No, madame, this is the nineteenth. None of your Lady Teasles, your flirtations behind French screens, with female impropriety a source of amusement! A lady is expected to act like one. The coronation of Queen Victoria was a boon to this country as well as her own. In less than ten years she has set a high moral tone I can only applaud." He made a gesture of consulting his pocket watch. "Tonight I intend to sup at my club. You will discourage further attentions from the Irishman or suffer my extreme displeasure. To me, marriage is sacred. I intend that ours shall endure." He nodded at her imperiously and strutted ponderously out.

Without Jane Anne, the house felt strange, silent and oppressive as a tomb. The voice of the maid startled her. Annie stood outside the dining room carrying the big tray used to clear the table. "Will you be wanting your dinner now, ma'am?" Elizabeth moved to the dining-room door, looked at the half-consumed roast leg of mutton. For all

323

his outrage, Isaiah had eaten voraciously. The day's excitement and disappointment abruptly ebbed, leaving her stranded and without volition. She ascended the stairs to her room, and with each step the house seemed to assert an authority equal to Isaiah's. Could she really escape?

As she reached the top of the stairs Melonia came out of Jane Anne's room. She started to Elizabeth, then paused, pointing back. Her white pleated maid's cap was slightly askew, which exaggerated her troubled look, the round brown eyes. "Do you want I should tidy up in there?"

"Didn't you do that after we left this morning, as I asked?"

"Yes ma'am. But—" She shook her head. "I just can't hardly believe he'd do a thing like this."

Elizabeth went to her side, saw the form Isaiah's anger had taken. At the foot of the bed was a tangled heap of what had been dresses, now ripped apart, topped by a smashed bonnet. Scattered about were the torn pages of childhood books, dismembered dolls. A small bisque hand and wrist lay by itself, tiny palm upward. Near it a cotillion program bore the dark imprint of a boot heel.

She turned to Melonia. "He did this and then went down and ate half a leg of mutton?"

Solemnly, Melonia nodded. "Always was a man of hearty appetite. Yes, ma'am." She went to the heap, shook her head. "All this seems fit for is to get bundled up for the rag and bone man." She knelt, picked up the doll's hand, and looked up at Elizabeth. In the sunny room her face was full of fear, eyes staring. "The devil took him over, body and soul."

The cotillion program, solidly filled with young men's

penciled names and bearing now the mark of Isaiah's heel mesmerized Elizabeth for a long moment, and seemed to epitomize his possessiveness, his hatred of those rivals. "As soon as you finish here, will you ask Annie to help you with my trunk? The old one in the box room. Bring it into my room, please." A doll's hand, a dance program, some torn cast-off clothing—what small things really to weigh so heavy in the balance! And yet, she thought, one drop of blood can convict a murderer.

First she sorted her books and papers, packed those she would keep, then opened her wardrobe and began to select and fold clothing. As she did a parade of past dresses went through her mind: the high-waisted, slim-skirted one she had worn to the regatta on the Hudson when the Erie Canal was opened; the white one bought for the festivities in Washington Square Park on Independence Day in 1826, her country's fiftieth anniversary; the amber silk ballgown; and the rose silk. They seemed now like costumes in an endless pageant: The Faithful Wife of a man of substance had been her role. But the wife was no longer faithful and the man of substance had feet and other parts of clay and the time at last had come to end it.

There was a knock at the door. Annie's voice, subdued by the day's upheavals, said that Mr. O'Casey was waiting in the parlor. Elizabeth thanked her, then rushed to the mirror to hurriedly straighten her hair. The pleasure that filled her was tinged with a vague anxiety. Isaiah had said he would sup at his club. That would be normal on a Monday. But a strange Isaiah had been revealed to her today. She ran down the stairs to Tom, recalling Isaiah's threat about a duel, remembering his grandfather's set of pistols in a case lined with worn red velvet. She closed the parlor door after her. "I don't think we should talk here, Tom."

With an oblivious smile he strode to her and folded her in his arms. A long, sweet kiss reminded her that a happy future lay ahead. "You really did it! You saw a lawyer at last!"

"Jane Anne and Leo are in Philadelphia to get married. They left this morning. I went straight to Mr. Harris from the packet boat."

"You should have come straight to me instead, because I have a lawyer I like and trust. Mr. Jeremiah Ould, in the Lorimer Building on Broadway. I talked to him right after I got your message today. He expects you in the morning at nine. I'll have Harry take you there."

"Harris seemed very positive that no prostitute would testify. And wouldn't be believed anyhow against the word of a man like Isaiah."

"Imogene Fisher may prove the exception. I'll go down to City Hotel and try to persuade her. I'll go tonight."

The parlor door opened. Isaiah rushed in, finger pointing at Tom. "Caught you, O'Casey! Caught you both! Explain yourself, sir, and why you are here alone with my wife!"

"Why, sir, it is because no one else was present until you arrived."

"No Irish insolence. You know what I mean. Be careful, I warn you, not to pile on the straw which breaks my back!"

"Then you see yourself as a camel, sir?" Tom asked with apparent wonder.

Elizabeth was at first too startled to speak, but found her voice. "Stop this bickering, I beg of you both. I have had two difficult days. I refuse to condone your uncivil behavior."

Isaiah lowered his voice slightly. "You cannot make a joke out of it, O'Casey. I am aware, from one source and another, of your attentions to my wife. I resent them, sir, utterly. And I may well decide to post you, to seek redress, unless you agree here and now to desist."

"If you did challenge me, I would have the choice of weapons, wouldn't I?"

"You would."

"What would you say to shillelaghs? At ten paces?"

Fury burst from Isaiah along with a spray of spittle. "You choose to mock me? Stupid of you! Even if no duel ever takes place, I can harm your reputation by what I say of it when I post you, and you will find it hard to laugh that away, sir!"

"You'll also make a laughingstock of yourself. Duels belong in the last century. An antiquated custom."

A cunning look glinted from Isaiah's cold eyes as he smirked. "But not the custom of posting. Scarcely a month goes by without at least one such notice in some newspaper."

"You have no regard for your wife's good name, then?"

"My regard for it depends on her behavior and yours."

"Then post me and be damned. Not you or any man can dictate my behavior."

"Leave my house this instant, sir!"

A few tense seconds later Isaiah sputtered again, "You did not hear me?"

Tom, with elaborate scorn, turned his back on Isaiah to face Elizabeth. It seemed to her that he was almost enjoying the clash. "Unless you want me to stay, I will go about the business we spoke of just before Moss came in."

She had for a moment forgotten his plan to visit Imogene. "Go, by all means."

He turned to face Isaiah. "As your enemy I should warn you that I make a bad one, sir—worse than you yet know."

Isaiah watched him go, then turned on Elizabeth. Fury had left his face. Had he already begun to regret his threat? "You will obey me, madame. You will see no more of that fellow. If I find you together again or hear of it I will post him. You will be tarred with that same brush."

"What a fool you'll look if he does insist on shille-laghs!"

"Do you see the position you've placed me in?"

Her heart felt cold, dwindled. She tried to hide anxiety as she walked past him toward the hall stairs. From the bulge of his body she felt his animus vibrate. Elizabeth did not feel any ease until she was in her own room with the door locked behind her. The walls and furniture looked strange to her, as if she had not seen them in a long time. She thought of all the other rooms she had redeemed from dullness, from the dismal imprint of Isaiah's mother, that unhappy woman. But it was still his house. Endowed with the name and status of wife she had been no more than a tenant here, after all. It suddenly seemed unbelievable that she had stayed so long.

Elizabeth crept into bed aware at last of the toll the day had taken. The last thing she saw before she turned off the lamp by the bed was the rounded lid of the trunk, the same one which had come into the house when she had entered as a bride.

In a dream she went to the bank to withdraw her savings so as to leave the city. A banker who looked like the lawyer Harris told her marriage was a sacred institution. He removed a tuft of hair from one ear and reached out to attach it to her forehead. This was to mark Elizabeth Moss as a wife who had attempted escape.

The slow plodding of a horse, the milkman's or the iceman's, woke Elizabeth to a sense of urgency. This was the day that would find her immediate future decided. Would Imogene Fisher agree to be a witness? And would Mr. Ould take her case? She was waiting on the front steps when Tom's cabriolet rolled grandly up to the curb. The cheerful coachman secured the reins and leaped down to open the carriage door for her, politely touching his small-brimmed black hat with its jaunty cockade. "And a foine good morning to you, ma'am." Smiling like a jack-o-lantern, he held out a sealed envelope.

"Thank you, Harry." Elizabeth took the letter, got in. Her hands were shaky as she unsealed the flap.

Good news, my love! Imogene will be your witness. And it did not take any great persuasion on my part, even when I explained I could not offer her another goldpiece for this kindness as that could be construed as a bribe.

The champagne I brought may have helped, but Isaiah Moss did us a great favor in treating her as a common doxy after he felt her dependent on his financial favors. For Imogene does not regard herself as such, but rather as a fortune teller whom men cannot resist.

She no longer cares about her sister's opinion, in short.

I am eager to know the outcome of your interview with Mr. Ould. I will be at the Ferris mansion all afternoon.

Love—much love,
Tom

At the Lorimer Building there was no spot for the carriage to wait, of course, but Harry said he would return in an hour, circling the block if necessary. She went up the gray marble stairs to the lawyer's second floor office feeling free and daring, a woman taking her first steps toward changing her own destiny.

No clerk was in the outer office, so she knocked at the door of the inner; a sharp voice told her to enter. Jeremiah Ould stood at the window looking out. As he turned to greet her he shifted a wad of tobacco to one cheek where it remained immobile, a slight bulge. He was a small, wiry man of perhaps forty-five with ginger hair, a wide mouth with a curly grin, and alert eyes the color of raisins. Two comfortable horsehair armchairs faced his desk, which was not imposing. "Sit down and tell me who you are and why you're here." He sat behind his desk but leaned toward her, all attention, eyes taking in details of her appearance to his evident satisfaction.

"I'm Elizabeth Moss. I want a divorce."

"Why? Adultery? Wife-beating? Non-support? Drunkenness? He likes little boys? General philandering? Tell me why you want to fly in the face of custom, common morality, all the clergymen, and make your mother cry?"

"I've already heard a lecture on the perils of divorce."

"You won't get one from me." He leaned toward her, his sharp face waiflike. "I'm a rare bird, Mrs. Moss. A man with a particular sympathy for the plight of women. Born and raised on a rock-scrabble New England farm, all

330

work, no play. A hard-souled father with callused hands and a mind like an ingrown toenail. Mother bore seven children, spun, wove, baked, and churned the butter. Died at forty-five, plumb worn out. But she had made time to teach me to read and write and figure, and at last she cozened and badgered my father to let me apprentice myself as clerk to her brother, a lawyer in the nearest town of any size." He smiled shyly. "I was her favorite, you see. She wanted me to have a better life than the one I was destined for. It was after she died that I discovered my peculiar sympathy for women in general and unhappy wives in particular. I believe in the vote for women, in divorce, and in contraception. I know the story of my life doesn't interest you greatly, but I want you to know that in me you have found a champion."

"And I need one. I am told that a husband's adultery, that is with a woman who shares her favors among more than one man, is not a very sound complaint."

"You put it very daintily—a prostitute? Your counterpart?"

"Counterpart? I don't understand."

"I've made a study of the effect of all the lies people learn to believe about being male or female in this time and place. It's come to the point where quite a few men regard their wives as pure angels, and so turn their own natural impulses elsewhere except for the meager purpose of procreation. Besmirch an angel? Never! Finds a low woman to cavort with! Some poor servant girl or a whore. Did you know there are more prostitutes than Methodists in New York? That's a matter of statistics. I'd say more than Methodists and Episcopalians together. So we can say that this whore is your counterpart, which suggests that the intimate side of your married life has not been rapturous."

"You put it well."

"How did you find out about the doxy?"

"Mr. O'Casey learned of the affair and revealed it to me. She then affirmed it herself."

"Well, well! Unusual."

"She has also told him she will act as my witness."

"Rarer and rarer!" He eyed her. "A pretty woman like you, I'd guess there's a suitor in the offing. Am I right?"

She felt herself blushing. "Yes."

"Tom O'Casey?"

"We were childhood sweethearts."

"Don't turn red for me. I like the fellow. But you have to be very circumspect. If Moss gets wind of it, you'll end up in the soup."

"He already has got wind of it."

"How strong is the breeze? A typhoon? A gale?"

"Merely that we supped together recently at Grennell's."

"Pooh! A zephyr. Your husband is I. Moss, the tobacconist?"

"Yes."

"Good. You may come out of this with more than the clothes you stand in." He seized a pen. "Give me his business address, his bank, your home address, and the prostitute's name and address."

She complied, he scribbled. "But all I want is eighteen hundred dollars he promised to repay me eight years ago. And, of course, the money banked in my pen name."

"How much is that?"

"About four thousand dollars."

"Get it out. Goldpieces. Don't hide 'em around the house. Stash 'em with a loyal friend. When he learns you're divorcing him his first urge will be to cripple you financially." He leaned forward over clasped hands. "Now I have a question: why is that all you want?"

"Years of my life are not for sale."

"Noble. Foolish, too. I forgot an important question: Any children still at home?"

"No."

"Any children at all?"

"One foster daughter, gone."

"Foster daughter, eh? I begin to see the light. Do you blame yourself?"

"The flaw is mine, yes."

"So, having given the man no offspring, you feel entitled to no settlement, is that it?"

He had startled her. "Perhaps. But all I want is to be free."

"Your emotional bias will not prevent me from acting in your behalf." He stood up. "I'll have the complaint drawn up tomorrow when you can stop by and sign it. As soon as I get a property agreement I'll file your affidavit."

"Don't I owe you a retainer?"

He grinned. "I make the naughty boys pay me and court costs."

"How soon will my hearing take place?"

"Can't say now; that depends on the court calendar. I may decide on a circuit judge. But leave all that to me."

"Can I move out? I'm already packed, or nearly so."

"Absolutely not! Don't budge a step until I give the word. If you do he could claim desertion. Stay put. And don't whisper a word of your divorce to any good friend whatsoever; they talk. I want to take him by surprise." He walked beside her to the door. "And be sure to remember this Imogene Fisher in your prayers. A rare doxy!"

Later, the withdrawal of her money in gold took longer than she had imagined possible, but at last she held a heavy chamois bag containing forty hundred-dollar goldpieces. She wedged it into her reticule, grateful that Tom's carriage would offer safety from thugs and pickpockets. At the Pierpont's she dismissed and thanked Harry.

Dolly Pierpont was astounded when Elizabeth asked her to hide a bag of goldpieces. "But why?"

"Isaiah and I have had a bad row. I don't want him to rob me."

"Oh, dear, it sounds so awful, put like that! And it's a dreadful responsibility, dear. What if the house caught on fire? The only place I seem to be able to think of is my sewing stand. It has a little lock, because the children used to get into my embroidery thread and tangle the skeins all up." Upstairs in the bedroom she shared with her husband she pointed to the small rosewood stand under the window. "It doesn't look much like a treasure chest, does it?" From a silver-topped jar on the highboy she took a key, unlocked the lid, lifted out a wooden tray full of spools, and hid the chamois bag below an embroidery hoop. "There! You keep the key. Oh, Elizabeth, you're so strong-minded, you and your suffragist friends! But for women with husbands we can cozen into pampering us, principles like owning our own property don't really signify." Her sparkling dark eyes, fans of fine lines at the corners, peered into Elizabeth's. "There's a great deal you're not telling me, isn't there, dear?"

"But you'll be the first I do tell." She chafed at the lawyer's caution. Dolly was her true friend, surely to be trusted.

"Won't you even hint at what has you so angry

at Isaiah?"

"I've lost all faith in him. He's not as I thought."

Dolly's face grew shrewd. "A doxy?"

"How did you know that?"

"Men, dear, are men. Because you're my friend, I'll tell you a secret. A few years ago I received an anonymous message, evidently from someone with a grudge against Robert, telling me he had taken up with one of those ladies of the night. Well, my dear, I betook myself to A.T. Stewart's and bought a very costly new gown and a pair of high-heeled shoes which were just then coming into style, and I wore the dress and shoes that night when he came home to supper. I said I wanted to look as well to him as any other lady in town. He had the grace to look considerably uneasy. Take a leaf from my book. And get yourself one of those terribly expensive cashmere shawls from France; I tried one and it's like wearing a cloud. The best can cost as much as five hundred dollars!"

"I'm afraid that wouldn't solve my problem."

"Is it Tom O'Casey again? I'd be careful about trusting him too far. I mean, he's enjoyed bachelorhood for a long time, hasn't he? Sighing his heart out for you now and then to be sure. But single still. Such a man's apt to take you right up to the altar, then run like a hare. Better a plain house built on a rock than a pretty tent pitched on sliding sand."

"Sometimes a house can turn out to have been built on sand, Dolly, and then it's bound to fall."

"Horrors! That makes me think of Poe, 'The Fall of the House of Usher.' I can't say I entirely understand it, but it did give me the shivers. Poe is quite far gone in drink, I hear. Absinthe." She laughed. "Oh, dear, it was you who told me that. I'm such a scatterbrain. Tom O'Casey hasn't asked you to invest that money your father left you in his construction company, has he?"

"Certainly not! Haven't you seen the grand mansion he's built for Cornelius Ferris?"

"I must go up and have a look at it one day. Does it mean that Tom is getting rich? Robert pretends to believe he eats boiled potatoes and points to a bit of meat under glass the way they say poor Irish families do." Dolly laughed lightly. "But my husband would not be the only man who's jealous of that handsome, lucky bachelor!"

"You won't tell Robert about my goldpieces, will you? Or anything else we've talked about today?"

Dolly looked shocked. "Elizabeth, you're my dearest friend, and there are a number of things I don't tell Robert, much as I love him."

As they went downstairs the rest of the day yawned ahead. Would Isaiah choose to dine at home again today? She remembered yesterday's mutton leg and knew she could not bring herself to dine with her husband; with surprise it occurred to her that they had eaten their very last meal together. She turned to Dolly. "Would it be imposing if I asked you to invite me to dinner?"

"Indeed not. We still dine at three, though Robert has lately been urging four; the European dinner hour, you know. He thinks it more stylish. I'll eventually give in, but by then he'll know it's a great concession on my part." She smiled charmingly.

In the cozy downstairs sitting room the two youngest Pierpont children made a pleasing picture: a boy of nine did lessons at the round center table while in the opposite chair a girl of four in a pink puff-sleeved dress and lacy pantelettes carefully dressed her doll, a handsome bisque-headed one like Eliza. "They've all been such a joy to me," Dolly said, fondly, at which point the boy, with no warning, reached over to thump his sister on the head. "She's muttering to that doll!" he explained as his mother scolded. "How can a fellow think of sums with all that muttering going on?"

It was nearly three when Robert Pierpont arrived home, an evening paper tucked under his arm. After a warm greeting to Elizabeth, a kiss for his wife, a tousle of his son's head, and a hug for the little girl, he excused himself and sat in a large, comfortable armchair to read the news, a rosy, handsome man in the bosom of his family. "Horrible!" he suddenly whispered, shaking his head.

"What's horrible?" Dolly asked, looking up from her embroidery hoop.

With a significant glance at the children, he shook his head, folded the paper and set it on the table beside his chair just as the maid announced dinner. After the meal he left for his office, and Dolly and Elizabeth returned to the sitting room. Dolly pounced on the paper he had left behind and opened it. "Oh, it *is* horrible!" She held up the page so Elizabeth could see the headline: PROSTI-TUTE MURDERED.

Elizabeth rushed to Dolly's side. Her heart closed like a fist at the first words she saw.

Imogene Fisher, 24, was found dead on the floor of her room at City Hotel at eight this morning by a hotel employee. The deceased woman had been brutally assaulted with a heavy, blunt object which caused severe wounds to the head which had bled profusely.

"Poor Imogene!" Dolly was saying. "I always thought

337

her quite sweet. And now it turns out that while she served the ladies with a trip or a dark stranger, she was serving the gentlemen something else altogether!"

The newsprint had blurred; Elizabeth blinked her eyes to clear them.

Miss Fisher was last seen alive at ten the night before by Artie Graves, 16, a hotel waiter who performs room service. At a quarter past nine, he told the police, Miss Fisher asked him to bring her a dish of fried oysters for her supper and a bottle of wine. When he delivered them at ten she seemed in good spirits. The gentleman who arrived at her door at 9:15 had by then left, according to Graves, for she was alone.

Albert London, the police detective in charge of the case, is attempting to discover who visited her after the hour of ten.

The victim's profession, as well as the location of the crime, are reminiscent of the Robinson-Jewett murder of eight years past. A young and pretty prostitute, Jewett, was found axed to death in her hotel bed, the bedclothes having been set afire in an apparent attempt to conceal the fact of murder. The bloodsoaked bedcover failed to burn, however.

Since the killer was so careless as to leave his cape behind, he was apprehended. He proved to be the scion of a wealthy family. The motive attributed to him arose from the fact that he had become engaged to a lovely young lady of quality whom Miss Jewett had threatened to inform of their affair out of jealousy.

Brought to trial, young Robinson was found innocent, to the surprise of many. His reputation damaged beyond hope, Robinson left the city, fleeing the sobriquet that dogged him: The Great Unhanged.

"Oh, these newspapers. One murder isn't enough. They have to serve us with two!" Dolly complained, reading avidly.

But as to any motive for the brutal slaying of Imogene Fisher, none is yet evident. Her grief-stricken sister, a widely respected psychic of this city, believes the crime to be the work of a madman.

"Why, Elizabeth! What's the matter with you? You're white as paper! Do you want me to get the smelling salts?"

Elizabeth shook her head, saw a pale porcelain face turn to her from a carriage window: "Your bad old husband got him a girl, and it was me."

She stood up.

"Where are you going?" Dolly demanded. "You look as if you might faint. I had no idea you liked the poor thing that much."

Elizabeth knew then that she was going to Tom at the Ferris mansion. The sudden crushing of their hopes was too much to be borne alone.

XXIII

The hired carriage halted with a slight jolt, and Elizabeth looked out at the austere neo-Grecian facade of the Ferris mansion, pale above its shadow that fell across the foreyard, enclosed now by a spiked iron fence. On the columned portico Brian Ryan stood facing the angular, dark-clad figure of Cornelius Ferris, the taller for a high silk hat.

Asking the coachman to wait, she descended and made her way toward them up the cement walk. "I am certain I told Mr. O'Casey I'd be here at four," Cornelius Ferris was saying, "to discuss the final placing of my statuary."

Elizabeth's heart sank. Where was Tom? Her calm voice said, "Good afternoon."

Seeing her, Cornelius Ferris removed his hat, inclined his tall body in an angular bow. "Mrs. Moss! What an unexpected pleasure!"

"Thank you. You have graced our city with a most handsome home, Mr. Ferris. Everyone speaks of its classical lines." The shock of Imogene's murder was quivering just below forced good manners. Where was Tom?

Ferris glanced with satisfaction at the Ionic column to his left. "Yes, I am immensely pleased. There remains the task of furnishing the interior in a commensurate manner." He turned to Brian Ryan, now also hatless, his red hair blazing in the sunlight. "There was also the matter of the plumber. Has *he* arrived?"

"That's just what delayed Mr. O'Casey, sir. He went to collect the fellow."

With a nod, Ferris turned to Elizabeth. "My home is not yet furnished, but would you care to see my statuary? It has only just arrived from Europe."

As she nodded, the scene became dreamlike. Ferris offered his arm to escort her up the marble steps. "I take it you found yourself overcome by curiosity?"

"As many have, I am sure."

"Yes, there have been hundreds of gapers, quite as if my sole purpose were to create a spectacle. But what is the use of inheriting a great deal of money if one does not use it with a certain degree of dash? *Noblesse oblige,* in a sense." He made a wide gesture. "Look!"

In the large marble-paved entrance hall stood one tall unopened wooden crate and one white marble statue, a life-sized female nude—her head turned to one side, chin shyly lowered, wrists chained. Ferris gazed at it with admiration. "She is an authentic replica of the Homer Powers statue I saw recently in London where it created a great sensation. Despite the absence of drapery the highest-ranking clergymen of England have declared her to be pure art. She is called 'The Greek Slave Girl.'"

Startled, Elizabeth knew that the sculptor must have been moved by the liberation of Greece from Turkish rule, and she felt a fleeting remorse for a task she had abandoned, her unfinished novel.

"In the unopened crate," Ferris was explaining, "I have an authentic copy of a Grecian youth by Praxiteles. My first intention was that they should stand in those niches formed in the wall at either side of the central staircase. But now I am beginning to doubt the wisdom of offering so much nudity to visitors as they enter. Were you at all offended, Mrs. Moss? Be frank."

"No." The very smooth breasts, arms and torso of the statue seemed less like nude flesh than like marble most cunningly worked; more erotic, somehow, were the delicate marble chains that manacled the wrists, suggesting utter helplessness: the helplessness of women in general? Had Powers meant that?

"The male statue wears a fig leaf, of course," Ferris said. "Although I must confess that I had the sculptor create one that is removable. In all other respects, though, it is an authentic replica."

Wondering how a replica could be authentic, Elizabeth nodded.

"But my bathrooms are what people are going to be talking about," Ferris continued, with pride. "There are two, one on the first floor, one on the second. Indoor plumbing! A bathtub, a hand basin, a—well, all with running water. You simply turn a faucet handle and, lo, water comes out of a spout! There is either hot water or cold, depending on which faucet you turn. I got the idea after I saw those eight famous indoor bathrooms at the Tremont Hotel in Boston. They are all on the first floor, though. My upstairs bathroom represents a *tour de force*." His eyes suddenly roved from her face. "Ah, there you are! I forgive your tardiness because of the delightful conversation I've had with Mrs. Moss."

She turned. Tom stood in the doorway. He bowed to her. "The Boston plumber failed us," he told Ferris. "The boat from Boston has come, but he was not on it."

"Blast that man!" Ferris turned to Elizabeth. "Permit

me to present my builder, Mr. O'Casey. Mr. O'Casey—
Mrs. Moss." Over their murmurs he said, "I am still torn
between placing my statues here in the atrium as first
planned, or banishing them to the ballroom. You haven't
yet seen the ballroom, Mrs. Moss, nor my bathroom. May
I offer a tour?" He offered his arm.

Upstairs, Elizabeth admired a copper bathtub with
lion-claw feet, a porcelain hand basin on thin brass legs
(the lidded oak commode being decently ignored). Downstairs, she nodded approval of a library paneled in dark
wood, an arboretum with glass skylight, the dining room,
and the vast drawing room, with pale plaster walls, a
white marble fireplace and an immense, gleaming
parquet floor. Ferris's voice echoed as he asked, "Do you
feel that my statues belong in here? What does your
feminine instinct say?"

Politely, she pondered a moment. "The size of this
room will tend to dwarf them, won't it? In the entrance
hall I believe they will look most impressive."

"One up for you, Tom!" Ferris turned to him with a
smile. "You said the same, I recall. One in each niche,
then." With a startled look he reached into his waistcoat
and extracted a gold watch. "Alas, Mrs. Moss, duty
beckons. I must offer my expertise in judging a number
of paintings as to which are worthy of the annual Art
Lottery. I wonder, would it be possible for you to join
me? Your excellent taste would make your opinion most
useful."

"Thank you, but another appointment forces me to
decline." She offered Ferris her hand and a farewell smile
with the feeling that it had been carved in marble along
with the pensive mouth of the Greek slave girl, visible
through the wide hall doorway. With a bow, Ferris left

her standing with Tom in the center of the vast room into which late sunlight fell from the tall west windows.

Tom turned a bleak face. "Imogene's dead. Murdered."

"I know."

"I can hardly believe it yet. When I saw her last night she was in the best of spirits. Told me she'd just ordered her favorite supper. Oysters. The boy who took the order was just leaving as I arrived. She was pleased to see the bottle of champagne I brought. Made a joke about it. What favor did I want of her this time? I told her. At first she was edgy about the idea of being a witness for you, but then she shrugged and said that it would do her heart good to see Moss get what he deserved. Spoke most kindly of you, how you were far above him. And who on God's earth bashed her skull in I can't imagine. Or why."

"What do we do now, Tom?"

"You saw Ould?"

"I did. I like him. But he made it clear that my hope of a divorce rested on Imogene Fisher's testimony."

"Yes. What evil luck we're having, my dear."

Quick footsteps sounded on marble. Brian Ryan came through the doorway toward them. "Sorry to interrupt, sir. But there's a couple of coppers outside, askin' for Tom O'Casey." He came to Tom's side and the three of them faced the entrance hall.

The two policemen entered the front door, then stopped abruptly to stare at the statue of the Greek slave girl. One whispered to the other, who laughed. Both turned and came into the drawing room. One was a small, wiry man in a shabby dark blue suit and a leather-visored cap, his round copper badge dangling from a narrow chest. The other wore a new dark-blue uniform with brass buttons, his badge gleaming above a sturdy abdomen. "Are you Mr. Thomas O'Casey?" he demanded of Tom, and then looked nervously around as his voice resounded against the pale walls.

"Yes. What is it you want?" Tom looked puzzled.

"I have to ask you to come with me, sir. Down to headquarters. For to answer a few questions."

"I'll be glad to answer them right here." He spoke calmly.

"Sorry, sir, but that's not how it works. It's Detective London what wants to see you, sir. About the Fisher girl's murder."

Shock struck Elizabeth like a blow from a fist.

"There's nothing I can tell you about that." Tom frowned.

"That may well be, sir. But it has to be settled down to police headquarters with Detective London."

"Fact is, we know you was in the dead woman's room last night." The small, wiry policeman had an enormous voice for his size; its reverberation seemed to please him. "So on account of that, Mr. London wants to find out if—" A nudge from his partner silenced him.

Tom's face showed only annoyance as he turned to Elizabeth. "I'd best do as they ask and get this over with. Shall I have Harry take you home?"

"I have a carriage waiting."

"Good. Then I won't have to go in an omnibus and these fellows can ride in style." With a nod at the two police officers, he strode toward the door and they fell in behind, both casting a last surreptitious glance at the marble nude.

Elizabeth found that she was very cold. She closed her eyes as if to blind herself to the truth: it was because of her that he had been in Imogene Fisher's room.

"Mrs. Moss?" It was Brian Ryan's voice. She opened her eyes, found him watching her with concern. "It knocked me a bit off my keel, too, seeing him took in like some pickpocket, and I can well imagine it was worse on a lady like yourself. But as for Mr. O'Casey bein' in that woman's room, don't give it a thought. He's a man that's friendly with all sorts and kinds of people, and was probably there to do her a good turn. He can explain that to the detective in a wag of a lamb's tail."

Explain? she thought. Explain that he went to City Hotel to ask Imogene to help his mistress get a divorce? "A good turn, yes. I'm sure you're right about that."

As she moved toward the hall, Ryan beside her, a short, portly man in a checkered vest and somewhat battered hat puffed in through the open front door. He carried a large, scarred black leather case. He stopped dead to stare at the slave girl, then turned quickly as he became aware of being watched. Removing his hat, he fanned his plump face. "I'm looking for Mr. Tom O'Casey. I'm here from Boston to get the bathrooms working."

The plumber had arrived at last.

Jeremiah Ould was at his desk, reading a newspaper; his eyes still on it, he rose as she entered. "It's a bad setback, I grant. But no reason for despair." He thrusted the paper toward her, finger pointing to a passage.

For the past two years the murdered prostitute found it expedient to keep an appointment book which contains the names of her numerous gentlemen visitors. It is now in the hands of the police department.

347

"I know a journalist with a sharp nose. Let's see if he can find out whether the name of Moss is anywhere on those pages!" He grinned. "'All is not lost, the inconquerable will, and courage never to submit nor yield!' Satan said that in *Paradise Lost,* poor devil, but it's a good attitude when the odds are against you. So be calm, Mrs. Moss, be confident. And stay put."

"That will be intolerable. My husband has threatened to post Mr. O'Casey. I got my money from the bank as you suggested, so I thought I might go to a quiet hotel or perhaps a boardinghouse."

He shrugged. "Why hire me if you intend to do as you please? I have said 'stay put' which means just that. Are you in physical danger from your husband?"

"No, I don't think that."

"Then think, please *think*. The minute you pack up and leave that house for good you are a sitting duck, a fish in a rainbarrel. Until I file your affidavit, Moss can claim desertion, as I said."

"What I really came here for is reassurance. Tom was arrested today. That is, taken in for questioning."

"Inevitable. Don't worry, there'll be quite a few gentlemen questioned before this is done and one may even be the man who killed her. Tom O'Casey is not that man. So just stay put, Mrs. Moss."

She stopped at a refectory for tea and at home went straight upstairs to her room. She had bought two evening papers. On page three a noted phrenologist described the shape of the slayer's head.

As J.F. Gall has demonstrated, each mental faculty has

its seat in a definite region of the brain, with a corresponding protruberance on the skull. That of the savage slayer of Imogene Fisher should be marked by a low forehead, an apelike brow ridge and a cranium very flat in the rear, evincing a lack of the philoprogenitive and philanthropic tendencies. A low-bridged nose is also likely, indicating a lack of idealism.

In the next column a journalist deplored the dead woman's life of sin, and the fact that death had foiled her possible redemption, according to her heart-broken sister, Adela Fisher, "famed psychic."

Unaware until recently of her younger sister's true situation, having accepted a tale of legitimate employment to explain her many absences, Adela Fisher has revealed that she had succeeded in persuading her fallen sister that they must leave New York, begin a life anew in another city, a course of action suggested to her by the voice of their dead father while she was in a trance at a seance.

There was a tap at the door and Melonia's voice called, "It's just me, Mrs. Moss. Can I come in a minute?"
"All right."
At first glance she might have been a well-groomed stranger, bonnet brim framing her face. As she came forward, light from the window glowed on the rose silk gown Elizabeth had given her.
"Why are you all dressed up, Melonia?"
"I's just leavin' for choir practice over to my church, ma'am."
"I hope you don't plan to come home alone."
"No, ma'am. Rafe'll walk me."

"Rafe?" She recalled then who Rafe was, a tall, serious, graying Negro whom she had encountered several months before in the kitchen after he had walked home with Melonia from church. "Ah, yes, Rafe."

Melonia's face was troubled, yet even so this shapely, well-fed woman of thirty-three was a far cry from the waiflike young slave girl who returned with her from Philadelphia. "I come in to tell you I'll be leavin' you soon."

"Leaving? Why?"

"I'se getting married, ma'am. To my Rafe."

"When?"

"Tomorrow."

"Tomorrow? And when do you plan to leave?"

Thick lids hid Melonia's eyes as she stared at the carpet. "Tomorrow."

"You're leaving with one day's notice after eighteen years? What do you know of this Rafe?"

"He's houseman at the Pollards' for near nine years now."

A name to reckon with, Pollard: money, social standing, and a large house in the best section of Fifth Avenue. "I see. Is the wedding to be at your church?"

"No, ma'am, just down to City Hall. I didn't wish no church weddin'. Just legal is enough."

"But why? Not all brides are young."

"I know, but this is how I decided."

"Has this Rafe provided for a home of any kind?"

"Not exactly."

"Well, that doesn't matter. You can stay on here until he does."

"After I's married, you mean?" Melonia shook her head. "No, Mrs. Moss, ma'am. I can't do that!" Her eyes

350

were wide with alarm.

"But where will you live?"

The lids hid the eyes again. "The Pollards are agreeable that I share his room there." The air of duplicity was now unmistakable.

Suddenly angered by disloyalty, Elizabeth found herself on her feet. "What you really mean is that you intend leaving me to work for the Pollards. Look at me! Isn't that it?"

Her upward glance was reluctant; her eyes, glazed with tears, roved the room, avoiding Elizabeth's. "I can't live here, not after I gets married."

Elizabeth took a step toward her. "Why are you crying?"

Melonia stood looking down at the floor; her voice was a whisper. "It began with Mr. Moss eight years back. He came up to my room late one night an' woke me an' made his wish clear. It got to be his habit, over the years . . ."

Elizabeth's brain whirled. "What do you mean? Are you saying he seduced you?"

The brown, alarmed eyes stared past Elizabeth. The whisper was now barely audible. "Yes, that's what he done."

Elizabeth saw her own hand gripping Melonia's forearm, flung it away. "Why didn't you ever tell me this?"

Melonia bent the rejected arm, clasped the place Elizabeth had gripped. Staring past her again she asked, "How did I dare? If you was angry, I'd be throwed out. If he found out I told you I'd be throwed out. Niggers, we can starve in this city. So all I could do was keep silent, an' do what he wanted, an' put it out of my mind."

The abject pose, the lowered eyes, the cradled arm seemed suddenly to conceal the terrible inner triumph of

351

the slave who has caused pain to one of the whites who ruled her life. Although Melonia's voice was pleading when she raised her eyes and looked into Elizabeth's, the words seemed false. "I's sure, Mrs. Moss, you can find it in your heart to forgive a poor colored girl who never meant you no harm." She backed slowly toward the door, then turned and ran out.

Elizabeth's shaking began inside, a fine tremor. Then she was sucked down into a vortex, her thoughts and feelings all whirling around what Isaiah had done to Melonia. He seemed to be two men, the one she had thought she knew, and the one unknown until now. Why had a man who lauded purity chosen to sleep with a prostitute? Why had a man who regarded Negroes as an inferior breed made one his backstairs mistress over many years? Counterparts! Those hidden women were balanced by the wife duly involved with her charities, and by the young ward he thought too fine for any man. They had been accessories of the man he showed to the daylight world: solid citizen, Whig of Whigs, churchgoer, patriot. But when did Isaiah split into two men? How did the daylight man condone the other one? Playing the secret satyr, he must have felt deep self-contempt. Yet from the first he had made it clear that delicacy, not ardor, was what he desired of his wife. The purity of an adolescent girl with strict parents had allured him as strongly as a ripe seductress drew to her men less strange. For the first time his fondness for his young ward took on a sinister cast.

Elizabeth found herself pacing the room, arms hugging her body as if a blizzard blew in through the open window, and she knew she was frightened of both the men her husband had suddenly become. The shuffle of hooves in the street below and the squeak of a carriage brake sent her running to the window. Not Tom's. She shut the window and turned. The packed trunk in the corner by the hall door mocked her. Jane Anne was gone, Melonia would soon be, but she was still a prisoner here, tamely awaiting the return of her jailer, her lawful husband.

The urge to leave was stronger than a lawyer's shrewd advice, stronger than caution. She did not yet know where she was going as she ran down the stairs in a state close to panic, and out into the early night. . . .

A woman alone was not in great danger of being accosted on this street, yet she was glad to see the night watchman only a block away. He accompanied her to Broadway where she mounted a nearly empty omnibus headed downtown. At a corner near Five Points, below the street lamp she glimpsed two women waiting in the pools of shadow cast by their full skirts: ladies of the night. She knew now where she was going.

Wary eyes alert for a night watchman she hurried as fast as decorum permitted to the little cul-de-sac and the small house where Tom lived. Her heart was pounding as she got out of her reticule the key he had given her, turned the lock, stepped into the dark hallway. "Tom?" As she called she knew he was not there. Groping like a blind woman she made her way into the parlor and to the drop-leaf table against the rear wall where, she remembered, was an oil lamp. She found the box of matches beside it. Her hand shook a little as she held the flame to the wick.

It was a plain room: horsehair settee and the Windsor chairs which the affluent had banished to kitchens and servants' rooms. Like the perilous walk from the omnibus, it reminded her that a secure existence she had taken for granted was all but gone. She felt cold and rather sad. Kindling and coal were ready in the grate. She kneeled on the hearthrug to light a fire, eager for the cheeriness of flames as much as for their warmth. She heard the front door open, felt a gust of cool air. "Good God! What are you doing here?" Tom cried.

Elizabeth stood and faced him. "Not a very warm greeting!"

"Forgive me. I was startled to see you. I'd been trying to decide the best way to get a message to you, by Harry or a regular messenger boy." He had walked toward her as he spoke and now took her in his arms. "You couldn't have done a kinder thing than come here, my love. Even though it's probably risky, I'm deeply grateful."

"I'm anxious to know about London, the detective. What sort of man is he? Did he grill you?" Her own news could wait; it had not included possible jeopardy.

"He did. May I get an ale? I've been bone-dry for the past hour. Take a chair by the fire. I'll be only a moment."

He returned with two mugs of ale and after a long swig took the chair facing hers. "London is a tall, thin fellow with big hands and skin pitted from smallpox. His mouth is small and prim. He's left-handed, and says he can see in the dark. His ambition is to make something of the police department. He cannot believe I stayed less than half an hour with Imogene."

"I don't understand why not. She was perfectly willing, you said, to act as my witness."

He stared, shook his head. "No, no, I could not tell him the real reason why I was there!"

"How did they know you were there at all?"

354

"Pure bad luck." He finished his ale, then bent to set the mug down on the hearth. "As I reached Imogene's door, the lackey who took her supper order was leaving. She was in the doorway and greeted me by name. This Artie Graves remembered it and told the police. The hour of my arrival is clear enough to London. What he wants to have confirmed is the time I left."

"Any number of people must have seen you in the hotel lobby."

"It was the supper hour. The dining hall was full, the lobby nearly empty. I didn't stop at the bar for a drink as I was half-inclined. Nor at the Union Club rooms either. So much for old Franklin's advice about an early bedtime." He shrugged. "Are you going to drink that ale or shall I?"

Elizabeth held out the mug and he took it. "But there's your coachman. Harry must know the time you left the hotel."

"A bit more bad luck. He was eager to be off to a lady he knows. It had been a long day and the congestion at the hotel was fierce, so I let him go on his way, intending to hire a coach."

"Didn't you?"

He shook his head. "None came along, and the night was fine. I walked."

She felt a sinking sensation. To Detective London the absence of any witness at all might seem suspicious. "But there's no motive for you to have harmed Imogene Fisher. And London can't find one."

He shrugged. A bitter look crossed his face although he quickly smiled. "Don't forget my last name! Does an Irishman need a motive for violence other than the short temper all Irish are said to have? Oh, yes, to Detective

355

Albert London we are hot-headed devils, ready to fly off the handle for almost no reason at all. A crime of sudden passion is assumed, because of the murder weapon, you see."

"A heavy, blunt object, the paper said."

"It was the long-necked bronze vase on her writing desk."

"But none of this points to you!"

"Prejudice does, though. London took pains to tell me that he is of English descent. So was his late wife. Prejudice can do wonders at stamping out rationality."

"Well, at least the appointment book she kept is in your favor," Elizabeth said.

"Appointment book?"

"Apparently she had many—admirers. London will have to question all of them."

"But, though not an admirer, I was there shortly before she was last seen alive by Graves."

"But your name is not in her appointment book."

"I wish that were true."

Something shifted at the pit of her stomach. "What do you mean? That you visited Imogene in the past? Is that it?"

His voice had a teasing tone now. "How do you think I survived all those years without you? By debauching virgins?"

She found herself on her feet, staring down at him. "Are you saying that you slept with prostitutes?"

His eyes were devilish now. "Don't forget I was married young to the innkeeper's daughter. And men are men, Liza."

Elizabeth wanted to weep and scream, both at once. "Men are odious, odious! 'Men are men!' Don't you think women have desires too? We learn to live for years without . . . without . . ." She hated the sting of her rising tears. "How can you say you love me?"

He jumped to his feet as she turned blindly away from the fire, and from him. "Forgive me, please! It was a bad joke. Of course I visited Imogene before. When I gave her a goldpiece and a bottle of champagne and asked her to tell you the truth about your husband." His arms were spread wide. "Come. Come to me. Let me hold you. You're no silly girl. Be the woman you are."

She searched his face. His eyes seemed to belong to a person inside him she had never known but now yearned to know. Suddenly she wanted to yield, to feel his arms around her. She started toward him, then stopped. "No! You come to me!"

He took a stride forward, kneeled at her feet. "Here I am, your slave! Does that suit you?"

"No!" Elizabeth was laughing now. "Get up!"

He sprang to his feet, laughing, and without warning picked her up in his arms and carried her to the narrow stairs.

"No, Tom! No!"

"Yes, Liza. To the devil with it all, with everything but ourselves!"

Her delight at being carried surprised her. Yet she cried, "Please, I beg you!"

"For what?"

"To put me down at once!"

"Too late! There's something I want to discuss with you in the bedroom upstairs."

It was sweet to relax, to let him carry her there, her toes tucked in close against his thigh so that he could negotiate the narrow stairwell. In darkness Tom dropped

Elizabeth onto the bed, turned to light the candle beside it, then turned back to smile down at her where she lay with fingers locked under her neck. "What was it you wished to discuss, sir?"

Tom sat on the bed's edge, bent and kissed her lips. She felt her mouth warm under his. All the day's ugly surprises were suddenly of no importance. It seemed a splendid miracle indeed that two people could do this for each other. "Cool, cool water sluicing down," he murmured in her ear, and Elizabeth remembered his naked body, more comely than the "genuine reproduction" of a statue by Praxiteles.

From below came the distant sound of the door knocker. Three raps in slow cadence. In her mind she saw Isaiah standing in the cul-de-sac, his gold-headed cane in hand and behind him only the blind brick side wall of the stables.

Tom stood up slowly. Finger to his lips, he backed to the door, and she heard his footsteps gallop down the stairs. She stole to the dark upper hall to listen. The knocker sounded again, quicker and more impatient. The front door creaked as Tom opened it.

"London! You do work a long day."

"That is my habit. Meaningless diversion does not suit my nature." His was a hard, loud voice, tense as a clenched fist.

"Come in. More questions?"

"Yes, I fear so."

"Then have a seat over there by the fire, and ask away."

She heard footsteps. After a pause, London's voice said something she did not catch. It was fainter, which meant that they were seated at the far end of the parlor. Leaning

358

out over the upper staircase rail she could hear better.

". . . because events have taken a new twist in the last hour," London was saying. "I just questioned Graves again." A row of white headstones flashed across her mind, then she remembered that Graves was the waiter who had seen and recognized Tom. Artie Graves. "He's an ignorant young lout, with almost no capacity for logical reasoning. I have found that his earlier statement that the Fisher woman was alone in her room when he returned at ten with her oysters and wine had no real basis. He did not actually enter her room, you see. She took the tray from him at the door. From his position just outside the doorway, he could not possibly have been sure there was no one else in the room. Not possibly."

"I left twenty minutes before he saw, or did not see, that someone was in the room." Tom sounded calm, sure of himself.

"There's something else Graves recalled. As he neared her door at ten, he heard her speaking. She spoke rapidly and as if angry, although he could not distinguish any words. He heard no other voice. And he said she did not thank him as she usually did, nor give him a gratuity."

"I don't see how it affects me." Tom sounded cool, collected still. "Nor why you have come here to tell me all this."

"Come, Mr. O'Casey. Don't play the fool with me. You were in her room a short time earlier, and I have only your word as to when you left."

There was a short silence. Tom's voice was harsher now. "By questioning Graves a second time you invited him to change his first story, so he obligingly altered it!"

"Amended it. Amplified it. Oh, I do not accept as gospel anything he says. But there's no reason why he would lie about her taking the tray at the door. Someone could have been in there with her, and I must find who." There was a dry cough. "You are the chief possibility, at present."

Now Tom sounded really angry. "I am a man of good repute in this city. Are you saying that a hotel lackey's changed story puts me in jeopardy?"

"What places you in some jeopardy, and did before he changed it, is that you have no witnesses as to when you claim you left City Hotel."

Elizabeth remembered Tom's voice saying that all had gone well. Why had he said that if it wasn't true? Or had he deluded himself that it was? His voice below sounded assured, now, robust. "But I do, London! I do! Like Graves, I suppose I am entitled to recollect something I did not remember when you first questioned me?"

"You do, of course. What is it?"

"A little man in gray. Wearing a tall gray hat with a black band. He sat in an armchair in the City Hotel lobby, the one left of the door. There was a large brown leather case beside his chair. He was reading a newspaper. As I neared him I began to whistle. He knew the song, or liked it, for he lowered his paper and looked up at me with a smile. He nodded and I nodded back."

"What song?"

" 'There's a Good Time Coming.' " Tom whistled a few bars of a cheerful melody. "I heard it a few weeks ago at a minstrel show. Catchy tune, don't you think?"

Elizabeth straightened; relief made her feel light, unburdened. But her ears were alert for London's answer.

"Let's hope this music lover is staying at the hotel," he said. "And that he remembers you."

"I have no doubt he will." There was a pause; she heard footsteps and drew back into the darkness of the upper landing. Then she heard the front door creak open. It was only a few steps from the foot of the staircase; Tom's voice was so close now that it startled her. "If you believe someone was with Imogene Fisher at ten o'clock, you'll soon find that you will have to look for a man who got there after I left."

"Or before. And stood outside her door eavesdropping on your rendezvous."

"But who would do that? Why?"

"A jealous admirer, perhaps. I have found out quite a bit about this doxy's life. It was her system to have in tow an older fellow who paid her rent and visited kind of infrequently, and several younger men who kept her amused." The detective's disgust and outrage were plain.

"I saw no one in the hall or on the stairs when I left." Tom's voice was tense now. London seemed to Elizabeth a menacing figure attempting to trap Tom into a lie about this skulker.

"You brought with you a bottle of champagne, you admitted," London was saying.

"True. And no crime."

"Yet the twenty-odd minutes you were alone in the woman's room with her seems a very short time for the sort of frolic that champagne suggests to me."

"There was no frolic."

"Then what did you go there for?"

"A friendly chat with a pretty young lady who liked champagne."

"A gift of French champagne to a lady of easy virtue and naught else in mind but a chat? Come, now. I don't pretend to be much of a man of the world, but it

361

seems unlikely."

"Ah, but you're forgetting that we Irish are unlikely creatures, with a fatal affection for underdogs."

"You are unwise to treat frivolously a very grave matter."

"But you can't hang me for that. Nor for buying champagne and giving it away. You said you are not a man of the world. I agree, you are not. If so, you would know that a good many members of the Union Club who meet at City Hotel are acquainted with the late Miss Imogene Fisher and not always in a carnal sense. She is at present very much *a la mode.* You might almost say that she has a little salon there in her hotel apartment. So my visit was not so strange as you thought."

"I'm obliged for your enlightenment as to the manners and morals of your fellow clubmen," London said dryly. "You can be sure I'll try to find your little man in gray. This alibi will help both you and me. Good night."

His voice had grown louder as he spoke and Elizabeth drew back into the shadows of the upper hall. She heard the front door creak, then close, and went downstairs to Tom. He had returned to the parlor and was turning down the lamp. "London is after my blood," he said.

"I know. I listened."

"As soon as I've taken you home I'm going to City Hotel to find that little man in gray."

Home. Still the house on 10th Street. She was a woman between two lives, the past with Isaiah and the future with Tom, only a hopeful dream at present. "You don't trust London?"

"He said 'at once' which could mean tomorrow morning. And he didn't see the fellow. Even though I don't know his name I remember him clearly, and I'll have no trouble describing him in detail to the desk clerk."

It suddenly seemed to her extraordinary that so much should depend on an unknown man in gray who had liked a whistled tune. "Let me come with you. I'm not eager to go home, and I'm on tenterhooks about your finding him."

"In that case I'll have Harry drive us so that you can wait in the carriage."

By good fortune a place at the curb was vacated as Tom's cabriolet neared the portal of City Hotel. Before Tom got out he said, "Sit well back so your face won't be seen, Liza. London or your husband could come out of that lobby at any moment."

She nodded, content to lose herself in watching the people passing on the pavement. It was a motley parade: a beggar asking pennies; a black waif in rags, eyes big as dollars; a well-dressed couple who turned into the hotel; a thin man who did the same, his eyes on his big silver watch; and a large-bosomed woman who seemed pulled forward, her rear following docilely, and who reminded Elizabeth of Adela Fisher. Poor soul—her psychic abilities had failed her where her own sister was concerned.

Tom came out of the hotel at a fast clip. His face told her that the trip had been in vain. He sank down beside her, reached for her hand. "The night clerk can't remember any such man being a registered guest. The day clerk may." He nodded and mustered up a smile. "Yes, the day clerk may know who he is." He tapped on the roof for Harry to start. There were dark circles below his eyes. The optimism he tried to exude rang false, and Elizabeth knew he was beginning to be afraid.

She held his hand tighter. "Everything is going to be all right."

"Of course it is."

"I feel responsible for all you're being put through, and just when the whole city's admiring the mansion you built. If it weren't for me you wouldn't have gone to see Imogene last night."

"If it weren't for you, I'd be only half alive with no joy to look forward to." The power had come back to his voice. "We have a future together, and no murder and no detective is going to change that. So give us a kiss, my love."

Hand in hand, her head on his shoulder, they rode as peacefully through the night as two people unthreatened by suspicion. It was not until the carriage turned into 10th Street that Elizabeth realized she had not told Tom of Isaiah's second paramour—Melonia.

She had been too long a wife not to feel tarnished by her husband's actions. She turned to Tom, tense with shame. "I just learned that Isaiah has been tumbling the upstairs maid."

"Melonia? The Negress? She told you?"

"Yes. It's been going on for eight years. Since 1837." Ever since, she thought, I gave him the money to avert bankruptcy.

"The hypocritical old Whig fornicator has hanged himself, then! That is, if Melonia will be your divorce witness. But will she?" His carriage came to a smooth stop in front of the Moss house.

"You don't seem at all surprised. I was."

"You needed to maintain certain illusions concerning your husband. Will she be your witness? Or is she in too much fear of him?"

"I'll soon know." She got out quickly, blew Tom a kiss and hurried up the eight steps to the green door.

Fear of encountering Isaiah on the third floor made her decide to wait until after he had left for his factory in the morning to talk to Melonia.

She fell heavily asleep, as though no problems confronted her. When she went to Melonia's room in the morning she found it bare of all the servant's personal possessions. The disappearance saddened her, but only for a moment. She set her jaw, then went back to her own room to dress for the street with particular care.

XXIV

The Pollard's cream-white door, topped by a fanlight, was opened by a tall Negro man with graying sideburns and a serious face. Rafe wore gray livery and an immaculate white cravat. When she told him she wanted to speak to Melonia, he stepped back, opening the door to her. "Please to enter, madame. I will fetch her directly." With a lordly bow and a gracious gesture he indicated the open door of the parlor.

In several minutes Melonia appeared. Her face was blank of all expression. "Yes, ma'am?"

"I need your help, Melonia."

With an anguished look over her shoulder Melonia leaned toward Elizabeth to whisper, "Please, I don't want us to talk about nothin' in here."

Elizabeth stood up. "Very well. We shall go for a walk."

"I got to get Rafe's leave."

"Then do so."

Melonia returned in a few moments, looking relieved. "Rafe said yes, if I don't stay long." She followed Elizabeth out the front door, which the houseman opened, bowing the guest out.

"I'm very well impressed by your Rafe," Elizabeth said.

Melonia nodded, gratified. "Most every single darkie girl in church was after him." She glanced warily at her former mistress.

The street along which they walked past fine houses fronting on a small iron-fenced park was like etchings Elizabeth had seen of London's fashionable Belgravia. "I am in the process of divorcing Mr. Moss. You must aid me and testify to his mistreatment of you."

Melonia stopped in her tracks, her face a grimace of fear. "I can't do that!" She shook her head so vehemently that her little starched maid's cap went crooked.

"You must."

"You can't tell me *must* no more. I works for the Pollards now. I isn't just Melonia. Now I'm Mrs. Rafe Jefferson."

"You said you don't want him to know. Very well. I can arrange it with my attorney so that he need not. A deposition, perhaps. All you must do is attest to the simple truth."

A cagey look came over Melonia's face. "What if I lied to you?"

"Why would you tell such a lie?"

Melonia closed her eyes, then opened them. "To get even with Mr. Moss. He always paid me less wages than those Irish maids, and I was mighty distressed 'bout that."

"Now you *are* lying, aren't you?"

"I hopes you can forgive me for what I went and said about Mr. Moss and me." Servile, Melonia wrung her pink-palmed hands, her shoulders hunched. "I don't know what made me say such a wicked thing. But I knows that as a good Christian lady you'll forgive me. Yes, that I is sure of, ma'am." Alert brown eyes in the anguished face examined Elizabeth's for the effect of the speech.

"Stop this!" Elizabeth found her hands on Melonia's shoulders, shaking her. "Stop lying, stop cringing. You've been abused, misused! Stand up for yourself. You're not a slave. You're free."

A passing gentleman stopped to stare, then went on, shaking his head and smiling. Melonia straightened. "Let go of me, Mrs. Moss." Now she was erect, voice hard, face stoic. "I got a chance at a life with a good man. There ain't nothin' going to make me chance losing him. Nothin'. He's an elder of our church! If he was to hear any story 'bout Mr. Moss and me he wouldn't want no such wife. And then my heart would bust, an' I'd die."

Elizabeth stood staring into hard brown eyes, saw a mouth set like stone. From far down the street came the unintelligible urgent cry of a newsboy vending his papers. The door of the house before which they were standing opened and a little maid in crisp white apron and cap ran toward the sound, her fist closed on a penny for the paper.

"You hear that, Mrs. Moss? They finds out everything, those papers. You got in them just for goin' to abolitionist meetings or to a charity ball. You think they won't put your *divorce* in?" Beads of sweat gleamed on her forehead and upper lip. She drew a handkerchief from her apron pocket and dried her lip, looking up with tear-glazed eyes. Elizabeth was reminded of their first encounter as Melonia whispered, "You was so good to me. I never should of told you that wicked lie 'bout Mr. Moss."

They stood for a moment looking at one another. Elizabeth felt weary, defeated. "All right, Melonia. You can go

369

now. I wish you happiness."

Melonia bobbed a curtsey, turned and hurried back to the Pollard house and Rafe.

In Jeremiah Ould's office Elizabeth confessed her husband's affair with Melonia, and the maid's denial of it this morning. "Now I scarcely know what to believe. Did she lie when she accused my husband, or did she lie today in denying that accusation to be true?"

"She's now working at the Pollard's, you said? Good. I'll have a word with her. Because I believe what she first told you. Interesting that both his doxies peached on him. But perhaps your years of charitable work in behalf of prostitutes and unwed mothers set you on some sort of pedestal." He nodded. "Yes, I'll get this Melonia to cooperate, and never doubt it."

"She's terrified of her husband's knowing what she told me. I can't blame her for that. I would not want her happiness destroyed."

"Don't worry. I know how to handle the situation. Just muster up some patience. And be glad that time is past when only the State Legislature could pass on a Bill of Divorcement. That took forever." He reached for the folded newspaper on the end of his desk, then passed it to her. "Have you seen this? The *Herald* did not attain a circulation of fifty thousand by letting a murder of a beautiful blonde die down after only a day or two."

The first paragraph was a rehash, but the second held her eyes:

The only known visitor Miss Fisher received on the night of her death was Mr. Thomas D. O'Casey, a well-known builder, who arrived at nine-fifteen, according to the waiter, Graves, and the desk clerk who saw him enter the lobby. Mr. O'Casey states that he left at about twenty minutes before ten. A gentleman in gray who may have seen him as he left the hotel is being sought for questioning.

The victim's body, having been subjected to scrupulous medical examination, will shortly be released for burial.

Elizabeth looked up from the paper at Jeremiah Ould. "He didn't go there for the reason this story suggests. He went to beg her to act as my witness."

"Which he has not told the police?"

"No."

"Thank God for that. I don't know whether it was gallantry or shrewdness that prevented him, but he was right to keep his mouth shut. To abet a divorce would make him seem almost as wicked to some fools as the killer of Imogene Fisher."

When Elizabeth returned to the house on 10th Street that afternoon Annie said, "You have a visitor, ma'am. In the parlor."

Adela Fisher sat there, in black from head to toe, a mourning veil thrown back from a white face, large nose pink, the protruding brown eyes sorrowful. She rose and followed her bosom toward Elizabeth. "The quality of mercy is not strained," she said in her deep voice. "Who, I have asked myself, will attend the funeral service of my poor, erring sister? Who will stand beside me at her bier? You knew her in better days. Could you bring yourself to come?" From her black handbag she drew a black-bordered handkerchief and carefully dried a tear.

371

"When is the funeral to be?"

"Tomorrow at noon in the Sodder Mortuary."

"I'll plan to attend, Miss Fisher."

Adela Fisher was suddenly overcome by emotion. She gave a wrenching sob, stifled with the handkerchief. Elizabeth moved to her side to put a comforting arm around her shoulders, but Adela stepped back, black-gloved hand upraised. "No, no, do not comfort me! I was the elder, I the more sensible one, and I should have somehow been able to keep her from such a life as she chose. Instead I allowed myself to be deluded by her transparent lies about a kind old invalid lady of great wealth." Over the handkerchief the murky eyes stared humbly. "I have one comfort. Before she died I was able to persuade her to come away with me to St. Louis where we have distant relatives. It was the place my father's voice suggested to me at a seance. Had death not intervened . . ." She shook her head. "I must continue with my sad task now, pleading for the comfort of a few mourners. I knew you would be one, Mrs. Moss. I just knew it."

"How?"

"I have been told of your charitable effort in behalf of young—prostitutes." Overcome by the word she had finally spoken, she said good-bye in a cloud of sorrow. Elizabeth knew the poor woman was coping with grief and shame as best as she could, and marveled at her own lack of compassion for her. Had her own problems hardened her heart? She went upstairs to finish packing her trunk, clinging as she did to the hope that perhaps one more night here would be her last. Before dinnertime she left so as to avoid Isaiah. Returning at five, she found Dolly Pierpont at the top of the steps, hand raised to knock at her door. She turned an excited face, held out the folded newspaper her body had hidden from Elizabeth. "Just look at this! It's outrageous!"

"Oh, I agree. Tom O'Casey should never have been named!"

"You're talking about the morning paper. Yes, I read it. This is an evening paper. And just look at what's in that box in the second column!"

NOTICE!!
To the Public!

I, the undersigned, on my own personal honor and responsibility, do hereby declare *Thomas O'Casey*, a builder residing in this city, to be a BOUNDER of the lowest order; a SEDUCER of unwary women; a malicious SLANDERER; and a most contemptible COWARD: all of which charges I hold myself in readiness to prove or to settle on the field of honor.

ISAIAH MOSS

Elizabeth felt her body clench like a fist. She thrust back into her friend's hand those words that would be read with cruel relish by thousands. "It's venomous and vile!"

"What was Isaiah thinking of?" Dolly demanded. "As his wife, you're sure to be suspected of heaven knows what. Who will doubt that his anger has a personal cause?"

"It does. He hates Tom O'Casey." And Tom was, just now, most vulnerable!

"What if Tom accepts the challenge? What if one or both of them get themselves killed?" Dolly fairly crackled with excitement.

A hoarse voice spoke from the sidewalk. "Is one of you ladies Mrs. Moss?" The messenger boy had brought a note from Jeremiah Ould asking Elizabeth to come to his office as soon as possible.

Elizabeth went immediately to see the attorney.

Jeremiah Ould's little raisin eyes were bright below his ginger hair. He cheeked his quid of tobacco, rubbed his hands like a miser. "I worked hard today in your behalf, and came out pretty well. First, I paid a visit to Melonia. I convinced her to sign the deposition I had brought with me. That was so she could not later welsh on us. I told her that your case would not be heard in New York City. And that all her Rafe ever had to know was that she had testified to your husband's mistreatment of you. She was reluctant like molasses in winter, but could not defy a white male as determined as I."

"Poor Melonia!"

"Send her a wedding present and wish her well. I then talked to my journalist friend about Imogene Fisher's appointment book. So far London has given no one even a peek. But that's all right. Because Moss knows he's in it. I then sent a messenger to his factory asking him to see me in my office this afternoon. He arrived at four with the idea that it concerned a separation. Divorce stunned him, as did the news that his former Negro servant would testify against him. At this point he reminded me of a large, scolded child. His face was blazing and he was clearly in anguish that he could become known as a 'nigger-lover' in the strictest sense of the word. So I offered to leave out of the divorce complaint one qualifying adjective. The victim of his affections would be known as 'a female servant' rather than 'a Negro female servant.' In return, he agreed not to contest."

As he spoke of Isaiah's infidelity, Elizabeth felt a growing shame: not just for him, but for herself—for she was guilty of adultery, too.

"But when it came to a property settlement, all the man's chagrin left him. He became passionate over dollars. After much haggling, all I wrenched from him was the money you have banked in your name, payment of the eighteen hundred he still owes you, some railroad shares worth about three thousand, and your clothing, jewels and other personal possessions. And, of course, my fees and all court costs." His joy had dwindled. "It's pretty paltry, considering his net worth in Debrett of about a quarter of a million. But I could see he would risk the loss of his reputation before parting with a penny more. And you had made it clear to me that a swift divorce was what you wanted above all else."

She nodded. She had brought with her Dolly's paper, and looked down at the posting notice. It seemed more ominous now. She passed the paper to Ould. "Have you seen this?"

He read it somberly. "The timing is exquisite. This means you must file at once. My clerk has drawn up the document. All you need to do is sign it." He extracted a long legal sheet from his desk drawer, passed it across to her and offered a dipped pen. Inwardly shaken, she signed firmly, knowing that she had crossed the pale bounding polite society, all she had ever known, into a netherland where she would have no status whatsoever.

Ould's forefinger reached out to point to a sentence. ". . . and moreover the plaintiff avers that by the above-mentioned sexual congress with the female servant in his house, and by his consorting with the prostitute in her dwelling place, the defendant did fail in the performance of his conjugal duty." He drew the page back, smiling. "That failure as to conjugal duty, it's Justinian, ecclesiastical, oh, a real whopper." He stood up. "I have no fears as to the judge's decision. Lip service to the ideal of marital fidelity is in our favor. A wealthy, whoring Whig who flouts monogamy with servants and paid women?" He held up a warning finger. "Once free, though, you are going to face a hard time for a while. A lot of wives putting up with their misery will be envious, while too many husbands will resent you for defying their right to betray, beat, torture, or work to death their wives in the name of holy matrimony." He smiled as he took her arm to lead her to the door. "This is your last chance. Within the hour I'll have filed for your divorce. Speak up. Do you want to go through with it? To pay the price of freedom?"

"Yes, I do."

There was a knock as they reached the door. It opened. Tom stood there. His face was grim. His frown made him look older. For the first time she saw him as a man of thirty-seven and could not glimpse the young Tom at all. Clearly surprised to see her, he forced a smile, but forgot to take off his hat. His eyes were hard and green as they went to Ould's face. He closed the door behind him. "I believe I need a lawyer." He looked back at her and said, "The little man in gray was not registered at City Hotel. God knows where he is."

"You need a criminal lawyer," Ould said briskly. "Which I am not. But the famous Eustace Carmichael has his office just down the hall. I'll present you to him at once."

*   *   *

376

Elizabeth waited in Carmichael's empty outer office after Mr. Ould left to file her divorce affidavit. The bench on which she sat was hard. Across the room the clerk's high stool looked even harder, the top rungs worn where he had hooked his feet while working. The irony of her situation suddenly struck her: she would soon be free to marry Tom who might by then be under arrest. But irony, she had long ago decided, is commonplace. Justice is rarer.

What was wrong with her today? However bad things looked at the moment for Tom, he was innocent. No mysterious little man in gray could change that by vanishing. And at last she could leave the house on 10th Street. But for where? A boardinghouse? No, to find a pleasant one would take a search she did not feel up to at the moment. Astor House. That was her temporary solution.

The inner door opened and Tom came out, with him a large, portly man with bulbous nose and flaring gray sideburns. The imposing Carmichael bowed deeply to her, then paused to inhale a pinch of snuff from a small silver box he extracted with some difficulty from his waistcoat pocket. He sneezed daintily, turning his huge head aside. "Madame, my client has wisely confessed his affection for you, and his reason for visiting the dead woman on the night of the murder. His gallant effort in your behalf may have placed his neck very near the noose. In view of your forthcoming divorce action, I urge you to avoid one another's company entirely at all times. He insists on the need to communicate with you forthwith. My clerk has left, so I offer you the privacy of this office." He bowed, and retreated into his sanctum.

As soon as the door closed, Elizabeth and Tom flew

into one another's arms, kissed as if parting forever. When they drew apart, hands clinging, she said, "Mr. Carmichael frightened me with his talk of nooses!"

"Juries, he says, are unpredictable. With all the evidence against Robinson, a jury found him innocent. Despite the merely circumstantial evidence against me, one might find me guilty if I'm indicted."

"How can he talk of juries? You're innocent! How would London dare to arrest you?"

"Carmichael explained circumstantial evidence to me in this way: when a set of footprints lead to a room, but none come out, it is assumed that the one who made them is still within or, if not, left by another exit. The other exit at City Hotel is the back stairs. My footprints, without any witness, do not cross the lobby. Therefore the assumption can be that I left by the rear stairs and alley door. Question: why? Answer: I did not want to be seen leaving at a time after Imogene was dead, by my hand."

"But it isn't true. You didn't leave by the back stairs!"

"What *is* true seems less important than what can be assumed true in relation to other facts. The impulsiveness of the crime is the issue here. I was bold about entering, because I had not planned to kill her. And sly about leaving because I had smashed her skull."

"But no motive can be found, none whatever!"

"Two. That, as in the Robinson case, she had threatened to expose me where it would do me harm. Or that I was so enamored that I went crazy when she insisted she would leave New York with her sister. But why talk of this? There's good news, isn't there? Your divorce is under way at last."

"And I can leave Isaiah immediately. I intend to go to

378

Astor House for the present. Oh, it will be such a great relief! All I need is a drayman for my trunk."

"I know one in need of work. I'll see to that as soon as we leave here."

The door to the inner office opened. Carmichael filled the doorway. "One final word. Leave here separately, if you please. Because I would not put it past this London to have his only present suspect followed." He offered Elizabeth a severe glance. "And I cannot let my client be seen in the company of a divorcing woman. The taint, you understand, could be harmful."

"I do not consider this lady tainted, sir," Tom objected.

"What you consider matters not one whit! Either you will follow my counsel or find another attorney. And you, madame, if you care for this man, curb your desire for his company just now. He is in jeopardy, and must walk a very narrow line. Surely you can understand that?"

"I do."

"And do not write him any letters. These have a way of falling into the wrong hands." Nodding, he again retreated to his lair and she and Tom kissed good-bye. "Watch the Personals in the *Herald*," he whispered.

She left him there, painfully.

Elizabeth bought a valise at Wanamaker's before it closed, and entered the house on 10th Street feeling almost like an intruder. Annie came toward her, eyes on the new valise. "Would you be going away, too, ma'am?"

"Too?"

"Like Miss Jane Anne?"

"Yes, Annie." Reminded of Bridget, the cook, Elizabeth went to the kitchen, found her standing at the center

379

table to pour water from the kettle into the common brown teapot. "I've come to say good-bye, and to thank you for all your loyal service."

The cook put down the kettle with a thump. "You mean that you're leavin' for good?"

Elizabeth nodded. "There are some clothes upstairs in my wardrobe I want you to have."

"May God be with you, Mrs. Moss, and watch over you." She wiped one eye with the corner of her apron. "No one ever had a kinder, better lady to work for, and that's God's truth."

"Thank you, Bridget." The hyperbole was heartening. She was sure the servants knew more than could be acknowledged, and that her leaving Isaiah was not a total surprise; but she doubted that they realized a divorce was pending. Many wives, for many reasons, lived for years separated from their husbands, married spinsters bleakly preserving the status a wedding ring had conferred.

In the front hall she paused to glance into the parlor. The space that gaped in the center of the mantel between the two candlesticks epitomized the void in her marriage which had been filled by the child to whom she had given the absent rose glass. She knew she was looking at this room for the last time. The day was darkening; the pale light from the window told her that she must hurry so as to be on her way before Isaiah came home. There was only the new valise to pack now. The actuality of leaving this house was proving more harrowing than the mere prospect of doing so. Already she felt rootless, vulnerable.

In her bedroom Isaiah sat at his ease in the chair by the front window. He stood up with an effort, using his cane for support. "There is still time to come to your senses, Elizabeth."

"I have done that."

"Forget this divorce. Call off your attorney. I will hold no grudge, I promise you."

"The shambles in Jane Anne's room makes me doubt that." He seemed to have become grosser in the last day. His bulk and his thin voice wearied her.

He took a step nearer. "I admit I have my flaws. Men are men, sons of Adam, all of us."

"Your eagerness to admit this is not endearing." Where was the drayman Tom had offered to send?

"But I do not want you to suffer for my shortcomings. Abandon this divorce, I beg of you. If you do I'm even prepared to forgive Jane Anne, restore her as my heiress, second only to you." He tilted his head, smiled ingratiatingly, the crooked canine alarmingly wolflike. "And haven't I been a most generous husband?" He gestured with his cane at the bedroom walls. "French wallpaper! A velvet settee and chairs. Have I ever stinted you? Why, you have the clothes of a nabob's wife! A queen! How many men would lavish music lessons on a thankless orphan to satisfy a wife's whim?"

"How many men would abuse a helpless servant as you did Melonia?" The sudden fury she felt rang in her voice.

His face was now a mottled red. "Slanderous lies! Let me assure you that the nigger wench tried to seduce *me*. She failed. As everyone knows, black slaves consider it an honor to lie with a white master. Oh, many's the time she swished her behind at me while looking back a clear invitation over her shoulder. I rejected her advances and so she finally avenged herself by traducing me to you."

"The story seems familiar."

He pounded his cane on the floor. "Damn it, it's her

word against mine! You're still my wife and I tell you she lied. Is it me you believe or her?"

"Her. Poor Imogene Fisher, too."

"Then get your divorce! Wreck your life! I wash my hands of you!" He grinned, breathing heavily. "But don't count on the Irishman to be your future companion. If he accepts the challenge to dual which I have offered him today he is a dead man. If he ignores it, he accepts the truth of my accusations."

"Ignoring your challenge he's within the law and no one will think the less of him."

"You seem to forget he's suspected of murder!" He smiled his contempt. "How much do you think it would cost me to pay a false witness or two? To swear they saw him slink out the back door of City Hotel? The world is not made up of charity concerts and balls and abolitionist asses and silly suffragists, madame! It contains a good many people who will swear to what I wish on a stack of Bibles and for less than the cost of that gown you wear." As he spoke his chest had swelled out as if with pride.

"Did you kill Imogene Fisher?" she whispered. The words had slipped from her mouth without forethought and astonished her.

He moved with amazing swiftness. His hands locked themselves around her throat. He pressed her backward against the rounded lid of the trunk. His face glaring above hers was red with effort or rage, his eyes stared glassily. It was a dreadful parody of their first connubial encounter. Instinct told her to go limp. His hands loosened then left her throat. Eyes closed, she heard his hoarse voice. "You pressed me too far, too far. I lost all control. For this I apologize." He shook her shoulder. "Open your eyes. I know you're all right." Solicitously he helped her to her feet.

There was a knock at the door. "A drayman's here, ma'am. For your trunk, he says."

"Send him up, please," said Elizabeth.

Isaiah bent to recover his cane he had dropped to choke her. "I made an empty threat in anger. I am not the sort of man to pay anyone to bear false witness."

"I don't know what kind of man you are. But that doesn't matter now. There's no more to say except farewell." She opened the door for the drayman.

"But you will not fare well," Isaiah said in an icy voice. "You will regret leaving my home for the rest of your miserable life." Head high, he pushed aside the drayman in the doorway and went out.

"There's a trunk to go?"

"Yes." A trunk, Elizabeth thought, a valise and a woman between two lives.

XXV

Alone in the hotel room that was to be her home for a time, Elizabeth unpacked and arranged her silver brush, comb and hand mirror on the lace-edged runner of the mahogany bureau. Her eye was caught by the sign beside the gas lamp flanking the mirror.

> **DO NOT BLOW OUT THIS FLAME!**
> This is a gaslight.
> Turn the handle until the flame subsides.
> To blow it out will cause
> *DEADLY FUMES!*

The warning sign reminded her of shocking tales of numerous suicides at Astor House, purposeful and otherwise. Momentarily haunted by the unpleasant thought that her room's last occupant could have been such a victim of modernity, she inquired of a chambermaid in the hallway the location of the Ladies' Ordinary, that hotel parlor set aside for women traveling alone. It was a shock to find the austere, elegantly furnished room empty. In the middle of the round center table a large pitcher of icewater stood on a doily.

She looked about her numbly. Was she the only single woman in the large hotel? She recalled the merry evening of years before when she had tea at Astor House with Fanny Wright. How different this!

And then the hour struck her. Teatime. Of course! The women guests were all at tea in the dining room. Before she joined them she remembered a neglected duty: to advise Jeremiah Ould of her whereabouts. A message sent now might reach his office before he left for the night, or at least would be there first thing in the morning.

But even in the dining room with its long tables of other guests, some chatting, some austerely silent, Elizabeth felt alone. Where, she wondered, was her heroine Fanny Wright at this moment? In what part of the country or the world?

Strangely, after retiring early and reading a while by the inadequate light she turned down the gas fixture in the prescribed manner and slept long and deeply, without troubling dreams.

But in the morning a troubling reality intruded: Elizabeth had given her word to go to Imogene Fisher's funeral. So, at the appointed hour she dressed and left her room.

Within the bleak chapel of Sodder Mortuary a severe and pallid clergyman spoke of the wages of sin, of a wayward young life duly ended in blood, of a soul now facing God's stern judgment. But he included a reference to Mary Magdalene, asked those without sin to cast the first stone, at which Adela Fisher began to sob rhythmically. When Elizabeth filed with a dozen others past the open coffin in which the corpse looked small, flat, and crowded, she saw that the marble-pale face was framed by a violet silk bonnet to hide, no doubt, where her head had been bashed in.

Outside, a crowd had gathered on the sidewalk

between the mortuary door and the hearse at the curb, drawn by two black horses wearing sable plumes. "Will you attend the burial?" Elizabeth turned to find Adela Fisher just behind her.

"I cannot."

"You have been most kind. I wish to offer you a gratis reading of your Tarot cards."

"You will not leave for St. Louis, then?"

Adela drew back as if astounded. "How can I, with the murder of my sister as yet unsolved?"

At the streetcorner half a block away a newsboy's voice was suddenly raised: "Fisher murder! Fisher murder! Suspect arrested!"

Adela seemed not to have heard, her eyes now on the waiting hearse, into which mortuary attendants were inserting the coffin. She glided forward past the stares of the crowd, her black cascade of mourning veil lowered now to hide her face, and was aided into a carriage by one of the mortuary attendants.

Elizabeth hurried to the corner, shared by the newsboy, a grimy urchin, and a fat Negro corn girl in a red bandanna, her bucket of boiled cobs beside her on the curb. She stared up without curiosity as Elizabeth gave the boy a penny and snatched the paper he held out.

FISHER MURDER:
BUILDER AGAIN QUESTIONED.

Early this morning Mr. Thomas D. O'Casey, owner of one of the city's larger construction firms, was detained for further questioning as to his whereabouts at the time Imogene Fisher met with her brutal slayer. . . .

Blood hummed in Elizabeth's ears; the page blurred. The slow hollow thudding of hooves loudened; she turned her dazed head just as Imogene Fisher's hearse rolled grandly by.

Detective Albert London of the municipal police force asserts that there is at present inadequate evidence to conclusively implicate the builder. He is being questioned to discover if anyone other than 'the little man in gray' can confirm the hour of his alleged departure through the hotel lobby.

As the newsboy's voice again called: "Suspect arrested!" Elizabeth rushed to him, snatched from his raised hand the paper he held high. "He was not arrested! Only held for questioning!"

The boy's grimy hand grabbed his paper from her. "What's the difference? They got him, didn't they?"

Panic seized her; Tom was helpless against the malignance of mischance. As the one person on earth who knew he was innocent, she had been told to do nothing to prove him so. A passing carriage made a close turn at the corner, splashed mud onto her skirt. Anger flared, burned away the cloud of helpless doubt. There was only one thing to do: tell London the truth! She would be the witness to replace the man in gray. Minutes later she had flagged a public coach for hire. "Police headquarters!"

As she started to mount the steps an enormous figure emerged from the Municipal Court Building's arched entrance, and she looked up at the broad, rosy face and double chin of Eustace Carmichael. Tom, beside him, looked tall, young and startled. For a flicker of an instant the lawyer's bushy eyebrows arched astonishment above eyes that glared anger, but then his booming jovial voice belied both emotions: "Madame! How kind of you to meet me here. Thus, as I explained, we can discuss your legal options en route to my office in my coach." With surprising speed he came down the steps, offered a bulky bent arm, and whispered, "Do not speak to him, do not look at him, but simply come along with me!" Pulled along beside him, it did not occur to her to disobey.

Inside his massive old-fashioned coach he took a pinch of snuff, turned his head away to sneeze, then frowned down at her. "If I did not know somewhat different, I'd say you want O'Casey tried for murder! Did you not believe me when I said you and my client must not be seen together? Yet you learn of his detainment and rush down to comfort him."

"I came to tell Detective London the truth. That Tom was in her room on my behalf."

"May God protect me against a woman with a modicum of intelligence and a dab of education! Give me just a normal, ill-informed female who does as she's told! Do you know that had you carried out your willful scheme you would have handed London a motive for murder on a silver platter?"

"I fail to see how. If he knew the real reason why Tom went there—"

"London is never to know that real reason. Never! If he ever finds out Tom O'Casey intended to cozen and charm and bribe the dead woman into testifying against your husband in your behalf, you can kiss Tom farewell and buy yourself mourning weeds!"

"I do not follow your reasoning, sir. He had no reason to kill her, but rather every reason to want her alive. Imogene Fisher agreed to what he asked!"

A humorless grin bunched his cheeks into rosy globes. "So he told you. But what if he lied? What if the wench refused?"

"He did not lie! How can you say that?"

"It would occur to London. He has opportunity, but lacks a motive except for a vague fit of passion which he knows I can tear to shreds. But if he finds *why* Tom really went there, ah! Another story! You would give London a strong-willed, self-made Irishman in love with another man's wife! But unable to talk a doxy into acting as the divorce witness needed! In a fury of anger at her refusal, might he not have seized that convenient vase and brought it down on her stubborn head? Which brings me to a decision I had contemplated before I looked down today and saw you about to give my client to the hangman. It would be well for you to leave the city."

Crushed, Elizabeth said, "I promise you not to interfere again."

Above the rosy cheeks his small eyes were cold as pebbles. "Do you recall the Robinson-Jewett murder of nine years ago?"

She nodded.

"Who does not? Now please scan these facts: Your husband has posted Tom O'Casey as a seducer. Your divorce will soon be public knowledge. O'Casey was seen in the company of Imogene Fisher an hour or so before she died. In the same hotel where Robinson killed Jewett, mind you! I believe London will want to question you. I do not know that you could conceal your infatuation for my client. You surely could not deny having known him some twenty years, however innocently. London could construct a motive in minutes, based on the famous murder of Jewett: that Tom O'Casey killed a jilted whore about to rob him of happiness with a lady of quality—yourself—by revealing their carnal relationship. Do you have any relatives or friends living at some distance from New York whom you could visit for a time?"

"My mother lives near Philadelphia."

"Excellent!" Nodding and beaming, he glanced from the window. "Ah, the Lorimer Building. My colleague Mr. Ould would like to see you, I believe." In parting he offered a bow and a farewell rather seldom heard of late: "Your servant, madame."

Inside, Jeremiah Ould had a surprise for her. "Tomorrow a judge of the Circuit Court is going to hear your case. I have in mind old Merrifield. We'll take a steamboat up to Tarrytown and catch him before he leaves. He'll decide your case 'on circuit.' In addition to Melonia's deposition, we have only your statement that you learned by rumor of your husband's affair with Imogene Fisher, and that she admitted it was true. Detective London won't let anyone have a peek at that appointment book. But the charge is adultery, which need not be multiple. So if Merrifield doesn't quibble, you'll soon be a free woman. I'll call for you at eight tomorrow morning at Astor House."

The attorney was waiting for Elizabeth in the lobby when she went down five minutes early, and they took a quick breakfast together in the hotel dining room. Aboard the steamboat he proceeded to tell her what he knew of Judge Merrifield, whose circuit covered the southern tip of

New York State. "I don't envy him or any circuit court judge. Execrable roads to jolt the kidneys when passable by coach; otherwise it's horseback, and he's nearing seventy. But I chose him because I know he shares certain of my views about unhappy marriages."

They found Judge Merrifield in his large, dark green coach in front of the inn where Ould knew him to have stayed the night. A short, portly old man with chin whiskers, he invited them into his vehicle, which was furnished with a bookcase, a fold-down writing table, and a built-in bin for food and drink. "Thus I try to make myself a fraction more comfortable, but at best I have the life of a postboy, the liver all but shaken out of me by confounded potholes, and freezing in winters and roasting in summers. I was about to take my usual libation before setting off. Will you join me?" Elizabeth declined and Ould accepted a whisky. The judge produced from his waistcoat pocket a silver box containing a nutmeg which he scraped on the top of the box, perforated to make an adequate grater. After drinking his spiced whisky and sighing his satisfaction he produced a gavel, rapped on the folding table, and announced court to be in session. He slowly read Ould's brief and Melonia's deposition, nodded at the lawyer. Exuding compassion, Ould asked Elizabeth a number of questions, most of which could be answered "yes" or "no," so that her tension lessened. "Is there any possibility, in view of the long-standing backstairs affair with the Negress servant, of a reconciliation?"

"None."

"Negress?" The judge read again Melonia's deposition, then cast a shrewd look at Ould. "As a horseback opinion, I believe Mrs. Moss is entitled to her divorce. It is my custom to confirm such an opinion later in writing, marked 'rendered on circuit.'" He rapped his gavel three times, then reached up and tapped the roof of the coach, a signal for his coachman to start. "Unless you two want to travel with me to the next town—and I admit I'd enjoy the company—I bid you farewell."

"Then I am free?" Elizabeth asked as she and Ould made their way to the dock.

"Not until Merrifield's written opinion reaches my office."

On the steamboat to New York she was filled with memories of the time she sailed home from Tarrytown with Tom. She turned abruptly to Jeremiah Ould. "Are you sure Mr. Carmichael is right? That I should leave New York for Tom O'Casey's sake?"

"I agree so heartily that I arranged the swiftest possible hearing and in Tarrytown. Trust Carmichael. He's a wise old bird."

"I hate leaving Tom when he's in jeopardy. I refuse to leave without saying good-bye."

He smiled. "I'll see what I can do about a secret rendezvous in my office tomorrow."

In the Ladies' Ordinary at Astor House that night, just before supper, Elizabeth picked up a copy of the evening paper, open to the social page.

DIVORCE SOUGHT

Mrs. Elizabeth Moss, known for many charitable endeavors, has filed an affidavit to sue for a divorce from her husband, Mr. Isaiah Moss, wealthy tobacconist of this city. She was unavailable for comment. Her husband, questioned on the matter, expressed regret that he had permitted his wife to become involved with such suffragists as Fanny Wright, exponent of the vote for women and, it is alleged, 'free love.' Asked if he would contest the suit, Mr. Moss said he did not plan to do so.

To see in print her name coupled with the word "divorce" made her almost frightened. Had she really done this thing? But her uneasiness quickly subsided. Glancing about cooly at the other ladies waiting there, Elizabeth saw the writing desk vacant and wrote a short letter to her mother, preparing her for a visit if not giving the cause.

Next morning while she was at breakfast a messenger brought a note from Jeremiah Ould. "Mr. Eustace Carmichael, Esquire has refused to permit your meeting with his client. I can only agree that discretion is probably the better part of valor—and of devotion. Yours, J. Ould."

An hour later Eustace Carmichael contained his irritation at her unexpected appearance in his office; he offered her a chair and a glass of wine both of which she refused. "How long do you expect me to stay out of New York? I find it absurd that you refuse to let us say good-bye!"

"Do you want him arrested? Forthwith?"

"He's innocent. How can they arrest him?"

"They can arrest him, arraign him and I think I've punctured his belief that he can't be hanged."

"He can't! How can he be?"

"With a rope, madame. Like too many innocent men before him."

"But surely no jury would convict him?"

"I'm glad you understand juries so well, Mrs. Moss. I do not, and I've studied 'em for over forty years. I lost ten dollars betting that the Robinson jury would hang him. I would not bet a dollar that a jury would find O'Casey innocent. He has something worse against him than an unlucky visit to the victim. He's an Irish farm boy of humble beginnings who's made good. And in this land the very people who vote for candidates born in log cabins also believe that to be poor is God's will and that any man who rises in the world must do so by devilish means. Don't ask me to explain this paradox; I can't. The American hero of the future may be the lad who makes something of himself, but that's not true quite yet. And if Tom O'Casey ever faces a jury, it'll be made up of some men in mean circumstances who will hate him for the success he's had, while those in good circumstances will distrust him as an upstart, poaching on their God-given preserves." Weightily, he leaned further over the desk before which she stood. "My client is in danger of the noose because he did you a favor. Do him one now, madame, and vanish."

Crushed, Elizabeth ached with the knowledge that for her sake Tom had been in the wrong place at the wrong time. "Why haven't you found the little man in gray?"

"I think he's left New York. Probably an itinerant peddler—traveling salesman, as they like to be called now—who left the city before the newspapers described him as a crucial witness. The large brown case by his chair suggests that to me. I do not choose to consider two other possibilities, that the man does not want to come forward for personal reasons. Or is dead." He stood, a ponderous figure. "And now, madame, you must excuse me. I wish you a pleasant journey."

"May I leave a message for Tom with you?"

He passed letterpaper and an envelope across the desk, then studiously busied himself with making notations on a long legal document. She sat facing him, her pen far from facile as she expressed her sadness at leaving, her regret that it was in her behalf that he had visited Imogene. She gave Carmichael the sealed envelope. "In this length of time, if you had been kind enough to ask Tom here, we could have said our farewell in person."

"Indeed? Let me finish that pretty farewell for you. The sleuth London has undoubtedly set on Tom would have followed him to this office, and would be outside, eye to keyhole. Now tell me, when are you leaving the city? Today? Tomorrow?"

"Or the day after."

"Not a moment too soon!"

In part from affection and in part to feel less like a fugitive pariah, she had decided to say good-bye to certain friends. Clara Mason and two other Bread Ladies were not at home, so she left her calling card and went to Mrs. Penrose's. She was received.

Larger than ever, her hair now white, she took both Elizabeth's hands in her warm, pudgy ones, and stared into her eyes. "Only to think, if you had not lost patience with him you could have been my successor, dear Elizabeth. A credit to our sex, admired by all, instead of otherwise. What will you now do with your life?"

"Live it!"

"That may prove a hard row to hoe. Did you plan to say farewell to our poor fallen girls?"

"I will, if you think it best."

"Perhaps not. They may ask difficult questions. Leave them the example of your kindness when you were a woman whom they could look up to and admire.''

At four-thirty, after dinner at the hotel, she went to Dolly's. The maid told her Mrs. Pierpont was dressing to go out to a tea, so Elizabeth waited in the cosy sitting room. On the central table she found the paper open to the society page. The paragraph headed DIVORCE SOUGHT stared up at her.

"Oh, Elizabeth, why did you do it?" Dolly, in an elaborate lavender gown hurried in, closing the door after her. "Robert simply can't believe it. I hardly can myself!" She came to Elizabeth in a rustle of taffeta and held out the chamois bag of gold pieces. "I guess you want this, don't you? Oh, Elizabeth!"

As Elizabeth accepted the heavy little sack she felt that Dolly, giving it, was unburdening herself of complicity. "Thank you for keeping it safe. I came to say good-bye. I'm leaving the city for a while.''

Eyes bright with tears, Dolly said, "This is just too much for me to grasp. I've always admired you so, and now you're suddenly going out of my life in disgrace!''

"I don't feel disgraced.''

"Where will you go?''

"To my mother's.''

"Your poor mother! What a shock this is going to be! But there, I mustn't add to your worries.''

"Can I trust you not to tell anyone where I am? No one, not a soul!''

"My lips are sealed. Oh, but I'm going to miss you, dear! I don't care what you've done, you'll always be my very dearest friend!'' She suddenly cocked her head, then rushed to the door and opened it a crack. "It's Robert. Home early to go to a tea with me at—You stay here while I run out and meet him and head him up the stairs. The truth is, he regards you as a fallen woman." She kissed Elizabeth's cheek, whispered, "Write me, dear," and bustled out.

After a few minutes Elizabeth let herself out. The gold pieces made her reticule very heavy, and it seemed to her that the coachman's sharp eyes were on it as she approached the waiting carriage. Pondering the safest way to travel with so sizeable a sum, she had the coach stop at a draper's where she bought two yards of wide grosgrain ribbon. Before supper she had sewn a compartmented money belt in which all but two of her goldpieces could be tied safely.

With the *Herald* open to the latest news from Texas, she remembered Tom's whispered command on the Municipal Court steps just before Carmichael whisked her away. None of the half-dozen messages was signed with a T. One was unsigned, address to "L."

"Tanner's son will arrive tonight at ten."

"L" for Liza? Tom the tanner's boy? She felt like laughing aloud. Her weariness vanished. So did much interest in supper in the ladies' dining hall. The solemn mahogany humpbacked clock on the mantel in the Ladies' Ordinary Lounge said half past nine. It would be better, Elizabeth decided, to eat something than to wait in her room for the next long half-hour. Food was tasteless. She passed the salt and pepper to the wrong lady, spilled tea on the tablecloth and was in her room five minutes early. The next five minutes seemed an hour. In another five she knew she had been mistaken and had hopefully ascribed to Tom a message meant for another "L." At seven past the hour a discreet knock sounded. She steeled herself to face a chambermaid, then opened the door on Tom.

An instant later the door was shut after him and he was holding her as if forever. At last she whispered, "Isn't this dangerous?"

"Who knows you're here?"

"Mr. Ould. And the drayman." She pointed to her trunk in the corner.

"I came by a devious route and not in my own carriage. I'm sure we're safe."

"No one saw you in the hall or on the stairs?"

"I have every right to be in this hotel. I am registered as Mr. Tanner."

For all his jaunty tone there was an air of desperation about this meeting. They both knew that it might be their last in a long time.

"As soon as Mr. Carmichael told me he had persuaded you to go to Philadelphia I made up my mind we would not be wrenched apart with no private moments," he said.

At first it was enough to sit at the table by the window, hands clasped across it, make plans for a shared life after the clouded present was only a memory. But soon the desires of bodies that had known together sensuous pleasure and explosive joy became imperious. His eyes roved to the opulent bed, turned down for the night, its carved mahogany headboard topped by an eagle with spread wings.

Elizabeth stood up. "I simply must show you my new moneybelt. I made it myself, from ribbon."

"You did? What a clever woman I am going to marry! Why do you need a moneybelt? May I help you with those buttons?"

"How kind! For my goldpieces."

"Beautiful *and* rich! Lucky tanner's son! Would a

bank draft be safer? I've knotted this ribbon of your camisole and I can't undo it."

"I will. Not according to Mr. Ould."

"They keep the rooms here very warm. I believe I must remove my coat."

"Only your coat?"

Soon the jests stopped, the deliberately light mood was succeeded by deep naked kisses, dizzying ones that led them by toppling inches to the bed where they gently tumbled. It happened that she was over him instead of under and she liked that much. "Stay," she whispered into his ear as she lay collapsed over his warm, panting body.

"I'll put out the light," he offered.

"Don't blow out the flame or we'll wake in Kingdom Come."

"I've just been there."

They drowsed in each other's arms. They knew passion would find them again before dawn sent him away from her. It did. When she woke to full daylight he was gone.

The same drayman brought her trunk to the steamboat. She boarded with ample time to spare. At the stern, above the wide white wake, she stood looking back at the city. At the Battery a big sailing ship from Europe had docked and from it would emerge hopeful immigrants in search of a better life than they had known. It struck her that she was leaving for the same reason.

Steaming past two flat little islands—Bedloe and Ellis—a sense of adventure took her unawares. She suddenly felt young again, and hopeful. The cautious old Carmichael became a laughable caricature. She had the faith he seemed to lack, faith in a future she and Tom would share.

400

A white seagull soared overhead, and she soared with it, smiling. Impulsively, she waved at the fellow peregrine, saw the gold gleam of her wedding band, the flash of her diamond. She pulled off both rings, and the urge came to throw them both into the sea. Prudence intervened as she remembered how the pawned diamond had paid her stagecoach fare when she rescued Jane Anne. So she tossed only the wedding ring into the boat's wake, put the diamond on the third finger of her right hand. There was a narrow band of white skin on the left where the rings had been, marking her as a bride of destiny.

In her old bedroom was the same three-drawer chest from her childhood, a poignant reminder of all that had happened since she had closed its drawers as a young bride about to leave for New York with Isaiah Moss. She unpacked with her mind knotted on the kindest way to break the shocking news to her mother and Cousin Amy. Both ladies had greeted her delightedly.

She started as her mother spoke from the doorway of the bedroom. "And Jane Anne will be overjoyed to see you. Leo, too. He is bound to do handsomely by her, I believe, even though medicine is not the most lucrative of professions. How is Isaiah?"

Elizabeth faced her. One look told her that those motherly eyes had seen in this sudden arrival more than a mere impulsive daughterly visit. "I have sued him for divorce."

After only a moment's pause her mother said, "Then I must suppose you had good reason. Do you wish to speak of it?"

It proved impossible to utter the word "adultery"

because of her own. "At the moment it would be quite painful, Mother."

"You have a home here with Cousin Amy and me for as long as you wish." Her face crumpled for just an instant. "Oh, Elizabeth, I'm truly sorry for you. We won't tell Cousin Amy just yet. Yesterday she had one of her palpitations of the heart. I don't want to agitate that frail organ unnecessarily." She reached up to pat Elizabeth's cheek. "Your father favored Isaiah because he was of a practical bent, to balance your youthful flightiness. But I had a reservation. He had devoted his energies to the manufacture and sale of tobacco yet believed it dangerous to the health. That showed an absence of concern for his fellow humans which I feared might take other forms. But your father could not see it that way, and I bowed to his opinion."

An early bedtime brought a sound sleep. Elizabeth woke to a comforting feeling of having reached a haven in her mother's home. At breakfast she asked that a family dinner with Jane Anne and Leo be deferred for a day. "I'm quite weary," she confessed.

"You look as if you'd been drawn through a knothole," Cousin Amy observed with her sweetest smile.

On her third morning in Allerton, the Philadelphia *Ledger* shattered repose. Her mother's shocked eyes stared out at her from above the open paper. "Tom O'Casey! Arrested for murder!"

Elizabeth leaped up, circled the table, took the paper from her mother.

NEW YORK MURDER

"A prominent contractor, head of the respected Dunbar Construction firm, has been arrested in New

York City for the murder of a young prostitute on September 3 in City Hotel. The suspect, Thomas D. O'Casey, originally of Allerton, Pa., had been seen with the dead woman only an hour before the earliest probable time of death. He was taken into custody in the early hours of September 9 after leaving a hotel where he had registered under a false name.

"A prostitute!" Her mother whispered the word.

Everything around Elizabeth seemed to blur, but she saw vividly the warning sign below the Astor House gas flame. She remembered lying in his arms below a carved mahogany eagle.

"The wages of sin is death." With calm precision Cousin Amy cracked the top off her boiled egg.

"Tom is innocent!" Elizabeth heard herself say. The words sounded as frail as the eggshell just slashed by a knife in the hand of a most virtuous old woman. Her mother's shocked blue eyes were stunningly aware of things unsaid.

Part Six

XXVI

The first six days of my marriage to Leo De Lange were idyllic. On the packet ship he had decided that we would be married by the mayor of Philadelphia, the father of a classmate. After the simple ceremony Leo and I set off together to find boardinghouse accommodations. Almost at once we came upon a snug, charming little suite, a bedroom and sitting room on the second floor of a nice old house with an affable landlady. There was even a small fireplace, and I at once put the Stiegel rose glass on the mantel above it.

It was not until my trunk was unpacked, my clothes in the wardrobe and drawers, that I gave way to a feeling of something like alarm. Here I was, parted from all I had known and about to begin a life with a stranger. Suddenly it all became unbelievable, and I looked with wonder at the narrow gold ring on my finger, proof of this extraordinary change. We went to tea at my grandmother's to be presented to a number of her dear friends. While we chatted with those ladies and gentlemen and partook of delicious viands which I scarcely tasted, I was keenly aware that the sun had set. Night—my wedding night— was upon me. Panic rose. The little I knew of connubial matters made me dread the moment when the door of that boardinghouse bedroom would close, leaving Leo and me alone with one another.

How little I needed to fear: Leo waited in the sitting room while I shakily took off my finery and put on my best nightgown of white lawn, trimmed with eyelet embroidery. I then sat pretending to read a book by the fire he had lighted in the sitting room grate while he donned his nightshirt in the bedroom. Looking very different from any Leo I had thus far seen he emerged, black hair touseled. Affecting great interest in the Dickens novel, I read aloud to him the scene of the death of Little Nell, he in the other chair flanking the fire. When I had come to the end of that touching passage, I looked up at him with tears in my eyes. He stood up, held out both hands to me. In almost a trance I put aside the book, went to him and took his hands. They were very strong and warm. "Let's make a good beginning," he said calmly, and drew me to him. In that kiss and embrace there was nothing of the shyness I had noted before. My eyes closed. He was warmer than the dancing flames. And I perfectly trusted him. . . .

His classes and his duties at the hospital kept us apart each day, but I managed to occupy myself although the sunlit hours that were only interims between waking in his arms and awaiting the sound of his footsteps at day's end. The other boarders were like phantoms at which I smiled vaguely. How had I ever believed myself alive before? I deeply pitied spinsters like poor Cousin Amy.

On the seventh day of my marriage, September 12th, came the stunning news of Tom O'Casey's arrest for the murder of Imogene Fisher. Leo first saw the brief item in the *Ledger* which he scanned every morning in the boardinghouse parlor before breakfast. He held the paper out so I could see it. "Can this be the friend of your

408

aunt who drove us home from Barnum's Museum?''

I nodded. My chagrin almost choked me, stronger than my shock. I could not look him in the face, and was keenly aware of other boarders also waiting for the breakfast bell. Would they read the paper and guess I had an aunt who was friendly with a felon?

There was worse to come. That evening Aunt Liza visited us in our little nest with a cake to warm it. As I sliced it and as Leo poured three glasses of wine, I tried to avoid the topic of murder. The rose glass was on the mantel and I thanked her for it effusively, skipped on to roses in general, the pretty bouquet Leo gave me for our wedding, and went from there to the flowered chintz I had seen that morning. When I stopped to breathe Leo said, "We read in the paper about the arrest of your friend. It must have been a shock for you."

Her voice had an undertone I had never heard, a tension that made it less mellow. For the first time I saw two very fine lines at the corner of each eye. "I knew he was under suspicion. But yes, it was a shock. He is innocent, of course. You may as well know now that I intend to marry him as soon as he is acquitted, as he will be. By then I am sure to have my divorce papers. The circuit court judge is sending them to my attorney, you see."

Divorce! A divorced aunt bent on marrying an accused murderer? It did not seem at all real to me, and yet all too much so.

Leo did not flinch. His expression was most compassionate. "What an excruciating time for you, Elizabeth, awaiting the verdict. You were wise to come here to be with your family, people who love you."

"Wise? I was forced to come. His attorney wished me unavailable for questioning by the police." She smiled in a new way, thinner. "I am, after all, notorious."

My aunt, notorious! Shame made my spirit cringe. "But at last you're free to go to Greece!" I offered.

"I'm not free while Tom is in jail."

"But what good can you be to him here in Philadelphia?"

"I could not put an ocean between us." There was a look of reproach on her face, as if she thought I should have been able to understand that without being told.

And I should have been. She was the only mother I had ever known, she had rescued me from a plague city, and yet I now resented her lost status, her love for a man accused of murder. What kind of a person was I?

Leo was staring at me as if I had soot on my face. He turned his eyes to my aunt. "I think you may be in need of some diversion. Would you like to see the new play that opens next week at the Arch Street Theater?"

"I accept with thanks."

My husband's generous gesture somehow eased my discomfort over my own behavior, my strange feelings. I clapped my hands and prophesied a grand time. If I had known then the outcome of that evening at the theater, I would have begged Leo to tear up the tickets and burn the pieces.

The play was *The Rakehells of Quaker City* and subtitled "The Mad Monks of Monks Hall." My aunt had read the novel on which it was based, and had not agreed with the outrage of the clergy and many reviewers. "The book contains gory murders, seductions and rape, also a monster named Devil Bug and an evil preacher in a Gothic mansion where rich rakes lure the female victims of their lust," she said with a smile. "But it was a good read and stabbed hard at hypocritical males who wear one face in church and another in Monks Hall." All she knew of the author, George Lippard, was that he had been orphaned young, had inherited wealth, and had made even more from his book, which had caused a furor.

At the Arch Street Theater on opening night it caused a riot. We could hear angry voices as we rounded the corner. A crowd choked the sidewalk before the box office in the outer lobby. A big man with a paunch was waving his fist in the air and bellowing, "That young whelp Lippard should be stoned!" A white-collared clergyman screamed that the cloth had been insulted. Around the two milled men and women with cold, angry faces who muttered of immorality, obscenity and vice.

We made our way toward the box-office, but ended to one side of it, facing the outer lobby across a velvet rope an usher would undo to admit the audience. "There he is!" someone yelled from just behind me. "That's Lippard!"

A rather remarkable figure had emerged from the theater into the outer lobby and came forward, surveying the crowd. In his early twenties, Lippard had dark hair to his shoulders, large intelligent eyes, a white face, and a crooked smile. He wore a black opera cloak and carried a cane. He waited for silence. With a sudden, easy motion he unsheathed from it a sword which he pointed out at the mob, then held it across his chest at the ready. He smiled. "No fools may enter!"

There was a gasp, a roar and the mob surged forward, pushing over the post that held up the rope. My aunt, Leo, and I were propelled toward Lippard. The ugly murmur from the people behind us I found frightening. An obscenity was yelled. Leo had my hand in one of his, Aunt Liza's in the other. "Run for the inner lobby," he told Lippard. "Or they'll trample you!" The smile left the author's face. As Leo intended, we served as a screen. Lippard was inside and so were we when a woman screamed, "He got away!" Lippard and Leo slammed the double door. Lippard shouted, "Follow me!" He sped down the center aisle, his cape billowing after him, sword aloft. We raced after him, past the pit, up onto the stage, into the wings, and down a corridor where we were met by a squat, hunched, fanged, pop-eyed little monster who made me scream. Devil Bug! "Run for your life!" Lippard panted.

I was panting, too, as we burst out a rear door and into an alley, and down its dark length to a side street. "If you people don't mind crowding in; I offer my carriage," Lippard gasped. It waited near the mouth of the alley, a sizeable two-horse coach. Lippard himself opened the door, bowed my aunt and me in, then Leo. Finally, he got in himself, followed by the panting Devil Bug, who crouched on the floor at our feet. By then the startled coachman had whipped up the horses, and soon we were headed away from the theater at a good clip to the receding howls of the mob in the alley. To my amazement, George Lippard started to laugh.

"What a night! All the papers will be full of it! You won't be able to buy a seat for love nor money! Those asses have just guaranteed me full houses for the run of the play!" He wiped away his tears of joy with a long, pale forefinger. "Now, please tell me to whom I am indebted for such kindness in this City of Brotherly Love."

"I am Elizabeth Aller," my aunt said, to my surprise, for I knew her divorce was not yet a *fait accompli*. Then she introduced Leo and me.

George Lippard glanced down at his feet where Devil

Bug sat crouched. "And just below us is Mr. McCready, of London, the most talented of my actors."

"Charmed indeed," said Devil Bug in a cultured voice.

Mr. Lippard insisted on driving my aunt to Allerton, but first took Leo and me to our boardinghouse near the theater. She told me later that they discussed literature and President Polk's territorial ambitions in about equal measure, and that she had found Lippard most entertaining. He asked if he might call and she gave him permission to do so. It seemed to me a harmless friendship, since he was a dozen years younger.

Equally harmless seemed her keen interest in Greenacres.

The *Ledger* offered the public the advertisement which had caught her eye, and which she showed to Leo and me when she took dinner at my grandmother's the following Sunday.

GOLDEN LAND OF OPPORTUNITY!

A large Federal Land Grant near the Western Shore of that Queen of Rivers, the Mississippi, now offers the Wise Investor the opportunity to OWN LAND. Rich farmland is for sale at a mere $12 an acre, TOWN LOTS as low as $200! The best are going fast. Take part in the westward growth of OUR NATION! GREENACRES office, 111 Arch Street, Rm. 12.

"I do not see how one could go wrong," my aunt said. "As an investment, such land is bound to appreciate in value. Don't you agree, Leo?"

"I don't know enough about this Greenacres Land Company to agree or disagree," he said. "All I do know is that the west bank of the Mississippi is a long way from Philadelphia.''

She nodded, and it struck me as odd that the distance seemed to her less a deterrant than an attraction.

Dolly Pierpont sent my aunt several New York newspaper clippings concerning Tom O'Casey, and I was surprised to discover that his arrest had brought into sharp conflict the social and political forces there. The Irish were clear that it was just one more blow below the belt for the Hibernians, a view seconded by liberals of all stripes; a cartoonist in Horace Greeley's *Tribune* pictured a handsome Tom O'Casey with a shamrock in his lapel chained to earth by Lilliputians—a skinny, hawknosed figure labeled "London" holding a hangman's rope. Tammany members stormed the municipal jail demanding Tom's release on bail. The clergy fulminated against prostitution, fornication, and the City Hotel; the Temperance Society made much of the bottle of champagne Tom had carried, claiming that without it what happened behind that hotel room door might never have occurred.

The delay in holding the trial, demanded by Tom's lawyer so as to prepare an adequate defense, was, I believe, as hard on my aunt as on Tom.

My first strange resentment, which I attributed to my intense and selfish joy with Leo that desired no reminder of life's harsher aspects, of course vanished. I felt a gnawing concern for my aunt, not because she wasted away, or wept, or complained, but because of her optimism that clung to a vision of a happy future with the man she loved. For my part, the long delay seemed ominous, indicating that even so seasoned a criminal lawyer as Carmichael could not find the witness Tom so sorely needed, could not frame an adequate defense.

Leo agreed. Indeed, he saw with a wider view than

mine. No happy future in New York seemed likely to him, even if and when the little man in gray were to appear and Tom was released from jail, the case against him dropped. "O'Casey has struggled against odds to get where he was before this murder occurred. But those odds did not include being arrested as prime suspect. To try to live that down will be to waste his energies, to seek frustration."

Unfortunately, he expressed these views in my aunt's presence, apropos of her remark that Tom had written that Brian Ryan was keeping the business going if barely. Her anger was immediate. "You don't know Tom O'Casey! He's far from a fool, I assure you. And furthermore, I do not believe the people of New York, or any Americans in any city to be so heartless as to punish a vindicated man with doubts of his honesty."

We had gone for a walk after tea at the boarding house, the weather being pleasant for late October. She turned on her heel and left us without a good night. I knew then that the optimism she had clung to had shallow roots indeed.

XXVII

In daydreams Elizabeth watched Tom walk down the
steps of the Municipal Court building a free man, cheered
by the crowd gathered on the sidewalk below. In a night
dream he had no luck: the little man in gray sneered and
said he had never seen Tom in City Hotel or elsewhere,
and so Tom would be hanged.

Angry though Leo had made her, his dark appraisal of
Tom's future in New York impinged on her wishful daydream. It was one of the advertisements of Greenacres
Land Co. that inspired a vision of a quite different happy
future—on the banks of the Mississippi. The town lots
for sale would turn into a town; Tom and she could be
among its first citizens. A magazine article concerning
the new "balloon" type of construction whereby a home
of five rooms could be put up in as many weeks thrilled
her. Tom was not tied to New York. After the injustice he
had already endured there wouldn't he be willing to
shake its dust from his feet forever? He could sell his
business and the little house he inherited and begin life
anew with her in Greenacres. Yes!

The office of Greenacres Land Co. was not impressive;
more so was Mr. Noble, portly and cheerful in a staid
dark-blue hammertail coat, pearl-gray waistcoat to match
his sideburns. "We have no need of showy offices as

some companies do," he said after greeting and seating her. "What we offer is solid value, a real prize for forward-looking Americans. You look to me like a lady who follows politics, so I need not tell you that President Polk will not be satisfied until our United States extend across this continent from sea to sea. Greenacres, in southern Missouri, will not seem far to the west when we own California, now will it?" He leaned forward, spoke intensely. "Think of it! By putting down roots in Missouri, you and your husband . . ."

"Husband-to-be . . ."

". . . will be taking part in the historic development of our great nation!"

The brochures he showed her were not impressive: a daguerreotype of a two-story frame hotel, an architect's drawing of a city hall with pillars, other daguerreotypes of rustic log cabins, and two frame houses, smiling owners posed on the porch steps. "What about water?" she asked shrewdly.

"A good question. The wells provide a clear, sparkling *aqua pura* and need go down no more than thirty or forty feet to reach the watertable. Rainfall is better than average. Most householders have truck gardens, but staples and other necessities can be bought in Cairo, across the river, which is easily crossed."

"Speaking about rivers, what about flooding?"

"What an astute lady you are! Towns fringing the Mississippi are prone to inundation from time to time, which is why Greenacres is situated on a plateau several miles from the shore."

"This may seem a foolish question, but what about Indians?"

418

He chuckled. "Hostile Indians, you mean? You are thinking now of the far west, the Dakotas, the distant Oregon territory. The Indians living in the region of Greenacres are an asset; they provide cheap labor. Oh, if only Greenacres were closer I would urge you to go there, see it for yourself. As it is, I can merely urge you to avoid delay. All but a few of the choicest lots are gone." He spread out before her a map of the town, divided into cross streets, and with his pencil pointed out two corner lots, shade trees sketched on each.

"And lumber?"

He beamed. "Greenacres landing is, in fact, a fueling stop for wood-burning steamboats. Trees abound."

"What about other women?"

"Greenacres attracts families, not mere male adventurers. As a matter of fact, a lovely lady, Mrs. Jakes, runs Greenacres Hotel, a place where you would stay in comfort until your home is ready for you."

"I have to give such an important decision further consideration," she said as she rose. "But I'm quite sure I'll be back."

Clutching one of the brochures, Elizabeth walked homeward with her head in the clouds, fluffy white clouds floating above her new home on a large corner lot in Greenacres, Missouri.

Tom's first two letters were encouraging and probably meant to be: Carmichael was arranging for bail, and had advertised widely in some two dozen newspapers for a man in a gray suit who had been sitting in the lobby of City Hotel on the evening of September 3rd and may have noted a man who left whistling.

The third letter contained bad news that made Elizabeth's heart turn over: "London has produced a shabby old fellow with a saggy paunch and broken cheek veins who looked me over and said I look like the young gent in fine togs who came out the rear door of City Hotel at half after ten on the night of September 3rd. The old man was waiting in the alley for his daughter, a scullery maid at the hotel whom he had walked home with. He squinted at me, cocked his head this way and that, looked dubious, but said I *could* be the gent he saw that night. If London prevails on him to be more positive, I am in a bog over my head."

But two days later he wrote to relieve her anxiety: "London has slipped badly! Do not worry about the witness in the alley. Carmichael at once queried all the kitchen staff at City Hotel and found that the daughter did not work on the night of the 3rd so that he could not have walked home with her as he said. His memory joggled, he amended his wait to the night of September 1st."

But she felt as though Tom were ripe to be the victim of any false witness who, for whatever reason, might come forward with a damaging lie.

Dolly Pierpont proved a faithful correspondent. Her letters, liberally punctuated with dashes, revealed such news as Clara Mason's elder daughter's wedding, the probable insanity of the poor Belmont boy, and the death of old Mr. Penrose, leaving his wife immensely rich. "But I'll warrant she will still hold her charity events—the Bread Ladies have fallen apart—that does sound strange—without your leadership, dear Elizabeth."

Her letter of October 20th contained a lengthy folded newspaper clipping, the headline of which was the first thing Elizabeth saw on opening the envelope.

O'CASEY WITNESS FOUND

James P. Sullivan, a salesman for the Continental Shoe Company of Wooster, Massachusetts, appeared yesterday at the Police Department to announce that he was the man in gray. As to why he had not come forward earlier, his explanation was simple. He left New York the evening after the murder of Imogene Fisher at City Hotel, before suspicion had attached to anyone, and before the elusive "little man in gray" had been alluded to in the newspapers.

Mr. Sullivan then covered his usual territory before returning to the metropolis. Dining at City Hotel he inquired about the murder which had occurred there the day before he left. He learned of the arrest of Mr. Thomas O'Casey and of his claim as to a missing witness who saw him leave the lobby whistling. Realizing that he was the man sought, Mr. Sullivan set out for the police department forthwith.

Detective Albert London, in charge of the case, has revealed that Mr. Sullivan gave an accurate description of Mr. O'Casey and moreover whistled the song the suspect said he was whistling as he left the hotel. The song's title, revealed to no one by the police, was also known to Mr. Sullivan, as well as the song's composer, a Stephen Foster of Pittsburgh. "There's a Good Time Coming" may prove prophetic for Thomas O'Casey.

As to the crucial matter of the hour when Mr. Sullivan and Mr. O'Casey so briefly crossed paths, the small, stocky gentleman was precise: "Two minutes before a quarter to ten." He had looked at his watch because he was to meet a friend there at a quarter to ten to take supper with him in the hotel dining room.

421

He described Mr. O'Casey as "a tall, well-set fellow on the middle thirties, broad in the shoulders and dressed in taste like a gent. Dark hair, a merry smile, and a good trill to his whistle. He could carry a tune to a T, like myself." Confronted with half a dozen men of that general description he pointed to Mr. O'Casey without a moment's hesitation.

Mr. Eustace Carmichael, the attorney for the accused builder, was emphatic as to the significance of Mr. Sullivan's appearance and testimony. "For the State of New York to consider bringing my client to trial after this vindication of his innocence would be outrageous. The sole alternative is a dismissal of all charges against him, forthwith."

Detective Albert London stated that in the event that said charges are dropped, his investigation of the case will continue until the perpetrator is brought to justice.

In the opinion of this paper, the shadow cast on Mr. O'Casey's reputation is to be deplored.

Exuberant relief filled Elizabeth; she felt light as air. Tom was cleared! Holding the two long ribbons of newsprint, she felt that she was holding the two most precious objects in the universe. Bless Dolly Pierpont! She continued reading the letter she had set down.

But I hope that the old saying won't prove true—that you can't touch pitch without being defiled—or have pitch touch you either—People seem so much more willing to believe ill than good—At the Union Club, Robert has told me, the members were divided about asking for Tom O'Casey's resignation—you can guess who has been most loudly in favor of this—Robert says Isaiah has already pointed out that Sullivan is an Irish name and the Irish stick together like glue!

Do hope my news was pleasing—even if perhaps no surprise—

Your loving friend,
Dolly

No surprise? What could that mean except that Dolly assumed Tom had revealed the good news before she read it in the newspaper? Why hadn't he? A trickle of her elation seeped out of her, but she read the news item again, savoring every word, then hurried downstairs to tell her mother and Cousin Amy that Tom was vindicated and all but free. She found them in the parlor with George Lippard.

As he rose, Cousin Amy said, "Mr. Leopard has been telling us about his visit in Baltimore."

"Tom's cleared of all suspicion!" she cried, waving the newsclipping. "I must tell Jane Anne and Leo at once!"

"Mr. Leopard's play was a great success in Baltimore," Cousin Amy continued, and cast a quite doting glance at the lithe young playwright. "The setting is a monastery."

"Didn't you hear me? The little man in gray has appeared and has exonerated Tom!"

"A friend of yours, you mean?" George Lippard asked.

"The man I intend to marry!"

"Marry?" Cousin Amy's small spectacles framed blank eyes. "But you're married to Isaiah Moss!"

Jane Aller stood, one hand reaching imperiously for Cousin Amy's. "Come with me upstairs, dear. There's something I must explain to you in private."

It had been decided by Jane Aller that the word "separation" was better used for the present in describing her daughter Elizabeth's marital condition. This word had gone out into the town and made Elizabeth a respectable woman, somewhere between a spinster and a widow. "She'll explain that I am divorced," she told George Lippard, "although as yet I lack the circuit judge's written decision."

The man who had written of rape, murder, and the seduction of innocents struggled to put on his worldly smile again. "I admit surprise. You do not seem the type."

"Is there one?"

"Apparently I have always thought of a divorced woman as declassée, which you are certainly not. Shall we celebrate your fiancé's freedom, your divorce and my play's really heartening Baltimore run?"

"First I'd like to tell my niece and her husband the good news."

"And then will all three of you take supper with me at a restaurant I favor for its shad roe and brandy flips?"

The evening was a total success, and began most happily in his coach on the way to the city with his praise of *The Ironmaster's Bride*. She had lent him a copy before he left for Baltimore. "You must no longer abandon writing, Elizabeth. Markets for fiction have widened in the past dozen years. *The Saturday Evening Post* pays well for serial pieces and you can retain the book rights. Double pay!" He smiled and nodded.

The easiness that had existed among the four of them since that first wild meeting at the Arch Street Theater prevailed again, and although the season was wrong for shad roe the roast beef was tender and deep pink and the brandy flips exhilarating. Jane Anne was particularly warm and loving. "I know everything will work out beautifully, Aunt Liza."

Despite a very early supper it was after eleven when

she reached her mother's house. Lippard saw her to the door, cape billowing behind him as he strode back to his waiting carriage. Was he aware of the Byronic air his cape and sword cane gave him? As she let herself in she was surprised to see that the lamp in the parlor was still lighted. The new maid Gerda was often careless so she went in to turn it out.

Tom stood up, pale and smiling and thinner. Her whole being blazed with joy. "Tom!" As she rushed toward him she became dimly aware of her mother and Cousin Amy side by side on the Queen Anne settee, but could not slow her pace or keep her arms from reaching out toward him. He took her hands in his, bent to kiss the back of each. She saw a few gray threads in his hair. "My good news preceded me, but here I am, anyway." His eyes looking down into hers were different. There were new lines beside his smiling mouth. He winked.

"Early to bed and early to rise," her mother said, rising. "Come, Amy."

Cousin Amy painstakingly tucked her crocheting into her knitting bag and rose with the effect of creaking gently. "Makes a man healthy, wealthy and wise. And a woman, too, I have always dared to suppose. Good night, Elizabeth. Good night, Thomas. And just remember those wise words of the Reverend Hackett: 'He for God, she for God in him.'"

Alone, Elizabeth and Tom rushed to each other's arms. She was at once aware of a change in him, of the tenseness of his body and the lessening of the remembered warmth that once had poured from it. Yet the long kiss dizzied her. At last, arm in arm and unable to separate, they sat close together on the canework Queen Anne, fingers interlocked, smiling into each other's eyes. Then they both began to speak at once; they laughed. The words she had wanted to say were ridiculous: that the irises of his eyes looked as if they had been shattered and expertly mended, shards of gray, green and blue radiating from the black pupil as before.

"You're as beautiful as all my dreams of you," he said, "and may we never spend another month and a half like the last!"

"Oh, Tom! This has been so hard for you. Your eyes look different. But now it's over. We have a future again. Together."

He raised the hand he clasped to kiss it. "And things will right themselves, given time. My worst fear was not that I might be hanged, you know. It was fear of being sent to prison—a prison like the old mine where felons are chained to the damp rock walls and left there, cold and half-starved, to go mad." He shook his head, impatient with himself. "But now it's the future I must plan for. And in jail I had ample time to think things through and put reality ahead of preference."

Was this grim-faced man her jaunty Tom? She tried to awaken his old jaunty self. "Oh, my dear, how lucky we are! It's a new beginning for both of us! How few people can seize the chance to start afresh, as if the past with its mistakes and misfortunes had never happened! It's like being given a whole second life to live!"

His smile was dubious. "Second life? My only desire is to mend the one I already have. I'd be a fool not to face the damage done me by that damned arrest."

"Damage? What damage?" Dolly's letter flapped bat wings in her mind. "You are free! You're innocent!"

"Yes, I'm free. But the taint of suspicion will cling awhile. People who once returned my smile or bow turn their heads and pretend not to see me. Do you remember that building contract I lost? One of the first things I did was to go to the man and ask him to honor his word. He said he had already signed a contract with another builder. True? Maybe. The president of the Union Club a week ago sent me a polite letter asking my resignation 'under the unfortunate circumstances.' I ignored it. Now a majority of members want me to stay, I hear. But I don't know how that vote will finally come out." The shadows under his eyes defined the shape of the sockets, giving his face a deathly look. "Sometimes I think I'd be better off if I'd faced a jury. Robinson was The Great Unhanged. Well, I'm The Great Untried. There are people who think I got off lucky because I hired a top-notch attorney. I have to fight this chimera, and I will. I'll show them all!" Now he looked more like himself. His face had some color and there was a jut to his chin. "A rich friend of Cornelius Ferris wants a mansion to rival his. I'll get that plum, or my name isn't Thomas Dunbar O'Casey!"

"New York isn't the only place where a builder can use his talents, Tom."

"New York's the place where I was headed for the top of the heap until my arrest. My outrageous and unjust arrest! I wanted to sue London, the whole damned police department, but Carmichael said it was unwise, protesting too much. He urged instead a sweet and noble announcement in the papers saying American justice had triumphed over all and thanking all those who had continued to believe in my innocence. And damned few they were! But, as you say, that's all past. Believe me when I tell you I'll go back there and hold my head high

427

and be on the way up to the top again within a few months at most."

"Of course you will, if anybody can!"

"I can! I will! Just keep believing in me, Liza!"

"You know I do!"

The future melted away. Only the present mattered, at last. With a tired wheeze the hall clock gathered its ancient forces and began to chime midnight. He slipped from the sofa, knelt before her, head pressed against her body, arms encircling it. "Oh, Liza, if you knew how I've yearned for you. To touch you, to hold you!" He tilted up an almost boyish face. She bent her head, kissed his mouth. "I must be with you," he whispered as she straightened.

"We can hardly bed down here."

"I have rented a room in a small, discreet hotel in Philadelphia." He smiled. "I signed as Mr. and Mrs. Byron, to amuse you."

With a pang she remembered that he had signed as Mr. Tanner at Astor House. "No, Tom."

He stood up slowly. "You don't want me?"

"Oh, I want you and love you to distraction. But at this hour I can't go with you and get back here in time to preserve the decencies."

"The place I picked is on the outskirts of the city. I could have you back, oh, let's say by two?" Now his look was mischievous.

"Will you give Mrs. Byron a moment to get her wrap?"

"That's my Liza!"

That brief hour in his arms had a new flavor. They reaffirmed their love in all the ways they knew. Awareness of time's flight was halted for ecstasy that gave them the precious knowledge of their uniqueness as a pair of lovers unmatched since time began.

"I'll see you tomorrow morning before I go, of course," he said as he drove back to Allerton in his hired carriage.

"Go?"

"Back to New York."

"No! You can't! We haven't had any time at all!"

"You're right. Forgive me, Liza. It's just that I have so much to do to begin to set things right."

"I know you've suffered. But it's been you, you, you! You haven't even asked about my divorce, if Judge Merrifield has confirmed his verbal opinion yet."

"Has he?"

"No!"

"But he will, won't he?"

"I don't know!"

He reached for her hand, squeezed it. "No matter. Married or not, you're my Liza and will always be."

That night she lay wakeful for a long time, shivering in her lonely bed. Her brief flare-up had left her spent and rather sad. Sometime before sleep came she knew she must convince Tom that there was an alternative to the hard struggle he had set for himself.

He appeared at the door in the late morning and delighted her by suggesting a walk to their old oak grove. The tree still stood. Grinning, he reached up into the hollow where they had left their letters. "There's something in there!" She reached up too. It was a small velvet box, in it a ring with a ruby and two small diamonds. "It's not as fine a one as I'll have for you one day soon," he said. "But it'll serve to keep you reminded of me."

"My dear, I need no ring for that." Her arms went around him and he held her close and their hearts beat together. "But I dearly love this ring and I'll always wear it."

As they strolled back to the Aller house after a long walk he told her he had spent the early morning with his mother and father. "He's drinking less, it seems, and they have a hired hand who's a good worker. I should have left before I did, right after Tad died." He looked at her half-reproachfully. "You should have, too. Years before. Jane Anne would have survived."

"'Might-have-beens' do no good at all," she said crisply. But with a sinking feeling she believed he might be right. "My mother wants you to stay for dinner, you know."

"The whole day'll be gone!"

"We eat at two."

"I'll say I'm taking you to the theater. That'll give us until midnight, at least."

He praised the soup, was ecstatic about the chicken, pretended to swoon at the apple pie, and so managed to charm Cousin Amy, who had baked it. As for Elizabeth's mother, she seemed barely able to take her eyes from the self-assured, stylishly dressed gentleman who had once been the tanner's boy. He leaned back from the table, a man clearly fed to the brim and well satisfied. His eyes flicked around the room. "Ah, when I think of what it would have meant to me as a boy to have dined here with the Aller family! But past is past and at last I'm at this table." He glanced at Elizabeth, smiling.

An uneasiness took her by surprise. Did he see life only in terms of attainment? The Aller table, the top of the heap in New York, the woman he had always wanted? When he said that it was time to go she was startled to realize her destination: A room in a discreet hotel, except that Mrs. Byron did not require a dark veil. . . .

In a wide bed, window curtains drawn before the setting sun, Elizabeth's passionate joy burned away the little doubts that had arisen. The silky, sliding touch of skin against skin was even more raptuous than last night, and she had not forgotten how it felt when he kissed her throat, her ear, her breast. He took her to a blinded dizzying ecstasy that left her not caring where she was so long as it was with him. In the dusk of the room she drowsed, head on his shoulder, until the touch of something cold against her cheek roused her. Startled, she opened her eyes, saw his hand holding just before her eyes a stemmed glass. "Wine," he smiled. "Red wine for my beloved."

She sat up against the pillows, pulled the spread up to her waist; Tom lay propped by a bent elbow beside her; the rims of the glasses touched with a soft ring. She felt suddenly animated, twice as alive as she had felt ever since waving at a seagull when she left New York behind her. She had put the Greenacres brochure in her reticule, pointed to it on the bureau. "If you'll be so kind as to bring me that, I have a surprise for you."

Wearing a gratified look, he lay down beside her as before. She took out the brochure and handed it to him. His eyes went over it; he looked at her blankly. "What's this?"

"What does it look like?"

"A brochure. But what does it mean?"

"It means I can afford to buy a corner lot for us in Greenacres, Missouri. A town in the making. Your talents would be put to good use there, Tom."

He sat up, put aside his wine glass. "Now wait just a minute, Liza! What makes you think I want to move to Missouri?"

"Westward lies the course of empire!" she smiled. "And our course!"

"Westward?" He stared as if she had gone mad. "My course is upward! Upward in the city of New York. Where I own an office and warehouse and home, and where I'm known to be first-rate at what I do."

"And where your reputation's been damaged, and where there may be no future worth mentioning. In Greenacres there's also good farmland for sale!"

"Farmland? Are you crazy? Do you want me to run a few cattle so I can tan hides again? Do you know how to milk a cow? Liza, we're city people! The rustic life is not for us. Can't you see that? Do you think I want to throw away all I've attained for myself—for us, just because of this whim?" He was angry now.

It was catching. "All you want is to swagger about New York! In this huge country, you've made that one city your universe. The pity is you're a bigger man than that. You could build a whole new town and you're willing to settle for another rich man's mausoleum. All right! If you love New York more than you love me, it's time I found that out."

He seized her wrist, held it, and smiled. "You can't compare a city and a woman. Did some smart salesman for one of these fly-by-night land companies get hold of you? Did he pump you full of nonsense? Is that it?"

"Please don't try to make me seem a fool, Tom. I'm not. I simply think it might be good for us to start a new life together in a new place, with none of the rags of the past clinging to our souls. In New York they will, I fear." Trying to sound rational despite his smashing of her dream, a clog came in her throat and tears filled her eyes.

"Don't try that trick, Liza! Tears lured me into a marriage I didn't want, and there I was, stuck with a sloven who had the intellect of a duck. Don't cry at me, because it won't work, Liza!"

She wiped her eyes with two savage strokes. "Go back to your beloved New York. But I won't live there with you!"

"By the time that's feasible you'll have forgotten all about this Greenacres." He reached for the bottle, poured wine into both their glasses and put one into her hand. "In fact, let's forget it now." He raised his glass to her, drank.

"What does that mean, 'by the time it's feasible?'"

"It means it isn't feasible to marry for a while to come."

"Why not?" The room was much too cold. She put down the wine, covered herself to the chin and still shivered.

He pressed his warmth close. "Time must pass, time for people to forget that posting of me and your divorce. To marry now, to set up housekeeping, would just mean another scandal to live down." He took her hand, kissed it, and then each finger, his lips moist and warm. "I love your hands! No, I've thought things through with care. With divorce laws differing as they do from state to state, New York's the place where we must marry. And I want no furtive wedding. But we have to wait awhile." He propped himself up on one elbow, looked down into her eyes. "And don't say I'm being over-cautious. You've been down here, safe from mean tongues. You're 'that Moss woman' in New York. And I'm 'The Great Untried.' A fine pair!" He smiled.

"All the more reason to consider a place like Greenacres."

"I don't intend to slink out of New York with my tail between my legs! A whipped cur! I intend to face them down—to regain the respect I've unjustly lost. It's the only way. Believe me, Liza, the only possible way."

"You there, I here?"

"But I'll be down to see you often, and write you often, too. And before long, my dear, you'll be Mrs. O'Casey and I'll be the happiest groom the world ever saw!"

On the way back to Allerton he told her he intended to return to New York in the morning. It was long after midnight when she silently entered her mother's house and heard Tom's hired carriage clatter away.

Her girlhood bed seemed cold and strange without him, and lying awake in the darkness with only the memory of his embraces it occurred to her that their early youth was repeating itself, she here alone filled with love for him and he elsewhere. She smiled then at the great difference. This time no one could keep them apart: nothing could.

He wrote to cancel the visit planned for two weeks hence.

Please, please be patient and do not be hurt by this, Liza. Here in New York I already see signs of change for the better. There are fair-minded people here. Maybe they had their doubts, but now some treat me with courtesy, even friendliness. I do not yet have the contract for the mansion I spoke of, but at least I do have one for a modest home, to keep me in bread and butter. I can't deny that my financial state has not been this bad in a long time. Carmichael's fee was not low, and my expenses do not cease because of the contract I lost due to my arrest. So please know I am doing my best to retrieve the situation here. I know I will not fail.

Love,
Tom.

She refused to deny her disappointment, but told herself he was doing the right thing. A letter from Dolly seemed to confirm this:

Saw Tom O'Casey at the small soiree given by the Brewsters—he waltzed past with their very plain elder daughter Enid who seems to have more than the usual number of teeth—could not decide if she was merely smiling or about to bite—he does seem to be somewhat living down that stain on his reputation—'twill take time, to be sure—I must add that the tale going the rounds is that your divorce was because of Tom—that wicked posting of Isaiah's—Do not, I beg you, consider returning to New York yet—let another few scandals come and go. . . .

The one that began to take shape like a cloud on the horizon that may or may not bring a thunderstorm was reported by Tom a week later.

First let me tell the good news. I am reinstated in the Union Club, a fact reported to me by Robert Pierpont and with apparent pleasure. This is a mixed blessing as I can never feel quite the same ease in the place. But on Thursday I stopped in for an hour at cards. I was at once aware of the peculiar atmosphere in the card room. At one table of whist the play stopped entirely while four faces turned in my direction, not a smile or greeting, then turned away as if I had not entered.

I continued to the table where some gentlemen were playing loo, and where I was expected, though I prefer the game of poker. One gentleman left after that hand, his manner toward me aloof. I pretended not to notice, played a while, and left when another player did. He stopped downstairs at the bar for a toddy and offered me one. I told him of the unfriendliness I had noticed, or thought I had. For the trouble with having been under the shadow I was is that one becomes absurdly sensitive to anything that seems like a slight.

He revealed the rumor spreading among club members. That I hired a thug from Five Points to cosh my uncle! Yes! Knowing myself his only heir, I had him done in so as to inherit, says this charming gossip!

The hurt and anger and outrage I felt were such that I slammed down the toddy glass I held and broke it. But I contained myself fairly well after that. The only source for this story, I pointed out, would be the thug himself. But would he tell anyone? Who? Why?

My acquaintance at once said he did not believe a word of it, had denied the possibility to the man who repeated this gossip to him. I got his name. If the final source of the calumny is who I think, then, my dear Liza, you may be a widow before you are a divorcee! I will post Moss and I will give him that duel he wanted.

She wrote and told him that if he did that he would step right into a trap. Isaiah Moss would have the choice of weapons, would choose pistols, and was a good shot. "But if, by chance, you killed him, then you would be guilty under law of murder! Please bear with this ugly tale, ignore it, laugh at it, but don't post Isaiah!"

Dearest Liza:

You are right about not posting Moss. I talked with

Carmichael, having had the second thought of suing Moss for slander, but was discouraged from this notion as well. Rise above it, is his advice. Build another mansion, cut Moss dead at first chance. The last is easy, the first harder. I did not get the contract I hoped for. It was given to a fellow not near as capable as I have proven myself. The hell of it is I will never know for certain if false accusation and slander turned the tide. Forgive that hell, but it *is* hellish. In my weaker moments I almost feel you are right, that I should let injustice triumph, leave New York, start anew elsewhere. But then I know I'm not so easily discouraged. One stupid and slanderous tale, one contract lost and I throw in the sponge? Not Thomas Dunbar O'Casey. Tammany loves me. I may be mayor yet!

A sudden, daring thought struck her. What if she took matters into her own hands and bought a lot at Green-acres? With the land bought, there would be a small anchor to windward if the troubles he faced in New York were to prove to be harbingers of the climate he would have to endure there forever. Her pulse racing, she went to the strongbox in her bottom drawer and got out two goldpieces, then went straight into the city to the Green-acres office. Mr. Noble urged the purchase of farmland too, and then of the small lot next to the corner one she wanted, but she held firm and he reluctantly agreed that more land might be purchased after she had seen Green-acres. When at last she held in her hand a receipt giving her title to the property, she felt a thrill of ownership, and was only a little uneasy about having used her maiden name of Aller instead of Moss, but surely a horse-back opinion was worth something?

Tom's reply to her letter proclaiming the land

purchase was a reprimand.

You have been too impulsive. You should have investigated this land company first. Speculators can get ahold of the land by cheaply buying scrip the government issues to veterans and good for fifty acres. Then the land company subdivides, at least on paper, and resells at fancy prices, moving on to another city before there is time for the gulled purchasers to discover that the promised amenities do not exist. How long has this Greenacres Land Co. been in business in Philadelphia? Have you talked with anyone who has seen the town?

She returned to the Greenacres office and confronted Mr. Noble with Tom's suspicions. He was nodding agreement by the time she finished speaking. "The gentleman you quote to me is a shrewd fellow, and quite right about dishonest land companies that take advantage of the credulous. I only wish they could be put out of business, for they give a bad name to honest companies like my own. I am sorry I cannot put you in touch with anyone who has seen Greenacres, other than myself, for buyers naturally remain there to put down roots." She learned that the route he recommended was to Cincinnati by train and stage, then down the Ohio River a mere 300 miles by steamboat. "And there you are!"

She wrote to Tom that she was satisfied as to the honesty of the Greenacres Land Co. "Whether the town is one we would choose to live in is another matter and cannot be determined until we can go there and see it, of course."

His reply ignored Greenacres entirely. He promised to arrive for Thanksgiving without fail; and he complained about the distance between them. "To be with you is the joy of my life, but until we can marry, and until I am securely on my feet again here, our visits will be rather few and far between. The cost in money and time is heavy just now."

She knew that what he said was both true and honest, yet the words made her feel like a burden, a detriment. She at once wrote Jeremiah Ould to ask what had happened to Judge Merrifield's written opinion, without which she and Tom could not marry. At the same time she asked his own opinion concerning Tom's chances in New York.

He wrote: "I have sent a reminder to Judge Merrifield that we still await his final word. As for Tom O'Casey, I have a couple of doubts. The grim fact is that what was, was. I mean the murder accusation. It's a heavy load to carry, and that would be true whatever the nationality of his father. As to that, his surname impedes him less than his own reaction to it. He may have to give a thought to our expanding frontier, as Greeley has advised in his *Tribune*."

To find out that her convictions were held by so sane a man as Jeremiah Ould lifted her spirits, as did the news that Fanny Wright was speaking in Philadelphia in two days. . . .

The lecture hall was filled to capacity, and the tall figure which swept across the stage to the lectern was as compelling as it had been nine years ago. Elizabeth, looking up, could remember, too, the nineteen-year-old beauty in yellow silk standing beside the Marquise de Lafayette. Her nearly fifty years had not dimmed Fanny's fire and eloquence. Now no lights were turned off, no choking fumes conspired against her, and her final words

drew vigorous applause: "Women cannot continue slavishly to accept superstitions that brand us as inferiors.
The suffragist cause is far from won and may not be in my
lifetime. But I assure you of this: every time one woman
finds the courage to rebel against a society blind to her
honest needs, the cause of all women is a fraction
advanced!"

Uplifted, Elizabeth was among those who rushed to
crowd about the lectern. Although Fanny Wright
greeted her warmly, she at once regretted that they could
not have a real visit; she would leave on a morning train
and had promised to sup with old friends. "But do at least
ride with me to my hotel so we can chat on the way."
Seen close, the large, fair-skinned face was not without a
few wrinkles and sags, but the huge eyes still shone with
hopeful idealism. On learning of Elizabeth's divorce she
congratulated her. "You are a woman of courage.
Nothing and no one should down you now!"

But Tom's next letter did. He would not, after all,
spend Thanksgiving with her in Philadelphia because of a
soiree Cornelius Ferris had chosen to hold on that day,
and to which Tom had been invited.

I beg you to understand the importance of this to us both.
My being seen there among the nabobs, and my name in
the papers as one of the guests, will make it clear to the
world that Ferris regards me as fit to mingle with the best
people in New York. It will eradicate the stigma I have
unjustly suffered from, financially as well as otherwise. I
know you understand. One Thanksgiving together is not
too much to pay for such a boon, now is it?

She remembered suddenly the day he had boasted that

one day he would eat with the silver-fork folk. The balance had tipped. Now he would, and she was excluded, hidden away in her mother's home in another city. But soon enough she had to tell herself that except for her and his love for her Tom would not be facing the struggle he now faced, would not have been in Imogene Fisher's room on the night she was killed.

George Lippard called that afternoon, moving so lithely in his black cape and dark trousers that she knew why Cousin Amy had called him "Mr. Leopard," though undoubtedly thinking of a black panther. At his ease on the stiff Queen Anne settee he aptly said, "I'm about to show my talons to the critics, clergy, and hypocrites of four more cities. A road tour, with my principal actors. The supernumeraries are hired in each city, of course. I set off on November 20th for Cincinnati, Ohio."

She remembered Mr. Noble's description of the route to Greenacres: by train and stagecoach to Cincinnati, then down the Ohio by steamboat to the Mississippi. "I almost wish I could go with you! I've bought a small property southwest of there, in Southern Missouri. I need to see it to find if I was bilked."

"How amazing of you. Why?"

"Pastures new!"

"Why not come? What holds you here? We'd have a splendid time."

She shook her head. "I can't possibly do it. Not just now."

"Better take advantage of this unusually mild fall and early winter, or else you'll have to wait until spring."

"I know."

"Wouldn't a trip be more interesting than waiting here in a sort of limbo?"

"Don't tempt me, George Lippard."

"Have you ever had a secret yearning to act? I ask because I have. I think quite a few writers share this foible. You could play the beautiful woman who defies Devil Bug and saves the girl from violation in Act Two. A stage name, of course."

"Appear on stage? I think I've defied convention enough."

"Ah, well. Do consider the change of scene." He leaned forward and whispered, "It's deadly dull in Allerton."

That night she wrote to Tom:

I find I have the opportunity to travel with new acquaintances as far as Cincinnati and I've half-decided to view Greenacres, only a charming riverboat ride from there. Although I will welcome the change of scene, my main reason for going would be to reassure myself that we have a possible future place of residence. I would leave on November 20th. So if there is a change in your Thanksgiving plans you must let me know at once.

Before she opened his answering letter she knew he was angry by the heavy penstrokes, the spatter of dots by her name.

My dear, headstrong Liza:

I am calling your bluff. Your threat to go westward without me won't work, my love. I am amazed that you fail to understand that I must be in New York on Thanksgiving Day and evening. I will be in Philadelphia on the evening of the 26th. We can celebrate our own belated

Thanksgiving then. Forget all about this foolish journey you have threatened.

Love,
Tom

Her first reaction was anger. Then came hurt. He saw her as a mere manipulator, did not realize that she wanted to spare him another disappointment if he failed to turn the tide of ill fortune in New York. Could that be true? That she had tried to manipulate? She searched her soul, found it not so. She did find that she resented being treated like a naughty girl. She was a woman, a woman whose freedom had thus far offered no scope at all for her new wings.

She was prepared for the stunned objections of her mother and Cousin Amy, but not for Leo's forceful ones, nor Jane Anne's tears.

"Cincinnati?" she wailed. "Missouri? It's the far frontier!"

"It's not nearly as far as Greece, which you seemed to favor only a short time ago."

"But Europe is a civilized place!"

"Good God, Elizabeth, do you see yourself as a pioneer woman?" Leo demanded. "A Mrs. Whitman, perhaps? If so, let me remind you that her husband was tommahawked to death in Oregon by an angry Indian! You're a cultured gentlewoman, accustomed to life in a large city, not amid savages, border ruffians, farmers and all sorts of trash!" He added, "Forgive me for saying so, but your divorce seems to have unhinged you."

"From someone who swam a river naked at age ten your fears for me seem quite exaggerated."

What turned the tide was, surprisingly, the arrival at

last in Ould's office of Judge Merrifield's written opinion: her divorce was granted. She was free, and free to marry Tom. The letter from him following this news contained no proposal of marriage, however.

He wrote: "It's a great relief to me to know that we can marry, and I believe that in another few months I will be on my feet again, financially and otherwise. By then, too, Imogene's murderer may have been found, for I understand that London is still quite obsessed with the case. . . ."

In her return letter Elizabeth included the address of Greenacres Hotel which, oddly enough was a box in the post office at Cairo, Illinois. "But Greenacres will merit its own post office very soon," she added, quoting Mr. Noble although refraining from his comment about Rome.

On the day before she was to leave, her mother, Cousin Amy and she filled a picnic hamper with food for the train trip. That night, after Elizabeth was ready for bed, her hair down in two long braids, her mother came in, also in her nightclothes. She looked more determined than Elizabeth had seen her in years. "I want you to do one thing I will ask of you, without qualm or question. Will you?"

"Of course, Mother."

Jane Aller raised her hands and twisted off her narrow wedding band and held it out on her palm. "Wear this. You have removed your own, which I gather has painful memories. But wear this. I am not a traveled person as you know, but all I have heard and read informs me that a single lady, traveling alone, does not receive the same courteous treatment accorded a married one. It will greatly ease my mind to know you have this slight protection."

Elizabeth stared at the small gold circle on the extended palm. "I really can't, Mother. Have you ever had it off before?"

"Several times, for one reason or another. Kindly humor me."

"I doubt it will fit. Your hands are much smaller."

"But you have slender fingers. Try it on."

It slid down easily to the second knuckle, stuck. "I really can't get it on Mother."

"You're not trying!" Her mother seized her hand, twisted the ring into place. "There! Now I'll rest more easily. People will probably take you for a widow, which is all to the good."

Elizabeth looked down at the narrow gold band. She had left Allerton long ago wearing a wedding band, and now would leave wearing another. She kissed her mother's cheek. "I appreciate your concern for me."

"And don't take it off. I don't want it lost."

Next morning at eight, her money belt around her waist and the deed to Greenacres in her larger valise, she boarded the train. Excitement filled her as the whistle shrilled, the great iron wheels squealed, and the train jolted once, then slowly chugged forward toward the Appalachians, and whatever lay beyond.

XXVIII

I went to my Grandmother Aller's the day after Thanksgiving so that she could help me puzzle out the letter I had received that morning from my Grandmother Clark. She lived in upper New York State near Mount Washington and the family spool cotton factory and had become quite senile though only some ten years older than brisk Grandmother Aller. The letter, in a fine, spidery hand, went on and on about a wedding gift she would make me and a small Philadelphia house she had been renting, though in no need of the income, and her sorrow that we had not seen more of one another. She enclosed a recipe for spongecake.

After reading this letter several times, Grandmother Aller said, "I believe she intends to offer you this small house as a wedding gift." Her tone was rather strained. "It must be the house where you were born. It belonged to her husband, became hers on his death."

At this moment the door knocker sounded. It was Leo. I was most pleased for I had thought he would have to work at the hospital that evening. It delighted me to tell him about the house, to have at last something other than myself to bring to the marriage. "It was the house where I was born!"

The knocker sounded again, and Gerda admitted Tom

O'Casey; he strode into the parlor, smiling and self-satisfied, or so he seemed to me. "Where's Elizabeth?"

"She has left," my grandmother said.

"Left?" he looked around the room again as if he thought she had lied.

"For Greenacres," I said.

"But I told her I was coming here today!" His look of amazement was nearly comic.

"Today is not yesterday," I said.

He looked at Leo. "You didn't try to stop her? As the man of this family?"

When Leo was annoyed his Southern drawl, as a rule scarcely noticeable, came back. "To ask me that shows me that you have considerable to learn concerning the character of the lady in question."

Tom O'Casey did not seem to hear. "I very clearly explained to her that I would arrive here this evening."

"Perhaps she did not take you seriously," Grandmother Aller said. "Since you broke your promise to spend Thanksgiving here."

Tom suddenly exploded, paced the room, one hand clenched in a fist, which he waved. "It's just too damned much to bear! Too much! Here I am, struggling, yes, struggling to make a future worth living, and she treats me like this!"

"Didn't she tell you she was leaving?" I asked. "And give you her Greenacres address?"

He nodded impatiently. "Yes, but in *my* letter I told her not to go."

Leo drawled, "I did not know you had any such authority over her, sir. By what right did you dictate this?"

"Damn it, I had every right! I'm the man she is going

to marry."

"I find this conversation most disquieting," my grandmother said. "You must recover your manners, Tom. No good will come of swearing and shouting."

His effort to recover his emotional balance was evident, like a man struggling into a tight garment. He bowed most gallantly. "Forgive me, Mrs. Aller." He turned and offered another bow to me. "And you, Mrs. De Lange." And then, as if tearing off the garment he had just donned he cried, "But she'll be the death of me yet! I thought her so reasonable, so far above the average flighty female! And now she does this to me! She's maddening—maddening! What made her change into someone else entirely?" His thoughts took another turn. "She wrote of a new acquaintance she intended to travel with." His eyes were on my grandmother now. "Do you know this person? Approve? Who is this new friend?"

Cousin Amy had quietly entered after her usual afternoon nap. "Mr. Leopard," she said.

Tom whirled. "Leopard?"

"Mr. Lippard," I corrected. "An author."

"Author of what?"

"Books. Plays." I hoped to escape mention of *The Quaker City* for fear he might possibly be aware of its controversial nature.

"I want to get this clear," Tom said. "She went off west with an author she recently met, is that it?"

"He's quite a bit younger than she," I said, "but they have much in common." I felt the situation was not only out of hand but verging on the farcical. "And there were others in the party, including two ladies."

"What party?" Tom asked, now bewildered. "You mean all these people were going to this Greenacres?"

449

"Well, to Cincinnati, which is en route."

"A troupe," said Cousin Amy, who had got out her crocheting. "Mr. Leopard's troupe."

"Troupe?"

"Of actors," Leo said, quite as if it were the most usual thing in the world.

"Will you stay for tea, Tom?" my grandmother asked, as if all were resolved. "We'll be sitting down in a few minutes and I would be happy if you could join us."

"Tea, Tom?" he asked, with a most peculiar smirk. "No, Tom will not stay to tea, but thank you kindly all the same. Tom will take himself off now, if it's all the same to you, and I'm sure it is. Tom has never been overly fond of tea, and today Tom will have a whisky or two in a hotel bar." He clapped on his hat, stood looking defiantly around at all our faces, ending at my grandmother's. "You still think your daughter's too good for me, don't you? That's why you let her go off roving with a troupe." He threw back his head and laughed. "With Mr. Leopard!"

I stepped forward. "Aunt Liza loves you. You know it. Don't pretend otherwise."

He stepped back, still smiling, but now I could see hurt and puzzlement in his eyes. "Most certainly she must! That's why I'm here and she's there. What better proof of affection could there be between a man and a woman than a few hundred miles of railroad track?" He bowed, turned, and left us, slamming the front door behind him.

For a moment no one could think of a thing to say. Cousin Amy then remarked as if to her crochet thread: "Breeding will always tell, won't it? Even when absent."

"I don't think things can be going too well for him in New York," Leo said, frowning.

It was nearly three weeks before we learned that all was going very well for my aunt. Her letter from Cincinnati was sent to her mother but addressed to all of us. The tone was light, amusing. The train that took her on the first lap of her journey had one of the new "sleeping cars" and on the first night she performed gymnastics to disrobe on a bunk behind a green curtain in a railway car filled with men similarly undressing to their underwear. Mr. McCready, the actor who played Devil Bug, was very good company, like Mr. Lippard. At first the two actresses were less friendly. As if aware of their low status they maintained their cultured "stage" voices during the first few hours, but then found she was not a bit "high-falutin'" and dropped the pose. George Lippard had also brought an ample amount of food as well as wine, so the whole train journey had the mood of an outing indulged in for its own sweet sake. She passed lightly over the balance of the trip, by stagecoach with overnight stops at crowded inns with dreadful food and worse sleeping accommodations.

Cincinnati is surprisingly large, a long scattered city on a deep slope flanking the Ohio River where a line of at least twenty steamboats and other vessels were drawn up, an impressive display though below average, I learned. At the top of the slope is a new observatory, recent monument to the science and culture of citizens who believe their city will soon rival Chicago. George is enthusiastic about the theater, the sizeable stage, the fixed seats, the gallery and boxes for an audience of over a thousand. Posters for *The Quaker City* are everywhere. In my clean private hotel room the management provided a portable folding tub for a luxurious hot bath, the water being brought by chambermaids in what seem metal milk cannisters. I mention all this to reassure you that I am a long way so far from venturing out to where civilization ends, my dears! This city merits another day at least, before I sail down the Ohio on the splendid new paddle-wheeler called, prosaically, the "Chas. C. Carroll." It boasts a bar for refreshment, a hairdressing salon, and a barber shop. The main salon with its long row of pillars and a rich carpet and elaborate chandeliers is described as "palacial." I am torn between leaving on this paragon of steamboats or waiting to attend the opening of George Lippard's play. Choices! Sometimes I believe we would all go mad if we knew in advance the blessedly unforseen chain of events that can spring from one simple decision!

I soon had a decision of my own to make. My Grandmother Clark did indeed intend to endow me with a house. It was in fact the house in which I had been born. I had forgotten at first that it was also the house in which both my father and mother had died.

I went to view it with very mixed feelings. It was a narrow red-brick row house on a narrow little street. On the white door with the shiny brass knocker I imagined a black funeral wreath. And I knew I did not want the first home Leo and I shared to be shadowed, for me, by the Grim Reaper. I decided to rent it out just as my grandmother had done.

Leo could not grasp my feelings at all. "If no one lived in houses where someone died, cities would have to be torn down and rebuilt every generation. Someone may have died in the very bed we sleep in." I told him that was a horrible thing to say, and although we did not argue long, I was reduced to tears by his appalling lack of appreciation of my delicate sentiments. I did not realize, or chose not to, that the sudden burden of a wife to support made

452

the prospect of a free roof over our heads a great boon to him. Blind to all but my own sensitive feelings, I found his blunt practicality appalling, and told him so.

"Only a boor, an oaf, would insist that I live where my poor parents both died!"

He gave me a peculiar stare, reached out a palm and felt my forehead. "Do you feel ill, Jane Anne?"

"No! I feel sick at heart, which is worse!"

Very soon I would know what those words really meant.

XXIX

Later Elizabeth knew that the most important event of all the long journey to Greenacres took place on the platform of a small station where the train stopped for water and coal. The passengers got out to stretch their legs, surveyed by a cluster of townfolk who had apparently come to view the occasion, standing in a group like a well-behaved audience. She and George Lippard paced the rough boards, slick with a coating of ice below the watertower. To pass the time she had been telling him of her unfinished story of the Greek slave girl, for he had read *Kathleen of Killarney* and had asked again why she had abandoned novel writing. Suddenly he paused, faced her. "Why a *Greek* slave girl? Why not an American slave girl?" Freed, perhaps, by means of the Underground Railroad. Facing all sorts of perils in New York?"

"A Negress? Could I sell such a book? Wouldn't it tend to turn into an abolitionist tract? Or be taken that way?"

He nodded. "You're right. This country isn't ready for a book dealing sympathetically with Negroes, of either gender." The train whistle let out a blast, and they returned to their seats. As the wheels began to turn, leaving the station behind, Elizabeth saw a lone figure standing apart from the townsfolk and farmers, nearer the tracks, a slim young Negro girl in a shabby shawl—

her golden brown face tilted up, brown eyes staring at the passing train windows in wonder. For an instant it seemed as if their eyes had met in a greeting. The whistle blew again and looking back Elizabeth saw the other watchers begin to disperse. But the girl stood there as if enchanted. At the same moment one of the actors began to play his harmonica, a tune Elizabeth knew but could not place at once. She remembered Jane Anne singing, and then the words of the song came to her: "Oh my pretty quadroon, lovely flower that faded too soon." She closed her eyes and saw a face, a beautiful quadroon, magnolia-skinned with black hair and eyes that stared straight into hers, sad eyes with some secret behind them. Rozalia. Her name was Rozalia.

She turned to George Lippard intending to ask, "What about a quadroon?" But the words would not emerge. Rozalia had not yet been born, had to grow in secrecy, and reveal her secret self. "How pleased you look!" he said. She could only smile at him and nod.

Eager as she was to view Greenacres, Elizabeth could not risk hurting George Lippard's feelings by failing to stay a day longer so as to see the opening of his play. They viewed it together from the box he had procured. It was clear from the start that the evil ways of Philadelphia gentlemen in no way angered a Cincinnati audience. After the last scene when the brother of a seduced and murdered girl shoots her slayer and does a victory dance about the body, declaiming his joy at the gushing blood, the curtain closed to enthusiastic applause. The actors took seven curtain calls and Lippard had to leave her to bow from the stage after cries of "Author!" arose. As they rode together back to their hotel later he said, "Oh, there's nothing like justified murder to make an audience happy! If you ever get back to your writing again, remember, I beg you, to give your villain a gory end!" He nodded, still smiling as at the ovation in the theater.

"I may have my central character. What would you think of a beautiful quadroon?"

But he had not heard. "Tell me the truth. When I took my bow as author, did this cape I affect seem, well, just a trifle too *much?*"

"It suits you."

He nodded. "Dramatic yet elegant, I have always felt."

She had her penny and her cake, for the steamboat she sailed on was, after all, the *Chas C. Carroll*, a day later than scheduled. George Lippard gallantly saw her off. As the whistle blew and she waved to him from the railing she saw a small figure race toward the riverside from the mouth of Ludlow Street. It was the actor Mc Cready, carrying a bouquet. He pushed his way through the watchers, saw her, tossed the flowers up to her. She leaned out, caught them, blew him a kiss, and waved to George Lippard. Then the paddlewheel began to churn and the steamboat moved forward. She last saw her friends backed by a four-story brick building with the prosaic signs "Ship's chandlery—Boat stores—Groceries—Liquor." She looked down at her bouquet, took it as proof that other friends as yet unknown lay ahead. Out in the channel another steamboat chugged toward them; the whistles called greetings.

The main salon, filled with well-dressed travelers, soon bored her and on a tour of the boat she at last found the captain with the helmsman, both staring through the enclosing panes of glass at the bright waters. "Our

Hudson River steamboats don't travel as fast as this!" she told them.

The captain, in peaked cap and brass-buttoned uniform, nodded. "I get up a good head of steam. But never beyond the limit of safety." He stamped the boards vibrating to the threshing of the great paddlewheel. "You're as safe here as in your own home!" He firmly escorted her from the pilot house, deploring captains who risked the vessel and the passengers' safety to set a record for speed or beat a rival's. "I've seen Mississippi riverboat races with folks lined up on shore day or night to watch competing boats steaming past at a breakneck clip!" For better speed, he said, every unnecessary weight was removed, lifeboats as well as furnishings. Sometimes crews even shed coats, caps, hats, shoes, and parted their hair in the middle and plastered it to their heads to offer the least resistance to the air current created by the boat's speed. "But speed exaggerates three dangers. I mean your shifting sandbars, your drifting, half-submerged snags, and your burst boiler. Disaster!" Seeing her alarm he recovered his calm. "You have boarded, I assure you, a safe vessel, ma'am—with a pilot who knows these waters like the back of his hand and a captain who sets human life above the vanity of holding a speed record until another fool exceeds him in recklessness!"

The Greenacres landing proved to be no more than one of the points along the Mississippi where steamboats sometimes stopped to replenish their supply of wood. A natural jetty fingering out into the slow river had been augmented by a crude wharf from which three shabby fellows waved to the vessel and then when it had pulled up to let her disembark rushed to heave aboard the bundles of firewood stacked on the dock. The shore, once well-wooded, showed the ravages of this practice, denuded of all but stumps. Her acquaintances at the rails of the *Chas. C. Carroll* looked amazed when her two valises preceded her to the Greenacres landing; she was the only passenger to disembark. Wood loaded and money counted into the palm of the oldest of the men, who wore a plaid shirt and a coonskin cap like Daniel Boone's, the steamboat's whistle hooted and it slowly steamed out into the current, its wide white hull disappearing downstream beyond a curve in the rivershore.

She turned to face that portion of it where she found herself, and the three men on the wharf. "I am expecting a stagecoach to meet me here from the town of Greenacres. I wrote from Philadelphia to reserve a room." All she could see ashore was an ancient ox-cart and a couple of dejected mules.

"It ain't here yet. Most folks wait in my saloon." He pointed to the log shack with a black smokestack near the end of the jetty. "They's a stove and your pleasure as to drink, barrin' fancy wine." He snapped his fingers at the larger of the two young men staring at her with open mouths, who at once seized the handles of both valises and trotted shoreward. The other, told to mend the fire, followed, looking back. "Fer two bits I can send one of my boys up to the hotel to tell 'em you're here waitin'," he offered. She nodded, deeply dispirited. As she reached the weathered door of the cabin on which the skin of a small animal was pegged out to dry, she saw the youth who had mended the fire glumly putting a saddle blanket on the back of one of the mules. The man in the fur cap thrust open the cabin door for her; a gush of warm air hit her. In the room's center a black, pot-bellied

459

stove threw out heat for the benefit of herself, her two valises, three cots, a pine table, hard chairs and a trestle bar propped on two whisky barrels. The frontier life, and no doubt about it, she thought, and settled on one of the chairs with a sigh, ready for a long wait.

She heard a thudding of hooves minutes later. The door opened. "Looks like you're in luck, ma'am. It's the diligence from Greenacres, for sure."

Her mood at once lightened, and she hurried outside, her host obliging with the two valises. The Greenacres diligence was very old, open on all sides below a flat top with three rows of seats, the driver seated above the rump of the horse. He was a large, broad man with black hair to his leather-jacketed shoulders, on his head a very old tricorner hat. He nodded thanks as her valises were put aboard by the man in the coonskin cap who also aided Elizabeth to climb in. With a thrill, she realized the driver was an Indian. He clucked to the horse, slapped the reins on its rump, and the diligence labored forward. She turned to thank her old host, found that he and his two sons were watching her departure with enigmatic faces.

The dirt road wound its way through a wide swath of stumps and tangled undergrowth that attempted to conceal the devastation. Elizabeth found her eyes fixed on the driver's long black hair. Was he one of the fifteen thousand Creek Indians put on the road to Oklahoma in 1836, having listened, like the Choctaws before them, to President Jackson's promise of government reimbursement for their ancestral lands? Was he a Chickasaw, similarly deluded and cheated? Or a Cherokee? She knew that of the seventeen thousand Cherokees who had migrated westward in 1838, four thousand at least had perished of hunger, disease, and perhaps heartbreak along the way. Could it be that the man now driving her to Greenacres had taken part in that tragic "Trail of Tears?" "What is your name, driver?"

"John."

"Just John?"

"John Whitehawk."

"May I inquire to what Indian nation you belong?"

"Cherokee."

In that one word, all! Only eight years ago he had marched west to the siren tune of the most popular President since Washington. "I am one of those who deplore the theft of your land, John. I am ashamed that my President chose to flout a Supreme Court decision in your favor. The brilliant attorney William Wirt who argued your case could not keep Jackson from winning the Indian's trust, alas." The long silence following these remarks convinced her she had intruded on John Whitehawk's deep, proud sorrow.

"I never heard of him," he said at last.

"Who?"

"That William."

"Wirt."

"That William Wirt."

What seemed like several dreary miles passed in silence. Clouds began to move across the sky, obscuring the sun then passing to let it shine forth again. Was she doomed to arrive at Greenacres in cold grayness, maybe snow or sleet? She watched the clouds, wondering about her chances of a fair and therefore cheerful first glimpse of the town she had come so far to see.

"You're the first lady alone I picked up," John Whitehawk observed at last.

Lady alone. And by her own choice. The sun went in again. Elizabeth shivered. For the first time she faced the fact that mere chance had been a large factor in her decision. If an author had not said he was going to Cincinnati, would she be here now? Should she have listened to the warnings of the people who cared for her?

As they continued westward and always slightly upward the road became two mere wagon tracks, but the further they went from the river the more bearable became the scenery. The tracery of black branches against the winter sky let her imagine how pleasant this trip from the river would be in spring or summer, below green foliage. But then the trees thinned out, sparse on a sloping savannah where she saw one small log cabin and a woman in calico hacking with an ax at a log upright on a stump. Turning to look back she could see the Mississippi. "Aren't we nearly there?"

"Up ahead's the tableland," John said.

His name for it proved accurate; flat as a low table it stretched toward the distant blue of mountains. Ahead she saw human habitations, scattered dwellings and a few trees breaking the monotony. The largest building bore a striking resemblance to the hotel in the daguerreotype Mr. Noble had shown her. The diligence turned into the dirt road leading toward it, pulled to a stop in front of the steps. John jumped down, flung the reins at a hitching post, reached in to seize her two valises. "Is this the Greenacres Hotel?" she asked.

"This is it." He helped her down, followed her to the porch where he put down her luggage. In his small black eyes she thought she saw a distant amusement. He turned, mounted the diligence, clucked to the horse, and drove away. She stared to the left and right, saw three scattered log cabins, one small frame house, a clutter of timbers on which a peaked shingle roof sat like a dropped hat. The clouds had defeated the sun. Nothing in the gray landscape stirred but the dustcloud following the diligence away.

She heard the hotel door open. An ample woman in dark blue calico sprigged with rosebuds, her red knit shawl open to show a cameo brooch, stood with arms akimbo, sunbleached hair piled carelessly atop her head. A faded prettiness haunted her weathered face, but her gaze was as direct as a man's. She looked from Elizabeth's bonnet, her gloves, and down to her shoes, taking in the russet, fur-trimmed pelisse on the way. "And who might you be?"

"Elizabeth Aller. I wrote and made a reservation."

"Then it's still in the Greenacres P.O. box over to Cairo. Otterby ain't got over there in more'n a week. He's the fellow down to the wharf." She picked up the larger valise; Elizabeth took the other. "So you bought yourself a town lot or two and some nice rich farmland, did you?"

"Only a lot."

"Come on in and get warm. I'm Mrs. Jakes, Floride Jakes, Florrie for short." She offered this over her shoulder as she led Elizabeth into the saloon of the hotel, a large dim room with pine plank walls, a fieldstone fireplace, several round tables and chairs. At first it seemed empty but then she saw a man standing at the far end of the bar, two others listlessly playing cards at a corner table. "Set yourself down over there by the fire. I'll just put your valise down by you until your room's ready." Numbly, Elizabeth obeyed. "I'm a widow lady,"

Florrie Jakes said, arms again akimbo as she stood over Elizabeth. "Since you got no man with you I take it you're in my same boat?" The query went unanswered as Elizabeth stared down at a mouse sitting upright near her foot, eyeing her without fear. "Oh, scat!" Florrie cried, stamping a worn shoe at it. The mouse skittered away. "It's just one of them field mice. Creep in by the dozens this time of year. I got some coffee on the stove. Want a cup?"

"Please." On the hard wooden settee Elizabeth found she was bone-weary. She closed her eyes. The fire was low and meager, but its slight warmth had at least a hint of cheer. In a minute Mrs. Jakes returned, a cup of coffee in one hand, in the other a sugarbowl from which a spoon handle protruded. "Hope you don't take cream because we got none since my cow died. Sugar? No?" She watched as Elizabeth sipped. The coffee was strong and bitter. "I make a good pot of coffee, if I do say so myself. An eggshell's the trick. I got a few chickens out back. So you only bought one single solitary lot?" She turned to the room at large to announce, "They didn't nick this lady for much. One lot."

From the glum silence a sepulchral voice spoke; one of the card players. "I bought me two and a hundred acres to farm. Near to wiped me out. Soon as the wife back home gets together my fare back, I'm goin' to the law."

"Much good it'll do him," Florrie muttered to Elizabeth.

"There must be some kind of law against a land company's claiming a town exists when it doesn't," Elizabeth said.

Florrie put the sugarbowl on the mantel, sat down on the facing settee, leaned forward. "Sure there's a town.

Granted this here hotel is mostly it, but there's a town of sorts."

"I was shown a city hall and post office and a pretty tree-shaded street."

"The P.O. shanty blew down in a blizzard two years back. Never was no *real* P.O. The City hall never went up. That fellow over there talking about going to the law should save his time and money. It's been tried, I don't mind telling you. By law, he didn't get bilked, or you. The land's here. You got a title to your piece of it. How can a body prove in the court the hot air a smooth salesman got him to swallow? So maybe they call a hunk of windy tableland Greenacres? They could call it Paradise if they was of a mind. Do you s'pose they got camels and them pyramids over to Cairo, Illinois?"

She saw Mr. Noble's smooth face, remembered Tom's advice to investigate the land company. "So you admit the intent was to defraud."

"Admit? Sure I admit. I'm a sucker too, along with my dear departed. That's what Mr. P.T. Barnum calls folks that get gulled. I met P.T. Barnum once, personal, down to New Orleans."

"You don't sound like a Southerner."

"Born near Trenton, New Jersey, raised in St. Louis. But my older sister married her a New Orleans gentleman and I went there to visit with her after he passed on." She smiled cannily, lowered her voice. "And don't think I won't again. They think I'm stuck here like a fly on flypaper, but that just ain't the size of it."

"Who are 'they'?"

"Why, Greenacres Land Company, that's who! My late husband, God rest him, was just about Greenacre's first sucker. Four years back two fellows smooth as silk,

465

names of Noble and Faversham, they hooked him in like one of them harpooned whales. Bought up six town lots, two hundred acres of farmland. They put up half the cost of building this here hotel, the idea being he'd have a nice income from it once the mortgage was paid off. They also made him mayor. Mayor of fieldmice, gophers, jack-rabbits, and prairie dogs! The trouble's water, you see. The water table's more'n two hundred feet down and sinkin'. One pore little well for a whole town, an' you try farmin' on that! But Jakes was a believer if there ever was one. That is, he believed what he had to believe, which was that he was no sucker. Every time some pore dogged soul paid John Hawkeye to haul lumber up from where the trees grow so as to put up a cabin or shanty, Jakes would crow and say the town was building, slow but sure." Florrie Jakes heaved up a big sigh. "I was kinda pretty when I married him. Got so I hated to look in the mirror to comb my hair." Her hand went up to the frowzy mass atop her head. "Jakes died the same blizzardy night the so-called P.O. blew down. I think it must of been his heart wore out. Leaving me a widow lady twice."

A sullen black-haired Indian girl appeared and stood with hands folded against a dirty white apron. "I made up the room."

"Clean sheets and pillowcases? This here lady ain't used to mattress ticking under her."

"Sheets, yes, and swept up good."

"All right. Make up the fire in the kitchen stove now, because I got to get supper started pretty soon." Florrie turned to Elizabeth. "Meals are included in the bill which is four dollars a day."

"They only charge two at Astor House in New York!"

"Then you just stay at Astor House!" Florrie leaned

forward, arms akimbo, defiant. "Ever since Jakes died I
been saving to get out of here. I been just living for the
day when I cross that river to Cairo, buy me a decent
dress, and climb on a steamboat for New Orleans! Leave
Indian John and Becky the maid to run this hole and
cheat me blind for all I care! Though nights it livens up a
bit. There's fellows out there running a few head of cattle,
living in shanties they flung up, and nights they come in
here to get a little drunk and play poker. Think they're
vaqueros, like down to Texas. Without that much
company I'd be crazy as two loons by now." She sighed,
put her hands on both knees, heaved herself to her feet.
"Don't imagine you plan on staying around long?"

"I think not."

"Got any money?"

Wary of mentioning the golden hoard inside her
money belt Elizabeth said. "A little. And funds in a Philadelphia bank I can draw on."

"If I was in your shoes I'd go home by way of New
Orleans, now you're this close. There's a place to see!
The river comes right into the city, and—oh Lord—the
life and bustle on that waterfront! Cotton bales stretch-
ing out like a town. Ships from all over this world. Shrove
Tuesday, and Mardi Gras! Those Creole ladies, grand?
Snooty rich French families in mansions—but, oh, the
life in the streets, the cafes! And old Marie Laveaux and
her magic spells! Black Snake Power! She peddles her
hexes and owns huge quadroon bordellos, and servants in
most every house in the city are her spies. I went to her
cottage in St. Anne Street but I was afraid to go in. She
has a wishing spot on Bayou Street where anything you
wish for comes true if you drop money in a hole in this
old tree stump. And you can bet what I'll wish for! A

nice gentleman with an eye for a lady that's full-formed. And I have a place to stay, because my sister runs a boardinghouse. The meals she puts on that table! Lord, but I am sick of cornmeal mush and rabbit stew!" Her face had lighted up but now clouded. "Drat it all! That reminds me I gotta go cope with those jackrabbits Indian John brought in. You can't believe how quick a skinned rabbit goes bad on you!"

The Indian appeared in the doorway as she spoke and she asked him to take Elizabeth's valises to her room. He obliged silently. Elizabeth closed the door, flung herself onto the bed, heard the straw mattress crackle under her, and began to sob. She had no idea why the miserable mattress should be what released her misery as she tried to stifle her sobs in a hard pillow that smelled faintly of sweat and something else, perhaps bay rum. Then she knew why. She might at this moment be in a comfortable home with Tom less than a day's journey away! She might be making plans for their wedding! What had possessed her to defy his expressed wishes like this? Pride! Well, she had fallen, and there was nothing else to do but confess her foolishness and go back where she belonged.

Self condemnation demanded denial. She admitted a touch of pride, allowed herself justified concern about life in New York as the notorious bride of a once-accused murderer, and felt better.

Before supper she bathed with the cold water in the ewer, did up her hair again at the small mirror, and descended, ravenous, to rabbit stew and cornbread at the largest table in the saloon on which Florrie Jakes had spread a cloth. The five men who dined with her were most polite, and Florrie had tidied her hair.

That night Elizabeth dreamed about Rozalia, in New

Orleans. She woke elated. The dream, though fading fast, had given her Rozalia's secret. All her life she had believed herself a Creole, but suddenly learned that she was really a Quadroon with a Mulatto for a grandmother, and this just after falling in love with the scion of an old French family. As she went downstairs she thought, I must see New Orleans. It would not even be a detour. I'd just be taking another way home.

She found Florrie Jakes in the kitchen in a faded wrapper, bent over the sink, her head a lather of suds. On the floor beside her was a washtub filled with water, a ladle hooked over the side. "What you told me yesterday about New Orleans was most fascinating."

"Is that Becky here? I can't see for the soapsuds in my eyes."

"No, she's not. I decided this morning that . . ."

"Then could you grab that there ladle and rinse me off?"

"Of course." She bent and straightened, rinsing off the foam. The water had been heated.

"That's rainbarrel water." Florrie Jakes tugged at a lock of her dripping hair. "There. It squeaks." One hand groped and found the towel hung over the back of a chair. "What was you saying about New Orleans?"

"I've decided to go there."

Florrie straightened, grinning, tipped her head to one side and briskly towelled her long hair. "That's real nice. So have I! I do believe it was seeing you that done it! I got enough to get there, and pay my sis a bit for the food I eat, and I ain't about to pine around here no longer. Believe it or not, I look like a lady too when I put myself into it!"

Two days later after they crossed the river on Otterly's raft they learned they were in luck. The new and elegant steamboat, *Cairo Belle,* was due that afternoon. Elizabeth helped Florrie select a new bonnet at the general store, and then went to the post office where she wrote brief notes to Jane Anne, Leo and her mother, another to Dolly Pierpont. The one to Tom was harder to write, because she had to confess her mistake in buying even one lot in Greenacres.

And so it was also a mistake to come here, of course, but to make the best of a bad bargain, I shall come home by another and somewhat longer route. It's not that I don't miss you, for I do, and ask you to be patient about this little adventure I now embark upon. I have chosen to return via New Orleans, which I yearn to see. I leave shortly on a splendid steamboat called the *Cairo Belle.*
I love you dearly, beg you to forgive me for being head-strong and not listening to your sound advice.

                                                             Liza

She paid the maximum postage and went across the tree-shaded street to the general store to which Florrie had returned, impatient with the letter-writing. Now people were strolling in the direction of the riverfront. A distant steamboat whistle sounded. Florrie dropped a pink shawl she was examining. "Come on!" As they started toward the levee she stopped in her tracks. "Drat! I clean forgot to see if there was any Greenacres mail at the P.O."

They crossed the street to the post office, and a moment later Florrie turned from the counter. She handed Elizabeth a letter, saying, "One for you!" Elizabeth's heart leaped as she saw Tom's handwriting. "Oh, do hurry," Florrie said. "You can read it on the

Cairo Belle!"

They joined the people flowing riverward. Pickaninnies skipped in the dust; grownups moved more sedately. Spotlessly white and well-filled with passengers, the steamboat churned toward where Elizabeth stood. At the foot of the short gangplank a white-uniformed officer flanked by a sailor holding a cashbox took twenty-two dollars for passage to New Orleans, the nearer townfolk observing the rite.

Aboard, Florrie Jakes settled her bonnet, touched the red bow under her chin. "Isn't this simply grand? I feel like a new woman already!" Swiftly, the steamboat picked up speed, and watching Cairo recede Elizabeth felt the sparkle of her daring.

"Let's go get us a seat in the grand salon," Florrie urged.

"You go. I'll join you when I've read my letter."

"I'll save you a chair."

Most people on deck were watching the shore sweep swiftly past. Elizabeth went to the opposite rail to open Tom's letter. Pleased anticipation filled her.

Elizabeth:

My anger is no less than when I arrived in Allerton and found you had left. I have tried without success to understand this. I told you I would be in Philadelphia on the 26th. Why did you let me look the fool to your family? Why?

As for this Leopard or Lippard who is apparently your escort, what kind of man do you believe me to be? Do you imagine I want a wife who consorts with other men? I do not.

This journey of yours leaves me to choose between two conclusions: you have managed to conceal until now a degree of lunacy, or you believed I will be coerced into abandoning my plans to follow you. Is that the game?

I have better things to do than try to understand you. Go to your Greenacres or to Hell if you please. Your recent behavior relieves me of the need to care which.

Tom

She began to shake. First her insides quivered, and then her whole body clenched and shook as if in biting cold. After a time—she never knew how long—she tore the letter in half, then in half again, reached out, opened her hand, and watched the white fragments of paper twist and whirl away toward the wide white wake.

In the long, vast salon filled with people and voices she saw Florrie standing, waving, pointing with the other hand to an empty chair beside her. As Elizabeth reached it a small, thin young man at Florrie's other side popped up. "This here is Mr. Hector Bassett," Florrie said. "He's a colporteur, he tells me, and travels all over the place."

Introductions completed, Hector Bassett put on his wide-brimmed black parson's hat, parted his black coat-tails and reseated himself. He had the face of a farm boy with freckles across his nose, but the manner of a man of years. He was, he revealed, one of two hundred and ten agents of the American Tract Society who traveled throughout the middle and southern states and territories selling and sometimes giving away pamphlets of a religious nature. "I am by way of being a lay preacher," he said modestly, "and my special meat is Papist families. This past year I got seventeen Catholics to throw off their bondage to Rome and turn Protestant. In the past six months I sold 1,383 pamphlets, which is something of a record.''

''I bet we're setting one right now,'' Florrie said, nodding happily. ''This boat's just humming along!''

Elizabeth was aware then of the slight vibration, of the rapid, churning slosh of the great paddlewheels.

''You have noted the speed?'' Bassett asked. ''By God's grace I survived a steamboat sinking only last year. I don't look forward to another.''

''Now don't be so gloomy!'' Florrie slapped at him playfully with the folding fan she had bought in Cairo. ''My friend and I just left our troubles all behind, and we look forward to a jolly cruise down to New Orleans.''

''I get off at Memphis. You might be smart to do the same.''

''Memphis! Who wants to go to Memphis?'' Florrie demanded. ''Talk about something cheerful or else keep mum!''

Evidently taken with Florrie, he obliged and told how he often made his way into remote hinterlands, to isolated cabins and hamlets where he was welcomed as a visitor from the great world. Elizabeth tried to listen, but again and again bitter words and phrases from Tom's letter, spoken in his angry voice, drowned out the colporteur's. The vibration of the vessel under her feet disturbed her more and more as she recalled what the captain of the *Chas. C. Carroll* had told her about the dangers of speed. She became aware of a dull ache in the small of her back, yearned to lie down, away from people, from voices. She stood up. ''I'm going to a stateroom to rest awhile.''

''Don't forget the first dinner gong sounds at two. The first serving is apt to be best, I find,'' Bassett said.

"I'm not very hungry, so you two go in without me if I'm still resting then."

Torpid on a stateroom bunk she heard a melodious gong and the footsteps of passengers on the deck outside. In a half-sleep she summoned up the face of Rozalia, but Tom's kept returning, tears trickled until anger dried them.

There was a tapping at the door and Florrie came in, the slight figure of Hector Bassett just behind her. "You feel some better?" Florrie asked, hopefully.

"I have urged Mrs. Jakes to leave with me at Memphis," Mr. Bassett said. "I have been asking some questions of a deckhand. The captain, as I feared, is known as a record breaker. I think the risk we run may be considerable."

Elizabeth sat up. A sharp twinge in her back was followed by a dull ache which seemed oddly familiar. "How soon do we reach Memphis?"

"In two hours, I'm told."

"I'll leave when you do."

"Oh, Elizabeth Aller, don't be so scared of nothing!" Florrie Jakes pouted. "You know good and well how anxious I am to get to New Orleans!"

"Then go on without me."

"I'll do no such thing!"

Hector Bassett backed toward the door. "I'll see about getting a portion of your fares refunded."

"He's just a smart aleck, and I don't care how many Bibles he sells!" Florrie said as soon as the door closed.

"I tend to believe him. But whether we're in danger or not, I intend to get off at Memphis. I'm not at all well." She knew as she spoke the words that they were the truth. Could any letter, however shocking, account for

474

her now acute discomfort?

"Oh, drat and damnation! I did so want to go steaming into New Orleans in real grand style!"

"Then do. I'll follow when I'm myself again. You can leave me your sister's address."

"What kind of a friend do you think I am? Just because I talked mean about my departed do you think I got a heart of stone? And anyways, I never been to Memphis."

Hector Bassett not only got four dollars refunded on each of their fares, but knew of a hotel that was clean, pleasant, and inexpensive. Florrie insisted on a room with two beds for it was a trifle cheaper for each of them. Making herself comfortable, the ex-tavern keeper fell asleep almost instantly.

Elizabeth passed a miserable night, unable to find any position that was comfortable. Her feelings about Tom's letter fluctua.ed wildly. He had not received her last, humble letter of this morning when he wrote those cruel words. He might have had some crushing disappointment in New York. Thus spoke logic. Anger said none of this mattered. With despair she knew that he had not dashed off the letter in the heat of fury; every word had been precisely formed by a steady hand. Had he really ceased to love her? She tried to imagine a future without him but could not.

She woke in the morning from sad dreams, unable to distinguish between her physical and mental misery. Her brain felt thick, dazed, while a dull pain nagged her lower back, radiating out over her abdomen. When she sat up, nausea made her groan. In the other bed, Florrie stirred. Elizabeth lay back, frightened. Florrie sat up, stretched, yawned loudly. "What time is it?"

"I don't know." To speak brought back the nausea;

she got up, stumbled to the washbasin, and retched. Nothing came up. "I'm sick." She tottered back to the bed, stood staring down at the bloodstain on the lower sheet. "I don't know what's wrong with me. I think I need a doctor."

"Just lay down. I'll get one if there's one to be got." Eyeing her, Florrie hurriedly dressed.

Fighting down terror, Elizabeth waited, staring up at the ceiling which a leak in the roof had marred with several stains, one shaped like the map of Africa. Tom's letter receded to minimal importance. Nothing mattered but the mysterious nagging ache and whatever disease it signified.

The doctor was named Cavendish and had a long yellowish face, hollow cheeks and a white mustache. His eyes were dark, sad, and knowing. He heard of her back pain and of the blood. "Have you missed a period?" he drawled.

"Period?"

"Your monthly, ma'am."

She thought a moment. "Yes. It's the change of life, isn't it?"

Moving swiftly, he got the pillow from Florrie's bed, raised the foot of Elizabeth's mattress, thrust the pillow under it so that her feet were several inches higher than before. He then lifted her head, took the pillow from under it, added that one below the mattress. Now she lay at an incline, her feet higher than her head. "If you don't stay quiet in this bed, you're goin' to lose this baby."

"Baby!"

"Yes, ma'am. Baby. Didn't you know you're expecting?"

As soon as he had gone Flossie Jakes said, "Don't that

476

beat all? I was took the same after my first husband up and died on me!"

Elizabeth did not hear her. On the ceiling the stain near the map of Africa was now an impish face. It seemed to be grinning down at her, the mask Fate wore when up to its tricks in Memphis, Tennessee.

XXX

I doubt that the news of a steamboat disaster on the lower Mississippi River would have had prominent mention in the Philadelphia *Ledger* had not a Pennsylvania Congressman been among the missing. As it was, the explosion of the boilers of the *Cairo Belle* in mid-river near the town of Jackson, Mississippi, and the ensuing raging fire and the sinking of the vessel before the eyes of the horrified and helpless viewers on shore was reported in grim detail as the worst such disaster in over a year. It had occurred at seven in the evening, the sound of the explosion alerting the townfolk who rushed to stare at the inferno of flames out on the water and the spectacle of human creatures leaping into the river from the floating holocaust which slowly sank. Of the nearly two hundred passengers only forty-two had made it ashore at Jackson, though others may have made it to the river's opposite bank or could have floated downstream, clinging to bits of the wreckage.

It had long been a matter of pride, I read, for steamboat captains to try to outspeed their rivals, with the result that the stokers work like demons piling more and more wood in the furnaces, producing such a head of steam that the boiler bursts. The explosion sends flaming wood in all directions to ignite all that was flammable.

Even though I knew that the steamboat my aunt had embarked on in Cincinnati was the *Chas. C. Carroll* and that it had sailed on the Ohio River, the very fact that the last words of her last letter to us had referred to a steamboat journey left me with a feeling of uneasiness. I recalled her comment in that letter about the choices we make, and I wondered about all those poor people on the *Cairo Belle* and why each one might have chosen to sail on that particular vessel, that particular day.

My aunt's second letter arrived two days later. Short and hastily written it said that Greenacres had been a disappointment and her stay a short one. She was, in fact, writing from the post office of the town of Cairo, to which she had crossed on a raft. A raft? To imagine my aunt in the stylish russet pelisse and bonnet in which I had last seen her standing on a raft was an effort. She went on to say that she had met a lady who had convinced her it would be foolish to be this near New Orleans and not see that remarkable city. "And so I shall do so, returning to Philadelphia by ship around Florida and up the Atlantic coast, less arduous and more interesting than my former route, I think. I leave in minutes on the splendid *Cairo Belle.*"

I remember that I snatched up the envelope and ran with it to the window for better light. She had paid 25¢ postage on December 6, the day the *Cairo Belle* had exploded.

The postmark blurred. Then the envelope. I felt the room whirl, melting into mist. This time Leo was not there to catch me. I came to myself huddled on the floor below the window. The first thing I saw was the white envelope I had dropped, the hateful envelope bearing that fatal date in small neat lettering in the upper right-hand corner.

Then feverish, scurrying thoughts found denials of the dreadful conclusion my mind had come to. Wait, wait! How far is Jackson from Cairo? Those steamboats go up and down the river. Was the *Cairo Belle* heading for New Orleans, or returning upriver? My aunt, I told myself, could be safe and sound in New Orleans. A map—I needed a map. I needed Leo!

I went to the hospital. He went to the heart of the matter: the list of survivors. The *Ledger* might well have those names. I went to the newspaper office. The only name sent had been that of the drowned or at best "missing" Congressman. The editor was sympathetic, realistic, and busy. "The dispatch we got said a lot of the bodies that washed ashore were pretty badly burned. In this kind of disaster identification is apt to be slow. About all you can do right now is pray for patience and hope for the best. Give me your aunt's name, and if I find out anything I'll let you know at once."

I made my voice firm, unwavering. "Elizabeth Aller Moss." I paused. "Elizabeth Aller, I meant to say."

"Well which? Moss or Aller?"

"Aller."

Leo and I agreed to say nothing to my grandmother just yet, since the one letter for all the family had been sent to me. I went about in a kind of daze; it did not seem possible that my aunt could be dead, yet I suffered horrible visions of her drowned body floating in that wide river toward New Orleans.

We went on Sunday to Allerton to dine, committed to the task of silence. The task of eating was also difficult. My grandmother poured tea with a steady hand while complaining of her daughter's negligence. "It is inconceivable that she has not written since that letter mailed in Cincinnati. I shall again inquire at the post office tomorrow."

"Now that the U.S. Postmaster is a member of our President's cabinet, one would expect fewer such fumbles," I said, sounding so much like Aunt Liza that I could have wept. Leo offered an anecdote concerning two families with the same surname who so regularly redelivered each other's mail that they became fast friends. Eventually a marriage took place between a young man and woman who otherwise might not have even met. "They now have two children who would never have existed without the U.S. Post Office, thus responsible for two deliveries it knows nothing about." Our mild laughter kept us from hearing Gerda admit a guest.

It gave me a strange feeling to look up and see Tom O'Casey in the dining room doorway, as if time had reversed itself, all the clock hands in the world spinning back to that other visit of November 26th when he had left in a rage. The man who strode in seemed a different one. He looked as if he had been bled too drastically for some ailment, lips pale, eyes hollow. His voice was bloodless too. "Has anyone heard from her since she wrote from Cairo?"

"Cairo?" My grandmother looked from him to me, alert.

"No," I told him.

Grandmother Aller was astonished. "Jane Anne, look at me. Did you receive a letter from Elizabeth of which you said nothing to me, nothing at all?"

"It was only to spare you worry."

"Worry?"

"There's a slight possibility that she may have been on the *Cairo Belle*," Leo said, with a cold look for Tom.

"Oh, Jesus!" Tom looked even whiter. "Is there nothing I can do right any more?"

"You can remove your hat," my grandmother said. "Jane Anne, please bring my smelling salts from my upper left-hand bureau drawer." Her eyes were on Cousin Amy. When I returned Amy was still upright and my grandmother was saying, "Borrowing trouble is an occupation fools enjoy. I do not. That Elizabeth mailed a letter from Cairo does not mean that she boarded the *Cairo Belle*."

Leo and I exchanged a long look. His slight nod corresponded to my feeling that further deception was pointless. "She intended to," I said gently.

"Intentions are one thing. Actions are another," she said. Tom made a sound like a groan, or the ghost of one. Plainly annoyed she commanded, "Do sit down, Tom. I have no whisky but I can offer tea, as before."

"Thank you, Mrs. Aller."

As she poured, my grandmother said, "My late husband had a saying which I believe you will all do well to keep in mind. 'Do not trouble trouble until trouble troubles you.'" Her hand was still steady and I realized that her mind had refused to accommodate the possibility that she had lost her last remaining child. . . .

Tom left when we did, which was earlier than usual. Outside a chill winter sunset glared behind stark trees. He at once exploded into self-recrimination. "How could I know that poor old lady knew nothing? You must forgive me. I guess it was the same for you as for me? First the news of the *Cairo Belle* disaster, then the letter written before she boarded?"

I nodded. "Then the story was in the New York papers, too?"

"Assemblyman Charles Weldon was on his way to New Orleans for his honeymoon. That was a short marriage. Do you happen to have a likeness of your aunt? A daguerreotype?"

I was shocked, thinking he asked a memento. "I have, and now more treasured than ever."

"Will you let me have it? Oh, I'll return it, but I need a likeness of her for a time."

"Why?"

"I'll wait another week to hear from her. Then I'm going to Cairo, Illinois. If I have to knock on every door in town I'll find who was at that steamboat landing when the *Cairo Belle* left on its last voyage. I'll find if a woman of her description boarded it."

"By enduring uncertainty a while longer you'll learn the same thing," Leo said.

"If I do any more enduring I'll go insane. I'm already half-crazed from knowing that if I'd spent Thanksgiving in Philadelphia instead of New York she wouldn't have left for Greenacres. If I'd married her the moment that was possible, she'd be here now. Yes, here with me now!" His voice had grown thick and harsh and he turned abruptly toward his rented coach. In a moment he had got control of his voice. "Do you want to ride with me into the city?"

At our boardinghouse I got out my daguerreotype of Aunt Liza in its folding case of maroon leather. He opened it and stood brooding down at her likeness. "She was my dream, you know, a dream that lured and prodded, both. And when it became reality I did not value it enough." He closed the case, hooked the tiny brass fastening, and put it into his inner breast pocket.

After we said our farewells he hesitated, then added,

"If you should hear from her, I beg you to let me know at once."

"When we hear, you will too," I said.

"I wrote her an angry letter that I will regret for the rest of my life. So be kind. Let me know of any word from her or of her."

I promised, hoping as I did that I would very soon be keeping my word.

My aversion to the house where I was born now seemed a trivial reaction indeed. I received title the day before Christmas, and the key. We found it to be in need of paint, wallpaper and other refurbishing, but all-in-all a nice house that seemed almost spacious after our boardinghouse suite. We hired a man to paint the woodwork and paper the walls.

My grandmother offered to help me choose the paper. The passasge of so much time—nearly a month since that fateful sixth of December—had not apparently affected her belief that her daughter was alive, and I thought of old Aaron Burr seeking word of his lost Theodosia.

Leo praised me for my calmness under distress. A letter from his mother shattered it. She had decided to marry a gentleman named Mr. Rufus Pinckeney. She summoned us both to Barclay Shore. "I want you here well before the wedding so that I can show off my son and daughter-in-law at certain gatherings, so do not say no."

"Maybe we should go down there for a week or so. A change will do you good."

A virago replaced his calm bride. "Good? I never heard such idiocy. Good? The only thing on earth that will do me good is to find out if Aunt Liza's alive or dead!" I went on to accuse him of being a hard, unfeeling man who had forced me to select wallpaper when all I wanted was to

485

read Dickens. "In Charleston, how will I find out if she drowned?" His patience was a marvel.

The scrawl I received from Tom O'Casey on January 3rd seemed to settle that question. No fewer than five people of Cairo had seen her board the ill-fated vessel. She had been wearing the russet pelisse in which I had imagined her crossing the river on the raft.

Hearts may break—at least in books they do. Mine accepted the truth it had already glimpsed.

XXXI

To induce the sleep he believed vital, Dr. Cavendish left a
tincture of laudanum. The opiate brought Elizabeth
relief from the emotions that besieged her on learning
that she was pregnant: rage because of the lie she had
believed about herself, astonishment, joy, fear, anxiety,
wonder, and bitterness at the irony of the timing. Again
and again in memory she tore Tom's ugly letter and let
the pieces blow away.

Florrie proved a faithful friend and nurse, brought
meals which went almost untouched, read aloud from the
Bible Hector Bassett brought, and waited on Elizabeth
hand and foot. "Flat on your back, the doctor said, if you
want to keep this baby. Though why you *do* want it, I'm
kind of hard pressed to figure out."

Sometimes, after the opiate got to work, the bed
seemed like a life raft to Elizabeth, she and the unborn
child safely carried along toward the future. Her intellect
had nothing to do with her decision to obey the doctor's
injunction. She knew the child was Tom's; she knew she
wanted to bring it into the world if she could. She did not
know if she would ever see him again, but this did not
seem to matter. Drifting in and out of drugged slumber
and almost enjoying unusual and complicated dreams,
Elizabeth passed two nights, and on the third day in

Memphis woke up hungry. "I think I'll go down to breakfast," she told Florrie, and did.

They continued their southward journey that same day on a steamboat called *The Brooklyn*. Now the climate became noticeably warmer, and she shed her pelisse, gave herself over to a dreamlike appreciation of the scenery and returned good health. The New Orleans waterfront burst on her eyes in all its color and motion and sound, close-packed ships' masts by the dozens swaying gently; and sailing in across the Gulf of Mexico she saw the great white sails of a Yankee clipper, from some far port perhaps halfway across the world.

She felt that she was in an exotic foreign land as she rode beside Florrie in an open calash. Such balmy breezes in December! She knew she had come to Rozalia's city. A tall, full-skirted woman, her face ebony, a pink headcloth arranged in elaborate stylized folds, walked by. Elizabeth soon saw others like it; she knew that the head scarf, once a badge of black women's inferiority had here been transformed into an assertion of dignity, proud as a banner. And she realized that more than melodrama lay under Rozalia's plight—that sudden knowledge of her black blood. It epitomized the plight of all women, whom priests had tainted with Eve's sin, whose mothers whispered the shameful secret of monthly blood—that hidden badge of womanhood—their doom and their destiny.

A stunning thought struck her: what if the revelation of Negro blood were a lie? What if Rozalia really was white? To learn so at the story's end, after paying a terrible price for believing she had a mulatto for a grandmother?

"I do think you've gone deaf," Florrie said. "I'll tell

you again: we're here."

The calash slowed and then stopped before a large, white two-story house with two fat white columns flanking the steps and to one side a large, glossy magnolia tree.

After Florrie knocked, the door was opened by a thin Negress in a flamboyant green turban. In moments a plump blond woman with very white skin had appeared and flung her arms around Florrie, laughing and crying, babbling in a heavy Southern accent about a sight for sore eyes. Then she turned round, her sky-blue eyes on Elizabeth. "It's just purely astonishin', you two comin' here today like this. Would you believe that two of mah gentlemen just left me? One got married and the othah up an' joined the army to go off to Texas to fight those Mexicans if it comes to that. So Ah got two perfectly lovely rooms, one overlookin' mah rear garden. Come an' see foah yo'self."

In the garden room, shuttered, cool, dim, Florrie's sister opened the jalousie at one window. "Smell mah roses! Smell mah jasmine!" Through the lacy leaves of the tree by the house Elizabeth saw at the far end of the garden a lattice summerhouse, and centered on the lawn before it a pedestal bearing a big mercury gazing ball.

Elizabeth turned to her. "Your sister told me the St. Charles Hotel is the best place to stay, but it can't be as lovely as this!"

"I do thank you kindly. How long was you plannin' on stayin' here in New Orleans?"

"Two weeks, at least."

"That'll be just fine. Mostly Ah prefer gentlemen, but for a friend of Florrie's Ah'm just bound to make an exception. Ah been gettin' seven dollahs a week for this garden room, which sounds a bit steep, but wait 'til you see the table Ah set!"

"I have just one request. Do you have a small table or desk that could be put there by the windows?"

"Table? Desk? Whatever for?"

"I want to start work on a novel."

Laurinda Bolling took the announcement in stride. "That's perfectly all right. We all have our little ways, Ah always say."

The first two weeks swiftly melted away. Not only was there a whole new city to explore, but its history to read about. She spent hours at the table by the window, writing descriptions of locales, the backgrounds of her major characters, trying to forge a plot. In the evenings she could, if she wished, take part in a pleasant social life, thanks to Florrie Jakes' unusual sister.

Laurinda Bolling may have been born in New Jersey, but she had married a Louisiana Bolling young and wore it proudly. Her accent was a buttery drawl, her gowns fluttered and flounced their ruffles and lace, and in the evenings she displayed a full, milky bosom, cleft up to just below her double chin. Her eyes had golden lashes and she rinsed her hair in lemon juice, spoke tartly of the men who had wanted to marry her. "But Ah never did have such an all-fired good time in bed as to wish to share the one I now got as a well-off widow, mah children grown an' gone, an' the time to pleasure mahself a bit." Her pleasures were modest, evening conversation in the parlor with her gentlemen boarders and various other guests, and occasional games of poker in the library which she had turned into a gaming room with a round green baize table. "Sizey stakes" were her preference, no penny-ante, and she won more often than not. Meals were "sizey," too, as she had boasted, and accounted for the three gentlemen who had been long-time permanent boarders: a retired riverboat captain, a white-haired naval officer who had fought in the Battle of New Orleans, and a young willowy artist with blond locks to his shoulders who lived on a remittance from his wealthy Virginia father. "Ah'm not a black sheep," Dalton told Elizabeth, "but rathah a white blackbird. Mah three brothers adoah horses as' gamblin' an got no'mal professions: a lawyah, a divinity student, an' a cadet at West Point. An' so one day mah Daddy said to me he didn't mind mah paintin' pictures, but would appreciate if Ah did it somewhere else." Dalton's interest in Elizabeth bounded upward when he found she was in the first stages of writing a novel. "We're kindred spirits, you an' me!"

A week after her arrival Elizabeth went to the big St. Charles Hotel, white as sugar frosting outside, more elegant than Astor House within. The manager welcomed her to New Orleans with exquisite courtesy and promised to see that any letters sent to her would be placed in his own mail compartment. Returning to Laurinda Bolling's she had a moment of doubt that she had ever written anyone of the St. Charles. The strange three days in Memphis had left much of what had happened before the moment of reading Tom's letter rather vague in her memory. But better safe than sorry!

In two weeks she went again to the St. Charles and was received with the same courtesy. No letters had arrived for her. This time the manager took her address and promised to send to her any correspondence. She returned home a trifle despondent. It seemed to her that Tom, on receiving her humble letter from Cairo should have repented his harsh one.

Back at the neat boardinghouse, how welcoming her room seemed! She drifted to the window to look out at the mercury gazing ball. If only she could see her future in it! But that was as dim as the ball was bright. Only within the little world of her novel did she not feel at odds with herself and the actual world. That night she wrote to her former editor at Ticknor and Fields asking his opinion about a novel, with a New Orleans locale, a white girl under the misapprehension that she is a quadroon.

She joined the others in the parlor just as the riverboat captain was delivering his opinion about a steamboat explosion: "A boiler is built to accommodate only so much steam pressure. There is a gauge to show that pressure, but on occasion it ceases to function properly. Since a stoker has no more wish to be blown to Kingdom Come than you or I, it is perfectly clear that a gauge failed on the *Cairo Belle*."

Elizabeth turned to Florrie. "Then Hector Bassett was right!"

"In the dining room in the Memphis hotel I heard a couple of men talking about a steamboat that exploded and caught fire, but I didn't hear them mention the name," Florrie said.

Elizabeth turned to the riverboat captain. "When did the *Cairo Belle* explode?"

"The *Cairo Belle* did not explode, only a boiler. The steamboat then caught fire and soon sank."

"But when?"

"The night of December 6th."

"Can you believe we was on it?" Florrie demanded.

"Mrs. Aller and me got off that afternoon at Memphis. God bless Hector Bassett!" As she told about the Godsent colporteur, Elizabeth was remembering that she had mentioned in at least one letter the steamboat's name because it had seemed such a charming one, redolent of the Mississippi. Would its fate have been mentioned in Eastern newspapers? Was it possible that her family— and Tom—thought her dead or missing?

She excused herself to write to her mother and Jane Anne. But when she started a letter to Tom her mind cramped. She looked down at the first painfully slow sentence: "In case you may have been concerned about me in view of the *Cairo Belle* disaster, I am writing to say . . ." She crumpled it, tried again. That attempt seemed worse. Slowly she tore the page in half, then in halves again. As she did, she remembered tearing in the same way Tom's cruel letter on the *Cairo Belle*.

In a moment she reached for another sheet of paper. She found herself writing words she had never intended. "I am still hurt and angered by the letter you sent to Greenacres. It was hateful and undeserved. I do not know what made me think we might have a future together there or anywhere. You have so far offered me only the life of a secret mistress. Even when you knew I was free you did not want to set a wedding date. All I have ever meant to you, apparently, was as a prize, a token to prove your worth. Revenge on Isaiah, on all the Isaiah's of the world, always lurked under your desire for me, I believe. But I am worthy of better treatment than you have lately accorded me. . . ." Her eyes skimmed the words. She threw down the pen, tore that letter to small shreds, dropped them into the wastebasket.

Then she addressed the letter to her mother, and the

one to Jane Anne and Leo. The effort slightly calmed her
boiling emotions. If Tom wished, he could find where she
was from her family in another ten days or two weeks. As
she turned down the oil lamp on her desk she knew that
she had made a grave decision: she would never beg him
to act as father of their child!

The next day, when Elizabeth and Florrie paid a visit to
the "Wishing Spot" on Bayou Street, Florrie's wish was
not hard to guess: "A gentleman with an eye for a lady
that's full-formed." But two crucial wishes occurred to
Elizabeth: that the Ticknor and Fields editor would
approve her going on with *Rozalia, A Creole Bride;* and
that Tom would write to her and all be well with them
again. "Only one wish?" she asked Florrie. Not that she
believed for a moment that a coin dropped in a hollow
tree stump could change her destiny, but like her visits in
the past to the Fisher sisters, the rite offered the chance
to pretend that there might be mysteries in the universe
that defied rational explanation.

"Only one," Florrie nodded. "That is, one per coin, I
guess. I put in two bits."

Elizabeth wished twice. Bending over with her ear
close to the gnarled stump she heard the faint clink as her
last coin struck the others piled within, and wondered
how many other wishful humans had that day enriched
the sorceress.

One wish came true. The editor urged her to go on with
her novel.

XXXII

Leo and I moved into the house where I was born before we journeyed to the plantation where I had once dreamed of living with poor Jonas. It was smaller than I had imagined from his letters, less handsomely furnished, too, although perhaps the cloud of grief in which I walked subdued its Southern charm. I met and liked Henry, the Negro slave whom Leo as a child had taught to read and write and who now oversaw the field hands. The house servants were of course darkies, and altogether I was quite surrounded by black faces. Nor had I been prepared for the great number of mules. Gray-brown, stubborn, and rather ugly, these beasts, Leo said, were as essential to Southern agriculture as the slaves. I had imagined the tobacco fields as having plants as tall as a man and bearing pink blossoms. They were not blooming in January, so I found them unimpressive. The row of brick slave cabins were not as large as I had believed, and the slaves were shabbily dressed.

But Emily Harth De Lange was much more than I had expected. A beauty at fifty, with lustrous dark eyes and hair, her daintiness and frills did not deceive me. She was chatelaine of this castle and ruled it without seeming to. She said I did not look like a Northern young lady, but was unclear about what a Northern lady was supposed to look like. Her marriage to Rufus Pinckeney, a noble-looking gentleman of impressive lineage, took place in one of Charleston's many beautiful churches, was well attended. At the later reception in her father's home her many friends drawled pleasantries at me which I could barely understand. I told Leo it was lucky he had lived so long in the North when we met or I might not have understood his proposal!

Leo confessed that the marriage was a great relief to him. For me it was hail and farewell to the plantation that had once figured in my girlish, romantic dreams. But as Emerson says, there is a law of compensation. It was at Barclay Shore, I later discovered, that I had conceived my first child.

The first thing I saw when we returned to our new home in Philadelphia was the Stiegel rose glass Aunt Liza gave me on its little shelf below the parlor window. Seeing it made the tears start to my eyes.

"Jane Anne." Leo spoke behind me, quietly. I turned and saw him holding the several letters he had picked up from the hall below the mail slot. One he gave me. The postmark was New Orleans, December 29. My aunt's handwriting stared up from the envelope. I tore it open with the eerie feeling that I was about to read a message from beyond the grave.

Dear Jane Anne and Leo:

I do hope you have not been at all worried. I have just learned of the fate of the *Cairo Belle* on which I probably wrote you I was sailing. I did, but became rather ill and disembarked at Memphis. There is not much likelihood that you have heard of the explosion which sank her, but just in case you have, my friend and I had a lucky escape.

The steamboat's speed was alarming indeed.

New Orleans is fascinating and I have embarked on a novel with this locale. I am at present hoping to attend a hoodoo or voodoo ceremony in the Vieux Carre cottage of a local witch. I believe a chicken is sometimes killed, but as I enjoyed one last night in a fricassee, I think I can bear it.

I shall remain here much longer than I once intended, there being no need to rush back to Philadelphia. I hope your Christmas was happy, and do forgive this belated wish. Down here amid palms, magnolias and cotton bales, December just hasn't seemed like it. I am writing my mother and Dolly Pierpont to let them, too, know I'm not lodged deep in Mississippi mud. The river's quite brown here at the delta, as though it had Negro blood.

Love to you both,
Aunt Liza

I gave the letter to Leo and began to laugh and then to cry, and Leo put his arms around me and patted my shoulder as a mother would have done. The stronger a man's character, the more gentle he can be when sympathy is required. He understood that they were tears of pent-up anguish, belatedly escaping.

What struck me next was the almost awesome way in which circumstances had conspired against my aunt and Tom O'Casey. If she had embarked for New Orleans on any other steamboat but the *Cairo Belle* . . . Choices!

I remembered the promise we had made Tom O'Casey and wrote to him that my aunt was alive and well in New Orleans and included her address. When I wrote to her I ended with words I hoped would please her: "And if I have a little girl, I will name her after you."

XXXIII

The letter Elizabeth at last wrote to Tom was brief. It told where she was, and that she had been hurt and angered by the letter he had sent to Greenacres. It even revealed that she had gotten off to a good start on a new novel. It did not say she was bearing his child. Even though she tried, she could not bring those words out of herself and onto paper. She knew she was guilty of pride, perhaps a foolish pride. But she wanted to know first that he cared for her still, had yearned for her, perhaps even had mourned her as dead. She could not—would not—be only another Betsy to him.

After sending it a feeling of helplessness gripped her. If he ignored this letter too, then what would she do? She fought down the brief panic that followed by telling herself the answer: she would continue to write her book as Mrs. Aller, the pregnant widow. And after the book was done, the child born . . . ? Her mind balked. Like the mercury ball in the garden, it could reflect only the immediate world.

In that world two letters loomed large. The first, from Jane Anne, told of Tom's trip to Cairo with her daguerreotype, which outweighed the news that Elizabeth might have a namesake.

Dolly Pierpont's letter arrived two days later. After

scolding Elizabeth for not writing sooner and admitting envy concerning the trip to New Orleans, she continued:

And now, my dear, since I am bursting with it, some perfectly astonishing news—believe me when I say it has all in New York agog—Imogene's murderer is now known—although perhaps I should write *murderess.* Adela Fisher killed her own sister!

This was revealed in an extraordinary way—no clever work by the sleuth London was involved—She confessed! If that confession came from the deeps of a tortured soul it emerged in a bizarre fashion indeed! For at a seance the voice of her dead father spoke again through her lips and told her to go to the police and tell the truth about the slaying of Imogene! There were nine of us taking part in that seance—all stunned silly!

As the newspapers tell it, Adela Fisher went to Imogene's room at City Hotel, arriving shortly before ten. She had just received a letter from relatives in St. Louis kindly inviting them to live at their home until getting settled in suitable quarters of their own. Overjoyed, and despite the hour, she hastened to her erring sister with this news, only to meet with rebuff. Imogene, it seems, had no intention of living a better life. Her refusal led to accusations—rage mounted in Adela's heart—said she had no recollection of seizing that bronze vase and striking her sister repeatedly—saw the body on the floor, the weapon in her own hand—cast it aside and fled. Did you ever? Cain and Abel reenacted with a female cast!

What a pity Tom O'Casey was not here to learn all this! As to him, I must tell you he has shocked many by his strange behavior. I gather you and he have had a falling out—he upset me greatly with his wild tale that you had drowned when a steamboat exploded—Robert will not reveal the details of some kind of bad joke he played on the president of the Union Club while very drunk. And now he has simply disappeared. I ran into Cornelius Ferris, the dear, who says Tom talked to him about joining the army—can you believe it? A soldier at his age? And without even a war yet to justify it. I do believe, Elizabeth—*if* I am right about that falling out between you—that you are far better off without him.

Do not dare wait so long before writing me again.

Affectionately,
Dolly

Too numbed to weep, to dazed to think, Elizabeth flung herself across the bed and lay staring out over the white counterpane. It seemed a vast wasteland where she was lost. Emotions buffetted her mind, thrummed on her nerves. First she cowered from the notion that she had dared defy the wisdom of the ages as to her subservient female role when she went west to Greenacres without Tom's approval. She clenched her fists, shook her head. No! A riverboat captain out to break a record had brought about all this grief—to say nothing of dozens of deaths. And that was not her fault. Simple chance had brought her to the *Cairo Belle* on the day of that last, fatal voyage. Chance? No, too simple! She boarded that particular vessel on that particular day because of everything that had happened to her up to that point. And she had been spared from death by drowning or burning because of carrying Tom's child. Would she have disembarked at Memphis without the malaise of threatened miscarriage, solely because a colporteaur thought the speed excessive? No. Love had saved her!

She sat up, and the first thing she was aware of seeing

501

was the neat pile of manuscript on her writing table. She had left the lid off the inkwell again.

Tom and the others she most loved were far away. But Rozalia remained, and Claude Demarest and Madame Joliet and the evil Gaspard.

She walked toward her paper people and in a moment took up her pen.

On February 20th Elizabeth stood on a low stool while Laurinda Bolling's dressmaker ("a clevah French lady who can look at a pictuah in Godey's Ladies' Book and copy most any gown perfectly lovely") knelt on the floor pinning up the hem of a dress of rose-pink challis. Of the three gowns Elizabeth had packed in the larger valise only one could be worn because of letting out tucks in the bodice. She was sure that as soon as she appeared in the new dress her secret would be evident to the gentlemen boarders.

Her attempts to find out where Tom was had failed. A letter sent to his New York house was returned, much battered and marked "NOT HERE." Cornelius Ferris had heard nothing, nor Mr. Carmichael, nor Jeremiah Ould. Even Brian Ryan, managing to eke out a living with small building jobs, said he was waiting hopefully for a letter.

And so she had come to terms with a hard truth: she could do nothing but wait to learn where Tom was, if he was anywhere to be found. In the meantime she dreamed of him, wrote her novel, and coped with such minor matters as confronting in her new maternity gown the gentlemen in the parlor.

But they were too engrossed in trading their knowledge and rumors concerning the threat of war with Mexico to notice at once anything so minor as a thicker waist. Captain Petard was speaking, his weathered face with its drooping gray mustache animated. "President Polk warned General Zachary Taylor against any unfriendly acts against the Mexicans, quite true. But he also commanded Taylor to take appropriate action if any hostile act were committed against us. And there, you see, is the crux of it. If the Mexicans persist in obdurately regarding the Nueces River as the boundary of independent Texas, our 28th state since December, and therefore cross the Rio Grande and make any sort of fuss in the area, why then, gentlemen, Taylor has orders from his President to drive them back. And that'll mean war."

Captain Blatty, the retired naval officer ran a gnarled hand through his white hair as if to calm his own excitement. "Our *navy* will play a crucial part, don't forget. While Taylor and his troops engage the Mexican army at the north border our fleet can take a second army down to Vera Cruz on Mexico's eastern coast, said to be ill-defended. Our soldiers and marines can march up to Mexico's capital just as the Spaniards did over three hundred years ago. What they did then, we can do now. Take the damn city!" He turned to where the women sat. "Your pardon, ladies."

"I'll pardon your 'damn.'" Elizabeth said. "But I won't forgive Polk if he pushes us into an unjust war against a weaker nation."

The men stared at a woman with such a forceful opinion. The retired naval officer spoke: "'I see you are unaware of the many past provocations before this problem at the Texas border. The year before the Alamo, twenty-two Americans were executed by the Mexicans.

503

Debts to Americans totaling several million have gone unpaid. American ships have been detained and captured by Mexico. Americans have been robbed and murdered on the high seas!"

Captain Petard said, "Our great mistake, ma'am, was ever to recognize Mexico as a nation at all. Ever since it won its freedom from Spain in '22 it has been shaken by revolutions, led by men out only to plunder it. Mexico is merely a state of anarchy, a late stage of the breakdown of the Spanish Empire!"

"Does that justify our attacking her now?"

"We will not attack," Captain Blatty explained, patiently. "We will only retaliate."

Laurinda Bolling interceded to restore peace. "Ah just do not understand, Elizabeth, why you get yo'self so riled up over a wah that's bound to be, no mattah what we-all say. The whole entiah South is *fo'* this wah, an' don't you forget it!" A glance at Elizabeth's waist conveyed her belief that her friend had more real and important concerns.

One was a snag in her plot. The first two hundred pages seemed fine: Rozalia learns she has black blood, her mother a quadroon, not white like her dead father. So Rozalia renounces Claude, scion of a fine old French family. This leaves Rozalia in jeopardy from evil old Gaspard, who wants to make her his secret mistress. But at last Madame Joliet confesses that she is Rozalia's real grandmother and gave her illegitimate daughter to her trusted mulatto servant to raise. Claude learns the truth and all is well. But it now seemed to Elizabeth that Claude must offer marriage while still believing Rozalia to be an octaroon. *Then* comes Madame Joliet's confession of the truth. A nobler Claude emerges, and the theme is not betrayed.

Shut in her room, the pen moving smoothly across the page or lying idle while her brain was clenched in thought, it sometimes seemed to Elizabeth that she was a little mad, so much more real were the creatures of her imagination at times than any of the actual people around her. It occurred to her that like the heartbroken glass-maker Stiegel she was coping with loss by pursuing beauty, though of another sort.

In late March, aware at last of her pregnancy, the gentlemen boarders showed an excess of the courtesy due a mother-to-be, and particularly one to whose interesting condition was added the touching aura of recent loss— the death of the non-existent Mr. Aller. Dalton was particularly considerate. Although it was not proper for a lady who was *enciente* to be seen in public, he gallantly escorted her to the Mardi Gras parade, of which she needed a vivid description for her novel, knowing no Northern publisher would consider a New Orleans locale valid if it did not include that famous event. She could not, however, induce Dalton to furnish her with a description of the inside of one of Marie Laveau's octaroon bordellos. "Mah deah Elizabeth, I assuah you that if one of those women in theah was to approach me with lascivious intentions, Ah would most likely faint dead away."

She had heard nothing of Tom's whereabouts by late April when a *Picayune* headline brought the news that presaged outright war:

MEXICO ATTACKS TAYLOR TROOPS

Her eyes raced over the lines below: Mexico, viewing

Taylor as wrongfully occupying Mexican soil gave him an ultimatum to withdraw. In the absence of communication with Washington, "Old Rough and Ready" had to act on his own authority. He cut off supplies to the Mexican troops to force them to withdraw instead. But on April 24th a force of 1,600 Mexican soldiers had crossed the Rio Grande, encircled a scouting party of sixty-three Americans and killed them all.

"American blood has been shed on American soil!" was the cry Polk raised in his ensuing message to Congress. "A state of war now exists with Mexico, notwithstanding all our efforts to avoid it!"

The South, said the *Picayune*, was wild with excitement, and volunteers were enlisting by the thousands. War fever everywhere had begun to blaze: "Mexico or death! Ho, for the halls of Montezuma!" In the Bolling parlor Elizabeth stood alone, the only pacifist, for Dalton seemed to straddle both fences.

"But, ma'am, they attacked us! Invaded us! Killed our men!" cried Captain Petard.

"Invasion is debatable."

"American blood has been shed on American soil!" the naval officer affirmed.

"It was not American soil, as the young Congressman from Illinois firmly stated."

"Abe Lincoln is a Northerner!"

"Born in Kentucky."

"No matter! He's a traitor to every one of our twenty-eight states if he can't see we must arise in our might when American blood is spilled!"

Abraham Lincoln had not swayed many other representatives, who cast only fourteen votes against war with Mexico. In the Senate, John Calhoun, gray and weary, urged that Congress must move with "forbearance, dignity and calmness." There was no war yet; only Congress could declare war, not President Polk, he had said. Senator Sam Houston did not want war either. Henry Clay had announced that the war urged by Polk was "unnatural, lamentable." Daniel Webster said that it was "founded on pretexts and unconstitutional." But it was Calhoun of South Carolina who went about pleading with Senator after Senator not to vote for war. The defeat of Mexico would mean acquisition of a vast new territory which the South would want as slave states, the North as free. His fear was a fatal disunion. On the day Polk's message to Congress was read Calhoun stood before the Senate and, eyes blazing, said that before he would vote for war he would plunge a dagger into his heart.

The Senate, like the House, voted for war.

For Polk now had the pretext he wanted and could exclaim: "The cup of forbearance with Mexico is exhausted!" That the soil upon which American blood had been shed could not be proven to be American soil at all did not seem to matter: legitimate national pride had deteriorated into arrogance, concealing with a nationalstic slogan a very real greed. On May 13, 1846 war was declared. Congress appropriated $10 million for initial expenses; a call for 50,000 volunteers was quickly met. The majority were Southerners, dreaming of a huge extension of Southern lands, even of a Southern confederacy.

General Zachary Taylor defeated the Mexican army at Palo Alto and marched south to Monterrey. Soon the *Picayune* announced his triumph over a large army at Buena Vista. "American know-how and superior weapons!" crowed the naval officer, Captain Blatty. "We have Colt revolvers and long-range howitzers. The Mexicans still use copper cannonballs. They fall short and just roll along the ground. Our men can jump over 'em!"

"I doubt the war can last more than another month or two." Captain Petard stroked his mustache, smiling.

It soon became clear that the scope of the war was to be far wider than Northern Mexico where Taylor's men were fighting and winning: The United States fleet would bear General Winfield Scott and his men to the waters off Vera Cruz, all primed and ready to follow the route of Cortés nearly three hundred hard miles up to Mexico City. And the rumor ran that another army was poised and ready to march toward the remote territory of California.

And where was Tom?

In June Laurinda Bolling recommended a midwife. "Mizz Thompson. She delivahed mah last chile, been practicin' here in N'Orleans more'n twenty-five years, an' she don't hardly evah lose a mothah nor baby—'cept the ones born blue."

"Blue?"

"Stillborn. But that's a seldom thing. Ah just do wish you to see Mizz Thompson, let her sort of examine you, deah. Ah mean, with mah gentleman livin' heah, Ah jest can't have yoah watah breakin' at the supper table."

She sent a maid for Mrs. Thompson, a large, wide lady of perhaps fifty with capable-looking hands. Noting the pinkness of the palms in contrast to the golden tan of the backs, Elizabeth looked up into wide-spaced brown eyes. "Yes, Mrs. Aller. I *am* a woman of color." She had

Elizabeth lie flat on her back, and with eyes shut felt her abdomen in various places, then nodded. "Your baby's placed right. No fear as to that, at least. You're about a month from delivering this child."

"But Mizz Thompson does have her little ways," Laurinda confided later. "Spankin' clean sheets, an' all the windows closed."

With the end of June the humid heat of summer closed in on the city. Motions became languid, and palm-leaf fans slowly waved to move the air. It became harder and harder for Elizabeth to keep her mind on mere words, yet she was determined to finish her novel before her child was born. In mid-July she wrote, "Finis." There was still the task of making a clean copy for Ticknor and Fields, but that was simple compared to forging this first draft. She had remembered the advice of George Lippard and had given Gaspard la Roche a gory end.

When the first of August arrived without a sign of a labor pain she revealed to Mrs. Thompson her concern about the baby's tardiness. First children, she was told, are often late. "Soon enough you'll have your hands full!"

But the white wicker bassinette at the far end of the room remained empty.

On August 3rd she learned where Tom was. Jane Anne enclosed the letter he had just written to them.

Dear Jane Anne and Leo:

Under separate cover I have sent the daguerreotype of Elizabeth you lent me. I have had a copy made, and thank you.

The tragic outcome of that journey I made to Cairo left me in a state of mind I find it hard to describe. I can recall only unrelated moments of my long journey back to New York, this being due to the great amount of whisky I consumed, being too cowardly to endure the pain of my loss.

In New York my earlier determination to live down the aftermath of my unjust arrest seemed senseless. I found I had great contempt for public opinion. This led to words and acts that shocked those who had liked and trusted me, and gave satisfaction to those who did not.

In short, I sold my home for ready cash, put my business, such as it was, in the hands of a trusted employee, and headed West. When I reached St. Joseph, Missouri, I volunteered to serve in the army. I write this from Fort Leavenworth, Kansas Territory, as a soldier in the Army of the West. My commander, Colonel Stephen Kearney, is a tough and valiant man, a Catholic, and has already raised my rank. I have bought a horse, and hope for a transfer to the cavalry.

Our ultimate destination is California. I welcome the long march ahead. As to outdistancing the loss of my beautiful Liza, I know that can never be.

> Sincerely,
> Sergeant Thomas O'Casey

As she finished reading, the baby fiercely kicked. She rushed to her desk and penned an answer.

Dearest Tom:

For the distance that lies between us now, I take full blame. By luck I got off the *Cairo Belle* at Memphis. I did not know it had sunk for two weeks, nor that you knew. I was not able to behave any more wisely or kindly than I did. But that is past and now our child's birth is very near. Yes! You did not love a barren woman, after all. The midwife I have engaged is competent. I have two close woman friends and a large, pleasant apartment in this boardinghouse. As soon as you get this letter I beg you to write to me the words I now write with all my heart:

I will love you until I die.

Liza

Her joy could not be concealed, nor did she wish to hide it from her friends. She revealed the existence of a man she loved and hoped to marry, showed them the letter he had sent Jane Anne and Leo. Laurinda Bolling was deeply moved, and had to wipe away a tear. "Mah stahs, it's like a book, ah sweah it is! Think of him thinkin' you was drowned, an' you thinkin' he no longah loved or cared!"

Before dawn next morning, her labor pains began.

Elizabeth had imagined that her courage was equal to this ordeal; it was her private belief that some women made much of it both because they had been told to expect agony and to emphasize the importance of what they saw as their most important function. But what Mrs. Thompson called "hard labor" was worse than she could have believed possible, and went on for twelve hours. At the end of the first three she was given a clean sheet to tear, to bite on, to muffle her groans, animal sounds that she was ashamed of yet could not contain. The room was stifling; she pleaded in vain for an open window, and at last Mrs. Thompson allowed in a little air from the garden. The sheet was nothing but shreds now and she was given another. "Bear down!" Mrs. Thompson urged for the hundredth time, and she did, thought she felt the child trying feebly to get out, in vain. In a pool of sweat, fainting and coming to, she screamed "Open all the windows!" because outside it was dusk and a breeze touched her. Grunting, she bore down with all her might, felt something gush from her, and bore down harder; then she heard a strangled wail and knew the baby was born.

"You have a little boy," Mrs. Thompson's weary voice said.

When the bright pink baby in one of the white gowns from the layette was placed in her arms Elizabeth looked down at the face with bulging eyes slitted in sleep and felt tenderness for the poor little thing, stunned as he was from his arduous journey into New Orleans. . . .

A week later when Elizabeth glanced through the paper the words KEARNEY MOVES WEST caught her eye, and she read that the Army of the West had moved out of Fort Leavenworth and was marching toward the Santa Fe trail bound for New Mexico. "The American battering ram will soon push at the farthest reaches of the old Spanish Empire in the New World."

At her breast the infant sucked contentedly. Its peaceful oblivion brought home the awesome probability that her letter to Tom had not reached Fort Leavenworth in time, that this baby's father did not know of its existence, and believed that she was dead. And now he was marching farther and farther away with each passing day across the western half of a vast continent with all its unknown perils.

She held Tommy closer, her body rocking as she sang to him, comforting herself and taking strength from this cherishing.

In a neat pile on her desk stood the finished novel. It seemed an artifact from another lifetime.

*　　　*　　　*

During her languid lying-in period, her room shuttered against August heat, the gentleman boarders tiptoed in with offerings of flowers and fruit. The cook's thin young daughter Juliette was hired as nursemaid; she reminded Elizabeth of the young Melonia. After a week she felt perfectly able to resume a normal existence and in spite of protests by Laurinda went for a walk in the early evening. A period of rest of at least two weeks and up to a full month was customary. But the realities of Elizabeth's existence took no account of this. The five hundred dollars she had brought to Greenacres was melting away. In the Philadelphia bank were 3,200 dollars. Ould was still trying to get Isaiah to part with the money and railroad shares promised in the property settlement.

No sooner had Elizabeth completed a clean copy of the first chapter of *Rozalia* than the baby became colicky and fretful. The sugar tit Laurinda brought it proved ineffectual. The middle of the night seemed Tommy's favorite time to cry. Weary and distraught, Elizabeth would nurse and soothe him. "Ah hope yo baby don't turn out to be one of these bawlers," Laurinda said. "Ah got mah gentlemen's rest to considah, to say nothin' of mah own. Maybe you better think about findin' yo-self a small house to rent."

It was an enormous relief when Tommy's colic passed abruptly, bringing silent nights and a return of Laurinda's sunny disposition. That same day Elizabeth dressed in the coolest of the gowns she had brought with her—delighted to find it only a little tight—and continued with the second draft of her novel. This task lacked the enchantment that had transcended reality. With cool eyes she found flaws, but in two months she mailed the fair copy off to Ticknor and Fields in Boston.

With no other focus to distract her, she set about the pleasant business of enjoying her child. It did not take long to find that the charms of a young infant were limited. She would hold Tommy, look into the dark blue eyes, observe the little grins that came and went, wipe away a bubble of saliva, wonder why she felt no surge of adoring love such as mothers were said to experience. And Tommy was such a pretty baby. Everyone smiled down at him with pleasure, and she thought how fortunate it was for an infant to be pretty, so that his first experiences of other humans consisted of beaming faces and cooing voices of approval.

An insidious despondence took over her being.

What is wrong with me? she asked herself. Was it that there was no father to take pride and joy in the child? Was it because the responsibility for its rearing was hers alone and might always be? Why could she not feel what mothers are supposed to feel? She had known more strongly maternal feelings for her sister's child. What was wrong?

She decided that what she had learned of life since she brought Jane Anne home had disabused her of many fallacies, so that the reality of bearing a child was now no supreme experience of a short and innocent life, but seemed no more than an animal process she had endured. Seated by the bassinet she stared down at the small sleeping face, so touching and vulnerable in contrast to the disproportionately large organs of procreation.

Strangely enough, it was Dalton who offered an explanation that seemed to lighten the post-partum depression of which only he and she seemed aware. "It seems to me, Elizabeth, that you-all know one of yo' babies is jest fine. But yo don't know a thing about the other."

"The other?"

"Yo' chile of ink and paper! Is Rozalia a healthy creature, or too pore an' sickly to live?"

She nearly hugged him. "And I can't do a thing about Rozalia, but I'm letting her spoil my pleasure in Tommy!"

"Ah do feah that's the case." He squinted at the canvas on the easel before him. "Hold the pose jest a few minutes moah, please." He was painting a Madonna and child, sure to find a buyer in largely Catholic New Orleans. Elizabeth held not Tommy but a small bolster in her arms, for the moment.

To hold onto her belief that Tom was still alive and that one day she would hear from him she had sent several other letters to him at Fort Leavenworth in the hope they would eventually reach him. In late August the *Picayune* offered heartening news of the Army of the West. After a long grueling march along the old Santa Fe trail, sometimes on blazing carpets of flowers, past massive buffalo herds, often parched by thirst, always weary, tormented by mosquitos and buffalo gnats, they had easily occupied the New Mexico town of Las Vegas, promising protection from the Indians and freedom of religion. From there Kearney's forces had quietly taken town after town and at last Santa Fe itself, called by his soldiers "Mud Town" because of the adobe houses. Not a shot was fired except for a noisy salute as the Stars and Stripes glided up. "'Mud Town' would seem an inadequate name for a sizeable and vigorous small city, its inhabitants friendly, the men with slit breeches, silver spurs and flaring capes, the women, though barelegged, clad in full skirts and vivid colors, all as gay as the

515

'fandangos' danced there with frequency and abandon to the thrum of Spanish guitars and other instruments."

Barelegged ladies? Dancing fandangos? She turned her thoughts from them and sternly suppressed the thought that unless her letters sent to Fort Leavenworth had caught up with him, Tom did not know she was alive, would not necessarily feel obliged to remain faithful to a drowned love. She ran to the bassinet, picked up the baby, danced around the room, rocking him in her arms. "Your Daddy's alive and happy in Mud Town! Dancing a fandango! Maybe in silver spurs!"

But early September brought crushing news. At Santa Fe, Kearney had split his forces. He and his 100 Dragoons were riding to California. The rest, a thousand men, had marched toward Chihuahua under Colonel Doniphan, across a dreary sagebrush desert known as *Jornada del Muerto:* Dean Man's March. "Doniphan's Thousand" would of course join General Zachary Taylor's army, fighting hard against considerable odds in Northern Mexico. And where was Tom?

She hoped he was en route to California, where a naval squadron under Commodore Sloat had landed blue jackets on July 7th, it was now known. But on the chance that he was marching into Mexico with Doniphan, news from that hub of the war became of vital interest. After a victory at Palo Alto, won by bullets, not morale, according to a young West Pointer named Ulysses Grant, Taylor's troops marched on to Monterey, a city said to be a natural stone fortress, bristling with cannons.

In mid-October United States newspapers were blazoning news of another victory, sent by the new electromagnetic wireless "At Monterey our troops advanced through thorny bushes, driving rain and heavy Mexican fire. Undaunted, they stormed up Independence Hill to the top of the rampart and unfurled the Stars and Stripes. A howitzer shattered the line of enemy soldiers and our troops took and held the Bishop's Palace. After two days of street fighting, to the wild and eerie battle cries of Texas soldiers, Taylor's troops on September 14th took the city of 15,000, though to heavy casualties. . . ."

And where was Tom?

The old gentlemen in the Bolling parlor seemed to know more about the war than the *Picayune* did. They took a fierce delight in bloody battles, excoriated Polk for trying to place old "Fuss and Feathers" Scott in supreme command, a post he wisely refused. The honor thus fell to old "Rough and Ready" Taylor. They insisted that Polk was jealous of him because he had been born in a log cabin, grew more popular with each report from the front, and was clearly Presidential timber. They were familiar with the names of the young West Point officers and had their favorites: Ulysses S. Grant, Robert E. Lee, Thomas L. Jackson, Jefferson Davis, George Meade, and William T. Sherman. The riverboat captain favored Lee, perhaps the handsomest in a group of handsome young men, but the retired naval officer liked Grant best, even after his compassion for Mexicans, expressed in a letter to his fiancée, leaked out: "Weak and corrupt, Mexico is no real enemy. Her people have been victimized by decadent leadership. Their splendid courage is all for nothing, their losses usually double ours. With a soil and climate scarcely equalled, Mexico has more poor and starving subjects who are willing to work than any country in the world. The rich keep down the poor with a hardness of heart that is incredible," he was quoted as saying.

"Grant's a Northerner," sneered the riverboat captain, "probably an abolitionist too. He's thinking of the Mexies as Nigras."

"He's an honest man, doesn't puff up our victories by making out the enemy's worse than it is!" the naval officer said.

But both loved old "Rough and Ready" when he defied orders from Washington; Taylor went ahead and occupied Saltillo, the chief pass through Mexico's Sierra Madre, in November. Then at Buena Vista General Santa Anna, learning that Taylor's forces were depleted, surrounded the Americans and demanded surrender. The Americans refused. "The forces were so close that the next morning the Americans could watch Mass being celebrated by the enemy, see the fumes from incense and hear Latin chants." It was Colonel Jefferson Davis who was ordered to lead the Mississippi Rifles in a charge. "Badly wounded in the foot, he displayed consummate strategy, ordering his men to ride forward in a V, open-end toward the Mexicans. A brigade of the enemy rode into it, and at a cry of 'Fire' our troops massacred the Mexican cavalrymen whose riderless horses galloped in all directions."

But where was Tom? And where was *Rozalia, a Creole Bride?*

Aware of the long distance it had to travel to Boston, Elizabeth had made another clean copy while the changes from the first draft were fresh in her mind. Now with November nearly over, should she assume that at some point the package had gone astray, been lost? Should she send Ticknor and Fields the other manuscript? Surely nearly three months was a long enough time for her editor to have received it, read it, come to a conclusion and written to her, if only a rejection.

She had written him a letter explaining her fear of loss in the mail when the letter from him arrived at last. A letter! No returned manuscript. With shaky hands she opened the envelope, eyes racing along the lines of the letter: "considerable hesitation . . . a heroine who is believed part Negro from page 35 and for most of the rest of the story . . . but, amazingly . . . interest in her plight, despite . . . have decided to publish . . . same terms . . . advance on royalties and written agreement to follow. . . ."

Suddenly limp, she sat down. It was all right! She had earned her keep and the baby's for a while, need not worry about dwindling funds, need not worry except for . . . Tom.

The truth must be faced, she told herself, the truth I have been hiding from. There has been time for the letters I sent to Fort Leavenworth to have caught up with Tom. But it could be a long time yet before I hear from him.

Jane Anne's ecstatic letter made her laugh aloud. It was short and ended, "I told you that if I had a little girl I would name her Elizabeth, and I did!"

Florrie and Laurinda were as pleased as when she read them the letter telling that *Rozalia* would be published. Florrie said that the only thing that kept her from turning green with envy was Mr. Brewster. "He's already talkin' of marriage, and we only met last month!"

A son, a book to be published, a namesake! Blessings, indeed. On Thanksgiving Juliette came in from the garden, carrying Tommy against her shoulder. "He just said a real word, plain as could be. 'Da-da' is what this chile just said!"

Elizabeth reached for Tommy, swung him high, swung him in her arms. "Now say, Mama. Mama?"

"Da-Da!"

"This chile, he has a will of his own!" Juliette nodded.

Like mother, like son, Elizabeth thought. It did not seem possible that more than a year had passed since she last saw Tom.

"Da-Da!"

Sometimes his face was as vivid in her mind as if she had seen him only yesterday. But at others it was indistinct, blurred by the veil of time that had passed without him. Was her face as blurred to him? Or was he where no memories existed, in a shallow Mexican grave along with others of what had been Doniphan's Thousand?

"Da-da!"

The letter from Tom arrived on Valentine's day, 1847.

San Diego, California,
December 10th, 1846

My Dearest Liza:

No words can ever tell you what it meant to me to receive your letters! To know you are alive! To know you have given me a son! That he is a marvel! What words are there to render such emotion as I felt then, still feel?

Your letters to me, reaching Fort Leavenworth after I had left it, apparently accumulated there, four of them, for about six weeks. Then they were sent in a mail pouch down the Missouri to the Mississippi and to New Orleans whence they sailed by ship around Cape Horn to Monterey, California, a voyage of many months, as you know.

By that time Monterey had been taken by the American forces of Stockton and Frémont, they having come down from Oregon to Sutter's Fort and thence to Monterey, which was easily taken due to the disorganized state of affairs in this territory. Its people are so far from the capital of Mexico and feel anyhow more loyalty to Spain, living as the wealthy Dons do on vast royal land grants. None of the commoner folk are too well informed as to the state of affairs in Mexico due to the continued revolutions and changes in the government there. But to return to your letters: I was nowhere near Monterey, which is to the north, but rather in the far southern part of Upper California which the Army of the West reached in early December. By then some Mexican inhabitants had staged an uprising, had re-taken the pueblo of Los Angeles, and hundreds of Mexican Californians were in arms—so that instead of an easy march to the port of San Diego we had to fight our way there and at a place called San Pasqual, our small force was badly mauled.

I suffered a wound of an odd sort. A musket bullet hit my spur and drove it deep into my foot. I was able to ride out the fray, but dismounting fell to the ground with a boot full of blood. The prearranged plan was that we should meet up with Stockton's troops in San Diego, they having arrived by sea from Santa Barbara to the north (every town or village here seems to be named for a Spanish saint) and before that by sea from Monterey. Whence they brought your letters (and others too, of course.) I was by then somewhat loony in the head due to the fact that my foot wound got badly infected causing some kind of fever to the brain.

When my overdue mail was handed to me by an orderly, the two on top were from Ould and Ryan, now jointly in charge of my business. Too uncaring of how things were in New York to bother to read them I shuffled them off as you do cards, and sat staring at your well-known handwriting. At that moment I believed I was seeing things not there, shook my head, looked again. Had the fever made me crazy entirely? But the letter was real and I opened it, the first one, sent in June. As I realized the whole mix-up, stemming from your having got off the *Cairo Belle* at Memphis, I began to laugh. I laughed so wildly and so long that two of my comrades in arms sneaked in with a rope to tie me down to my cot for fear I'd do harm to myself or others in my derangement. I tried to explain that you were not dead but just kept laughing and had to kick the one with the rope with my good foot which somehow convinced him I was in my right mind after all. The truth is, I have never been so happy in my life. The joy kept coursing through me in wave after wave.

Who was it that said, "What fools these mortals be"? Well, we are mortals and have both richly proven it. But God is good after all, and we will be together again when this war is finally over. And may Polk rot in hell for fomenting it. In a few days or less we Dragoons will head north for Los Angeles, a small inland pueblo, to take it back again. When we do, all California, from Sutter's Fort southward, will be secure, I think. Would that Mexico itself could have been so easily taken! As for this beautiful land—as unlike the Eastern coast as can be imagined, with the sun shining warm and flowers blooming in December—we have wrenched it away from the descendants of those Spaniards who colonized it. I hope to God it was indeed our "manifest destiny" to do so, for otherwise we are no more than bandits.

I cannot help remembering how you pleaded with me to seek a wider horizon, and I must tell you now how right you were, for it is in this beautiful land that I would like to live forever. But any place where you are will do as well, my love.

This letter will come to you, I have made certain, by

the overland route, via Santa Fe, and so should reach New Orleans in no more than a couple of months, possibly less.

Kiss our son for me, and to you, my dear, *muchos, muchos besos y mil abrazos.* Many, many kisses and a thousand embraces. I live for the day when I will embrace you in more than just dreams.

Your Tom

May your Christmas be a merry one. Mine will be the best I have ever had, the finest gift already given me—by you.

XXXIV

My little Elizabeth was born on the second of November. Oh, but that was a joyous Christmas, even though the woman I had named her for was not with us. Leo was in fine spirits even before her birth because on October 16th a dentist, W.T.G. Morton showed a number of surgeons how to save their patients pain by the use of ether anaesthesia, an event so well publicized that Leo was filled with joy, yet also a trifle annoyed as he believed his friend-by-correspondence, Dr. Crawford Long, deserved the honor and praise accorded Morton. But I said Doctor Morton deserved much credit for his successful demonstration and for making sure that it got in the papers, so that people being thus informed could demand of conservative members of the medical profession that this wonderful anaesthetic be used. For, as Leo said, there are medical men so hard-headed that they would go right on using a slug of whisky and a bullet to bite on.

My little Elizabeth was not one of your "bouncing babies," but small and delicate. Such tiny hands! With minute dimples at the bases of each finger. Her feet were no bigger than the length of the palm of my hand. The delivery, especially for a first child, was not as hard as I had expected. The only flaw one could find was that she was born with a faintly yellowish pallor, but this passed.

On the fifth of February I went in the morning to her cradle—the same quaint little cradle in which I had once lain, my Grandmother Aller having saved it all those years. In it my baby was lying on her face, very still. I knew the truth when I saw her, but gently turned her over. She was dead.

I do not remember much about the following several days—only Leo holding me on his lap as if I were a little girl, rocking me, assuring me I would have other children. Telling me that such sudden deaths of infants happened from time to time, mysteriously, as though God had reached down and taken to Himself their tiny souls. I was too bogged down in my own grief to realize what a double blow her death was to Leo; not only had he lost his firstborn, but in January he had been awarded his medical degree half a year after the rest of his class due to time he had lost from his studies. To be a new-fledged Doctor of Medicine and promptly to lose his child I know now was a horrendous experience, not only because of the pain of the loss, but because of the grim reminder of how little any doctor knows, and what mysteries of the human body he will face each day of his life.

I tried to write to Aunt Liza but could not. A strange obsession overtook me. I believed my aunt was ill, possibly dying. I think the horror of my child's death had made me doubt the goodness of God, so that like a poor savage I lived in a universe where the baby's namesake might be doomed, too. When Leo pointed out the irrationality of my fear for her, I insisted that there was an undertone to her letters which had always disturbed me, even the cheery one telling us that her novel would be published. "Why has she stayed away for more than a year?" I demanded. "I want to see with my own eyes that she's well, Leo."

"Go to New Orleans?" He was flabbergasted.

"Yes!"

"No! It's ridiculous."

"We could go by packet ship around the coast of Florida. Don't doctors recommend ocean voyages for people in distress of mind?" I would never have asked for such a holiday if it hadn't been for the sale of his share of Barclay Shore to Mr. Pinckeney. I knew there was enough money in the bank so that my wish could be granted without hardship to him.

"You can't go running to her whenever life deals you a hard knock. You have me." I saw then that he was put out that I could need anyone but him in my grief.

"I don't want to get comfort from her but to give it in case its needed."

"There's nothing whatever in her letters that suggests she's ill! That's all in your head. I refuse to humor this whim."

By then I knew Leo better than to persist in arguing. I merely continued to eat little or nothing until I looked so wan and thin that he became alarmed. "All right. You've made your point," he suddenly said one day at dinner. "If I don't give in you'll starve yourself to death, is that it?"

"I can't seem to swallow. My throat closes."

"If I agree to New Orleans will you eat your dinner?"

"Oh, yes, Leo! As much as I can!"

"More than that!"

"Yes, Leo."

The white house shaded by a big magnolia tree looked

most Southern and charming, as did a maid in a bright turban who admitted us after Leo told her who we were. I was full of that sly, eager excitement that goes with giving someone a happy surprise. I had not written Aunt Liza that we were coming.

I was nearly as surprised as she, for the suspected invalid who swept into the large, airy parlor radiated life and joy. She gave a little scream of pleasure on seeing me, and in a moment her arms were around me and I felt suddenly safe and protected, as if all would be well. Before I could speak she held me at arm's length, smiling into my eyes. "Did you get my letter? No, you couldn't have. Tom's alive! Oh, what a wonderful letter he wrote me! He's in California. Safe and sound except for a wounded foot!" She sat facing us, leaning forward, and told us Tom's adventures, and how by now he had gone North from San Diego with Kearney's dragoons to retake a town called Los Angeles.

Leo and I both expressed our pleasure, though our own news, as yet untold, must have made our voices a bit strained. And of course the next topic was a question: "Whatever made you decide to come to New Orleans?" With a noble restraint Leo could not fail to note I told only a half truth, that Leo had his medical degree and was free until he opened his practice, and that I had yearned to see her. Why smash her happiness, thrust my sorrow into her lap as I had once put my broken doll?

"And little Elizabeth? Is she with my mother? Who will nurse her? Wasn't it a great wrench to leave her?"

The multiple questions allowed me to answer the last. "Yes, it was." I thought of that tiny casket. I thought I heard a baby crying.

"Do I hear a baby?" Leo asked.

My aunt stood up. "Would you like to see him? Come." Leo took my hand as we followed her out of the room, down a hall and into a large shuttered bedroom. A white wicker bassinet stood in the far corner. Aunt Liza went to it, bent to lift out the baby, silent now. She turned to face us, holding it cradled in her arms, turning to display the rosy little face. "This is my Tommy. I named him after his father."

My voice was as shrill as a little girl's. "You never told us you and Tom got married!"

"We didn't." As I stared she went to the rocker near the bassinet, undid her bodice, and began to nurse her child, her body modestly turned so that the frill on her dress hid her breast. Rocking gently, eyes on her infant, the very picture of serene motherhood she asked, "I kept my secret well, didn't I?"

No apologies, no explanations! The woman I had looked up to all my life was the mother of a bastard. I looked at Leo, sure that he shared my shock.

He seemed impervious. "What good luck that Tom went to California instead of Mexico. The casualties there are already high, and bound to increase, and the notion that General Scott can easily take Mexico City is a pipe dream. 'Manifest Destiny' is going to cost many thousands more American lives before this damnable war ends."

What had happened to his sense of morality, talking of luck, casualties, a popular slogan?

My aunt responded in kind. "Manifest Destiny! I loathe that term and the kind of nationalism it stands for. 'It is our manifest destiny to overspread and possess the whole of the continent which Providence has given us for the great experiment of liberty!' What outrageous twaddle! Providence did not give us this continent. We are killing Mexicans and Indians to get it. We are grabbing it with a howitzer in one hand and a Colt revolving pistol in the other!"

"How can you talk like that?" I cried. "Nursing your baby, how can you talk like that?"

She looked down at Tommy. He sucked noisily for a moment, then relaxed into a sudden satiated doze. She closed her bodice and looked up at me, smiling. "Babies are not very delicate creatures. Neither are we, Jane Anne. I hope your marriage has taught you that. And I hope, more than you know, that your judgment of me will be tempered by understanding." She stood to carry the baby to bed, then turned to face us both, her head high.

All I could think of was my own dead baby. Why had mine died while hers had lived? "I am shocked," I said and began to weep. "And ashamed of you. Carrying on with Tom O'Casey like an immoral woman!"

"Jane Anne!" I turned to see Leo's frowning face. "Don't speak like that to your aunt." He turned and left the room.

My aunt took a step closer, reading my face. "Jane Anne! What's really wrong? Tell me!"

It came out in a wail. "My baby's dead!"

"Oh," she moaned, understanding now. Her arms opened and I went to her, sobbing. "There, there, my poor dear, my poor darling . . ."

"Don't tell me I can have more babies!"

"I won't."

"It was this baby I loved. My first."

"I know, I know."

I had put my broken doll into her lap after all. She could not mend this one, but she had comforted me. I raised my head, dried my eyes, and met hers. "I'm sorry for those awful things I said. It was just . . ."

"The unfairness," she said. "I know. I understand."

"And I understand about Tom. He was the great love of your life, and you were his."

She smiled. "That's putting it very prettily. But at least we love."

"I know," I said. My eye caught a gleam of silver; behind her on the bureau her hairbrush brought back memories of past nights, of confidences shared. I went to pick it up, then turned smiling. "Do you remember how I brushed your hair for you?"

Her hands flew up to unfasten the tortoise-shell pins from her chignon, and she sat before the mirror, her hair cascading down. She talked about the lies we live by as if they were immortal truths. And about pride, false pride—her pride and Tom's that had nearly destroyed their lives. And we talked about my dead baby. "You are a small but strong woman," she said, "and you will have other children. In your place, I would never again speak to Leo about the dead child. He feels pain, too, but he can't let it out as you have done. Look to the future. Look to life!" Her reflected face smiled at mine in the mirror. "As I am doing!"

Her bravery touched me. She must know, as I did, that the war would be a long one. Mexico had to be defeated in her heartland, and General Scott was not Cortés, whom it had taken two years. I stroked the brush soothingly through her hair in which gleamed a few threads of gray. "Tom will come back to you when the war's over. I know he will."

"Oh, I don't intend to wait for that!"

The brush in my hand stopped stroking. "What do

you mean?"

"I've arranged with a bank here for the transfer of my Philadelphia funds. There's also the advance royalty on my book. I'm going to California."

"California? With a baby?"

"I couldn't bear to leave him behind," she smiled.

In the mirror I saw the two of us, a tableau, the silver brush I held motionless. I began to brush furiously. "It's a terrible journey! And dangerous. Indians, privations unspeakable! Only the strongest survive. Didn't you read about the Donner party, trapped in the snow in the Sierras last fall? They ate each other!"

"I wouldn't dream of a covered wagon. I intend to book passage on a clipper ship around the Horn."

"The what?"

"The Southern tip of South America. I've already written Tom of my plan and I'll advise him as soon as I know when the ship can expect to reach Monterey, California. That's where the American Presidio is, army headquarters. Ships stop first at San Diego for tallow and hides."

My husband's voice spoke from the doorway. "I left a scene of incipient battle and return to a hairdressing parlor."

"She's going to California!" I cried. "Around the Horn!"

He stared at her, transfixed, then at the bassinet. "What will you do with the baby?"

"Take him with me!"

"You can't take a baby of six months around the Horn."

"Why not? I can nurse him another six months. After that there's always bread sopped in rice water."

Leo strode toward her. "And how do you know the man'll be alive when you get there? You don't know if the American troops have retaken Los Angeles. In short, isn't this more of the same headlong willfulness that sent you galloping off to Greenacres?"

She stood up, her long hair giving her a girlish look. "Yes, I'm a willful woman, Leo! But now I have an important reason to be. I will not live out this endless war as a widow. I'm sick of lies. And I intend to give my child a father in spite of Mr. Polk's war, and nothing can stop me!"

We stayed in New Orleans for three more weeks, until Elizabeth sailed for California on a big new Yankee Clipper. Some passengers were accepted at a stiff price—nearly five hundred dollars. Her friends Florrie and Laurinda and all the gentlemen boarders had come down to the wharf with us to see her off. She looked small in her russet pelisse, standing at the rail near the stern, holding her baby. The anchor was raised, the sails bellied as they caught the wind, and majestically the great vessel left the shore behind. Her friends Laurinda and Florrie were both weeping, but I did not want to cry. I felt uplifted by her courage, and I waved smiling, wide waves of my arm. She raised hers in a salute of farewell. It seemed to me a good omen that the ship was named the *Rainbow*.

XXXV

The *Rainbow* was a cargo ship primarily, for not even a war of which they did not approve could keep New Englanders from the rich rewards of trade with California and the Orient. But passage across the Gulf of Mexico and the Caribbean went without incident. Of the dozen passengers, Elizabeth became friendly with Belle Greene and Lola Parmenter, pretty young brunettes who had brought a piano and intended, they said, to open a boardinghouse in San Diego, having learned through Lola's soldier brother of the wonderful climate. Donald Farr was a Harvard science student who, like Richard Dana fifteen years earlier, had left school after a severe illness to recapture his health on an ocean voyage to California. Like Elizabeth, he had brought two dozen books and as many periodicals—among them *Journal of Researches* by a Charles Darwin who had voyaged along the coast of South America and around the Horn on HMS *Beagle* at about the same time Dana had gathered material for his splendid book, *Two Years Before the Mast*. Elizabeth found the *Journal* heavy going.

Then there was a missionary couple, Reverend and Mrs. Lemuel Vernon, who hoped to bring knowledge of Christ and decent clothing to natives of Oahu, near

Hawaii. Though gentle-spoken, they were tough-minded. Mrs. Vernon told Elizabeth she did not think it was a boardinghouse that Belle and Lola intended to open. Gaylord Drayton, a cynical Boston bachelor lawyer, was sure his services would be needed to settle land disputes as soon as the war was over if not before. The other half dozen passengers were less outgoing by nature and seemed to suffer often from seasickness, except for a man with a fancy waistcoat and a well-tended mustache who looked like a riverboat gambler and tried to strike up an acquaintance with Elizabeth of a more intimate nature than she wished.

But everyone was charmed by Tommy.

Since winter in the Northern hemisphere was summer in the Southern, they sailed into ever-warmer temperatures so that the russet pelisse was stored away in the trunk and the coolest summer clothing came out. Very soon Elizabeth learned why doctors had long recommended sea change: the rest of the world and its troubles vanished over the horizon at the stern. Small routines on shipboard were what mattered; and what would be served for dinner became the most important daily matter.

The fare was surprisingly good. Mangoes, bananas, and papayas graced the table after the first stop at a tropical port, Parimaribo. Elizabeth had brought a small strainer for the purpose and at dinner that evening pureed mango with banana, which Tommy gobbled greedily. She hoped he would prove a late walker. Such was not the case. Just before they came to Rio de Janeiro, and despite rather high seas, she went on deck for her usual afternoon walk while Tommy napped. She had circled the deck twice and had just passed the door to the cabin when she heard a sound behind her, turned and saw Tommy standing just outside the open door, both little arms wide for balance. Then he sat down hard and her heart turned over as she rushed to gather him in her arms. After that she not only closed the cabin door when she left him napping, but locked it so it could not possibly swing open in high seas.

It was some days later that she saw from the ship's railing a tragic sight—a weathered sloop, its mast snapped off and sails in rags, wallowing in the sea, not a soul aboard. Captain Abernathy, remote of eye and rather hard on his sailors (though not as hard as he might have been if Dana had not written his book about the life of sailors), said that such unmanned vessels were all too common. Whether the passengers and hands had abandoned ship for good reason or been swept off in a storm would perhaps never be known. And she thought of poor Aaron Burr looking for his Theodosia, never found.

The days, the weeks, the months melted one into the other. She worked sporadically on a journal of this voyage, but there was very little to say. She started a novel, but abandoned it. The yearning for Tom became a torment and seemed to worsen the nearer she came to the moment when she would see him again.

Rounding the Horn she knew to be a very dangerous passage, one which had lost many ships and lives. She tried to ignore a secret anxiety that began to gnaw at her nerves as soon as the captain told them at dinner that in another day's time the ship would reach that rocky tip of Patagonia and begin its westward journey. A second anxiety joined the first, born of her knowledge of life's frequent irony. What if she reached San Diego only to find that Tom had died in the long interim since his last letter? There was that strange wound to his foot. What if it had become infected, gangrenous? Her stomach felt hollowed out by fear. That was the trouble with giving in to worry. Worry bred worry, *ad infinitum*. It was natural to be anxious about the dangerous passage ahead. It was unnatural to worry about Tom.

It occurred to her then that she was certainly not the only anxious passenger. What could be done to lift all their spirits? She remembered the piano in the hold. She found Captain Abernathy in his cabin. "It's a waste to have a perfectly good piano sitting unused down in the hold. Could it be brought up to the salon?"

He gave her a gelid look. "Why?"

"I'm frightened of the Horn. I imagine others are. And music has charms to soothe."

He considered this. "Can you play it?"

"Certainly. So can the owner, I imagine."

"If this sea calms down I'll see if it's feasible."

That night the upright piano stood in the dining salon. Through mists and fogs and showers that all but obscured the rocky coastline, the *Rainbow* toiled around the Horn to cheery piano duets by Miss Lola Parmenter and Miss Belle Greene, who also sang nicely, and occasional etudes and one concerto from Elizabeth. Best of all two male voices were raised in lusty song: "Sailing, sailing, over the bounding main, for many a stormy wind shall blow e're Jack comes home again . . ." At last, from their cabins, the other six passengers crept in to warm their frightened hearts at the sounds of music.

In her last letter to Tom—which went overland via

Santa Fe and would presumably reach him about the time her ship began its journey northward along the west coast of South America—Elizabeth had told him that when the *Rainbow* docked at San Diego she would look for him, and if he did not meet her there she would continue on the ship to Monterey.

He did not meet her ship in San Diego. The most beautiful blue bay she had ever seen suddenly seemed stark and empty. "Da-da?" Held high in her arms, his fat little legs straddling one hip, Tommy pointed to the little town.

"He's in Monterey." She found the captain. "I'll be continuing to Monterey as I told you I might."

"And as I told you then, I will have to charge you an extra thirty dollars if you do."

"Yes."

They sailed into summer sea again in late July. She said good-bye to all her friends of the voyage except Reverend and Mrs. Vernon who would continue on the *Rainbow* to distant isles. Having told them, like the others, that she was journeying to join her son's father, she decided not to ask them to perform the marriage ceremony when Tom met the ship.

It was nearly impossible to contain her combined excitement and anxiety when the captain told her they were nearing Monterey. Elizabeth stood at the prow, Tommy in her arms. The ship rounded a curve of shore and there it was, a deep blue bay and on the far side a high headland thick with pines that marched right down to the water—and above all a blue morning sky with one sunlit white cloud.

The captain's voice startled her. "The Reverend just

told me your husband's one of Kearney's Dragoons tha[t] helped us to win California."

"My child's father is a Dragoon, yes."

"Someday that little boy is going to be mighty proud [o]f his father!"

An hour later the captain pointed out the Presidi[o] where, presumably, the brave Dragoon was statione[d.] "The near building at the end of that wharf is what th[e] Spanish call the *aduana*," he said. "A sort of custom[s] warehouse, it was." Two sailors carried off her trun[k] followed by another with her two valises. She had put o[n] her bonnet an hour ago and had worn a rose-red challi[s] dress because Tom had once said he liked that color o[n] her. Tommy wore his best embroidered gown and bonne[t.] He disliked bonnets and would soon pull the bow loos[e] and get the headgear off. She followed her luggage dow[n] the gangplank to the wharf, thanked the sailors, an[d] turned to wave a last farewell to the captain and the mis[-] sionaries, waving from the rail.

When Elizabeth turned to face California, Tom wa[s] coming toward her from around the warehouse. He wor[e] a bright blue cavalry uniform with a darker peake[d] cap. He looked tanned and splendid, and such joy fille[d] her heart that she thought it would burst. She wen[t] toward him and put his son into his arms. It felt lik[e] something she had done before, and she had in man[y] daydreams.

Tom held his son high against one shoulder, encircle[d] Elizabeth with the other arm, and drew her hard agains[t] him. Their kiss went on and on, forever and a da[y] forever. . . .

"Da-da!"

They drew apart, laughing together. Tom swung hi[s]

son high in the air above his head and the baby waved his arms, laughing too. When Tom looked at Elizabeth, there was the suspicion of tears in his eyes. He whispered, "Thank you, my love." And she knew that there was nothing they could not attain together in this far land to which their love had brought them.

Part Seven

XXXVI

Lucas was born a year after Aunt Liza sailed away. I was reading of the Women's Rights Convention at Seneca Falls, New York when the first labor pains began. Then came Jonas, born in 1850. John, named for my father, was born in 1853, the year Fanny Wright died, mourned by all the suffragists she had inspired. I wanted to name our fourth son Leo, but my husband was against it so we named him Louis. Our fifth son, Leo, was born in 1858, shortly after a vigorous argument occasioned by a surprising letter to my husband. It was from The Hague and had been forwarded by Emily from Barclay Shore. It informed my husband that as the only male descendant of a Baron Henri De Lange, the title was rightfully his, as well as any property accruing after he had made his claim. To me it was as though a window had opened, shedding a romantic light on my rather circumscribed life. A baroness! But Leo showed me the letter he had written in answer: "As a citizen of the United States I have no wish for the title of Baron and would regard my assuming it a repudiation of all I believe concerning the sacred principle of human equality." I could not budge him and I never became a Baroness, but when I insisted that our fifth son was to be named Leo, he gave in.

By then we were living in a large old three-story house

in Bordentown, New Jersey, having long outgrown the little house I inherited, and because Leo considered that pleasant little town a better place in which to raise our sons than a large city. In the year before our first son was born Leo had attended the Dental College in Baltimore, and practiced both as a physician and a dental surgeon. "I wear two hats in two offices," was his joking way of putting it. His main office was in Philadelphia, to which he commuted four days a week by train; he had taught himself to go to sleep at once on the homeward ride, the conductor waking him when he reached his destination: "Bordentown, Doctor!" He also had an office above the drugstore in Bordentown where he worked two days a week, an associate being there the other days. Leo's skill as a dentist brought patients considerable distances for his services. He could turn from filling a molar to setting a broken arm with the greatest of ease. I need not say that he utilized ether whenever he knew he had to inflict severe pain.

The time we spent together was most precious, for busy as he was away from home, I was busy in it. Even with three servants (the usual cook, upstairs maid, and downstairs maid) to raise five boys was demanding. Louis, named for a pirate, was at first a handful. He would vanish in his Sunday clothes, return black from head to toe, and explain, "I was helping Mrs. Jones' man get in the winter coal." They had a chute to the basement and I could just see him riding the coal down. But his nature changed when Leo bought a piano. Louis sat beside me watching my hands as I played, then, though not yet five, he sat in my place and improvised a charming tune. He was there next day, doing the same, and the next, so I started him with Mrs. Bates for music lessons. I called im "my little Mozart."

In 1860, with the horrible shadow of the Civil War darkening all our lives, I became pregnant for the seventh time. I was sure that at last I would have a little girl. "And if not, we can name him Chestnut," Leo said—"chestnut" being argot for a joke too many times told. We named our sixth son Alexander, after Grandfather Harth. "It's most peculiar having a Yankee grandson named after my Daddy," Emily wrote, but the old gentleman seemed not displeased.

For Leo, the War Between the States (as the South preferred to call it) was mind-rending. He saw, as many did, that the Treaty of Guadalupe Hidalgo of 1848, ceding to the United States the vast Mexican territory that encompassed what became Texas, New Mexico, Arizona, Nevada, and California, had surely laid the ground for the Southern rebellion, his own state of South Carolina having been the first to secede. "The Mexican War was a rehearsal for this one," he told his sons, and it was true that all the young West Point officers who had learned the craft of war in Mexico were now generals, though no longer comrades-in-arms. To me it was strange to think that Robert E. Lee and Ulysses S. Grant had once been friends.

"Passion and reason, self-division's cause," said my husband. Leo's anguish of mind came from the sharp division between his principles and his emotions. In principle he believed the Union must be preserved. In principle, he knew a Northern triumph would mean emancipation of the slaves, and knew this was right. But he had a mother and an aged grandfather in Charleston: there his roots were, there his forebears had struggled and survived. When we stood at the curb watching a

547

dozen young volunteers marching to the railroad station to fight Johnny Reb, Leo's face was a battle ground with no victory in sight. Had he not been a man of forty with large family to support, I have often thought he might have gone marching off with them. Lincoln was his hero long before he became a popular one, while cartoonists mocked with wicked pen his long, spare frame and jokesters mocked his high-pitched voice. Leo told such a fellow one night, "What Lincoln says will be remembered, not how he sounded saying it."

In the third year of the war a letter from Rufus Pinckeney informed Leo that his mother and grandfather had died within a fortnight of one another. Her will left to Leo her house at Barclay Shore and the acres surrounding it to which she held the title, as well as the town house in Charleston, "an increasingly valuable property providing the Blue Bellies don't blast it to rubble." That obviously disappointed gentleman then offered to see to its rental, if Leo so desired. "Otherwise I shall be pleased to occupy it during the summer season as your mother and I were wont to do." The very next day Leo was out in the street teaching a gaggle of adolescent boys to march, wheel, turn, barking orders as the drillmaster at Ashley Military School must have done. When he came in I protested that it was Sunday, but he said, "They might as well go off to war with a few of the rudiments." But this Sunday game did not suffice him long; knowing of the great need of doctors to treat the wounded, he left me with six boys and was gone more than six months, until after the war ended. He would never talk of what he saw and did. By then Lucas, though not yet sixteen, had run away to enlist. He was among those who returned North on the steamboat *Sultana*. Dangerously overloaded with veterans wild to get home, its boiler exploded and it sank. Lucas was not among the survivors.

But before this tragic news, and before Leo's return to us, I was astonished to receive a letter from Isaiah Moss. He had learned where I was from Dolly Pierpont and wished to see me. From her I had learned that he had some years ago married a much younger widow whose health was poor, had continued to prosper but still lived in the house on 10th Street, still talked of building a mansion on upper Fifth Avenue. At this time I knew nothing of his deplorable double life, but still was of two minds about granting the invitation he had asked me for. I had been deeply hurt that he had made no overture toward me even after the loss of my first child and the birth of those following, of which he had surely learned from the Pierponts with whom we were both in touch. And since Leo absolutely forbade me from "kow-towing" to Isaiah Moss until he extended the olive branch of an apology for manhandling me, I had not seen him since the night before my elopement. Nearly seventeen years! My curiosity overcame such scruples.

He arrived in a dark green, old-fashioned carriage with a liveried footman aloft. At seventy-one he looked little different except that his jowls were saggier, his eye pouches bluer; but when he removed his high black silk hat he was entirely bald except for a gray fringe. His small cold eyes attempted a kindly look. As he remarked that Time was a great healer, I wondered what he wanted of me. Soon after he arrived, Louis returned from school and began his daily practicing on the piano in the sitting-room. At six he played remarkably well; Uncle Isaiah cocked his head to listen. "Quite a sprightly touch," he remarked. "And a handsome boy, too." I had offered him

Madeira, remembering his fondness for that wine, and after a second glass he became expansive as to his wealth and success (fourteen cigar stores in three states!). He had remarried, yet still lacked a son and heir. But he wanted to die knowing that his name would survive. Leaning toward me he proposed that he would like to adopt one of my sons.

Astonished, and angry that he would think I would give away one of my children, I refused. "And I do not believe the child of living parents can be adopted," I added.

"Adopt was too strong a word. Nor do I propose taking the boy out of this home nor away from your care. No, all I wish is that he bear my name: Moss. A legal change of name. What is that to you? The mere scratch of a pen. And I will make the boy rich when I die. A trust fund, set up at once. Possibly even more later, if he continues to please me. I want the little pianist. Louis." Eagerness shone in his eyes.

"My husband would never agree to what you ask."

"Ah, but you tell me he's away at the wars. He doesn't need to know until it's a *fait accompli*. Think of what I can do for that little musical genius! The best education possible. Paris. Rome. Or wherever." He leaned forward again. "Can your husband, with so many sons to educate, provide that?"

"He works very hard and provides well for us!"

"Then you would be doing him a favor to lighten his burden." He tried playing on my sense of justice. "After all, I gave you a good home and many luxuries. Now you can show a little gratitude at last. The mere scratch of a pen. Louis Moss. Louis De Lange Moss, if you wish it. A change of name is one of the simplest legal procedures,

I assure you."

I had decided that the old man was senile, no matter how many cigar stores he owned. "Since you know the law, you must know that by law a child belongs to his father. Leo will have to agree to this name change, not I."

He sat back, looking dour. "Yes, of course. But you can persuade him. You can bring out the arguments in favor." He grinned with gray teeth and looked quite evil. "The first being money, the second being lucre, and the third being pelf!" He became solemn as he leaned toward me again. "I speak of a *ten thousand-dollar* trust fund."

"I will convey to my husband your sentiments," I said.

When I wrote to Isaiah Moss that Leo had refused his strange request (though not including any remarks Leo made concerning him, of which "senile dementia" was the kindest) Isaiah honored me with a brief reply. "A selfish father has cost his talented son a fortune, a mistake in judgment he will live to regret."

Only belatedly did I try to puzzle out why it had been one of my sons Isaiah had wanted to bear his name. After all, he could have adopted any number of sons years before. After Leo came home and we got over our first grief at losing Lucas, we talked about it one night. "I guess," I said, "he really did think of me as his daughter."

Leo stared up at the ceiling above our bed. "Or as his wife."

"What a peculiar thing to say!"

"Not so peculiar as wanting to pin his damned name on your son."

"For ten thousand dollars, don't forget."

"The man's never learned that people don't really change; they just get more like themselves. Did I tell you

that the Charleston town house was smashed to smither-
eens, just as poor old Rufus feared? I guess the plantation
of Barclay Shore will be only a memory pretty soon, now
that the Negroes are freed." He heaved up to put out the
lamp by the bed, gave me a goodnight kiss, fell back into
his pillow, and turned over for a well-earned sleep.

How strangely things turn out! Five years or so after
the war ended, a rival tobacco company began the calcu-
lated task of putting Uncle Isaiah out of business. By
then his good ten-cent cigar had been equalled by them
and they wanted the entire market for their product. So
they opened a store of theirs near an I. Moss store and
undersold him. He, in turn, undersold them, and it went
on until a man could buy a ten-cent cigar for three cents.
Every one of the fourteen I. Moss stores had a competing
Union Cigar store to reckon with. But Isaiah would not
give up. He opened new stores, which soon had rival
Union stores competing as before. It became a mania
with him to triumph over Union Cigars. He sold one of
his lots, expanded his factory and staff, continued to sell
his cigars below cost. He sold the other lot a year later and
continued the battle. Union Cigars had shown the first
sign of defeat, jumping their price up to six cents, when
Uncle Isaiah had a heart attack in front of his old store on
Merchant Street, and died at the feet of the wooden
Indian saved from the fire of 1835. His business went
into receivership; he was bankrupt. All that was left was
the house on 10th Street, left to his ailing widow.

By this time Louis was eleven; he and I both knew that
one day he would be a famous concert pianist. I
remembered my aunt's wish for my musical career, never
fulfilled. Although while we still lived in Philadelphia,
Leo had permitted me a brief fling when Mr. Mendel

reappeared in my life shortly after our second son was born. By then Jenny Lind, under the auspices of P.T. Barnum, had made her triumphal appearances in the United States. "The Swedish Nightingale" had reminded him of me, and he pleaded with me to allow him to book me as "The Jenny Lind of Philadelphia." I enjoyed a few weeks in the limelight, though of course could not go on tour with his revue. Afterward I sang at a number of charity events, until we moved to Bordentown. A few times, when miffed with Leo, I used to muse on how different a life I might have lived had I defied Uncle Isaiah and run off with Mr. Mendel's Ethiopian Revue. It was a joy to me that my son Louis had so much talent, and I would watch him at the piano and imagine vast audiences clapping and cheering him.

That dream was to end in the same year that brought the realization of another, almost as dear to me: to see again my beloved Aunt Liza.

All her earlier letters to me from California were lost during our move to Bordentown when the trunk containing them did not arrive with the other belongings. It was never located. But I had read them all many times, and I can still clearly visualize her first years there, vividly described by her. The first great moment was when she placed Tom's son in his arms, for she felt that life had returned to him the little boy he had lost. Since Catholic priests cannot marry a divorced lady, they were wed by a *justicia* and later found a Protestant minister to marry them again. After the Mexican War ended in 1848, they traveled from Monterey to San Francisco because soldiers in Stockton's army had spoken of the beauty of the bay, a magnificent natural harbor. A city to build was the lure. Tom had ruled out Los Angeles: a tiny pueblo miles from a seaport and on the banks of a river that often ran dry, its future did not seem promising. In San Francisco Tom made his final break from New York. He sold his warehouse, Jeremiah Ould acting as his agent, and urged Brian Ryan to bring his family to California where they could build them a town overlooking the best harbor in the world! He spoke flamboyantly, but land was cheap and roofs were already needed, for more and more Americans were filtering into California every month that passed. And he sent Ryan a list of scarce things he was to bring or else send: tools such as saws and hammers, also nails of all sizes.

As all the world knows, the discovery of gold at Sutter's Mill in 1848 brought ships from all parts of the world crowding into San Francisco Bay. The gold-mad passengers who disembarked lived transiently in a spreading tangle of tents and crude shacks on streets that were like bogs when it rained. A jerrybuilt wooden box containing two dozen small cubicles called itself "Astor Hotel." Wood was plentiful, my aunt wrote, if in the wrong location: in the bay more than four hundred ships were abandoned by passengers and crew and left slowly to rot. People lived on the nearer ones. A city in the making was not what San Francisco seemed, but rather a helter-skelter limbo between arriving ships and the gold fields. There was a section called little Chile, a French quarter known as Keskedee, a wandering band of dangerous Australian convicts. The influx of Chinese offered a plethora of laundries—a clean shirt was one of the few things that was affordable. And as for building a city, one nail cost ten dollars!

In disgust, Tom wanted to put on a red shirt, buy a burro and pickaxe and set off for the gold fields. Aunt iza had another idea: "We'll open a restaurant."

"Where?"

"In a building you'll put up on our lot uphill away
from the waterfront."

"With nails at ten dollars apiece?"

"I think they built log cabins without nails."

"You want me to build you a log cabin—to use as a
restaurant? You're crazy, but I'll do it."

"With a room in back where we can sleep."

He managed it, employing Chinese who had not yet
opened laundries or headed for the goldfields, and each
log hauled was a long distance by mule. In several months
was up. A large sign above the door read FOOD. Aunt
iza began with a thick fish chowder of her own inven-
on, fish being in good supply. The purchase of 30 bowls,
n iron stove, and thirty spoons cost over six hundred
ollars. At first there were only narrow counters around
hree walls where people ate standing up, but later Tom
ound a carpenter who built them tables and chairs. The
tove and the worktable were against the fourth wall.
When I read this, it was hard to imagine my aunt at that
tove stirring an iron cauldron of fish stew.

"In a place where a sheet of paper costs $150, no one
alks at paying $20 for a large serving of really good
howder," she wrote. "The cornbread is $2 extra. I have
wo waitresses. I can accommodate twenty people at a
me, and often we are full with folks waiting. Yesterday,
erving dinner at three and supper at nine we made over a
housand dollars and could have made more but the
howder ran out. I make the dinner chowder and Tom
akes the supper. Our net profit per day is never less
an five hundred dollars. I tell Tom it's a lucky gold-
iner who pans that much, day in and day out. He says

that's easier work. But we'll hold up, and I'm training Chinese cook to help out."

After the gold fever passed, and poor Sutter had los his property on which hundreds of illicit claims had bee staked—the government giving him no justice no redress—the time was ripe for Tom's skills: out of th chaos left in the ebb of that wave of fortune seekers decent city had to be built. And that's when the Bria Ryans arrived, having crossed the country in a wago train. They had brought the nails and the tools, and in th years that followed, all prospered. Aunt Liza, already well-known local figure because of what was calle "Lizzie O'Casey's Chowder," became in time known a the wife of one of the city's most prominent men. She wa noted for her style in dress and her many charitabl endeavors. Her indignation at the treatment of th Chinese was intense; she established a home for Orienta orphans, then expanded it to include those of all races Tom built her a handsome American Gothic house o which she sent me a photograph; they had a Chinese coo with a pigtail, which epitomized for me how much mor fascinating her life was than mine. She and Tom had ha one other child, a little girl they named Rose. My aunt' fourth novel, *The Daughter of Don Pedro*, enjoyed con siderable success, and vividly pictured the days of th great California *haciendas*. It concerned a Spanish gir who loved a Yankee, her father's sworn enemy.

Although from time to time my aunt expressed he desire to see her grand-nephews, Tom was always to busy to join her, and I knew that after their agonizin separation during the Mexican War they did not wish t be parted by a wide continent. I had higher hopes afte 1868, when train tracks laid from the West met those lai from the East at Promontory Point, Utah (thanks to the labor of ill-treated Chinese and Irish "gandy dancers"). Instead, she suggested that we visit her.

For Leo, of course, it was impossible. As for me, I still had the younger boys, though Jonas was enrolled at the University of Pennsylvania to study medicine and John would be ready for college the following year. Louis was still at home, as well as little Leo and Alexander. I could not take them with me unless we traveled in the heat of summer, and I could not leave them behind. My husband was something of a disciplinarian with his sons, and had stern punishment for what he considered serious crimes: lying, deceit, and deliberate disobedience. For these they were deprived of privileges. For disobedience which endangered their lives, they received a thrashing—not severe, but most humiliating. I know Leo feared I would ruin the boys by being too gentle with their faults; but I was very much needed after the fuss and bawling was over to affirm that their father loved them, too. So the years passed and I did not go to California.

The year I became fifty was an extraordinary one. Jonas, on becoming a doctor, decided to practice in England, and left us. A handsome, bearded young man, he wrote us that he was often taken for the young Prince of Wales, Edward. John had decided to study dentistry in Baltimore, and Louis had been enrolled nearly a year at the University of Pennsylvania. Sometimes, with little Leo and Allie both gone at school much of the time and my husband working the long hours he did at both offices, the house seemed strangely empty. I was looking forward to the change of scene in late July and August, when we always went to the summer home Leo had bought five years before: a Swiss chalet facing the ocean in Asbury Park. I often wondered, seeing it crying for alpine scenery, why we Americans chose to copy foreign or ancient architecture so slavishly—and why French words and phrases had so permeated the language. In that Centennial year of 1876 it was *comme il faut* and *a la mode* and *soignee* and menus were a mystery to many. The *modiste* replaced the dressmaker, hats became *chapeaux*, and a farmer from the hinterlands had a hard time in New York or Philadelphia.

In that amazing year, and more astonishing than the departure of Jonas for England or John's desire to practice dentistry in South Africa, was the day my husband said he intended to have a look at the silver mines of Colorado, for now it was silver fever that sent men hastening westward. But silver, it seemed, was less a lure for my husband than an excuse. "I intend to cross the whole country by train, see the West—the buffalo herds, the Indians, all of it—before it's all gone. Because it's vanishing, Jane Anne, vanishing." He added politely, "You are welcome to come, of course, if we can make proper provision for the boys."

I looked at a broad-shouldered, rather short man of fifty-five with a dark mustache but a good deal of gray in his beard and his once-black hair. His eyes, though, were those of a young man as he spoke of the Indians and buffalo herds, and I remembered the day he told me of his first ride on an express train. Never once in the twenty-nine years of our marriage had he ever taken a good, long holiday from his patients or his wife and children. For a moment I thought of San Francisco and Aunt Liza, but I said, "No, I don't think I want to join you, Leo. I'd be worried about the boys, and that would spoil your whole trip." There are things in a marriage you do not say; I did not tell him I knew he wanted to go without me.

Enthusiastically, he explained the plans he had already made: he had capable assistants in each of his offices, and in summer there were always fewer patients. "And I seem to need this change. I feel weary too often, and my hands are slower."

I praised him for his decision. That night was our happiest in years, as if we were both young again. He left in early May. By mid-June I knew I was pregnant. I could not believe it at first, and I was a little afraid. For a woman of fifty, bearing a child is perilous, and Leo was far, far away. That he would surely be back before my time came seemed to make no difference. I felt abandoned.

But happy news lifted my spirits. At long last my aunt was going to travel east to visit me! "I want to celebrate our Centennial Fourth of July in the place where I was born. Tom insists on spending the great day here in San Francisco, so I'm coming alone."

Just a few days before she was to arrive, Louis came home for vacation with his right arm in a sling, a cast on that hand and lower arm. I screamed at the sight. His right hand!

Quietly, he told me what had happened. He and a few friends and some girls they knew had hired a sailboat and taken it down the Delaware. Suddenly the boy at the helm yelled to Louis, pointing ahead where a low draw-bridge was closing. There was a strong breeze and current and no time to heel the boat around. None of the girls could swim. With only an instant to think, Louis climbed up the mast and as the boat reached the bridge he planted his hand against it and by the strength of his arm held bridge and boat apart until the bridge began to open wide enough to let the mast slip through, the forward part of the boat being under the bridge. But his hand got crushed between mast and bridge. "The doctor says every bone is broken or splintered. Says I'll never get back enough use of it to play the piano again."

With oft-imagined applause for him ringing in my head I said, "You did a brave thing. I'm sure you saved lives."

"Brave isn't wise, Mother."

"No, not always, but who ever said wise is better than brave?" I smiled cheerfully. "And maybe the doctor's wrong."

"And maybe I'll become the best one-handed concert pianist on earth!"

"Maybe!"

My unwelcome pregnancy, Louis' tragic accident, Leo's absence—none seemed to favor a joyous reunion with my aunt. I could not have been more wrong.

I went alone to the station to meet her train, hoping I would recognize her. Although we had sent each other photographs down the years of our families and ourselves, she was now sixty-eight, an old woman; and I, the troubled girl she had waved to from the *Rainbow,* was nearly fifty. Would we recognize one another?

The train chuffed in, a thrilling sight to me, however commonplace now. It groaned to a stop. The whistle blew. Porters in red coats leaped down to place small wooden platforms below each door. And then, framed in the doorway of a car that had come to a halt near where I stood, I saw her. Her hair was silver now, below a small, dashing hat heaped with roses; her waist was still slim, her long sleeves puffed wide at the shoulders in the latest style. She paused there a moment, head high, her slim furled parasol canted to one side like a dandy's cane. Her eyes skimmed the dozen people on the platform and passed right by me. I knew then I had changed more than she: a small, rather dumpy middle-aged housewife bore no resemblance to the girl she had kissed good-bye in New Orleans. Ignoring etiquette I cried, "Aunt Liza! Here I am!" Her head turned sharply; she nodded, smiled, and, aided by the Negro porter's upraised hand, descended like a great lady from a private coach. Heads turned as she swept toward me.

Seldom have I felt such emotion as we quickly embraced, then stood apart, hands clinging, to look into one another's eyes—as if trying to learn in a moment all the years of small, intimate happenings our letters had not touched on. "You . . ." I began, just as she said, "You . . ." We laughed. I waited for her to speak. "You've changed. You look contented," she said with a smile.

"You've hardly changed at all!" The silvery hair was now like a wig she had put on for a whim, and the lines in her face were only another disguise through which the same direct blue eyes looked at me.

"I have. I'm old." She raised her parasol of rose silk, and opened it. "This serves two purposes. A sunshade and a cane when my leg gets gimpy. I broke it last year, or did I tell you that?"

"No."

"Not important. What shall we do about my trunk?"

We hired the old drayman at the station to bring it home and put her valise in my gig. We started talking during that ride home and scarcely stopped for three days.

. The boys were very good, for I had made them understand how much this time with Aunt Liza meant to me, and Louis was there to keep them amused; he was a wonderful storyteller and most inventive about things to do in that small town in the lull of summer. About his smashed hand, Aunt Liza said to him, "Who knows what it will lead to? We seldom know what's good or bad for us while it's happening. Awful things can lead to fine outcomes, and vice-versa. If you can't be a concert pianist, you're still a composer of music. Think of deaf Beethoven! His Ninth Symphony!" I was to remember her words to Louis years later when I heard a Philadelphia audience applauding the musical comedy for which Louis had not only composed all the music, but had written the lyrics, libretto, and dialogue, and which made him famous overnight.

During the first week of our reunion Aunt Liza and I enjoyed the rarest kind of companionship, an utter candor, nothing held back. Every single night we talked until one or two in the morning, each dressed for bed, in my room or hers, revealing to each other and sometimes to ourselves our deepest feelings and perceptions, some of which neither of us had shared with no one else on earth. I learned for the first time of Uncle Isaiah's secret life after I told her of his wish to change my son's name to his. I revealed my secret hurt that Jonas had gone to England, my belief that he had escaped his strong-willed father to whom he felt inferior. Young Tom O'Casey had escaped in another way; he had a ranch across the bay where he raised horses. As for daughters, her beautiful little Rosie had run off and married a handsome young Italian fisherman though ardently wooed by a young man from the wealthy Sutro family. She told me she was grateful that I had been such a good grand-daughter to her mother, she having proven so distant a daughter. I told her that Jane Aller was holding up remarkably well at eighty-six, and that Cousin Amy, eighty-three, still enjoyed her palpitations and still crocheted as Grand-mother Aller read aloud: they had just finished *Moby Dick*. They now had a splendid Swedish housekeeper who did not treat them like frail old ladies but with great respect. They had refused to share our home. Amazingly, quite a few of their old friends were still alive, one of whom at three had seen George Washington in the flesh.

This led to the holiday we would soon celebrate, and to the fact that in the year I was born, 1826, the last of the Founding Fathers had died: Jefferson and Adams, both on the Fourth itself. I told her I had already reserved rooms in a Philadelphia hotel for the Fourth. "We can't stay with Grandmother and Cousin Amy because of the boys; there isn't room." Hopefully, I added that there would be fireworks in the Bordentown park in case she decided on a quieter celebration of our country's hundredth birthday. The truth was, I rather dreaded a night and day in a hotel with the three boys, all that fuss and bother just for a parade and some more elaborate fire-works. "Don't you like parades any more?" she demanded, and that led to the wonders of the Mardi Gras parade in New Orleans which she saw while expecting young Tommy.

I asked about Florrie Jakes and her sister, and found out that Florrie had married her "gentleman with an eye for a lady that's full-formed." A farmer, he had enforced her reluctant return to Greenacres. The soil was not hopeless, the dowser he knew found an unsuspected underground stream not far out of the "town" and they at last made a go of the place. Laurinda Bolling had never remarried, and at seventy-eight she still had her little way of holding five of a kind to a straight flush.

Of her four grandchildren, my aunt loved best a little girl who was the image of my mother. She told me then of her envy of lovely little Jennie. "Listen to me! Talking of all that as if it any longer mattered! It's hard to believe that pokal of Jennie's even meant so much to me. I stole it, you know, the day I brought you home with me. I imagine it's long since shattered in this houseful of boys."

I smiled, went to my highboy, and from the bottom drawer I drew it out. "I put it away years ago. It seemed to attract small hands like a magnet, and I didn't want to find it in pieces on the hearth. But sometimes I take it out and put it on the windowsill up here while I'm sewing or reading, and let the sunlight shine through the rose."

She held out her hand for it and I gave it to her, holding it so the lid wouldn't topple off. She was in bed by then, and sat up to hold it against the bedside lamp, staring at the rose with its dewdrop, then gave it back to me. She laughed, and looked quite young in spite of two silvery braids. "I have always supposed you thought it not very much of a wedding gift."

I was startled. "I regard it as a precious heirloom. Maybe someday I'll pass it on to my little girl."

"Girl?"

In a rush I told her perhaps my one unshared secret, that I was two months pregnant.

She tipped her head, thoughtful. "You'll be fifty. Didn't you consider an abortion?"

"No!"

"I'm in favor of abortion, adequately performed, when

the need is obvious, though I'm even more in favor of contraception."

"I'm against both," I said firmly.

"Why?"

"Well, they're not natural."

"Nature, my dear, may be thought of as a giant, mindless ape who knows nothing of Malthusian theory, nor of the Industrial Revolution. Large families have ceased to be a blessing, as numbers of ill-fed children laboring in factories, fields, and mines all too shockingly prove."

"That may be, but I regard my large family as a blessing no matter what you say!"

"For a man once so passionately concerned about mistreatment of Negroes, Leo has turned his wife into a brood mare."

I was shocked, hurt, and angry. "I wanted my babies! Every one!"

She spoke soothingly. "And you can certainly be proud of the children I've met. That Louis! And a doctor in England, and a dentist-to-be down in Baltimore. Yes, you can be proud of them, my dear."

"And maybe this last one will be a little girl," I said.

I have no idea how we got from my hopeful expectation to Adela Fisher. "Has anything been heard of her in late years?" my aunt asked. Long ago Adela had disappeared from New York. There had been, I recalled, a long delay between her confession and her later trial. Eustace Carmichael had defended her and very well, considering that the jury found her guilty of mere manslaughter and recommended clemency. Carmichael had managed to establish the fact that she was a virgin; his peroration had presented her as a virtuous woman driven temporarily insane by her corrupt sister's scornful refusal of her plan

565

for a reformed life. Reaching blindly out for a means to castigate such corruption, her hand had chanced to fall on the murder weapon; in raising it against the debased Imogene, had she not acted in behalf of social morality itself? The judge had sentenced Adela to five years in prison, and then suspended the sentence. "No one knows where she went or where she is now," I said.

My aunt looked thoughtful. "I can't help remembering how pretty Imogene was, in contrast to plain, lumpy, sallow Adela. It's very strange to think that had she only confessed sooner Tom and I might have been spared the most dreadful year of our lives." She gave her sudden, robust laugh. "But there I go, belying what I told Louis and truly believe! If she'd confessed at once, Tom and I would never in this world have ended in California or known the grand life we've had there! Oh, Jane Anne, isn't it wonderful! If the voice of Adela Fisher's father had told her to confess *before* Tom was arrested, my entire life would have been different!"

The discovery seemed to tickle her, so I laughed with her, and didn't remark that if Tom had gone down to the City Hotel one day later than he had, it would have been different too. It does not pay to dwell on such matters, in my opinion. Our characters make the final decisions. Liza being Liza, and Tom being Tom, they'd very likely have ended in California anyhow, one way or another.

Of the three possibilities I had offered Aunt Liza for spending the Centennial (all five of us in Philadelphia, at home in Bordentown, or possibly an early summer exodus to Asbury Park where there would be fireworks by the pier), she contrived a fourth. "I have a perfect solution! You don't want the bother of the boys in the city, and I don't to stay here or go to your summer house.

So we'll leave the boys here and have a little fling in Philadelphia, just the two of us!"

"Oh, I couldn't leave the boys like that!"

"Why not? You have three servants and Louis is eighteen. Those boys don't own all your life. You'll be tied down again soon enough with the new baby . . ."

"Shhh!" I had of course not yet revealed my condition, nor would I until Leo had returned.

"Cancel all but our two reservations at the hotel. We'll see the parade, listen to the speeches if we feel like all those proud platitudes, and at night we'll sally forth again and watch the fireworks."

"Two ladies alone?"

"I've traveled far enough alone to tell you there's nothing to it!"

Reminded that she had crossed a continent to celebrate this holiday with me and in Philadelphia, I could not disappoint her, although it would be the first time I had not spent the Fourth with my family. I was rather surprised that the younger boys took this change from the normal in stride; all they cared about was the usual Fourth of July picnic with their friends. Louis, busy composing a new *etude* with his left hand seemed relieved that we did not wish him to escort us. "See, you are not indispensable!" Aunt Liza said, not knowing this somewhat dismayed me.

Because the parade was to pass along Chestnut Street, I had reserved rooms in a hotel right on that thoroughfare, so that by stepping out the doors we would have front-row seats, as it were. But it turned out even better; our double room, on the second floor, fronted on the street. We could stand at the open window and overlook everything! "We have box seats for the parade tomorrow!" I exclaimed. We did not talk late that night, for tomorrow would be a long and exciting day.

Little did I dream how exciting!

The centennial started warm and turned hot. Standing at our open window—seeing the row of people at the curb below already wilting, men removing hats to mop sweaty foreheads, women fanning themselves and glancing enviously at those who had brought parasols—Aunt Liza conceded that our box seats were better than the first row.

We heard the band first. It played "Yankee Doodle" and was preceded by that staunch Revolutionary trio with drum and flute: the little boy, the man with the bandaged head and the old soldier limping bravely along. "The Spirit of '76!" read the banner two young marines held high between them. The women below waved handkerchiefs and the men waved hats, all cheering. Then the band marched by, all in Continental uniforms, and after them came the first float showing Washington crossing the Delaware. Then Paul Revere galloped along warning us that the British were coming, and then came a small float bearing a demure Betsy Ross sewing the first American flag. A big float showed the Founding Fathers signing the Declaration of Independence while the band played "Columbia, the Gem of the Ocean." A small model of Old Ironsides trundled after, and then a second band in the uniforms of Union soldiers approached playing "The Battle Hymn of the Republic," and the float that followed showed a white-haired General Lee surrendering to Grant, and the next showed Lincoln in a pose of agony signing the Emancipation Proclamation. . . .

Oh, it all brought tears of pride to my eyes, and I

wished with all my heart that Leo and the boys could have seen what I was seeing! Uplifted, I watched the last of the parade pass by, heard the noble strains of "The Star-Spangled Banner," and found myself singing the words as the colors passed, a huge flag carried aloft by a young soldier.

But the parade had not passed after all. "Look!" Aunt Liza cried, pointing down. On the heels of the grandeur had appeared a file of marching women. They held aloft lettered placards: "WOMEN MUST VOTE!" "GRANT US OUR RIGHTS!" "100 YEARS AS CHATTELS!" "EMANCIPATE WOMEN!" My aunt was now leaning far out the window, looking down as they neared. She drew in and turned to me. "I'm going to join them. Will you come?"

I looked nervously down. Now most of the male watchers had cupped their hands to their mouths to jeer. "Go home and take care of your children!" a man shouted. Another bellowed, "Whores!"

"No," I said. "And neither should you!"

But she was already out the door, her long white skirt floating after. I watched from the window; I saw her manage her way through the people at the curb, hasten out into the street, and fall into step at the end of the procession of women. How out-of-place she looked, so elegant in cool white, her stylish hat with the roses atop her silver hair! She had thought to snatch her parasol and opened it above her head. The distant band was playing "The Battle Hymn of the Republic" again as she passed down the street followed by a clot of skipping, mocking urchins. Just before I lost sight of her a young woman bolted from the curb to fall into step beside her.

When she had not returned by nightfall, I knew the

worst: arrest! Oh, if only my son Louis were here! Or, better, Leo. But as it was, I had to go alone to the City Jail. As I had suspected, the women marchers were under arrest.

I stood below a high brown desk looking innocently up at the officer in dark blue behind it. "But on what charge?" I asked.

"Disturbing the peace, ma'am."

"There was more disturbance from the men at the curb who shouted some very ugly epithets."

"That's the point. These crazy suffragettes, they cause disturbances of the peace."

"I've come to demand the release of my aunt. She's from California, you see."

"That so? Don't see how that signifies."

"She had no intention of breaking any local ordinance. I believe she was just carried away by the parade. She came all the way across the country to see it." Habits formed during thirty years with a stubborn man stood me in good stead. I was gentle but firm. "She is no more a suffragist than I," I lied.

"Which one is your aunt?" He was now evidently scanning a list on his high desk.

"Mrs. Thomas O'Casey. The tall, handsome lady in white with roses on her hat."

"Ah, her. She looked out of place to me. I'll see what I can do. You wait here." He nodded toward a hard oak bench against the gray wall. I sat down. Oh, if Leo could see me now! The officer at the desk was conferring in a low tone with another he had in some way summoned while I had made my way to the bench. I heard the words "old lady" and "California." I smiled a bit complacently to myself. My aunt might not enjoy the fact that I had

570

conveyed the idea that she was rendered a bit potty by a parade, but surely that was preferable to spending the night in jail?

The second officer appeared in a short time to tell me that my aunt did not choose to leave the jail until all the others had also been released. My dismay must have been plain, for he leaned over to whisper, "But there's a lawyer on his way, so it may not be too long now."

Rejected, I rose. "In that event, will you be so kind as to tell my aunt I shall wait for her at our hotel?"

I waited several hours, too agitated to eat, but by tea-time my appetite had returned with a vengeance. I had just decided to go down without her when the door of the room opened and she burst in. She looked quite drawn, but her eyes were shining. "This is the best Fourth of July I've ever spent!"

"I cannot say the same," I told her.

I was rather cool with her at dinner, but she, unaware, reveled in her recent experience: how splendid were the women she had been jailed with, how clever the sympathetic lawyer who had obtained their release with only a modest fine! "It's men like that who will make the difference in our getting the vote! It's been an inspiring day, and when I get back home I'll certainly do something worthwhile about the cause of feminine freedom!" She laughed. "How absurd that sounds. As if freedom had any gender."

She was favoring her bad leg a bit as we left the table, and I suggested that she might be too tired to see the fireworks. She was amazed. "Miss the skyrockets? Not a chance! I'll just lie down awhile with my feet up, and then off we go!"

Later, she seemed to enjoy the fireworks display

utterly, gazing up at those lovely explosions in the sky as full of wonder as my boys would have been.

After visiting her mother and Cousin Amy we took the train to Bordentown and I, at least, was rather weary, and very glad to be returning to the peace and quiet of my own home. That was the moment Aunt Liza chose for a serious talk with me concerning my circumscribed life. I should begin, she said, to set aside a corner of my life for myself, take voice lessons and throw myself into some worthy cause. Otherwise, where would I be when the last two boys were grown and gone? "A poor little bird sitting in an empty nest!"

"I like my life just the way it is."

"You do? "

"And as for empty nests, aren't you forgetting something?" Significantly, I glanced down at my middle.

"The baby!"

"Shhh!" I put my finger to my lips and cast a quick glance at the gentleman across the aisle, imperviously scanning his paper. Apparently no one had heard her indelicate revelation.

"Well, my dear," she said after a thoughtful moment, "I guess it takes both kinds of women to make a world. The kind you are and the kind I wanted to be."

"Past tense?"

"Not quite."

She spent a few days with her mother and Cousin Amy, and a week with the boys and me, then went to New York to visit Dolly Pierpont and see the Statue of Liberty. She returned briefly, but left for San Francisco after receiving a letter from Tom which made her throw back her head and laugh. Since she did not show it to me I gather whatever he had said was too intimate even for my eyes. As soon as she had gone I began to miss her. Of all our hours together, the way I was most often to remember her was marching for the rights of women under a rose silk parasol on the Fourth of July.

Leo came home without a word of warning in September, on my birthday. I was at the little writing desk in our bedroom when his voice from the doorway called my name. I saw a man who looked years younger, tanned, revitalized. As I stood up and went toward him, my arms out for his embrace, he stopped dead, his eyes wide in surprise or perhaps shock. So I did not have to tell him my news, but merely nodded. Having thought the matter over most carefully, I added, "And if we have a little girl, I've decided to name her Jennie."

ZEBRA HAS IT ALL!